Front & Center

(Book 2 of the Back-up Series)

By:

A.M. Madden

Front & Center

A.M. Madden

Published by A.M. Madden

Copyright ©2014 A.M. Madden

First Edition, ebook-published 2014

ISBN:9781495941238

www.ammadden.com

Table of Contents

Jack's Prologue

She came into my life and flipped it upside down.

She completely altered who I am as a person.

She wreaked havoc in my world.

And I love her.

I thought I had all I needed. I am blessed with good looks, a good family, and good friends. I have a rock band that is about to explode in popularity. I had sex whenever I wanted. I thought it was the perfect life.

I am such an idiot.

My so-called perfect life completely changed when we hired Leila Marino as our back-up singer. After meeting her, I was riding a roller coaster of emotions, most of which I've never felt before.

I'll admit in the beginning all I wanted was to get into her pants. I know it sounds crass, but it is my normal reaction when meeting a beautiful woman, especially a stunning, leggy brunette. I am prewired that way. She is very attractive, with her perfect body, long wavy hair, gorgeous topaz eyes, and the most kissable lips I've ever seen. Who could blame me?

The overwhelming sexual attraction I felt towards her in the beginning was very familiar to me. The stirring in my pants, the desire to bend her over, and carnal need to take her from behind was nothing new.

But then I heard her sing…*holy shit*.

And then I got to know her…*game over*.

That's when all hell broke loose. The feelings engulfing me were so foreign, I didn't know what to do with them. They infiltrated my subconscious to the point where I had visions of her while with other women. I had dreams of her while alone in my bed. The thoughts in my head were belying my normal sexual responses. I stopped having sex with random women. I basically stopped *having sex*. I was in a constant bad mood from wanting her so badly. I had no idea what was happening to me. I was slowly unraveling.

I only had one long-term relationship and in hindsight, it most definitely wasn't love. But this, what I was feeling about Leila, rocked me to my core. The revelation that I, Jack Lair, could be in love, fucking consumed me. I desperately tried to deny these new feelings, but it didn't matter. I was falling in love with my new back-up singer, and I didn't have a prayer.

For the first time in my life, I wanted to know more about her, to share things with her, and to spend time with her. I ached to hold her in my arms for hours. I wanted to make love to her. I don't mean to simply fuck her. I wanted an emotional connection. I wanted her in every way a man wants a woman.

What I wanted and what I should do became a punishing battle between my heart and my head. She was off limits. This only made me want her more. When we were apart, I was miserable. My misery influenced my better judgment. I lost control the night of my surprise party. I couldn't get enough of her. Tasting her lips, feeling her soft body pressed up against mine, and having her respond to me the way she did made it nearly impossible to pull away…which I probably wouldn't have done if we weren't so rudely interrupted.

Her reaction towards me fueled me on and encouraged me to push the envelope. I could see it in her eyes that she wanted me too. I loved it, exploited it, and flirted shamelessly.

We couldn't deny our mutual attraction. One night in her apartment, a moment of weakness pushed us over that line, the one we both tried to avoid. Once I had her, there was no going back. Admitting my feelings for her was a rebirth. I was a new man. Amazingly, she also admitted her feelings for me. Leila and I were finally together. I'd endure all the cold showers I took and all the misery I felt all over again, just to get to this point.

The weeks that followed were fantastic. No one knew about us, so we existed in our own little bubble. Leila felt vulnerable in her new career and worried our relationship would eclipse her talents. I understood, but I felt it would be beneficial for us to at least let the guys in on our secret. Since we would all be living together on a tour bus, we wouldn't have to be discreet around them. Thankfully, she agreed.

Last night was the start of our tour in New York City. The response we received was awe-inspiring. We exposed our relationship to the guys after our show. Hunter claimed he knew, Scott was shocked, and Trey couldn't give a damn. Now that they know, we can be together as a couple, no hiding, no sneaking around, and the back bedroom is ours for the taking. I can't wait to tour across the country while living with her. Having her with me twenty four seven, loving her daily.

I was on such a high. My band now knew Leila and I were in love. The show was outstanding. I couldn't be happier.

Then my world imploded.

My ex-girlfriend, Jessa, crashed our after party, while we were celebrating with our closest friends and family. She came to warn me about an ex-band member, Danny Sorensen. He was our bassist and is still feeling slighted that I fired him. I can deal with this psychopath who is after me. I don't regret letting him go from the band. His threat only solidifies what a lunatic he is. But if that fucker comes near Leila, I'll kill him with my bare hands.

The only upside to hiding our relationship is Danny hasn't a clue Leila is in my life. It's only a matter of time until he finds out about her. When he does, I'll be ready. Thankfully, I'll have her by my side every day for the next several months. Protecting her is now my priority, and I'll do anything to keep her safe.

Ironically, Danny's threat wasn't the worst thing Jessa told me last night. It was her claim that she is pregnant with my baby that leveled me. I had one stupid night with her right before Leila came into my life, and as it was happening, I knew it was a huge mistake. I'm not convinced it's mine. She has always slept around, and I'm sure she still does. Until she proves it, I won't believe it. Jesus, I wanted to punch something when she dumped her news on me. I felt like life needed to bring me down a notch.

Regardless if it's mine or not, I still had to tell Leila. Telling her about Danny was difficult. Telling her about Jessa and the pregnancy was the hardest thing I've ever done in my entire life. She reacted just as I worried she would. She withdrew and pushed me away. She said she needed time to think.

I aged a lifetime last night.

Minutes felt like hours as I waited for the love of my life to make a decision. I can't keep my promise to give her space. I need to see her.

Now.

Chapter 1 – Jack

"He emerges." Hunter calls out when he sees me.

I ignore him and knock on Leila's door. She opens it slowly, barely making eye contact. When she does, it's obvious she's been crying. I can feel my heart breaking from the pain I'm causing her. The feeling is foreign, and it's crushing me. I can't lose her. I would give up everything to avoid losing her.

"Can I come in?"

She moves aside and opens the door to allow me access. I immediately sit and prepare myself for the worst.

"Leila, I wish I could undo what I did. It was a huge mistake, and now the person I love the most has to pay the price. I'm so sorry."

Without warning, she launches herself onto my lap and into my arms.

"I love you, Jack."

I cling to her as if I was drowning and she was my life vest. I'm afraid if I let go, she'll change her mind.

"I'll support you, no matter what the results are." When she pulls away from my embrace, I quickly search her eyes. In spite of her declaration, her pain is still clear and evident in them.

"Jack, I'm not going to lie, it hurts more than anything I've ever felt before, but that's because I love you so much."

It kills me to know I caused her so much pain, and it's probably nothing compared to the pain we will be facing in the future.

"I don't want you keeping anything from me. No matter what it is, I need to know. No matter how bad. I'll need you as much as you need me during this nightmare."

"I promise, no matter what." I tighten my hold on her. "Leila, I don't deserve you."

I would move heaven and earth to make her happy. I would do anything to keep her safe…anything.

I love her.

She pulls away from me and walks over to the door, defensively wrapping her arms around her body. My heartbeat halts in my chest, while I wait for her to speak.

"Jack, last night after seeing the reaction from the crowd, I felt complete. I'm truly living my dream and that's not even the best part. It's that I'm doing it side by side with you. I love that I found you. You're my bonus."

"In spite of that," her voice is barely above a whisper when she continues, "I'm furious with you. I'm scared of how this is going to affect us. I'm angry at you for being with her."

"Baby, come here." Leila hesitates for a moment, and then comes to sit next to me.

"Leila", I take hold of her chin, forcing her to return my gaze, "I can handle you being angry with me. Besides, you aren't nearly as angry as I am with myself. What I can't handle is constantly worrying that you might leave me."

She waits a few moments before she speaks. "I don't think I could. That's what I kept coming back to last night. As angry as I am, I love you too much."

Relief floods through me. I would love to end our discussion here by proclaiming our love and moving on. But there is another concern I need to address, and I need to do it now.

"Jessa slept around. I'm sure she still does. Regardless, there's still a possibility it will be mine."

"I know," she nods, sadly.

"How do you feel about that?"

"I don't know."

She looks down as a single tear escapes. I tilt her head towards mine and gently wipe her tear away. "Leila, please talk to me."

"Ok…I hate that it may be yours. I hate that she would have that part of you."

"I hate that too, but I need you to keep remembering how much we love each other."

She nods as I pull her into my arms in a tight embrace. An unfamiliar silence falls between us, as we get lost in our thoughts.

Leila pulls away to ask, "Can I ask you a question?"

"Anything."

"Why would she think it's yours?" I guiltily look away, but she insists that I respond. "Jack, didn't you use a condom?"

"I really don't want to tell you the details. It was a stupid mistake."

"What if you aren't the only person she hasn't used a condom with?"

"I didn't even remember not using a condom until she reminded me last night. I know it's too late to change things, but I'll get tested as soon as possible. If it will give you piece of mind, I'll do whatever I need to." Holding her face between my hands, I will her to look into my eyes. "I'm so sorry."

"I know. I need to ask you another question that's been haunting me. I need you to be completely honest." I nod solemnly. "Do you have feelings for her?"

"No, baby. I don't. Years ago I thought I did. I was eighteen and I had no idea how much she manipulated me until I ended it. Now that I know what love is, I know that wasn't love."

She takes a deep breath. "I needed to know. Could we stop talking about what happened last night? I don't want to think about it anymore. I just want to be with you." She settles against me.

"Can I kiss you?" She nods, and I lean towards her. The minute my lips touch hers, I feel time stand still. She quickly responds, but then uncharacteristically pulls away.

"Just be patient with me."

"I understand." I soothingly rub her back as she clings to me.

"I'm so exhausted, but I feel bad that we've avoided the guys."

"I know…so do I. I haven't even congratulated them. I need to do that."

They have been up for a while now, yapping in the front of the bus regarding last night's show and the reviews online. More than once, I heard my name being mentioned during the conversation along with Leila and Jessa's. I'm sure they are all speculating on how Leila reacted to her visit or the real reason we slept apart last night.

"Hunter knows about Danny threatening me. I'm not sure if he told Trey and Scott yet. I didn't tell him about the pregnancy. I don't want anyone knowing."

Leila nods. "Ok." As she leans against my chest, her eyes droop from exhaustion.

"Do you want to take a nap?"

She shakes her head in defiance. "No, I'm fine. I'll wake up."

After a few minutes I offer, "Um…I can wake you up."

Laughing, she pulls away "That's not being patient."

"What? Four minutes isn't enough time to wait?"

She giggles adorably and settles back into my arms.

"God, I love that sound." Ten seconds later I ask again. "Seriously, how long do you need?"

"Trust me, I'm sure you'll break me soon. I can't resist that Jack Lair voodoo," she admits. "I had plans for you last night."

"You did? Damn it!" she laughs at my outburst. Smiling at her mood shift, I decide to tease her some more. "I have a confession to make, too."

"Another one? What did you do now?"

"Not funny."

She folds her arms and raises her eyebrows, waiting for me to admit my truth.

"For your information, Miss Marino, I was going to tell you I've been sporting a major hard-on since hearing you sing *Dream On* last night. I've never been so turned on in my entire life. Actually, I just lied. I was that turned on when I first saw you in that leather top at our photo shoot, but having you sing *Dream On* IN that leather top? Fuck, that was so hot."

"That is not what I expected you to say."

"It's true. Of course my hard-on died a horrible death, but now it's back." I smile, wiggling my eyebrows at her.

"You're impossible."

Pushing her hair behind her ear, I meet her gaze. "Babe, all kidding aside, I was so proud of you last night."

"Thank you."

"You were unbelievable."

"So were you. The guys were as well."

I nod towards the door and admit, "I guess it's time to go out there."

"Yep," she responds, but not too convincingly.

"Are you sure you don't want to stay here?"

"Nope. I want to be with you."

"God, I love you." I take her hand and pull her up with me. "Ready?"

"I am fucking ready."

"Wow…you rarely cursed when I met you."

"Well I learned from the best."

"I have much better things to teach you besides cursing." I bend to kiss her passionately. She digs her fingers into my hair, pushes up against me, and literally tries to consume me alive. I smile against her lips. "Changing your mind? I'm still good to go."

"You're insatiable." She pushes me away as I chuckle. "Do I look like hell?" she asks as she runs her fingers under her eyes.

"No baby, you look beautiful." I turn to say one last thing to her before we emerge as a couple. "Leila, I know it's going to be hard, but can you promise me one more thing?" She nods solemnly. "Please talk to me if something is bothering you. Promise me you won't pull away."

"I promise."

I take her hand, pull in a huge breath, and lead her out to join Hunter, Scott, and Trey at the front of the bus.

"Well, it's about time. We've been dying to show you something."

I head right for the coffee maker in desperate need of my first of many cups, while Leila pulls a yogurt from the fridge and a spoon from the drawer. She moves to sit in the booth across from Scott.

"What's going on?" Hunter asks again as I'm preparing my coffee.

"Nothing."

"Bullshit." He touts annoyingly.

"Really?"

"Really. What the hell is wrong with you? Aren't you curious what the reviews say?"

"Of course I am. We got about three hours of sleep, and I desperately need coffee."

Hunter looks over at Leila not buying what I just said. "Are you two fighting already? Honeymoon over?"

"Fuck off, Hunt." I finally lose my cool.

"You should be fucking stoked man. The reviews are awesome." Scott speaks up.

Taking a deep breath, I walk over to sit next to Leila. "First of all, the honeymoon is just starting. Second of all, I *am* stoked. Let me see."

Scott turns the laptop to show me what he was reading. I quickly scan the online article and nod. "Awesome."

Hunter watches me and shakes his head. Looking over at Leila he asks, "Honestly, what's bugging him?"

"He's upset about the news regarding this Danny character," she responds, without missing a beat.

Hunter looks contrite as he remembers what I shared with him last night. "Oh, that."

Putting my arm around Leila, I pull her closer. My girl is so smart. She effectively shut him up with one sentence. Why didn't I think of that?

Trey has been lost in his own world and only now realizes he is sharing a bus with us. "What about Danny?"

"Danny ran into Jessa. He is pissed he got fired and feels I robbed him of his career. He ran his mouth off about getting even."

"Is that why she showed up last night?" Scott asks.

"Yep." I avoid eye contact. I don't want to tip them off to what's really upsetting me. Hunter can usually see right through me.

"Fuck, that's not good." The quick look of panic on Leila's face causes Scott to retract. "Um, actually, he's just a nut with a big mouth."

I watch Leila carefully and take her hand in mine. "We do need to take him seriously, but I won't let him ruin our high. You guys were awesome last night. We couldn't have had a better start to our tour."

"We made *Page Six*, man." Scott beams at the open laptop. Leila moves it closer so we both can read the *New York Post* page that Scott has opened.

"If any of you were lucky enough to see Devil's Lair last night in New York City, you no doubt walked away exhilarated and maybe even a touch turned on. They opened with an exciting, rock the house, sexy as hell show to kick off the rest of their tour. Last night, they set the benchmark pretty high.

No doubt all you warm-blooded girls are well aware of the sexual magnetism their lead-singer, Jack Lair, exhumes, not to mention the rest of his band. But now all you warm-blooded guys can sit and drool over their new back-up singer, Leila Marino, as well. She's the perfect choice, if you ask me. She is sexy as hell, and the chemistry between her and Jack on stage is off the charts. If these two aren't doing it…they should be. But then again, maybe that's how Miss Marino cracked the code to this all male rock band.

How she got in doesn't matter once you hear her voice. This girl has the goods and brings it home. If she gets bored with her new band mates she can bring it to my home…I'm in love.

Along with Miss Marino, Jack Lair is at his all-time best, accompanied by his drummer-Hunter Amatto, bass guitarist-Trey Taylor, and guitarist-Scott Mallone. All in all, Devil's Lair brings back traditional rock with a new edge. As they begin touring from coast to coast, you

need to find their itinerary and buy your ticket. While you are at it, pick up their debut CD-
'Committed', a must have in your collection. Whoever said 'sex sells' said it with Devil's Lair in
mind."

Leila looks annoyed as she pushes the laptop closer to Scott.

"What?"

"It barely mentions my voice between all the sexual innuendos." She's right. The article
was definitely written by a man sporting a hard-on.

"The guy who wrote this is an ass, but it's a good review."

Scott and Hunter look confused. They don't know that Leila's biggest fear once we go
public with our relationship is that they will think she got the job for the wrong reasons. One day
into our tour and it's already loud and clear and in black and white on *Page Six* of the *New York
Post*.

Now's not the time to explain it to them and they wouldn't get it anyway. Anyone who
knows Leila or has heard her voice knows how deserving she is to be part of our band. Hell,
she's too good to be our back-up singer. She deserves to be front and center.

Watching as Hunter tosses the last bit of *Fruit Loops* into his mouth directly from the box, I
use it as an excuse to change the subject. "You ate a whole box already? You seriously need
help. How can you eat that shit?"

He looks at me wide eyed while chewing and ignores my comment.

"Hunter, what's with you and the *Fruit Loops*?" Leila asks amused.

"I wasn't allowed to have them when I was a kid. *Cheerios* only household, so I'm still
rebelling."

"That's pathetic. You're a grown man. The way you pound that crap down makes me
nauseous." Turning towards a smiling Leila, I pucker my lips for a kiss.

"Ugh. Watching you two is making me nauseous." Hunter says with another mouth full.

"Get. Used. To. It. Consider it payback for all those nights I had to watch you and Mandi
making out on the couch." I respond arrogantly before pulling Leila in for a real kiss. The sound
of three grown men gagging snaps Leila back to reality.

She pushes me away while shaking her head.

I smile devilishly as I look out the window. "Where are we, anyway?"

"Bumblefuck, USA." Trey deadpans.

I almost spit out my coffee from his comeback. "Well, as long as we are in Bumblefuck…" I look down at Leila, and she warns me with a pointed finger.

Leaning into her ear I whisper, "You are so hot."

"You are so dead."

"Is it time yet?"

She gives me a threatening look and I shrug, feigning innocence. "Hey Steve, how much longer until we get there?"

He meets my gaze through the rear view mirror. "A few more hours or so. We would have arrived by now if there hadn't been that huge delay last night. We'll get to the arena in time for rehearsal."

When we sat in the arena parking lot last night for hours, I had no idea why we hadn't left yet and at the time, I really didn't care.

"Why were we delayed?"

Hunter looks at me like I've lost a screw. "The bus wouldn't start."

"Why?"

Steve responds first. "Strangest thing, the fuel line was punctured. It looked like an animal gnawed on it. Must have happened as the concert was going on."

A quick shot of suspicion runs through my mind. Deciding that would be too convenient, I dismiss it.

"Well as long as we have a few hours, I need a nap. Lack of sleep and all." I hold my hand out to Leila. "Join me?"

"Jack, we just got out here."

Turning towards my band I ask, "Would you guys prefer me to make out with my girlfriend out here or in private?"

All three simultaneously yell, "PRIVATE!"

Shrugging, I take her hand. "Majority rules."

Leila shakes her head refusing to budge. I bend and pick her up, carrying her over my shoulder towards the back room.

"Jack, put me down. Jack!"

Tightening my grip as she squirms and kicks, I call out behind me, "I apologize in advance for Leila's loud…um…snoring."

Chapter 2 - Leila

Damn him!

As soon as he shuts the door and puts me down, I shove him onto the bed. He dramatically drops while laughing.

"What the hell?"

"What?" He asks with an adorable smirk, while I shoot daggers at him. Sitting up he shrugs, "Don't be mad."

"I'm beyond mad!"

He reaches for my hand and pulls me closer until he is able to reach my breast, which is conveniently at the same level as his mouth. He gently bites my nipple through my t-shirt and bra. I become instantly aroused from his sexual exploit, then remember what he did and quickly step away.

"I'm serious. I'm pissed at you."

"Why?" He asks with complete seriousness.

"Really?"

He shrugs like he truly doesn't have a clue.

"It's hard enough to be living on this bus with you guys, but I don't need them thinking I'm your fuck buddy who is at your beck and call."

"First of all, I'm *your* fuck buddy at *your* beck and call. Second of all, they don't think that."

"Yeah, ok."

"If they are thinking anything, it's how lucky I am."

Rolling my eyes, I retort, "Because you have a fuck buddy living with you."

He reaches for me again and pulls me onto his lap. "No, because I have my girlfriend living with me. They are jealous it's not them traveling with their girlfriends."

Ok, they probably are jealous, but still...

"You need to stop teasing me."

"I can't promise that." He immediately responds, while shaking his head.

"Jackson. I'm serious."

He holds my chin while staring into my eyes. "Jackson? You really are pissed!"

"Ya' think?" I say, folding my arms in total frustration.

"I'm sorry." Jack softly kisses the side of my neck and works his way towards my earlobe. "Am I forgiven?" He murmurs against my skin. When I don't respond, he moves down my neck. "How about now?" Shaking my head, he moves towards my lips. Pulling my bottom lip in between his own, he releases it and asks, "Still mad?"

"Yes," I sigh, and my eyes close on their own accord.

He sucks on my bottom lip, and I groan while his thumb makes small circles around my erect nipple. The desire I feel whenever he touches me is now spreading like a slow moving fire.

Damn it!

He makes it impossible for me to be mad at him.

Smiling, he looks into my eyes. "Let's talk about the teasing. I can't promise I won't do that, because it's so much fun. But I can promise I will always make it up to you." He unleashes his full CCDS smile. The one that shows off his dimples and causes my crotch to clench, thus causing me to shift uncomfortably on his lap.

Jack moves his hand between my legs and slowly strokes me over my shorts while smiling knowingly. "Clenching?"

"Why did I ever tell you that?" I should have never told him how his dimples do things to my lower region. I'm sure he's going to gloat over this for a very long time.

"Hey, I love that you told me that." Softening, I smile at him and he smiles back. "And I love you."

See what I mean? Who's pissed?

"So am I forgiven?"

"Damn you, just kiss me."

"I thought you'd never ask."

Jack holds my head, slowly leaning in until our lips touch. He repeats the motion that caused me to groan and pulls my bottom lip into both of his, sucking lightly. He continues with his kiss, soft, dry, and slow. It's my favorite kiss. It's the same one he gave me on the rooftop at his party. It always leaves me panting. It always leaves me wanting to consume him, and it's never too long before I attack.

Opening my mouth, giving him complete access, I practically climax from this one kiss.

He traces a line with his fingertip from my jaw, down my body to my breast, and circles my nipple slowly. My body is writhing from his touch, but my brain remembers the guys.

Somehow my brain becomes the chaperone at this party.

I pull away completely out of breath. "Jack, I lied. I'm still not ok. This is really embarrassing, because they all know what we are doing back here."

"So?"

"Jack…"

"Babe," he huffs out and adds, "we are going to be on this bus for months, and the guys know we are in love. You are just going to have to get over your embarrassment and get used to the fact they know what we are doing back here." He raises his eyebrows expectantly with his hand still on my breast.

I purse my lips and process his words. He's right. I'll have to learn to deal with it, or abstain. There is no way that's an option. You may as well cut off my oxygen supply. It would be a less torturous fate than staying away from Jack. One night without him and I feel like I haven't had sex in months.

As Jack decides to convince me of his logic, by continuing his erotic massage on my breast, I bargain with myself and conclude that I can worry about this tomorrow.

I fumble with the button of his jeans clumsily, while having absolutely no success.

Jack grins, showing me he knows he won this argument. "I adore you."

"I know," I grump, as I still struggle with his button.

"Need help?" He asks with his lips against my neck.

"Shut up," I pant, showing my cards way too soon. I'm such a hypocrite.

Jack chuckles at my flustered condition and stands us both up, to kick off his shoes and to strip completely naked. My eyes focus on his abs and slowly move lower, taking him in, inch by inch.

I don't think I'll ever get used to his beauty. My brain turns to mush, my heart pounds, my skin warms, and my nerves tingle at the sight of him. This man controls every part of me.

As I stand blatantly gawking at his nakedness, he takes control and peels off my clothes, leaving me completely bare for the taking. He then lifts me and places me dead center on our bed. I trace his lips with my fingertips, and he kisses them softly. He intensely stares into my eyes, his expression becoming somber.

"I missed you. I came in here last night and watched you sleep for hours."

"You did?"

He slowly strokes my cheek and nods. "You were so restless."

He reminds me of my anguish last night, and the pain I felt alone in this room. I was so mad at him while still wanting him so badly. Yesterday I felt nothing could stop us. Today I have no idea how this is going to play out. Our relationship is so new and can easily become victim to this situation, and it terrifies me.

"I don't want to talk about it."

"Ok."

He stares into my eyes, while continuously stroking my cheek with his thumb. His expression becomes mischievous. "I do miss you. It's been too long since we made love."

"It's been a day." I respond, although my brain agrees and quips, "*Way, way too long.*"

"Like I said, too long."

Smiling, I ask, "Well, what are you waiting for?"

"Finally."

We make love like it's our first time...slow, sweet, and gentle. The combination of staring into his beautiful eyes and his deep thrusts commences another earth shattering orgasm. Every encounter with him surpasses the one before. I've lost count how many times I've told myself, "*This time was the best by far.*"

I completely forget we are at the back of a bus, separated by a thin door from the rest of the band, or that we are barreling down a highway with cars and trucks surrounding us, or that damn woman and the news she so cruelly dumped on us, because Jack is able to obliterate the outside world every time we are together.

Biting down on my bottom lip to stop myself from screaming out, I whimper as my entire body spasms viciously from my release. His hands hold my head in place, and his eyes hold my gaze.

"Leila..." he whispers, as I feel his whole body responding to his release. He continues his sentence through his pants, with so much emotion that he causes my heart to literally ache. "...I love you so much."

We are so good together, and it's not just the sex part. He gets me, I get him, and we deserve happiness.

"I love you, too." I wrap my legs around him even tighter, not wanting to break our connection and let him go...ever. I'd be lying if I didn't admit I really could get used to making love every day and singing together every night. I really don't want to take one second of being with him for granted, especially now.

It's as we lie together afterwards, lounging lazily in the back bedroom and no longer immersed in the throes of passion, when I remember the three men sitting right outside our door. "Jack, we really shouldn't lock ourselves back here and ignore the guys."

"Why the hell not? I'd much rather be here, alone with you."

"Don't be mean."

Jack moves to my ear to whisper, "If we stay back here, I plan on getting you off again while you're on your back and I'm on my knees."

Holy fuck...

"You did not just seriously say that to me."

"What?" he asks innocently.

"We need to interact with our band."

"Says who?"

"I say." I lift to kiss his lips and add, "And you love me and you want to make me happy."

He lets out a deep sigh and responds grumpily, "Fine..." The sour look on his face makes me laugh.

As I try to get dressed, he keeps kissing me and it's driving me wild.

"This is not interacting with our band." His response is to pull me closer and probe my mouth open with his tongue, stroking the inside of my mouth so sensuously that he causes me to gasp for air.

"That's low."

"What?"

"You can't let every kiss lead to sex."

"Who says I can't?"

"You are impossible. Get dressed." I turn to leave, and Jack grabs my hand and stops me from leaving the room.

"I love you."

"I know."

His smoldering eyes set me on fire. So much so that I decide to stand and dressed. My eyes slightly unfocus, and my mouth gapes open awkwardly. As he ⸂ articles of clothing, he stands smirking, completely aware of his effects on me. He's person who can make dressing as sexy as stripping. I should have left, because now I'n and horny again.

Once he zips his jeans I scold, "You don't play fair."

"Nope."

The scene hasn't changed much since we slipped out earlier. Trey is still staring at the TV, Scott is still on his laptop, and Hunter is now eating *Pop Tarts*.

"Nice nap?" he asks.

"Epic. I'm totally rejuvenated." Jack says, smiling down at me while Hunter groans and Scott turns a bright pink.

I throw him a dirty look and slide into the booth next to Scott, while Jack fixes himself another cup of coffee.

"Whatcha doin?"

"Reading some of the posts after our show. They definitely love us. Some, not so much," he says, quickly glancing over at me.

"Ugh, I don't want to know. Wait - yes I do. They hate me, right?"

He looks embarrassed that he brought it up, just as Jack comes over and slides in beside me.

"Um, most of them don't hate you. The majority of them love you."

Jack slides the laptop closer to read some of the posts. After a few clicks, he begins to clench his jaw.

"What is it?" I ask hesitantly. Do I really want to know?

He slams the lid closed with such force that I wince from the noise. "Nothing."

I lift the lid and after searching for a few seconds, I stumble upon a page that was listed in recent history. There already is a blog on Facebook dedicated to hating me.

"So much for feeling I belong here and deserve this."

Jack turns my head and says, "Hey, knock it off. It's pure fucking nonsense."

Scott takes hold of my hand and says, "He's right, Leila. This shit happens all the time. I'm sure we all have haters, and every successful band before us has had them too."

Scott's words do nothing to calm my nerves. Jack takes hold of my chin, forcing me to look into his eyes. "Babe, there are like ten followers on this fucking page. It means nothing." He releases me and starts opening other pages until he finds what he's looking for.

"Look, this person thinks Hunter's gay and trying to hide it. Well, maybe some are true." Hunter flips Jack off without even looking over. Jack opens another site and adds, "This idiot thinks we lip sync." He moves the laptop away and takes my face in his hands. "Don't pay any attention to them."

Taking a deep breath, I concede, "Ok. I'll try."

He's right. There are only a handful of followers on this site, but regardless, deep down I know damn well I will not be able to ignore this.

We spend the rest of the long ride being lazy. The guys decide to try and take naps. Jack tries to coax me back to the bedroom and gives up after the third try.

"You're still thinking about those stupid posts, right?"

"Yep." I shrug, not able to deny it.

"You need a distraction." He gets up and loads a movie into the DVD player.

I'm surprised at the one he chooses. "The Notebook? You hate this movie."

He cozies up next to me on the couch. "I'll make the sacrifice for you."

"You're such a great boyfriend."

"It's so hot to hear you call me your boyfriend." He smiles wide and leans in for a kiss.

Squirming on the couch, he picks up my scent like a bloodhound. "Are you clenching again?"

I smirk before turning towards the TV to watch the movie, trying hard to ignore his dimples.

"Fuck, that's even hotter than calling me your boyfriend."

I smack him, while glancing at our driver. "Jack."

He leans in, his lips directly on my ear and says, "Your clenching causes my throbbing."

Oh my God...

"I really regret telling you that. Now shush, I need to concentrate on Noah."

♫ ♫ ♫

"Babe, babe, wake up."

I slowly open my eyes to see two long legs covered in denim stretched out before me. Even while being groggy from sleep, I can still appreciate long legs in Levis. I'm lying across Jack's lap, as he rhythmically strokes my hair.

"I don't want to," I mumble, turning towards him on his lap. I now see a delectable crotch covered in denim.

He bends to kiss my cheek and chuckles, "We're in Portland, Maine. We need to get in and start rehearsals." He waits a few seconds and starts stroking my eyebrows.

"Doing that is not going to wake me up. It's doing the opposite."

He chuckles again and turns my head so he can kiss my lips, nibbling and sucking, until he successfully wakes me up.

"Ok, now I'm awake and horny. Thank you for that."

"Shit. You can't say that to me." I feel his arousal growing beneath my head.

"Let's call it payback for the comment you made regarding me on my back and you on your knees."

"Well then...let's get this rehearsal over with so we can do something about our conditions."

My head accidentally pushes down on his predicament, causing him to grunt, "Oomph." His eyes cross from the discomfort I'm sure he's feeling.

"I'm so sorry," I plead, while trying to hide my smile, but failing miserably.

"Hey, it's not funny. I would like for us to have children someday," he teases, standing to adjust himself. Shrugging, he bends to kiss me.

Jessa immediately pops into my head. I'm immediately wracked with resentment from the possibility that she may be carrying Jack's baby. I stiffen awkwardly and take a step away from him.

"Um...I need to freshen up. Give me a few minutes?"

"Lei, are you ok?"

"Yep," I say over my shoulder as I walk towards the bunks, leaving my boyfriend totally confused. To be honest, I'm a bit surprised at my reaction. I guess subconsciously I'm already harboring resentment. The thought of having Jack's baby is heartwarming. I crave the day we can have a family together. I selfishly hate that Jack's first born may not be with me.

When I quietly open the bathroom door, he is on the phone with his back to me.

"Jennifer, quit being so dramatic...I didn't ignore your calls, my phone was off...Yes...Yes...No...Fine...One more thing, I need to talk to you about something important...Yes, it has to do with Danny. I can't now because we are heading to rehearsal...I'll text you when we're done...Yeah...Bye."

Raking his hand through his hair, he turns to see me watching him.

"Hey, are you ready?"

I nod and move to hug his waist. "Yeah, I'm ready."

"You ok?"

"Yep, I'm fine. Is our agent ok?" I motion towards his cell phone.

"She's just being Jen. She saw Jessa backstage, so I told her about Danny."

Thinking to myself, "*Who didn't see her?*" I nod wordlessly.

"Ready to do this?" he asks. Another wordless nod, and Jack takes my bag from my hand and leads me off the bus and into the arena.

He's hiding something from me, but I'm not going to nag him. He'll have to want to tell me himself.

As we walk silently, hand in hand, I attempt to lighten the mood. "Hey, do we have a few minutes to stop at a gift shop?"

He looks amused and asks, "What for?"

"I want to pick up a postcard. I'd like to have a postcard from each tour stop."

He smiles warmly and shakes his head.

"What? Corny?"

"No. Baby, you can have ten postcards. Come." As he drags me towards the gift shop, I'm still left to wonder what's running through his head.

♫ ♫ ♫

Our show in Portland was a repeat of New York City. The crowd loved us and unlike when in New York, where our adrenaline high was killed by the Jessa debacle, last night we were able to enjoy the effects of the awesome reception we received.

We were all wired because of it and decided to unwind by drinking and playing poker on the bus. They tried to talk me into strip poker, promising me Hunter was wearing underwear, but

Jack told them to take a hike. We had such a fun time. I actually told them I love when they are all nice to each other. I spoke too soon. Not ten minutes later, they started throwing cards with accusations of cheating, and I threatened I would ground each one of them. They all fled to their bunks pissed off and grumpy.

Jack and I then retreated to our room. I was tired and wanted to fall into a sleep-coma. My plan was thwarted when Jack started sucking on my neck. He can exist on very little sleep. It doesn't matter how drowsy I am, he is a professional at keeping me awake. If I weren't so addicted to him, or if I didn't completely love the mind-blowing sex, I'd tell him to piss off.

Needless to say, I was exhausted by the time we arrived in Buffalo the next day. We headed out as a group to have lunch. Of course, Jack and I kept it purely platonic out in public, which was hard as hell. Afterwards, he told the guys we had plans. He's fixated on the fact we've never had a real date yet and surprised me with a matinee. It was so sweet how he bought my ticket, popcorn, and soda. He chose the movie based on popularity, and we sat in the back row sharing the theater with six other people.

Jack pounced the minute the lights went out and we made out like teenagers. He took it to third base while muffling my moans with his kisses. It was a really good date. Just don't ask me the name of the movie or what it was about, because after our tryst I slept through the rest of it.

On our way back to the bus, Jack informed me that Jessa texted him while I was passed out. Apparently she will be taking a paternity test soon.

His news killed my good mood, causing me to clam up. He accused me of hiding how I truly felt, and I was. I couldn't confess that the news of her pregnancy is a shadow that constantly follows me. My brain knows it's there, but most of the time I forget. Then suddenly, when things are shiny and bright, it appears again to remind me…a film of doom coating everything. So of course, I kept it all in. I didn't want to upset him.

When we got back to the bus we had about an hour before rehearsals began. I excused myself, asking Jack for some time alone. His frown almost deterred me, but I was dying of curiosity. I needed to do some research on paternity testing. A few Google searches educated me. Most of the time the tests are performed once the baby is born. It is possible to have it performed in utero, but it's an invasive procedure and risky to the fetus. It can only be done during the second trimester, and the results could take a few weeks.

Would Jessa risk anything happening to her baby? I don't know her at all, but from what little Jack has told me, she doesn't sound like the mothering type. She may very well take the risk just to prove Jack is the father.

Aside from that, DNA is also needed from the father to perform the test. Does Jessa have Jack's DNA? I guess a hair sample or a toothbrush would supply that, but Jack said they had gotten together by chance a few months ago and it was in her apartment. How could she possibly know she would need his DNA? This didn't add up.

The more I read, the more I got annoyed. Frustrated, I deleted my history and opened up our website to read what our fans were posting. I quickly became engrossed with what I found. The website Jen set up lists the cities and dates of our shows, allows our fans to comment or post pictures of our performances, and to upload video as well.

I watched a video from our New York show. The quality was awful and the fan was so excited that the frame kept shaking, but to see our performance through her eyes was amazing.

Most of the posts indicated they love the new Devil's Lair and they love our sound. However, my anxiety with Jessa's test quickly was replaced with apprehension when I made the mistake of opening my haters' blog. They increased a bit in numbers. Although, still not that many, the fact that more have joined the group was worrisome. The posts were downright disturbing. How do they come up with this stuff? There were already speculations that Jack and I were doing it. Ok, so those were dead on, but there were also theories that I was doing it with Hunter, Scott and Trey. Apparently I was pregnant with Trey's child. Hunter is cheating on me, and I am cheating on him with Jack.

Some felt I couldn't sing for shit and those hurt the most. Not because I am insecure with my singing abilities, but because it's like they already smelled my fear and were pecking at my confidence. I couldn't believe so much gossip surfaced after only one night. What will be said as our tour progresses, and it's discovered we are a couple or that his ex is pregnant? I tried to ignore all the negative crap and concentrate on only the good, but it was extremely hard not to let the insults get to me.

Frustrated beyond belief, I was just about to join Jack and the guys when I received an email from Malcolm Reynolds, agent extraordinaire. He still wanted to represent me and felt he could further my career as a solo artist. This man is relentless. Since meeting him, I wondered what my career could become. For most of my life I've wanted to be a rock singer. That's been my one and only dream. I still want that, except now I want it with Jack. I think my dad would die of shock if he knew I had the opportunity to go solo so soon into my career and I passed it up. Evan, who has already assumed the role of my big brother to a fault, would absolutely kill me.

I am not a quitter and even if Jack and I weren't together, I wouldn't make any rash decisions to leave the band until my contract was up next year. At that time, I will have to think about where I want to take my career. For the moment, I cannot imagine being away from Jack. Remembering my dad's words before leaving on tour, '*Leila, I ask you to be true to yourself*', I know I'm being influenced by my feelings for Jack, but love doesn't come around often. I am a hopeless romantic, so I *am* being true to myself. Besides, why can't I have Jack and my dream career as well?

I responded to Malcolm and said when and if I decided to pursue a solo career I would let him know. No sooner did I hit the send button, than Jack came looking for me.

In an attempt to diffuse his concerns about our earlier argument, I made the mistake of telling him about Malcolm's email. He flipped out. He went on and on about how he was holding me back. After another heated argument that resulted in him sulking and me stewing, we screwed each other's brains out in my dressing room after rehearsals. Make up sex with Jack is pretty fucking awesome. He admitted we should argue more often.

After our show in Buffalo, it was only an hour drive to Rochester. Our three a.m. arrival gave us a decent amount of free time. Once we all woke up, the guys decided to go out for food. Jack wanted to stay behind, but I convinced him I really needed some privacy to call Dad and Evan. He reluctantly agreed and left with them.

I made a quick call to my dad to make sure he was ok. I gave him the run-down of how our tour was progressing, caught up with news about his job, and assured him despite what he read on the Internet, I definitely wasn't pregnant. Once I was done with him, I then called Evan.

We were on the phone for more than an hour. He and my friends have also read the good and the bad on the Internet. He personally didn't believe any of it, but was just concerned for me. I assured him I was fine and lied that I wasn't paying attention to the gossip.

He said he finally had dinner with Lizzy. She has been to Hoboken to see them play at The Zone. He's crazy about her. Secretly I'm hoping things work out with them. It'd be awesome if my brother and Jack's sister fell in love as well.

He casually asked, "How's your boyfriend?" sparking my suspicions he was totally on to the fact that Jack and I are doing it. I will have to fess up very soon. I'm just not ready yet. I decided that on our next day off I'd be making another phone call to finally come clean.

He filled me in on what's happening at home. His mom had her first chemo treatment for her breast cancer. He and Dad have been a huge support to her. Barb started her ordeal by carrying so much angst. Finally telling her son the truth about his father definitely relieved a lot of her stress. Dad said she was now concentrating on her recovery.

A few weeks ago, Evan was stunned with the news that he's my dad's son. I was too, but I understood the reasons Barb and Dad hid this from us. Evan, however, is still struggling with it. Aside from the fact I gained a brother and he a sister, it's the whole *"who am I?"* issue that's driving him crazy. He couldn't get past the fact that they lied to us. For his entire life he thought his real dad abandoned him. Only to find out his real dad was within arms reach the entire time.

Since then, Evan has been coming around slowly. He and Dad saw each other last Sunday for brunch. I felt that was a huge positive. I've been skeptical about getting my hopes up, but I see the Sunday brunch thing as a good sign. I am proud he is moving forward, even if it's one slow step at a time.

He dropped a tiny bomb on me that Matt, my ex-boyfriend and ex-band mate, has already broken up with his girlfriend Gina and is chasing Lori.

Lori?

I can't believe that. Lori chased Matt for years and finally backed off, or so I thought. She did not share this bit of info with me, either because she is not happy about it or maybe she is and she's afraid I'll kill her. I know she ended things with Trey before we left on tour, but I also know they still talk and text. I hope she knows what she's doing.

Evan said she's been doing a phenomenal job as their agent. She already has them booked to play in a charity concert for a New York radio station in a few weeks. They have been getting ready with some new material they wrote and they are all extremely eager.

Alisa and Logan are neck deep in wedding plans. It's driving the rest of them crazy to keep hearing about flowers and cake flavors. Evan asked me, "Isn't there like one kind of wedding cake?"

Joseph our drummer is dating a girl named Sandy. She is very petite, practically half his size. They met a week ago and she's already been to their show.

Nina is doing well as my replacement. She has also been helping Lori with her new job as the boys' agent. Since Alisa is so busy with the wedding, she hasn't been able to do so. Lori has proven to be most fastidious in her new role as agent to Cliffhangers. I knew she would be.

Ace the bouncer, and his wife Cindy had their baby boy. They named him Justin, a suggestion from their daughter Paige, who at the age of three is already a huge Justin Bieber fan. Ace is off the wall excited and shows off tons of pictures. Evan said Justin looks just like Ace, baldhead and all.

After hanging up with Evan, I called Lori, but she wasn't able to talk. I told her to text me when it was a good time and she promised she would. I can't wait to hear what the hell is going on with her and Matt.

The guys got back a few minutes ago. Although we still have a few hours before rehearsal, it's pouring out, and we all decide to lazily hang in the bus. As my mind wanders from paternity tests, to my Internet haters, to Lori hiding things from me, I'm pulled out of my reverie by something flying through the air. It looks like a pair of boxers, and they land right on Hunter's head.

"Waa tha fock?" Hunter says around his *Blow Pop*.

Jack is standing near the kitchen fuming. "If I find one more pair of your fucking underwear lying around this bus, I'll make going commando the least of your problems."

At first I think Jack is joking, until I see the look on his face. He is dead serious. It's true they are slobs, but Jack included. It's only been recently that he has been much more cognizant with keeping the bus clean. Mainly because he hates seeing me clean up after them. It's adorable how he'll pick up after himself, yet always making sure I know it. The neater he is the more he gets lucky. Since he's made this breakthrough, he expects his band mates to as well. He doesn't seem to understand that he benefits from being neater. His band mates do not.

Hunter calmly pulls the boxers off his head and the pop out of his mouth and says, "You can suck my dick."

"You seriously need to get laid dude. I'm sick of you and your walking hard-on." Jack responds without sympathy. He quickly looks over at me and says, "Sorry, babe."

I throw him a look and say, "Knock it off."

"Thanks for reminding me. Actually my problem is, I haven't gotten laid in way too long and it pisses me off that you are."

Jack shakes his head at Hunter and says, "That's a mother-fucking-shame."

Hunter gets up and wordlessly walks past Jack to his bunk. A few seconds later, we hear his music playing and a dull thumping.

Hunter's choice of heavy metal music is the last thing I want to hear right now, his being alone in his bunk is the last thing I want to think about, and the sound effects he has added are making me want to throw up.

Jack calls out, "Shut the fuck up!"

"Jack, he's going to pummel you."

"He can bring it."

"Stop picking on him...please."

"Fine. Only because you asked me to."

I can't blame the guys for their moods. We have claimed the bedroom as our own, and since Scott or Hunter didn't have their companions, there were no arguments. Regardless, it's still unfair that Jack and I get to sleep somewhat comfortably in a bed, while they are cramped in their little bunks. Jack said it's not the bunks that are making them irritable, but the lack of females in them. He further explained they are both *horny and annoyed* that Jack isn't. I guess he was dead on...Hunter just confirmed the exact same issue.

Jack has little patience and wants them to stop bitching about it. At the time he said, "It is what it is, and they need to deal with it."

Trey watches quietly. We all know he isn't horny, since he has been getting his fill backstage after our shows. He suggested Hunter and Scott should help each other out, and then they'd feel better.

The sound effects increase in tune to Metallica. Usually I escape to my room when they all start ragging on each other. The only reason I'm not in my room now is because I need an empty outlet for the laptop. I quickly decide to tune them all out and put in my ear-buds to watch my favorite movie.

Jack slides into the booth next to me. He pulls a bud out of my ear and inserts it into his own. "What are we watching?" he asks cheerfully, like he just didn't flip out on Hunter.

"*I'm* watching The Notebook."

"Again?" He rolls his eyes and gives me an -A*h hell, but ok, I'll watch it too* - kind of look. Ignoring him, I start the movie.

"I don't get your obsession with this movie."

"You mean besides Ryan Gosling?"

"Ppffit. He's got nothing on me."

"You're right, he doesn't." Kissing his cheek I add, "It's just a sensational love story. They are meant to be together and nothing stops them. Destiny…I believe in it."

"I'm your destiny, baby."

"If your band mates don't kill you first."

Jack doesn't argue and leans back in the booth, laying his arm along my shoulders. My level of horniness progresses as the movie does. First Jack traces patterns on my neck with his fingers. Then his hand finds my thigh as he slowly moves it up and down, getting closer to my crotch each time. Next his lips find my ear, tugging on my earlobe. My moan tells him that he's completely distracting me from a shirtless Noah.

"Let's forget the movie and make out," he whispers into my ear.

Trying my best to ignore the onslaught of ear nibbling, I concentrate on the tiny laptop screen.

"So, is that a no?"

"Jack, before they kill you they may castrate you, and that would be extremely upsetting to me."

He glances at me for a few seconds and blinks. "Good point."

The thought must be sobering and scary, because he immediately tones down his efforts. Soon enough Ryan Gosling is able to suck me in. I start to lose myself in the movie until I feel his chest rising and falling. He is passed out, his lashes fanning his cheeks, his lips parted slightly. He is so beautiful.

I pull the plug from his ear and put it back into my own. Jack shifts and leans his head against my shoulder. He smells so damn good. I can feel his soft hair brushing up against my cheek and it makes me want to run my fingers through it, but I don't want to wake him.

A little while later, Hunter walks back out from the bunks. I'm guessing his mood hasn't improved, because he scowls at Jack and asks, "Can you plug his nose and mouth and do us all a favor?" He says this with such complete seriousness that it causes me to laugh and my shoulders to shake.

Jack wakes up disoriented and sees Hunter positioned in front of the table aiming a pair of boxers at his head.

"Go ahead, I fucking dare you," he challenges.

"You two fight like an old married couple. Why don't you finally do each other and do us all a favor. I'm sure Scott and Leila wouldn't mind." Trey privileges us with his words of wisdom.

"He's fucking getting on my nerves!" Hunter barks out. "He isn't the first person in love. At least he gets to be with his girl. He's right, I am horny as hell and I miss Amanda. I don't need constant reminders." Hunter grumpily sits on the couch next to Scott. "Let's play *Call of Duty*, I'm in the mood to kill someone."

"Instead of playing those stupid games, why don't you guys do something productive, like cleaning up your messes?"

Hunter and Scott look like they want to slit Jack's throat.

"Fine. Forget I mentioned it."

"Smart move, Lair," Hunter barks.

"I don't know what your problem is, Hunt. You've gone longer than this without sex."

"Jack," I scold, as mediator mode kicks back in.

"What?"

Hunter releases a stream of curses. "I'm envisioning your face on each and every one of these dead motherfuckers." I've never seen Hunter so agitated.

Jack ignores Hunter's admission. After a few minutes, he instigates again. "Maybe Trey is right and Scott should help with your situation until Mandi meets up with us in Chicago."

"You're fucking hilarious, Jack." Now it's Scott's turn to be annoyed. A round of gunfire blasts through the bus, prompting Hunter to laugh and Scott to lose it. "FUCK! Stop killing me you dickhead."

"Blame Jack," Hunter says triumphantly.

"Stop busting their chops." I nudge him with my elbow.

He shrugs sheepishly. "Fine." Turning towards Hunter he adds, "Sorry, man."

"Thank you."

"Scott, is Patti able to meet us in Chicago also?"

"Not sure yet," he responds, as his body ridiculously makes the same motions his hands are making on the video controller. "Damn it, Hunter...I quit!"

"You're such a pussy. Man up and fight back." Hunter says, as he simultaneously unleashes another round of gunfire, taking Scott's last life. Hunter bursts out laughing when Scott throws the remote at him.

"Fuck off."

Their crude comments no longer faze me in the least.

Scott gets up off the couch and slides into the booth across from us. Shaking his head at Hunter, he finishes his earlier statement. "Patti's work schedule is nuts. She's hoping to meet us in Chicago, but won't know for a few days."

I feel for him. Touching his arm across the table, I try to make him feel better. "I'm sorry, Scott."

He blushes and shrugs. "It sucks, but iChat comes in handy."

Trey stands and announces, "You assholes are driving me crazy. No offense, Leila." Trey leaves the bus and doesn't look back.

"What the hell is eating him?" Jack asks Scott. Trey is a man of few words, but something is definitely bothering him.

"He's been going through some crap. He won't say, but we think it has to do with Lori."

"Really, how do you know?" I wonder if Lori admitted anything to Trey regarding Matt.

"He was on the phone with her yesterday and it didn't end well."

That girl has a lot of explaining to do.

"Leila, do you think she would come out and meet us?"

"I don't know, Scott. I can ask her."

I pull out my phone and quickly text Lori.

Still want to talk to you. Also can you meet us anytime soon?

My phone immediately buzzes with a response.

I'm too busy. I'll text you a time we can chat tomorrow.

"Um, she is crazy busy with Cliffhangers and can't get away right now. She said she'll talk to me tomorrow."

Jack watches me skeptically, but doesn't comment. Leaning down, he whispers, "Wanna take a nap?" He pulls my earlobe between his lips to convey his true intentions. Throwing him an exasperated look, he responds with an innocent, "What?"

"We have less than an hour."

"So, it will be a quick nap." He quips.

I glance at Hunter and Scott. Jack follows my gaze and argues, "They don't care. They probably rather we disappear."

"They'd rather *you* disappear."

"Smartass."

"Quit acting like we can't hear the two of you. Jack's right, get lost."

Jack shrugs and says, "See?"

"This tour will be our demise, because they are going to kill us." I nod towards our unhappy band mates.

"It'll be worth it."

Sliding out of the booth and pulling me with him, he announces, "We are going to go take a nap."

Hunter looks up from his game and smirks, "Just keep it down, please."

♫ ♫ ♫

Lying in bed, I thought Jack dozed off, until he suddenly asks, "What's going on with Lori?"

"Why?" I ask, confused.

"You looked like you knew something out there when you texted her. I can tell."

"Really?" I ask, looking up at him.

He nods, "I know your faces."

"Lori broke it off with Trey the night of our opening show. She didn't want to pine away for him while he was traveling the country. Plus, Lori was dead set on getting Cliffhangers discovered and is not taking her role as agent lightly."

Watching me closely, he adds, "I get that…and?"

"And what?"

"There's more."

"Jeez, how do you know?"

Shrugging, he waits for my response.

"Matt is chasing Lori."

"Matt is chasing Lori? When did that happen?" he asks, looking completely shocked.

"I'm not sure Trey knows about that part. Lori has wanted Matt for years. After I broke up with him she asked if I would mind, which of course I didn't. The problem was Matt wanted nothing to do with her in the romantic sense. It took a while for her to finally move on. Trey actually helped her with that. A couple of days ago, Evan informed me that Matt broke up with the girl he had been seeing and is now pursuing Lori. Lori has been tight lipped about the whole thing. I don't know if she is playing hard to get or if she's truly moved on."

"Wow. That's quite a bit of gossip. If Trey is really into Lori, this is not going to be good."

"I'll try to get some info out of her or Evan." I sit up and decide to let him know what I've been meaning to do. I decide this is as good of a time as any to enlighten Jack about my brother.

"It's time to tell Evan about us."

"Really?" Jack fails to hide the excitement in his voice.

"Yes."

"Finally." He regards me for a few seconds. "You miss him, don't you?"

I nod and smile, "Yeah, I really do." As I look away, Jack takes my chin to turn my gaze back to his.

"You're doing it again. You're hiding something."

"Do you remember the day I came to rehearsals late and then cried my eyes out?"

Jack simply nods, his expression shows he is clearly worried about what I'm about to say.

I hold his hand and take a deep breath. I begin to unleash my one biggest secret to my other biggest secret.

"Evan and I had just found out the day before that we are brother and sister."

A myriad of emotions pass through Jack's eyes, first relief, then confusion, and finally sympathy.

"Well, that's not what I expected you to say. How?"

I explain the friendship between Barb and my dad, Doug's role in Barb's unhappiness, Mom ending it with Dad and his turning to Barb for comfort. I describe what happened that fateful night between Barb and Dad. I tell him about Barb harboring her secret to protect my father, my mother, and Evan. I explain Barb's motives for keeping her secret from my dad, but reluctantly had to tell him the truth once Evan became sick. I tell him why Doug left and why Barb didn't want my mom or anyone to know, and the only reason she told Evan now was because she was battling breast cancer and wanted him to know who his real father was. I finally end with my dad's determination to build his relationship with Evan back to what it was, or better than what it was before. I happily admit I think Evan is finally coming around and is slowly forgiving his mom and my dad for what they did.

During my entire rundown of that significant day, Jack takes it all in quietly, never breaking our eye contact.

Still holding his hand, I wait patiently for him to process all the information I just dumped.

"Holy shit", is all he says while looking away for the first time. "Babe, how did you feel about all of this?"

"I was stunned. After the shock wore off, I slowly began to understand why Barb lied and why she wanted to protect my mom. I get why she wanted to protect all of us from her secret. Now, I am just thrilled to be related to my best friend. We always considered ourselves brother and sister and there's no disputing that. You are the first person I told. Evan wasn't ready to tell anyone and I'm not sure if he has changed his mind yet."

Jack pulls me into his arms and hugs me tight. "Thank you for telling me. I wish I was there for you when you were going through it."

"You were. You were really great that day. You allowed me to release without asking questions. It was exactly what I needed from you. Besides, you're here now and that's all that matters."

He kisses me sweetly and runs his thumb across my cheek. "I'm here now and every day from now."

My heartbeat quickens from his declaration. Caressing his beautiful face, I place a chaste kiss on his lips. "I know."

Chapter 3 - Jack

"Your name sir?"

"Mr. & Mrs. Sated," I respond, without looking at Leila.

"Ok, Mr. Sated. You are in room seven-fifteen. The elevators are on the right." The blonde points down the lobby as her eyes focus on my ring-less finger. "Enjoy your stay."

"Thank you." Taking our overnight bag in one hand and Leila's hand in the other, I walk with her through the lobby towards the elevators.

"Mr. & Mrs. Sated?" she asks, smirking adorably.

"Well, aren't we?" Bending to kiss her, the arrival of the elevator stops it from becoming our normal make-out session. The minute the doors close, I push her up against the elevator wall.

"I'm completely sated. But I have to warn you, I do have a *huge* appetite."

"Really, I hadn't guessed that yet. Speaking of, I was hoping to eat because I'm starving. I was also hoping to catch up on some sleep."

"We have plenty of time for that, after I fuck you. Then I'll feed you and then I'll devour you. After all that you can sleep."

"You're so accommodating."

"I know."

"We need to have our laundry done too."

"We will. I already warned the guys to not bother us, call us, or seek us out until rehearsal tomorrow. We are not leaving this room."

"Do I get to pee during this time?"

"Yes."

"Ok, sounds like a plan."

I've been bouncing off the walls in anticipation of our first night off in a hotel. During our show last night in Albany, my mind wandered so much with thoughts of Leila and I in a hotel room that I honestly don't know how I managed to sing the lyrics to our songs.

I practically sprint down the hall to our room, having us through the door and naked in less than a minute. I then proceed to do exactly what I promised, to fuck her hard and fast. And as promised, I then feed her and now it's time to devour her inch-by-inch.

"Mmm…you taste like coffee and your mouth is so warm." She says, after I kiss her slowly.

"Yeah? You like my mouth warm?"

She nods slowly. "What about when it's ice cold?"

"What are you talking about?"

"I have an idea." I grab my coffee and take a healthy gulp. I then lower myself between her legs and slowly drag my tongue through her.

She lifts her hips and gasps.

"More?"

"Yes."

I take another drink and repeat the motion. I continue alternately drinking my hot coffee and devouring her with my mouth.

"Jack, I'm close."

Her words cause my cock to stiffen to the point of discomfort. Once she comes against my lips, I move over her and kiss her deeply.

"Next experiment will be with ice. I'm curious which feels better."

She nods with her eyes closed, otherwise not moving or speaking.

"You just lay there, I'll do all the work."

I nibble on her lips as she lies lifelessly beneath me. I can never get tired of just kissing her. I love the feel of her soft lips and the silkiness of the inside of her mouth. I love the smoothness of her skin, especially behind her ear and down the side of her neck. Tracing a path with my lips, I love how she moans every single time I make that journey. I love the swell of her breasts, the way her nipple is already rigid by the time I reach it. I love the way her chest rises and falls once I pull her taut nipple in between my lips. I love how she arches her back when I swirl my tongue around her before sucking her with my mouth.

Moving my hand slowly down the center of her body, I love how her hands find my hair when I reach her clit. How her legs fall open allowing me to touch her, stroke her, feel every inch of her. I love how she says my name when I trace the path my hand made with my lips. How her one hand falls away from my hair gripping the sheets beneath her. How her other hand clutches my hair when I reach her with my mouth.

I love how smooth she is, how she tastes, how she flinches when I touch her with my tongue, and how she bucks when I pull her into my mouth. I lose it when she clenches around my fingers and how she trembles once she climaxes. I come undone when she pushes against me, saying my name for the second time. I love when she sighs once she's done and how her fingers stroke my hair lovingly.

I look up at her while resting my chin on her belly. I love when she looks down at me completely sated and content. A small smile plays on her lips as I move up until I am hovering over her. I love when she stares deep into my eyes before pulling me down for a kiss. I love sinking into until I am entirely connected to the woman I love.

"You own me…completely." I say, before making love to her.

But what I love the most is when she says, "I love you."

♫ ♫ ♫

Three songs into our show, I finally address the crowd. I have a different agenda tonight, so I'm a bit worried on how it will be received.

"Good Evening Boston!" A deafening roar fills the arena, supplying the instant adrenaline rush I've become accustomed to. "We are so happy to be here. Hey, so I'm a Mets fan and I hate that other New York team!" The crowd shows their agreement with another round of noise.

"Ok, let's not rub it in Leila's face." I cup my mouth as if telling a huge secret and whisper into the mic, "She's a Yankees fan." Boo's echo and all two thousand fans sound like one voice.

"Sorry, Leila, but please take a bow anyway. Ladies and gentlemen, Miss Leila Marino."

She smirks, feigning annoyance and curtsies to the crowd. I turn back to our fans to introduce the rest of the band, ribbing each of them like I always do.

"Ok, Boston…This next song is a new one and I don't normally sing solo. Since I got the approval of the three yahoos and lovely lady behind me, I wanted to sing a special song for a special city."

I am about to sing the song I wrote for Leila back when we weren't even together. I'll never forget coming home that night after spending a really nice time with her at her apartment, only to be wracked with frustration. I had no idea why I was feeling so unsettled, until I realized it was because I missed her and wanted to be with her. The love that I unknowingly felt for her even then fueled the lyrics and music in this song.

I am nervous to debut my ballad. I secretly shared it with the boys a few days ago and they all loved it. Of course, Leila has no clue I wrote it or that I'm about to sing it.

I sit on the stool provided for me center stage, taking my guitar from the roadie who ran out with it. Looking back at Leila, she looks confused and raises her eyebrows questioning what song I'm referring to. I give her a quick smile before beginning my new song.

I quietly say into the microphone, "This one is called, *The Reason I am*."

The stage goes dark, except for a single spot light that shines down on me. Closing my eyes while strumming the acoustic intro, I can clearly picture the woman I love.

My life was on track. Knew all of my plans.
I knew of my purpose. The reason I am.
But life has no rules, of this I am sure.
Just one glimpse of you, I wanted much more.

Baby, you're the reason I am.
Oh, baby you're the reason I am.
I need you to breathe, to walk on this earth.
You're my sole purpose, my cause for rebirth.
You are the reason I am.

It just took one kiss, to claim me as yours.
I see no one else, you've closed all of my doors.
If you were to go and leave me alone,
I couldn't exist. I couldn't go on.

Baby, you're the reason I am.
Oh, baby you're the reason I am.
I need you to breathe, to walk on this earth.

You're my sole purpose, my cause for rebirth.
You are the reason I am.

Stay with me, baby. Please don't leave.
My love for you is endless. You're my reason to be.
I know I deserve less than your soul and your heart.
But I'd rather die now than for us to part.

I can't guarantee a life free of pain.
But I'll protect you always, every second each day.
There isn't a doubt, my love runs too deep.
With my blood in my veins, it controls my heartbeat.

Baby, you're the reason I am.
Oh, baby you're the reason I am.
I need you to breathe, to walk on this earth.
You're my sole purpose, my cause for rebirth.
You are the reason I am.
You are the reason I am.

At the end of my song the spotlight goes out, briefly leaving me in the dark. I wish I could see her face at the moment. I wish I could bring her front and center and kiss her over and over.

Seconds later the stage is lit and the cheers and applause become deafening. "Thank you Boston! You like that one?" More applause and screams follow. "Yeah, me too."

I turn towards our bass guitarist and joke, "Trey, now you know how I truly feel about you."

Hunter hits a sequence on his drums just as Trey flips me off.

I shrug sheepishly. "Jeez, I guess the feeling isn't mutual".

As the crowd bursts into laughter, I turn my back to them to remove my guitar. Finally braving a look, I lock gazes with Leila. She stands stunned, her eyes glistening, a small smile on her beautiful face. I mouth the words, "I love you."

"Ok, Hunt. Take us into the *High Life*." Hunter's drumbeat fills the arena, followed by the rest of my band's instruments. Elation takes over and I'm having the time of my life. I'm engaging the crowd, busting on the guys, and singing side by side with Leila. It's a really good night. I will never forget the rush I feel here at this arena. The only thing missing is being able to show this crowd who that song was truly for.

The minute our feet leave the stage after our final encore, Leila leaps into my arms and kisses me passionately. This is unlike her. There are many eyes back here and it's not exactly private. I can't help but worry that we shouldn't be doing this if she isn't ready to expose our relationship. But her body pressed up against me, her hands in my hair, and her lips on mine irresponsibly squelch all my conscious thoughts.

A few minutes later, Jen's voice breaks our moment like nails on a chalkboard. "What the hell is this?"

Leila pulls away, wide eyed and panting.

As I turn, I notice a small audience gathered around Jen.

Damn it…

I know Leila is not ready for the wrath of Jennifer or exposure. We both lost our minds for a few minutes. I feel more responsible though and I should have stopped her.

Turning towards Jen, I quietly resign, "Let's go to the holding room. I'll explain."

The minute we enter the room and I close the door, Jen turns on me like a madwoman. "How long has this been going on?"

"Not that it's any of your business, but it's been a while."

"As your agent, THIS is my business. Is this the real reason you want security? Did your female fans get wind of this and want to hurt her?"

"Oh shut up, Jen! I told you I want security because of Danny."

Leila watches the exchange between us silently. I didn't tell her I asked Jen to request security from the label. I didn't want to scare her. At the time, Jen said we would discuss it in Boston. I kept it from Leila only because I really didn't have any info to share yet.

Trying to placate our agent, I choose my words carefully. "Jen, Leila and I are in love. This is more than a fling. No one knows except the guys and now you. We aren't ready to go public yet. When we choose to, we will discuss the methods with you to decide the best way to handle it. In the meantime, we would appreciate your support and silence."

Jen looks at me as if I lost my mind. "Are you crazy? The two of you haven't exactly been discreet with your attraction towards each other, and that little song you performed tonight was an announcement by default. Not to mention the dozen or so people who just witnessed your make-out session."

"Knock off the drama." I'm beginning to lose my patience. I'm getting tired of her attitude. If I didn't feel so indebted to her, I'd replace her ass.

"Jack, that song along with a ton of speculation will be all over the Internet tomorrow."

"So?"

She gives me another bug-eyed look. "I'm disappointed in you if I have to explain why it's not a good thing."

Leila interrupts, "Jen."

Our agent levels Leila with her gaze. "We're sorry we didn't tell you. That was entirely my fault. I wasn't ready and I convinced Jack to hide our relationship. If this caused you problems, I apologize."

Jen looks surprised by her apology for exactly two seconds. She then turns towards me, essentially ignoring Leila's presence and points a finger at me. "You should have told me."

"Jen, do not treat me as if I'm invisible." Jen blinks slowly, crossing her arms defiantly. Her face betrays her shock with Leila. Leila has never spoken up towards Jen. In an eerily calm voice she adds, "Like I said, Jack kept this from you because I asked him to. It was my choice to keep our relationship a secret."

"Until now? Jumping him backstage doesn't help your plan," Jen bitchily replies.

"I lost myself for a minute. It wasn't planned."

"I'm sure no one we need to worry about saw us," I add.

"Jack, don't be so naïve. If the label gets wind of this, heads are going to roll."

"Why would the label care? It's not their business."

"It is their business and we need to thoroughly think this through. Jack you were single and available when we signed with the label. You have a persona to live up to. A sappy love-struck relationship isn't part of that persona."

"Why are you being such a bitch?"

"It's because I am a bitch, that got you where you are right now. I need to think clearly since you obviously aren't."

"Screw you, Jen." Clenching my fists, I am now beyond angry. Jen shakes her head and turns to storm out. As she exits, I call after her, "Oh, and get me security...please!"

The minute she is out of the room, I turn to face Leila. "Do not listen to a word she said."

"I'm sorry I screwed up. It's that Jack Lair voodoo that gets me every time."

Smiling at her admission, I shake my head stubbornly. "You did not screw up."

"Yes, I really did. It was stupid."

"Babe, stop."

After a heavy sigh, she shrugs. "I guess we should have expected that from her."

"No. There is absolutely no excuse for her to act that way. She still works for us." Bending to kiss her gently, I ask, "Did you like your song?"

"You couldn't tell from my sexual attack backstage? Jack, that was so beautiful. I loved it! Thank you."

"I wrote it after the night we hung out in your apartment. Even then, I knew." Leila wraps her arms around me, hugging me tightly.

"Well, I love it. Thank you."

Kissing the top of her head, I quietly say, "Everything will work out. Let's get out of here."

We aren't on the bus five minutes before Jen and Dylan show up. Dylan looks like he just found out his best friend died. Confirming my suspicions that our tour manager does have feelings towards my girlfriend. This shouldn't be news to me. I knew he wanted more than friendship based on what Leila admitted to me in New York.

Dylan joined us this evening and will be traveling with us for most of the remainder of the tour. Now that he knows, it's going to be awkward to say the least. Thankfully, he's on the other bus with our drivers and roadies.

"So much for keeping it to yourself." I grumble at Jen.

Without any preamble or remorse, Jen says, "We need to figure this out, tonight. I may have to do some damage control soon, and we all need to be in sync with what our statement is."

"Damage control? Aren't you overreacting?"

"Yes, damage control and no, I'm not overreacting. You are on the way to being the hottest rock stars in the nation. I've worked my ass off to get you there. Relationships this new to the game can cause damage."

The guys all sit uncomfortably during our exchange. I'm sure they are wondering how this will affect them and their own significant others. I, on the other hand, have no doubt Jen is not referring to their love lives. She's always seen me as a sex symbol and has made no secret about it. The old Jack loved it but the new Jack…not so much.

I know we are supposed to be heading out to Hartford as we speak and I turn towards Tom, our driver to ask, "Will it screw you up if we pull out in an hour?"

"Nope, that's fine."

"Thanks, Tom. Jen, you have one hour."

No offense to my buddies, but I'm not having this conversation on the bus. This is way too personal to be discussing it in front of an audience. "We'll be back soon."

I lead Leila, Jen and Dylan off the bus to quickly find an empty holding room in the arena.

Once inside, Dylan speaks first. "You both need to be comfortable with the statement we need to prepare."

"Why do we need to prepare a statement?"

"Because, Jack, if we don't control the info we want everyone to know, rumors will be running rampant." Jen speaks to me like I'm a two year old.

"The rumors have already been running rampant. Where were you when all those posts were appearing from the Leila haters? Suddenly you are concerned about rumors?" Dylan flinches at my words while Jen sighs impatiently.

Turning towards Leila I ask, "I worry about you. Are you ready to go public?"

"Jack, don't worry about me. I'll do whatever is best for the band."

"Too late," Jen quips.

"Jen, I'm warning you. One more comment and we're out of here."

"Jack, she does have your best interest at heart." Dylan tries to pacify me. While glaring at Jen, he adds, "Even if her methods suck." She dramatically rolls her eyes and makes it difficult to appreciate all that she does for us.

Ignoring her, I choose to focus on Dylan. "We are getting nowhere. How do you think we should handle this?"

"I think…"

Jen abruptly cuts Dylan off. "We will say that Jack was in a relationship, misses her terribly, and wrote her a song. Leila is jealous and is trying to seduce you. The allure and drama of a love triangle will spark curiosity, but in a good way."

"No."

"Why not?" Jen throws her hands up annoyingly.

"Besides the obvious, which makes me look like a wacko, I thought relationships could cause damage?" Leila asks what I'm thinking.

"Not vague ones. The mystery will cause interest. Knowing you two are together may upset people."

If we insinuate I was seeing someone at home, it's only a matter of time before Jessa appears with a healthy baby bump, claiming she is the one. I am not ready to admit that to Jen or Dylan, but then again in a few weeks, I may have to anyway.

"This is ridiculous. Why would admitting we are together have people turn on us?"

"You are a hot commodity, Jack. Realistic or not, people connect with you and want to be with you. It's always a fan's fantasy to envision themselves in a relationship with the object of their desire." Dylan patiently explains, remorse in his eyes.

"Plus, the Leila haters will multiply," Jen adds.

My eyes move over to Leila. "Fuck."

"So, now I have your attention?"

"Jack, I don't care. I'll deal with my haters."

"Well I care." Ignoring her frowns, I turn towards Jen and Dylan. "Ok. I get it. We should be prepared. You can call the label and let them know the situation. Leila and I will call you tomorrow before our show to discuss this nonsense."

Jen and Dylan exchange looks. Jen goes to speak, but Dylan holds up his hand to stop her. "Fine. I'll arrange for a conference call tomorrow at three in Hartford." Dylan looks at Leila for the first time. "You ok?"

Shrugging she says, "I'm fine."

He nods, quietly walking out of the room. Jen leaves behind him, a bit more dramatically.

"Are you ok?"

She simply nods, but I can tell she isn't.

"Babe, don't worry. She is overreacting." I wrap her in my arms to hold her tightly. I hate being dishonest. Truth is, I am worried. I hate we need to even deal with this crap and this drama was exactly what she predicted.

She pulls away to look into my eyes. "Jack, you asked for security. You mentioned the hate posts. The same ones you've been telling me to ignore. Please, be honest with me."

"My worries all stem from Danny. Once we go public and the Internet starts buzzing about our relationship, that will firmly put you on his radar."

"Oh…"

"We are all spinning our wheels on the unknown. Who knows if that fucker was just making empty threats? We'll take it one day at a time. Let's go fill the guys in on what's going on, and then you and I will talk this through. I'll call my dad tomorrow for his advice. Ok?"

Nodding she doesn't look at all convinced. "Ok."

♫ ♫ ♫

After filling the guys in, talking through most of the night, and speaking to my dad, I feel like a week has passed by and not merely hours. We are both exhausted.

Why can't life be simple? You meet a girl, you fall in love, and you live your lives? Those rules apparently don't apply if you are Jack Lair.

At least my Dad was ecstatic to hear our news. He said both he and mom had their suspicions. Mainly due to the perpetual smile on my face whenever Leila was near me. I hadn't realized I was doing that.

Regarding our relationship, basically he said we can't worry about the "what if's" and what we are unable to control. Honesty would be his advice. I asked him to keep the news of our relationship to himself until I had a chance to call mom and Lizzy personally.

Leila and I agree with my dad and we rather not lie about our relationship. Hopefully the label feels the same.

So here we are, waiting for Jen to call in with the execs from the label. I personally feel this is all unnecessary and could give a crap what our fans think. I've said as much to Leila, but she worries the label will be upset with our relationship.

I've met Louis R. Vassler, owner and C.E.O. of L.R.V. Media a few times. He is a very influential man in the business with a hard-ass reputation. But those who know him personally say he does have a heart beneath it all. His heavy Texan accent and deep baritone voice overshadow the fact he is height-challenged. His executive vice president, Charles Landon is a lot taller and a lot smoother around the edges.

The tension in this room between Dylan and us can be cut with a knife. Conversation has been minimal or all together nonexistent. At three on the dot, thankfully the conference phone finally rings.

"Hello?"

"Dylan, it's me. I have Louis and Charles on the line as well."

"Hello gentlemen, I'm here with Jack and Leila."

Louis' deep accent comes roaring through the speaker. "Hello y'all. So I'm guessin' congratulations are in order for you two?"

"Hi Louis, It's Jack. Thank you, sir. I'm sorry to have to drag you into this."

"Nonsense. Love is part of life. Being a romantic myself, I don't have any problems with you two or what you do in your personal lives."

"Thank you, sir."

"Unfortunately, we are all involved in a fickle industry. One can never tell what can make the fans loyal or what can piss them off. Havin' said that, you two don't want negative bull crap affectin' your popularity so soon in the game."

My heart sinks at his words.

At my silence, Louis further explains. "Now kids, don't misunderstand. You boys, and Leila are talented and we stand behind that talent. Your talent will make you a success. But your fans will make you superstars and obviously the label would prefer the superstars. Hell...my wife would have my nuts if she found out I'd said that out loud. I'm no idiot. So I'm deferrin' the decision to the fans. Let them decide. Your contracts aren't dependent on the amount of fans you have. They are dependent on how much money you make. Hopefully, the stars will align on both fronts. Understood?" Leila and I exchange glances, both getting the point loud and clear. Bottom line...it comes down to money.

"Yes, sir."

"With the way today's youth just love themselves a scandal, this could sky rocket you right to the top. We'll have to wait and see. Another unfortunate or fortunate reality today, dependin' on how you look at it, is we live in the era of the Internet. We'll know soon enough what people are sayin' and if we'll have to announce your relationship. Bottom line, if needed, we'll do complete honesty and we'll ride the wave."

"We agree."

"Leila, darlin', are you ok with this plan?"

"Yes, Mr. Vassler."

"Darlin' you have the voice of an angel. I honestly feel as you become more recognized, your talent will influence public opinion. It would have been ideal if this little revelation came later in your success, but shit happens. Anyways, don't you worry your pretty little head about this, understood?"

"Understood."

"Perfect...our statement will be, *'Jack Lair and Leila Marino are ecstatic to be tourin' together as a couple. Their relationship is important to them, however, so is the success of their tour. They are dedicated to their fans and look forward to continuin' on their excitin' journey with the rest of their band mates in Devil's Lair.'* Period."

It's surreal, having people discuss your life as if you aren't part of it.

"Louis, its Dylan. I will call Publicity to fill them in."

"Fine. Hey Jack, Jen informed us you're requestin' security?"

"Yes, sir."

"Under the circumstances with this Sorenson character, I understand you'd rather be safe than sorry. But I'll have to get back to you guys on that. We'll see what we can do."

"Thank you, sir."

"Charles you need to add anythin'?"

"No, Louis. I'm comfortable with the statement. I will assign Krista in Publicity to Jack and Leila full time. We will be in touch regarding security."

"One more thing..." Louis's voice booms over the speaker once again. "Jack, that song you sang in Boston, are you lookin' to record it?"

"Um...I really hadn't thought about it, sir."

Releasing his deep throaty laugh, Louis says, "Boy, that song is pure gold. You think about it now. It'd be a shame to keep that beauty to yourselves. Hell, maybe those fans of yours will appreciate the chivalry. Every woman is a sucker for a romantic man."

Watching Leila, I smile warmly. Her returning smile calms me instantly. "I'll think about it, sir."

"Jack, its Jen. Hold on the line, I'd like to talk to you."

Louis and Charles both say goodbye and hang up their calls. Dylan stands and says, "Well, that went better than I thought."

"Really? He may have sugar coated it, but he's definitely not going to be happy if this affects our popularity." Leila challenges Dylan.

"No…you two should feel better now. Believe me, if he wasn't happy about your situation, you would most definitely know it."

Leila and I exchange another look that doesn't go unnoticed by Dylan. "I'll leave you two alone. I'm sure you have things you want to discuss. I'm going to get in touch with Publicity and prep them for what may come."

"Dylan. Hey, thanks man."

He nods and then smiles at Leila. "Yep, no problem." Turning, he leaves us alone in the room.

"Jack?"

"Yes, Jen?'

"Dylan is right. It did go over better than I thought."

"Ok."

"I want to apologize to you and Leila for the way I acted." Wow, the sky must have fallen outside. We just got a rare apology from Ms. Baxter.

"Jen, we know you were just trying to prepare us for the worst case scenario." Leila looks over and winks at me.

"Yes I was, Leila. Jack, I'll be in Chicago. Until then, I'll be in touch. Please be sure your phone is on and not off. Bye, children." That was one of the shortest-lived apologies I've ever heard, but considering the person it came from, I'll take it.

Once Jen hangs up, Leila expels a huge breath of air. Reaching for her hand, I tease, "I love that you think you can change her."

"I was that obvious?"

"Only to me. Are you ok with what Louis said?"

"Yea, I get it. We'll have to wait and see."

"That's all we can do." Of course, the next few days we will be sitting on pins and needles waiting for the shoe to drop, but we'll be sitting on them together. "Babe, I would like nothing more than to crawl into bed with you right now, but we have a show to rehearse for and we owe the guys an explanation." Pulling her into a standing position, I wrap my arms around her tightly. "Rain check?"

"Abso-fucking-lutely."

"You're a badass, Miss Marino."

Chapter 4 - Leila

@ammadden1- I love, love, love #Jack&Leila together, #Front&Center!

@madmaxi177 – they are so doing it! #JackLair, why couldn't you wait for me? #brokenheart.

@lulubelle555- at boston DL show. So hot. Love new song. #marryme.

@green-monsterpete- #DevilsLair boston show rocked. That new chick has him wrapped around her pinky. #whipped.

@queenofdanile1686-can you say F@#% buddies? Come on jack and leila…we are so on to you. #denial.

@boomboom.nyc1 – if I screw you, can I get in on ur band too? #JackLair

"Stop reading those tweets." Jack slides into the booth, reading over my shoulder.

"I can't help it, it's addicting." He turns my head to kiss my lips. "So far no urgent fires that are in need to be put out. A lot of speculation of who you sang that song to."

I look away and violently gnaw on my bottom lip.

"Ok, spill it."

"I hate that I can't keep anything from you."

Shrugging, he kisses my cheek. "Well?"

"Um…so my haters have doubled in numbers since the Boston show."

"So now there are what, twenty of them? Babe, L.R.V. Media's publicity department is on top of the situation. Please stop stressing over it. Come to bed, I miss you."

It's two a.m., and I've been scouring the Internet for the past two hours. Jack moves out of the booth, holding his hand out for me. "Come."

"Ok. I think my ass is numb anyway."

"Ooh, can I wake it up?" he asks, as he swats at my ass.

"Very funny."

A few grumbles remind us we aren't alone. "Ssh, the guys are sleeping."

Jack pulls me into the room, locking the door behind us. "You must be tired."

"I'm exhausted." The past twenty-four hours have been mentally draining. I've been running through all sorts of scenarios in my head, most of which can't be controlled anyway.

He moves behind me, wrapping his arms around my waist. "Would you like a massage?"

"I would love one."

"Well, let's get rid of this," he says as he pulls off my t-shirt, "and this..." he adds as he unhooks my bra. They both fall to the floor, at the exact moment that his hands mold over my breasts. Expertly, he massages my breasts at the same time. My nipples both immediately respond to his touch.

I arch my back, groaning from how good he is making me feel, and rest my head on his shoulder. "Lay down." He commands directly into my ear. Moving towards the bed, I lay on my stomach excited to feel his beautiful hands on my bare back. Jack straddles me, using both hands to firmly massage my shoulders, my back, and my arms.

"Oh God, Jack, this feels so good."

"Just relax, baby."

Those are the last words I hear as Jack massages me right to sleep.

I wake hours later and am mesmerized by his beautiful face while he peacefully sleeps beside me. My heart swells with how much love I have for this man. It's starting to scare me how much I need him.

The bus is parked at the arena in Pittsburgh, having arrived somewhere early this morning. We have all day before we are due for rehearsals. I would like nothing more than to spend the entire time lying here, watching him.

Jack reaches for me, pulling me closer. When I'm nestled against him, I softly kiss his chest and he opens an eye drowsily. "Hey, babe."

"Hey."

"What time is it?"

"Not sure."

Stretching, he repositions his body against my own…his gloriously naked body. "Mmmm. You're so warm." His lips find my neck, and he starts sucking and kissing and riling me up.

"How did I get naked?"

"No clue." He moves to my breast, pulling my nipple between his lips. As if on cue, his excitement grows against my thigh, setting my insides on fire. Rubbing my leg against him is just enough to clue him in to my desires and causes him to seductively say, "Hi."

"Hi."

It's rare for me to be the initiator. Somewhere inside me a switch is flipped.

As I kiss my way to his chest, his hands fall away from my shoulders. His smoky gaze penetrates me. His breathing accelerates at the same pace as my heartbeat. I love that I'm driving him crazy. Slowly I kiss my way down his body, until I reach the apex of his thighs. When I look up at him, he pins me with his smoldering gaze, watching me intensely, waiting for my next move. His lips are parted, his eyes are hooded, and he is so fucking hot.

Gripping his inner muscular thigh with one hand, and his base with the other, I slowly trace his ridge with my tongue. Jack's thighs flex beneath me and his forearms show the strain of his clenched fists. I can feel every cell in his body coiled and ready to burst.

I want to taste him…all of him. I want to drive him crazy. Putting my lips over his tip, I tease him for a few seconds. When I finally take his entire length, he takes in a shaky breath. I hollow my cheeks and suck with all the force I can muster in my mouth. The results are evident in his moans. I continue to pleasure Jack, as he starts to shudder beneath me. His fingers find my hair as he succumbs to my efforts. I take everything he gives, until he is totally spent.

I slowly kiss my way back up his body to his gorgeous face.

As I straddle his hips, I slowly lower myself over his tireless erection, never breaking eye contact.

"Baby…" He tightly grips my hips, holding me down, forcing me to accept his entire length.

"Jack, let me move. I need to move." He loosens his grip, allowing me to take him at my own pace. His hands slowly move up my back, as he sits up until we are face to face.

My hands find his hair, his hands find mine. Nose to nose, he silently brings me to the edge of reason. Nose to nose, I climax wordlessly. My panting is the only sound in the room. It is the most intense moment of my entire life.

Jack feels it too, because his first and only words are, "Marry me."

My already pounding heart quickens even more so. He must feel it against his chest. He removes his hand from my hair, placing it directly over my heart. "Marry me."

I'm unable to move. My eyes are pinned to his, and my chest still heaving from my frantic heartbeat.

"I love you. I can't live without you. Marry me."

Stroking his cheek, I gently kiss his lips.

"It doesn't have to be now. But I need your promise. I need your commitment."

I kiss him again and again. He must feel doubt because he adds, "Leila, I'll do whatever you want. If you want to wait, we'll wait. Whatever. But I need to know you'll be mine in every way."

It's a desperate plea. A desperate attempt to ensure I am not going to run away. I meant it when I told him I don't think I could ever leave, even with all his problems. But he obviously needs my promise. There's a hint of sadness in his eyes. Actually, it's more like that doom that follows me around. "The shadow of Jessa", but I love this man. I love him more than anything in this world. I can't be without him. I couldn't survive. With all the doubt and uncertainty I have towards what lies ahead for us, the one thing I am most certain of is my love for him.

"Yes."

He crushes me to his chest, burying his face in my neck, our bodies still connected. He kisses me over and over...my eyes, my cheeks, my lips.

"Really? You'll marry me."

"I will."

Pulling back he smirks, "I won't pressure you, but Vegas is only a month away and we have three days off. How do you feel about me, you, and an Elvis impersonator?"

Scrunching my nose, he laughs endearingly. "Ok...that's a no to Elvis."

"Don't take this the wrong way, because I love you and nothing will change that, but I really can't think about anything else until Jessa's results come in."

He blinks a few times. Nodding, he says, "I understand."

Kissing him deeply, the dread in his eyes is hard to ignore. "I'm sorry. I didn't mean to ruin our moment."

"Baby, you didn't ruin it. Leila, I love you. I'll wait as long as you want."

"I know. I love you too."

Our bodies still connected, I attempt to lift off, when he holds me in place. "Again?" I ask incredulously.

A slight shift of his hips and a devilish smirk clearly answers my question.

♫ ♫ ♫

Sitting on the quiet bus is a slice of heaven. No bickering, no raunchy comments, just quiet. The guys took off for food and said they would bring something back for us. I do have some calls to make. It's time to tell Dad and Evan the truth. I've put them off long enough. As I sit in the booth holding my cell phone and pondering whom I should call first, Jack slides in beside me.

"So what do you want to do? Check out the sites? Have sex for the next four hours? Play scrabble?"

"Scrabble sounds fun." His pout causes me to giggle. "I wanted to make some phone calls. I need to call my dad, Evan, and Lori. I want them to hear it from me and not from some blogger's website."

"Do you want me to sit with you?"

"No, I need to do this alone."

"Does that mean you are kicking me out?"

"Yes, you'll only distract me."

Sighing he looks up, pretending to ponder this request. "Fine, but only until you hang up. Then all bets are off."

"Deal."

"I actually wanted to make a few calls as well. I owe a call to Mom and Lizzy. You sure you want to do this alone?"

"Yep…wish me luck."

"Good luck. Love you." Kissing me, he scoots out of the booth and heads for the back bedroom.

With shaky fingers, I hit my dad's number.

"Baby girl, how are you?"

"Hi, Dad. I'm really good. How are you?"

"Fine. Busy at work, blah, blah. Where are you?"

"We just got to Pittsburgh. We have a few hours before we are due to rehearse." An awkward silence falls.

"Lei? You ok?"

"Um...yea. Dad I'm calling to tell you something."

"Oh my God! What's wrong?"

"Nothing is wrong. Just the opposite." More silence, but this time my dad patiently waits. "Um...jeez this is hard...um...ok...I'll just say it...I'm...I'm... seeing someone."

"Holy crap, Lei. You almost gave me a heart attack. I couldn't imagine what you were trying to tell me. Is it Jack?"

Gasping, I can't believe he guesses correctly so fast.

"What? You don't think I saw the signs? Hopeless romantic here, remember?"

"Yeah, thanks for that gene."

"Sweetie, you need to own it. So Jack, huh? When did you two finally figure it out?"

"Um, after my farewell party."

"Are you happy?"

"So much."

"Then I'm happy. He's a good man. Is he around?"

Uh oh. "Dad..."

"Relax...I just want to give him my blessing."

"Dad, he's not asking for my hand in marriage." Little does he know.

"Yet..."

"Dad."

"Do you love him?"

"Yes."

"Does he..."

"Yes," I interrupt his next question.

"Good. Then let me talk to him."

"He's on the phone with his parents. Can he talk to you later?"

"Sure, sweetheart."

"Ok. I have to call Evan now. Everything ok with you guys?"

My dad pauses for a second. "Um, yea…it's getting there. Don't you worry about us, we'll be fine."

"How's Barb?"

"Good. She's handling it like a champ. She sends her love. I gotta go babe, I have another call. You have that boyfriend of yours call me later, ok?"

He suddenly rushes me off the phone as if the topic of Barb has him uncomfortable. I worry he is keeping something from me about her recovery. "Sure…call me when you have time to talk. I love you, Daddy."

"Me too, baby girl, so much. Be careful."

Sighing with relief, I don't understand why I was so scared to tell him. Stupidly, I thought calling Dad would be the harder call. I now have to call my brother. And my gut tells me it may not go as smoothly as my conversation with Dad went.

"Hey Sis…how are you?"

"Hi Ev, I'm good. Miss you."

"Yeah, me too."

"How's your mom?"

"Good. She is remaining positive and has a really good attitude. It's like she is so relaxed and happy now, even with battling cancer. Very strange."

"That's great. Attitude is everything during recovery. Keep me posted."

"Definitely."

"You guys ready for that charity concert you're doing?"

"So ready. It's in two weeks."

"I wish I could see it."

"I know. Lori is having her friend video tape it, so she can put it on our website. You can see it there."

"I meant in person."

"I know. So many times I would turn towards your spot on stage to throw you a look, only to remember you aren't there."

"You're killing me, Ev."

"I'm sorry." He sighs into the phone. "Sal added karaoke night."

"Wait, what?"

"I know. It was all Lori. She said she needed a night for us to be seen. She rallied for Fridays, but he told her she was nuts. So they settled for Thursdays. She switched her shift with a Day-Timer so she can be with us. She really is perfect for this, Lei."

"I knew she would be."

"You were right. So, is touring with a famous rock band all it's cracked up to be?"

Taking a few seconds to choose my words, I admit, "It's even better."

"Better? That's cool. Your fans are loving you."

"Some."

"Most. Don't worry about those idiots."

"You were worried about those idiots last time we talked. Why the change in attitude?"

"Jack's right. They are jealous. The legitimate fans are loving you."

"So I keep hearing." Evan and I discuss our friends, like we do each and every time we speak on the phone. He fills me in on their latest shenanigans. I'm pathetically making small talk, going as far as asking what color are Joe's girlfriend's eyes.

"Why do you care?" Evan calls me out on my stupid line of questioning.

"Um…"

"What's wrong?"

"Nothing."

"Bull crap."

"Um… I just spoke to my dad. I wanted to let him know my news. I want to let you know as well."

"You pregnant?"

"Evan! Jeez. No, I'm not pregnant."

Chuckling, he says, "I'm kidding."

"Not funny."

"I thought it was." Evan laughs into the phone. "So spill it. What do you need to say?"

"Um…" Awkwardly I once again fumble for the right words. Why is this so hard for me to admit?

"Leila?"

"Jack-and-I-are-together," I blurt out.

A few seconds of silence from his end, then he says, "Stop. Repeat it slower."

Releasing a burst of air from my lungs, I repeat my news halfheartedly. "Jack…and…I…are…together."

"I thought that's what you said. When did this happen?"

Oh no…

"Ev…please don't be mad."

"Why would I be mad?"

"It started the night of my farewell party."

More silence…

Nerves take hold and prompt my frantic pacing back and forth in the bus, waiting for Evan to speak. "Ev…"

"What?" he says with a ton of attitude.

Sighing, I scramble my brain for something adequate to say. I come up empty.

Evan finally speaks. "Wow! Why didn't you tell me?" he asks, unable to hide the hurt he feels in his voice. "Ok, so I suspected. But I've waited and waited for you to confirm or deny my suspicions. I've given you more than one opportunity to do that. And you said nothing."

"Evan…you had a lot going on with your mom and my dad. I didn't want to worry you."

"Why would I be worried? Because he is walking sex? Your words, not mine! Or because you work for him? Or because you are trapped on a bus with him for months and you have nowhere to run if it doesn't work out? Or maybe because I've heard he has quite a reputation and he's not a one-woman man? Are any of these possibly the reasons you think I would worry?"

"Ev…"

"Leila…I'm not your father. But I am your brother and your best friend, and I have the right to worry about you. Are you sure you want this?"

"Yes."

Now it's Evan's turn to sigh heavily. "You said it was a crush."

"It's more."

"And what about all his conquests?"

"Evan. He's not like that anymore."

"I can't believe you just said that."

"Well, he's not." While Evan remains silent on his end, I take the opportunity to convince him that Jack is my soul mate. "We're good together. We didn't just jump into this. We got to know each other first. He's a good man. He's kind and considerate. Evan, he loves me and I love him." Tears well up as I sit on the phone, miles away from my best friend, enduring the torturous silence he's determined to unleash on me. I sit heavily on the couch, waiting for him to speak.

"Are you happy?" he finally asks quietly.

"Very much so."

Jack walks out from the back bedroom to witness me swiping away my tears. His face crumples with concern as he squats before me. Taking my hand, he squeezes until I make eye contact with him.

"Ev…are you there?"

"I'm here."

Jack motions for the phone. I shake my head because I'm not sure Evan would want to talk to Jack right now.

"Listen, I told my dad. He was happy for me. Besides you two, Jack's family and our band, no one else knows yet. But something happened in Boston, and you may start seeing things on the Internet. I wanted to tell you myself." When Evan doesn't respond, I add, "Call me back when you're ready to talk about it."

"Is he there now?" he asks, ignoring my comments.

"Yes," I respond while looking at Jack.

"Let me talk to him."

"Evan…"

"Lei…let me talk to him." Wordlessly, I hand the phone to Jack.

"Hey, Evan…yes, I understand…" Jack sits next to me while Evan rants on the other end. He wraps his arm around my shoulders, and then kisses the top of my head, patiently waiting for Evan to finish his tirade.

"Yes, I got it…crystal clear…I love her Evan…" There's another long pause before Jack adds, "Yes…it's not like that anymore…you need to trust me…I intend to…sure, hold on."

Jack smiles as he hands me the phone. "Hey…"

"Hey…I'm sorry I acted like an idiot. I just worry about you."

"I know."

"And I love you. Don't keep anything from me, ok?"

"Ok."

"Good. I'm happy you're happy. And he knows he'll have to retrieve my shoe from his ass if he hurts you."

"Great…"

"Bye, Lei."

"Bye, Ev."

Turning towards Jack, I shrug sheepishly. "Well, that went well."

"Babe, you had to expect that. He cares about you."

"I'm sorry he grilled you."

Jack laughs and says, "No worries."

"How did it go with your mom and Lizzy?"

"They are thrilled." He turns serious, and then asks, "What about your dad?"

"He was happy, I think. Strange. You must have charmed the pants off him. He wants to talk to you also, but I'm sure he won't be as crude as Evan was."

Jack laughs again. "That was the first time someone threatened to shove their foot and ankle up my ass." His phone buzzes with a new text. Frowning as he reads it, he quickly glances up at me.

"Who is it?"

Jack hesitates before answering. "Um, it's a text from Jessa. She had the tests done yesterday and says the results should arrive in a few weeks."

My heart drops at the sound of Jessa's name. I stand to put distance between us, but Jack takes my hand in both of his, stopping me in my tracks. "Hey…"

"Does she have a DNA sample from you?" I can't believe I just blurted that out. I wanted to talk to him about this, but I'm not prepared to do it yet, and definitely not while I'm in an emotional state.

"What?"

"Nothing. Forget it."

"Lei, what did you ask me?"

Not able to take back my question, I ask again. "Jessa? Does she have a DNA sample?"

"I don't think so. Why?"

"Did you research paternity testing at all?"

He looks confused. It slowly occurs to him what I'm getting at. "You think she's lying?"

"No. But I did some research. She needs your DNA to perform the test. It's also risky to the fetus to perform the test in utero. It's something to think about."

He sits quietly. It upsets me that he sat back, allowing this woman to dictate the chain of events in this nightmare. Jessa isn't here to take my anger out on. So unintentionally, I focus my anger towards him.

Pulling my hand away, I utter, "Let's not talk about this right now. I have some more phone calls to make." I know it's a shitty thing to do, but I can't deal with the black cloud that discreetly hovers above us. I'm too tired.

"Ok…" He watches me, waiting for me to say something.

I can't. I'm just not in the mood to pretend. Deep inside, I truly feel it is Jack's baby. A small seed of doubt festers from the fact that Jessa has been very elusive regarding this paternity test. I don't trust her. I think what upsets me is Jack seems to. I also feel the closer that we get to the truth, the more I panic. This is clearly my version of a panic attack.

"Do you want some space?"

Nodding, I pick up my phone and start to scroll through my contacts.

Jack stands before me, gently pulling the phone out of my hand.

"Lei…I love you." He stares down at me, waiting for my response.

Gazing back into his eyes, I respond, "I know."

My heart splinters a bit from the look in his eyes. He bends to kiss me and hands me back my phone before walking off the bus.

We promised each other to talk things out, and to not let this come between us. I feel awful, but I just can't help it. Feeling emotionally drained, I walk to the bedroom, closing the door behind me. I just need to be alone for a while. I need to remember all the things I love about him, and not the one thing I hate…specifically his pregnant baggage.

Chapter 5 – Jack

I would much rather be next to her, talking her off her cliff, instead of leaving her alone with her thoughts. I get she needs to be alone, and I'll give her the space she needs. I have no worries or doubts of her love for me. I know she's told me she isn't running, but I do worry that she's keeping things from me. Like how she truly feels about Jessa's situation, or if things do not turn out the way we want them to, does it scare her more to be with me than without?

Walking around to the front of the Rex Theater, I text Jessa.

where did you get my dna?

I don't beat around the bush. I will kill this bitch if she is lying to me. I decide to hail a cab. I have no idea where I want to go, but I need time as well. Jessa's text also mentioned Danny was at our opening show. A chill ran down my spine. Initially I disregarded the whole fuel line thing, but now I'm worried. It can't be coincidence. As I left the bus, I asked Tom to watch Leila.

"Where to?"

"Where's the nearest mall?"

"Ross Park, ten minutes."

"Fine."

Pulling my phone out, I decide to call Jen. "Hi, Jen."

"Hi, Jack. What's up?"

"Where's my security?"

"Actually, I was going to call you today about that. The studio feels there really isn't a specific threat to you."

"That's not acceptable. I think there already has been a specific threat to us."

"Why, what's wrong?"

"Jessa texted me. Turns out Danny was at opening night."

"So? A lot of people were at opening night."

"The bus didn't start after the show."

"I know. It caused hours of delay. So?"

"Steve said it looked like something gnawed on the fuel line. I immediately thought of Danny, but then decided it was irrational. Now that I know he was at the show, it's not so irrational anymore."

Jen remains silent on her end of the line for a few seconds. "Ok…it does seem too big of a coincidence."

"Can you let the studio know? I'll call Dylan. I need you to keep on top of this for me. I haven't asked for one Goddamn thing. I'm demanding security."

"Ok, Jack. I'll call Louis now. I'll also call the arena and speak to their security. Maybe they have tapes of the back lots where the buses were parked. We'll touch base after your show.

Hanging up, it's hard not to notice Jen's newfound level of compassion. She knows how pissed I was with her behavior and is trying to placate me. I have no problem using her guilt to my advantage. I'm not ashamed to admit that.

The cab lets me out at the mall, just as my phone buzzes with a call from Jessa.

"I assume you got my text?"

"Yes. That's why I'm calling you."

"Explain."

"I got it from the condom we used that night."

"What the *hell* are you talking about?"

Hearing a sigh over the phone, she waits a few seconds before she continues. "Jack, do you remember what I said to you that night?"

"Nope. I try to ignore you as much as possible."

"Lovely. Well after you screwed me without a condom, I called you an asshole and said you better not have gotten me pregnant."

"I vaguely remember that."

"Do you vaguely remember telling me there was no way my evil, overused womb could procreate?"

Laughing, the memory comes back to me. "Oh, yeah. I remember that."

"And you remember me throwing you out?"

"Yep. I had to call Hunt to pick me up." Hunter was furious with me for fucking her that night. I had to listen to him cursing me out the entire way home and first thing the next morning while fighting a raging hangover.

"Well, whether you believe it or not, I was devastated."

"Cut the drama, Jessa."

"Jack, I still love you. One of these days you'll believe me and realize you love me too."

"You've lost your mind. I don't love you nor have I ever."

"So you propose marriage to anyone you fuck?"

"Please. We were in high school. Everything I did back then was controlled by my dick."

"And what exactly has changed?"

"Hilarious. A lot has changed. I figured out what love is."

"You have? What you figured out is you're obsessed with her. You were obsessed with me too, once. I'm determined to help you remember your feelings for me and bring them back to the surface."

"You're insane. You were an easy lay, and I took it."

"This is exactly what I predicted the night you fucked me without a condom. You're stubborn as hell and impossible to talk to."

"What are you talking about?"

"I saw a clear glimpse of what would happen if I did get pregnant. I predicted you would deny responsibility. So I fished the used condom out of my trash, threw it in a plastic bag, and froze it. My insurance policy."

"You're sick."

"No, I'm practical and I love you."

"Oh my God! Am I talking to a wall? I do not love you. Is this what you are trying to do? Trap me?"

"Jack, do I look like the kind of woman who would have a kid to trap you? I hate kids. But since it has happened, I take it as a sign we are meant to be together."

"You hate kids, but yet you fished a used condom out of the trash in hopes you got pregnant?"

"No. I fished it out just in case I got pregnant. After you fucked me against the wall and called me a barren whore, I had a nightmare that night. I woke up in a cold sweat."

Is she for real? I have little to no patience for this song and dance. As I'm about to tell her so when she continues and catches my attention.

"I clearly saw my future, and your involvement in it. I knew you'd deny and run if I were to become pregnant."

"You are a delusional bitch."

"Now is that a way to talk to the mother of your child?"

"Let's make no mistake about this, Jessa. If, and I mean *if* this baby is mine, I will fulfill my financial responsibilities, but that's it."

"Really?"

"Yes, really. I do not love you. I do not like you. I do not want anything to do with you. I plan on spending the rest of my life with Leila. I'll never look back."

"Jackson, do you think Renata and Peter would allow their only son to turn his back on his child?"

A chill runs down my spine. "This has nothing to do with them. Leave them out of this."

"I intend to. I doubt *they* would stay out of this once they find out I'm pregnant with their first grandchild. What an exciting event in their lives. Or Lizzy? Turning away from her niece or nephew? What about that sweet little girlfriend of yours? I don't think she would want to be with such a cold, callous man."

The more she speaks the more I feel sick to my stomach. "Enough. I don't want to hear from you until you have the test results." I spit out through clenched teeth before ending the call.

I feel my blood pressure rising with every breath I take.

I wander aimlessly for a few minutes, trying to calm down. My thoughts go to Leila. I need to let her know what we are dealing with, that no matter what happens, she will always have my heart.

As I walk the mall, I get some stares from a clump of the guys hanging out by the food court. One of them is wearing a Devil's Lair t-shirt. I nod while they all continue to stare. The dude with the t-shirt opens his mouth to say something, but then quickly dismisses that it could actually be me casually strolling through a mall in the middle of the afternoon.

On impulse, I duck inside *Tiffany's*. I really should get back to the bus, but instead I find myself searching the glass display cases. I haven't a clue what it is I am looking for. It doesn't take long for the sales vultures to circle.

"Can I help you?" A woman with way too much makeup and way too tight clothing smiles at me like we are the best of friends.

"No, thanks." I spot a necklace in one of the cases and it stops me in my tracks. It's a thin silver chain with a small heart dangling from it.

The saleswoman keeps her distance, but barely. The minute she sees me looking up, she pounces. "That piece is exquisite. It's filigree eighteen-carat, white gold, imported from Italy. It comes in…"

"I'll take it."

She tries to sell me a few other things, probably because she thought I was a sucker for not even asking how much the necklace cost. I'm a minute away from telling her off, when she finally wraps my choice.

Back at the arena, Dylan is talking to our driver, Tom, outside the bus. The guys are still not back from wherever they went off to this morning. I don't think they are thrilled with the whole situation. I really should talk to them, especially Hunter.

As I approach the bus, Dylan notices me first. "Hey, Jack."

"I spoke to Jen."

"She called me and filled me in."

"How much pull do you have?"

"Normally, it would be hard to get a security guard for a tour of our size. Due to the whole fuel line thing, I'll see what I can do."

"Thanks, Dylan. I'd appreciate it. Tom, have you seen Leila?"

"She hasn't left the bus. She's still in the back."

Walking towards the closed door, I quietly knock. "Lei?" When she doesn't respond, I open the door to see her lying on her side sound asleep. Her right hand is clutching a tissue and her left is clutching my shirt.

I move to sit next to her, softly stroking her back. "Hey," she says, when she opens her eyes.

"Are you ok?"

"Yeah, I'm good. I must have nodded off. I called Lori, she exhausted me."

"And what did Lori say?"

"Well, she claims she knew about us. She said we were too obvious. She is happy I am finally," she raises her fingers to motion air quotes, *"getting some."*

Laughing at her expression, I lean over to kiss her gently. "Did you tell her you are more than *getting some?"* I mimic her motion.

"No way. That's none of her business. That kind of info would fuel her for years."

Chuckling at her admission, I ask, "Did she bring up Matt?"

"No. So of course I did. She said she has no intention of starting something with him. But I don't believe her. I think she's turning the tables on him and she's enjoying the chase."

"Interesting. Did you mention Trey?"

"Yes. She is trying to meet us in Chicago. I worry she's stringing him along though. If she has Matt on her mind, it's not fair to deceive Trey. I said although I'm dying to see her, I wasn't sure coming to Chicago was a good idea if she isn't planning on a relationship with Trey. She said they are both honest with what their relationship is, and Trey's a big boy. I think it's wrong, but hell, what do I know?"

"She's right. Trey is a big boy."

"I guess…" She stretches lazily. She seems in a better mood. I hate to spoil it, but we really do need to talk about what happened earlier.

"Want to hear something cool?"

"Yeah."

"I saw a guy wearing our t-shirt at the mall."

"Really? That's awesome. Wait, why were you at the mall?"

"Just killing time."

"Jack, you shouldn't be going out alone."

"I was fine."

Motioning toward the bag in my hand, she says, "What's that?"

"Oh. I picked this up for you."

Pulling out the small box, she looks up at me sadly. "I kick you off the bus and you buy me a present?" she asks and smiles warmly.

I decide to get it over with. "Lei, I spoke to Jessa again."

She sits up and her smile fades immediately. "Why?"

"I asked her how she got my DNA."

"Oh, and?"

"I rather not tell you this, but I want you to know I'll hold nothing back from you."

She takes a deep breath and nods, "I want to know."

I give Leila all the details of my fateful night with the bitch. I do edit where she claims undying love and predicts how my parents will react. That part she doesn't need to hear. When I'm done, Leila has the same sick look I had outside the mall.

"I don't know what to say."

"Babe, she is ruthless, conniving and calculating. I want you to know I don't trust her. I know she is jealous of our relationship. I want you to know you will always have my heart. You own me." She looks at the box as I lift it towards her. "Open it."

She opens the lid and lifts the chain until the small heart is eye level, swaying gently back and forth. "I love it."

"Can I put it on you?"

Nodding, she turns and lifts her hair. I place a kiss on the back of her neck and fasten the necklace. When she faces me, her finger is stroking the delicate heart as it nestles in the hollow of her neck.

"I know this doesn't begin to make up for all the crap I'm putting you through. I just wanted to give you something symbolic of how I feel, a reminder."

"Jack, I'm sorry."

Shaking my head, she continues, "Yes. I acted horribly. I'm sorry. I could have handled it better than I did."

"I feel so stupid for not questioning her. I should know better. I promise to get my head out of my ass, but you can't shut me out."

"Jack, sometimes I need time to calm down. I'm not proud of the way I freak out, but it is part of who I am. Once my brain clears, I'm then able to act rationally. I promise I'll do my best not to, but if I do I need time alone to reel it back in."

"Ok. I get it."

She leans over and kisses me deeply. "I love you," she proclaims, once she pulls away.

"I know."

Running her fingers through my hair, she leans her forehead against mine. "Are the guys back yet?"

"Nope."

She looks into my eyes, her gaze is filled with pure heat. "Is the door locked?"

Giving her a half smile, I get up to lock the door. "What do you have in mind, Miss Marino?"

"I'll show you." She reaches for my t-shirt and pulls me towards the bed. While on her knees on the edge of the bed, she takes the hem of my shirt and slowly pulls it up and off my body. Watching me the entire time, she drags her fingertips across my chest, down my stomach, towards the button of my jeans.

"Have you hit the tequila?"

"Nope," she retorts, as she unbuttons my jeans. She leans forward to kiss me. My hands snake around her body, pulling her flush to me.

"I love when you take control," I admit, in between kisses.

"Hang on…it's going to be a bumpy ride." She steps off the bed and stands.

Her gaze lights my cock on fire. She smirks seductively as she lowers my zipper. She slowly drags my jeans down my legs until she is kneeling before me. Her expression becomes predatory when she looks at my Calvin's. She kisses me through my briefs and places her lips on the exact spot I need them to be. My abs flex automatically as I wait for what's yet to come.

Hooking her fingers into the waistband of my briefs, she pulls them down, releasing my stiff cock in the process. She gently pushes me, until I am seated at the end of the bed. Bending to remove my pants and briefs that are embarrassingly around my ankles, she then positions herself between my thighs.

As we stare at each other, the electricity practically becomes visible. Leaning into me, she lifts her lips to kiss mine, my erection now an intrusion between us. Her kisses start out torturously slow, inch-by-inch, down my body. I close my eyes and desperately try to control my excitement, wanting this to last as long as possible.

She looks up at me one last time before she bends to take me. The warmth of her mouth surrounds me as her tongue works me over and over. Her hands spread on my inner thighs, her hair caressing my abdomen and her mouth on me are our only contact. The inside of her mouth feels like pure heaven. I can feel the build in every cell of my body each time she moves down. I'm losing the battle to hold back. She senses I'm close and increases her efforts until I groan loudly with my release. It goes on and on, and she doesn't let up until I'm done.

I lay back on the bed completely spent and panting from the exertion of my orgasm. Leila slows her methods, kissing her way up my body. Positioning herself in the crook of my arm, she waits for me to recover. My girlfriend is always sexy as hell, and our sex life is off the charts, but it's a complete turn on for me when she initiates.

I wrap my arms around her and grip her tightly. The only words I can manage to say are, "Holy fuck."

♫ ♫ ♫

Back stage after our Pittsburgh show, exhaustion is visible on each and every one of our faces. We are waiting for Dylan to discuss the picture that appeared online of Leila and me kissing backstage in Boston.

Krista from L.R.V Media's publicity department found it on the Leila haters' blog site and they aren't happy about it. Some of the posts from fans on our own website were also less than thrilled as well. Krista immediately called Dylan. He filled us in right before rehearsals, and he called Jen during our show. It's a matter of minutes before my phone will start ringing from her call.

It could have been anyone who posted that picture. There is no way of telling where it originated. Most likely a stagehand sent it to a friend and it spread from there. The fact it took days to materialize only supports this theory even more.

Hunter, Scott and Trey sit quietly. I had a sit down with them before rehearsal. Hunter spoke first and confessed he is worried how this whole mess will affect our careers. More importantly, he is worried about Leila and me. Scott said this isn't our fault, and it sucks it has to be this way. Even Trey said we are meant to be. Bottom line is they support us. It means the world to me to know how they truly feel. Their words touched me in a profound way.

Leila has been noticeably quiet. I attributed it to her freak out this afternoon, in conjunction with the news from Krista. I wasn't able to talk to her yet. I can't wait to get her alone to assure her the guys support us and the fans will eventually as well.

Our show was lacking. I could barely concentrate on the lyrics of our songs. I didn't engage with the guys in my usual ball-busting way. I also decided not to sing my ballad, as not to fuel the gossip mill. So all in all, it sucked.

Our current dour moods are a culmination of all the above, and here we sit and wait. Leila sits alone in a chair across the room. I know she's trying to keep it together for me, but she isn't very convincing.

Needless to say, I'm falling short in giving my band or my girlfriend words of encouragement at the moment. I just can't think of one thing to say to any of them. Deciding on honesty, I start with an apology. "Guys, I'm really sorry you all have to go through this."

"It's not your fault." Hunter says half-heartedly.

Unexpectedly, Leila quietly responds to Hunter. "It's my fault. I'm sure you regret adding me to the band."

"Lei…"

"No, Jack. All this crap is because of me. It's because I fell in love with you. If you and I hadn't gotten together, you wouldn't be saddled with this shit. I knew this would happen."

Her words stun me. Where the hell is this coming from? I clench my jaw and respond tightly. "We'll talk about it later."

The anxiety in the room becomes suffocating as Leila and I glare at each other.

Dylan finally appears. He takes a quick look around the room, first noticing the looks on our faces. "What's wrong?"

Sighing, I'm the first to speak. "I wasn't happy with our show." I don't want to drag Dylan into this.

"Oh, they loved you. Don't sweat it."

"It wasn't our best performance. I take responsibility for that. We all had that picture on our minds."

"You're upset about it being leaked?"

"Uh, yeah."

"Don't worry about that. Krista is on it, and in the next few hours she will be watching the Internet. She's prepared to release our statement at any moment."

He makes it all sound so simple. We all know the next few hours will definitely set the tone on how the fans will respond to Leila and me being together. "I'm sure Jen doesn't feel the same way."

As if on cue, my phone finally buzzes with Jen's number. "Jen."

"Ok, so the shit is hitting the fan." Just as I'm about to tell her off, she adds, "But we are prepared and we will deal with it. We are going to spin this in to the greatest love story ever told."

"What?"

"I've spoken to Krista. Why not put our own leaks out there?"

"Our own leaks?"

"Yes. Pictures of you two, fan sightings and gushing comments, all planted by us."

The rest of my band, Leila and Dylan all gape at me, wondering what I am hearing over the phone.

"It sounds like a good plan."

"It is, trust me. Malcolm actually gave me the idea. Why not control the gossip? It's going to happen anyway. Let's steer it in the direction we want it to go."

"Jen, I'm surprised and impressed, thank you. I honestly was prepared to fight with you over this."

"I'm full of surprises, Jack. When are you going to get it through your thick skull that I want you to succeed? I'm not the enemy."

"I know you do."

"I have more good news. We're adding shows to Vegas, Miami, and now ending in New York with two nights."

"Really?"

"Yes. You've sold out every show so far. People want to see you. We're going to give them what they want. The show we are adding with be in *The Garden*."

"*The Garden*?"

"Yes."

"*The Garden*?"

She chuckles and repeats, "Yes."

"Holy shit. That's awesome."

"Yes it is. One more thing. Your album is steadily climbing the charts. Krista arranged all major radio stations to play a Devil's Lair block on the same day next week, your top three songs. You will be doing an interview on *The Diane and Dean Morning Show* on WXLP in

Chicago on the same day the blocks will be played. After the interview, you'll play a song live over the radio."

"Holy shit."

"We will keep releasing tidbits about you and Leila, then you will be on every major airway, coast to coast. The buzz this will create will be priceless."

"Thanks, Jen…and tell Krista thank you. I'll give her a call tomorrow."

"Will do…I'll talk to you later. I have a lot of work to do. Tell Dylan to call me once you arrive in Cleveland. Dylan is handling the security part for you. He'll fill you in."

"Yes, boss." Smiling like a fool, I forget the other five in the room are still gaping at me.

"Well, that was Jen."

Hunter stands and says, "We know…and?"

"She and Krista came up with a plan. They will be leaking our own photos, planting our own comments and blog entries, steering the gossip towards revealing the positives of our relationship."

"That's it?" Dylan asks. "It seems so simple."

"I guess it is. But if done right, it can work."

"Well good for Jen, being a team player and all." Scott says.

"Yeah, it's kinda strange," I admit while shaking my head, I look over at Leila. She sits, staring at the floor while lost in her own world.

"What about *The Garden*?" Hunter asks impatiently.

"Oh. She said our album has been steadily climbing the charts. The label is adding shows to Vegas, Miami and we are now ending with two nights in New York, last one in *The Garden*."

"The fucking Garden?"

I nod and laugh at Hunter's bulging eyeballs.

"Holy Fuck!"

"Wait, there's more. All major radio stations are going to play a Devil's Lair block on the same day next week. We will be interviewed that day on the *Diane and Dean Morning Show* in Chicago."

The guys go ballistic, hooting and hollering about the news I just shared. As they carry on, I move to squat before Leila and take her hands in mine.

"You ok?"

"Yes." She stares into my eyes looking completely defeated.

"You're lying." I pull her up to a standing position. "Let's take a walk."

Leila allows me to lead her to an empty dressing room. The minute I close the door, I come right to the point.

"You really pissed me off with your stupid comment."

"I could tell by your clenching jaw." I give her a look she chooses to ignore. "I meant every word of it."

"You regret falling in love with me?" I ask dumbfounded.

"No. I regret you met me though."

"*What*? It's the same fucking thing." She stands motionless, not denying my claim. "Damn it Leila, knock it off! How many times do I have to tell you I don't regret any of it? Not meeting you, not falling in love with you, any of it!"

"You are biased, Jack. Those guys aren't. I can't help but feel they all regret the day I showed up."

"No, they don't."

"Now you need to knock it off. They deserve more than a mediocre tour filled with bullshit. That's what this will all be reduced to if the fans hate us together." She crosses her arms defiantly and turns her back to me.

"Did you just hear what I shared with them? Were you listening?" She turns and stares at me impassively. "It's a stupid picture. It's not a big deal."

"Exactly. Look at the shit-storm one picture is stirring up. Can you imagine what we'll have to deal with once the news of her pregnancy leaks? What the guys will have to deal with then?"

"You promised you wouldn't do this."

"Do what?"

"Shut me out."

"I'm not shutting you out. I'm telling you exactly how I feel. I wasn't considering the guys in all of this. I was consumed with you being a dad, what that meant to us, what that meant to me. I finally woke up today and realized how much this could affect them."

Sitting in the nearest chair, I viciously rake my hands through my hair. "*What* are you saying?"

"Maybe we should take a break."

"ARE YOU FUCKING KIDDING ME?" The volume of my voice causes her to jump.

"Just until all this crap blows over," she responds in almost a whisper.

I stare at her like she lost her mind. "How the fuck is that going to solve anything? You are asking me to live on that bus and not be with you? Pretend I don't love you more than anything else in this fucking world?" I'm not reaching her. I can tell because she won't even make eye contact with me.

"I'm asking for you to consider the guys."

"The guys don't care that we are together."

"They'll care if the fans do."

Taking a step closer to her, she steps back. "So you want to table our relationship for a bunch of what-ifs?" Again she stands motionless. What the hell has gotten into her?

"Leila, even Jen is fighting for us. *Jen*! How the hell are we going to make it if you won't fight for us?"

Leila sits heavily on the couch, still avoiding my gaze. Kneeling in front of her, I take her hand in mine and soften my voice in an attempt to get through to her. "You said you loved me."

"You know I do."

"Then why are you trying to deny it?"

"I'm not denying it. We've been in denial, pretending our relationship doesn't affect them." She pulls her hands away and adds, "I'm scared."

"I will not let anything happen to you."

"I'm not scared about my safety." She says impatiently. "I'm scared I'll be the reason you don't succeed."

"Baby, please stop. You aren't listening. We are moving in the right direction. The label is behind us. The guys are behind us. Please promise me you'll stop thinking this way."

She doesn't respond when I surround her with my arms. She suddenly stiffens and pulls out of my embrace.

"Jack, I need time."

"Ok. I'll give you a few minutes to calm down."

"No. I need time."

She meets my gaze for a moment, before turning away as one single tear rolls down her cheek.

Her steely stance, her detached aura, her indifference towards this entire situation angers me more than anything else. I thought I knew this woman.

I take a step forward until we are practically nose-to-nose, my hands clenched in fists at my sides, as a means to control the rage I feel coursing through my veins. It reverberates with every breath I take.

"I'll give you your fucking time so you can get your head on straight. But if you think I'm walking away from this just because you are having a fucking panic attack, you don't know me very well."

I storm out of the room and viciously slam the door behind me.

When I walk into the room the guys are sitting in, I instantly know they've heard my outburst. "Hunt. Please wait for her and walk her to the bus."

"What happened?"

"She's losing it. She feels she's ruining your chances to make it big, and she's fucking freaking out!"

I grab a beer and bolt from the holding room. I need air to squelch this dangerous feeling bubbling up inside. I've felt rage before, but this is different. It's tinged with desperation. It's so foreign, and I have no idea what to do with it. I've never needed another person in my life like I need her. The more I'm with her, the more I need her to survive. What the fuck has happened to me?

I storm out of the room, down the hall, and towards the bus. Pacing the parking lot isn't helping with my rage. I hurl the beer bottle through the air and watch it smash to a million pieces against the pavement. One of the roadies chooses to approach me at that unfortunate moment.

"Um, Jack."

"WHAT!"

Once he sees the look on my face, he retreats and falters slightly. "Um, Dylan wants to see you. He's on our bus."

I walk onto Dylan's bus to find him on the phone. He puts up a finger and I sit on the couch still seething. I need to convince her that she is so wrong. While I wait for Dylan to finish up, I quickly text Hunter.

do me a favor. talk to her.

Hunter replies immediately.

will do.

Dylan hangs up and watches me skeptically. "What's wrong?"

"Nothing." I respond through gritted teeth.

"Well, that was Krista. She reiterated their plan. I need to take a picture of the two of you and send it to them."

"What kind of picture?"

"I don't know, an embrace? A kiss? Something intimate. It needs to be in a public place so it would look like a fan took it."

"Fine. When and where?"

"Whenever, but the sooner the better. Also, the arena in New York found something on the security tapes."

My blood runs cold. "What?"

At my expression, he shakes his head. "Just someone lurking around the back. It was hard to see and it was grainy, but it was definitely a man...thin, average height."

"Can't be Danny, he's built and almost as tall as I am."

"It was probably a roadie or stage hand. You can't see the front of the bus because the other bus was blocking the shot."

"I guess it was a coincidence."

"You still want me pushing for security?"

"Yes. Is that it?"

"Are you ok? That's some pretty awesome news Jen shared. Why aren't you happy?"

"I am."

I stalk off the bus and run right into the roadie who said Dylan wanted to see me. He is leaning against the bus, busy on his cell. For the life of me I can't remember his name.

"Hey, I'm sorry, man."

He shifts uncomfortably. "Sure. No problem, Jack."

My gut instinct is to go back to Leila, but based on my frame of mind, I decide against it. I'm hoping Hunter is with her right now talking some sense into her.

Chapter 6 – Leila

I haven't seen Jack this pissed since he stormed out of my apartment the night Dylan's phone call interrupted our lovemaking. That night, he quickly reeled it in and came back. This time I'm hoping he gives me my space. I know if I'm near him, he will cloud my judgment. I need to think clearly and that wouldn't be a possibility being around him.

There's a quick knock at the door before Hunter asks, "Leila, can I come in?"

"No."

Hunter slowly opens the door, watching me cautiously. "Too bad." His posture is defensive as if I'm a caged animal about to attack him. It's almost comical. "He said you're freaking out."

"He's right. Did he send you here?"

He shrugs and slowly walks towards me, clearly out of his element. I feel sorry for him. I feel bad Jack subjected him to a situation he clearly has no experience dealing with...an extremely emotional woman.

"Um, so why are you freaking out?" He has always reminded me of Evan. Having him here with me, he suddenly becomes my substitute best friend, whether he likes it or not.

"I'm screwing things up for you guys."

"No you aren't."

"Hunter, please. Don't say things only because you know he would want you to say them."

"I'm not."

I give him an incredulous look. "Hunter, I heard you all talking. Please stop lying to me."

"Talking about what?"

*Crap...m*e and my big mouth.

"I heard you tell Jack before rehearsal that you and the guys are worried about how this is going to pan out."

Hunter frowns, confusion on his face. "Wait, we were all telling Jack that we are concerned about you guys. That we feel you deserve to be happy and we support your relationship. That's what you heard?"

"No."

"Then you heard wrong. We all told Jack, this sucks. You shouldn't have to go through this and we support you. You heard that part, right?"

"No."

"Ok then, are you jumping to conclusions?"

"No."

"Yes."

Hunter takes my hand. "Leila, hear me out. He doesn't always make the right decisions. He fucked up a few times since I've known him. He fucked up in college. He fucked up with how he handled your relationship in the beginning. He did not fuck up when it came to hiring you. He did not fuck up because he fell in love with you. He loves you. We all do. You joining us was meant to be."

I sigh heavily and he watches me for a few seconds. "Leila, I've never seen him this happy. I've never seen him this content. This was supposed to happen. You are supposed to be together."

"I keep panicking. I keep…" I quickly stop myself when I remember Hunter doesn't know about Jessa's situation. I was just about to confess how much the baby news is wreaking havoc on my mind and that's what I'm really worried about. Once that news is out, all hell will break loose.

I instead say, "I love him so much. I love you all. I wouldn't recover if our situation causes you to not reach the success you all deserve."

"Leila, we are there. A year ago we were playing in dive bars in the city. Now we are traveling the country on a cushy tour bus with sold out shows, and our album is climbing the charts. It's going to take a lot more than you and Jack's relationship to derail this train."

Like a rock-star having a relationship with his back-up singer, while his baby mama is home pining away for him.

Hunter waits for me to absorb his words. After a few minutes he finally speaks again. "Leila, he needs you. We all do. You need to stop this. We are not at all upset, concerned, or regretful that you and Jack got together. You are part of us now. We all adore you. We love seeing him this happy. We don't give a crap what anyone out there thinks. We are a talented bunch of fuckers and our music will get us where we need to be. Stupid internet gossip means nothing to us."

He stands and holds his hand out to me. "Come. I'm sure he's frantic by now." A vision of Jack sulking causes a pain in my chest. I don't want to hurt him. Ironically, my behavior is doing just that.

I take Hunter's hand. "Ok."

He pulls me into a hug before leading me out of the room. As we walk towards the buses, Hunter turns and asks, "No more freaking out?"

I can't promise that. So instead I joke, "What fun would that be?"

"So true."

Jack steps off the bus with his cell phone in hand just as my mine starts playing, *Tie Me Down*. We stand face to face, each waiting for the other to speak. Hunter squeezes my hand and stealthily slinks onto the bus, closing the door behind him.

"Hi."

"What the *hell* was that?"

"I overheard your conversation with them regarding our relationship."

Jack looks confused for a second. "And?"

"I heard Hunter telling you they were worried."

"And you heard that he and the guys support us, and are happy for us?"

"No."

"Jesus Christ. So now you understand they do support us?" When I don't respond, he steps away, agitated. "Really, Leila?"

"Hunter clarified they are happy for us. I still can't help it. There is a lot of crap riding on our success. Most of it because of us, and the worst is yet to come. Plus, Jessa's news is still not out, and I'm extremely insecure about the band's future once people get wind of it. Jack, I don't know how to deal with those feelings. You can't blame me for that."

Jack steps closer and strokes my cheek while his smoky grey eyes gaze right into my soul.

"Baby, I don't know how to help you with those feelings, but you need to detach them from us."

"How can I do that? Let's picture the Devil's Lair of a few months ago. What would you all be doing right now? Partying and celebrating that your album is climbing the charts and you are adding dates."

"We are celebrating. If you paid attention, the guys were stoked from the news that Jen shared. Besides, our success is because you joined the band."

"There is no way of knowing that."

"It's probable. We have to do this together. Because the alternative, being apart, is not an option." Jack searches my face for signs of doubt.

"Jack, you know how vulnerable I feel towards the powers of the Internet and my career. This is hard for me. I promise to *try* not to freak out anymore."

"You need to promise not to push me away."

"It wouldn't matter. I could push all I want, eventually you wear me down."

Rolling his eyes, he adds, "I love you, even when you are a royal pain in my ass."

"Ditto."

♫ ♫ ♫

Cleveland turned out to be my favorite tour stop so far. We arrived early, since it's only a two-hour ride from Pittsburgh. Jack canceled rehearsals, claiming we all needed the time to chill out and celebrate. We all went to a greasy diner for a late breakfast. Then we went straight to Horseshoe Casino. We gambled, we drank, and we laughed. It was just what we all needed. Jack and I slipped away, finding a bar in the casino that played Oldies.

We danced to Elvis' *I Can't Help Falling in Love With You.* I fell in love with him all over again. His lips on my ear and the sound of his voice sent jolts throughout my entire body.

It was the middle of the day and the bar was empty. He sang along to almost every song they played, while holding me close and swaying to the music. We finally had a perfect date.

When we got back to the bus, Dylan was waiting for us with news that the planted pictures and blog entries were released into cyberspace. The studio also released their statement on Devil's Lair's website after our Pittsburgh show. The announcement seemed to appease our fans. There were many posts of congratulations and well wishes. It's as if they were waiting for us to come clean. My haters not so much, but in comparison to the supporters, their numbers didn't seem so scary.

Our show that night in Cleveland was perfect. Jack introduced me by singing *Brown Eyed Girl.* He told the crowd it was a personal favorite. Once done, he sat on his stool center stage with his guitar. While strumming the chords, he asked the crowd for silence.

"So I have something to tell you guys." They responded with cheers and screams.

Chuckling, he asked, "Can you guys let me talk?" The crowd ignored him, the decibels only increasing with his request.

"Please?" Their response was to add whistling and hooting.

"No? Well I'm going to talk anyway. Have you heard my new song?" The noise level in the arena increased to a fever pitch. He waited for them to settle down and then asked, "Do you like it?" I actually felt the stage beneath my feet vibrating from their response.

He chuckled again at their enthusiasm. "Oh, good. I'm glad you like it. I was worried. I lied, though. I didn't write it for Trey."

Laughter filled the stadium. Jack laughed with them. "Seriously...I wrote it for someone very special to me. I wrote it for an amazing girl who changed my life and rocked my world." Jack paused briefly, still strumming chords on his guitar. While smiling wide, he continued. "So, I love her." The crowd went crazy.

"This one is for *my* brown-eyed girl." My heart pounded frantically from watching his performance and to the amount of emotion he stirred within me from his song. It was even better than the first time he sang it. This time, he allowed his own emotions to come through. He glanced over to where I was standing and searched my eyes, sending bolt after bolt of electricity through the air straight into my heart.

The crowd loved it. This set the tone for the rest of our show. Jack was ecstatic and it showed on stage. This sexy, talented, romantic, perfect specimen was declaring his feelings for me. It touched me more than anything ever had in my entire life.

He held my hand during our encore, confirming to the masses in attendance that we were together. The applause became thunderous.

He leaned over and said, "See, there was no need to freak out."

He was right.

As I scanned the hoards of faceless bodies, watching from the stage while they all applauded and screamed for us, while his hand tightly gripped mine, I decided I wouldn't want to be anywhere else at that moment. It felt perfect.

Our next stops were Grand Rapids, Indianapolis, then Detroit, all back-to-back nights. All three shows pretty much went the same way as our Cleveland show did. The only difference was Jack's flirting increased each night.

Once on the bus, I sat on the laptop scouring posts and comments and searching for any evil wishers that were tainting our success. We have officially been out-ed as a couple to our fans, and so far I haven't found any to be concerned about. The Leila haters were still out there, but their numbers weren't increasing all that much. If at all possible, their posts were getting more hurtful. Krista and Jen were constantly on top of the situation, interjecting *happy thoughts* wherever and whenever they could.

After our Detroit show, we all got rip roaring drunk. There wasn't a rush to pull out, so we all hit the closest bar and drank our asses off. Even Dylan and some of the roadies joined us. The redhead, who I suspect has a crush on Jack, came along as well. His name is Kyle and he's painfully shy. It was funny watching him watch Jack all night.

A few patrons recognized us, taking the opportunity to join our loud, obnoxious gathering. It was just what we all needed.

It was four a.m. once we stumbled back to the bus. The guys immediately crashed. Jack and I stayed out front, laughing and making out. At times we were so loud, they threatened to kick us off the bus *while we were moving* if we didn't shut up. Their crankiness fueled our antics even more. By five a.m., Jack and I took our party to our room and had drunk-induced, raunchy sex. He took me from behind as my naked breasts pressed up against the darkened window. It was so erotic. Even though no one could see me, the illusion was enough to enhance my already *mind-blowing* orgasm.

"Ok, you need to fess up."

"Huh?" I respond sleepily. My eyes drift closed again just as I feel Jack pulling a taut nipple in between his lips. I'm so conflicted. I'm exhausted, but I'm also now aroused…again.

"Jack…What are you doing? I need sleep." Swirling his tongue around my nipple, he sucks hard until my eyes fly open. "Jack, it's so early. You're killing me."

"No, it's not, it's late."

"Can't be." I am so tired. It feels like I've been asleep for minutes and not hours.

"It is. Actually it's like ten. We need to get up." Kissing my other breast he asks, "Do I have your attention?"

"Yes."

"Good. You need to fess up."

"About what?"

"My ringtone."

Oh crap.

I was hoping it didn't register with him that his ringtone is a song about tying me up and fucking me senseless. Absolutely nothing gets past him. I meant to change it. I totally forgot. This is almost as bad as me confessing his dimples make my crotch clench.

"Well?"

"Um…I think it's pretty self-explanatory."

"That it is. I can't wait to get you into a proper bedroom to fulfill your fantasy."

"I promise once we get to a proper bedroom, you can fulfill my fantasy."

"Good. Especially since that will be in less than an hour."

"Then can I sleep?"

"No. Definitely not."

"You're mean."

"I'll make it up to you. Thank you for choosing that ringtone."

"Thank you for reminding me that I need to change it."

"What? Why?"

"It's embarrassing."

"No, it's not. It's hot as fuck."

"Jack, I was mortified when Evan accidentally heard it. I need to change it."

Jack frowns adorably. "What will you change it to?"

"I don't know. What do you have as my ringtone?"

Without missing a beat, he proudly replies, "*Layla,* of course."

"Really? I love that."

"Well, I love you. I set it after our first night together. I told you I love Clapton and now more than ever."

My heart melts at his admission. I smile warmly. "Oh, I know what I want."

"What?"

"My song. I'll download it from YouTube."

"Really? I love that." He repeats my words back to me before bending to kiss me softly.

"Can I go to sleep now?"

"Nope." Jack pulls my earlobe in between his teeth, tugging gently. "You need to get up. We'll be arriving at the hotel soon, and we need to pack and check in. But don't pack too much. I plan on having you naked most of the next two days."

"Can I wear clothes to the radio interview?"

"Uh, yeah. I don't want anyone else seeing you naked."

"You're so considerate."

"I can be." He reaches down between my legs, skimming a fingertip over my sensitive skin, over and over and over and over, until I climax.

♫ ♫ ♫

We arrived in Chicago mid-morning and we have the entire day to ourselves. Sure, we have rehearsals and our show to perform tonight and an early radio interview in the morning, but who cares…we have two nights in a hotel.

Bliss.

Patti and Mandy flew out to meet us. They were originally only going to spend the two days with us in Chicago, but they decided to move on to Des Moines and fly home from there. I'm really looking forward to having some female company on the bus. Lori was not able to make it. I was disappointed, but simultaneously relieved that she took my advice not to string Trey along. Trey pretended he didn't care in the least. I'm not buying it, though.

As we walk through the lobby, it is hard not to spot Hunter and Mandy, Scott and Patty sucking faces. They are literally blocking the walkway, forcing people to walk around them to get to the elevator banks. Some mothers are giving them dirty looks, but most of the dads are enjoying the show, as well as a few teenage boys.

"We need to get them to their rooms or they're going to get arrested."

"That could be kinda fun."

"Jack…"

Laughing, he pulls me over to the love fest, breaking them up long enough to convince them to check in and get out of the lobby. We agree to meet at rehearsal, all wanting to spend every minute locked behind closed doors. Trey takes off in the opposite direction, out into the parking lot.

"I feel bad for Trey. We're all paired off." I voice my concern while waiting for the elevator.

Jack looks down at me. "That's what he does. Even before you joined us, we would all go out to a bar, and Trey would disappear minutes later."

"I still feel bad."

"He's fine, babe."

Hunter and Scott are down the hall fiddling with their room keys as their girlfriends do a-*hurry-up-and-open-the-damn-door* jig behind them. The more they bounce, the more their boyfriends can't get the doors open.

Jack laughs out loud at the sight. Our room is right between theirs and these walls better be soundproof. I'm not very concerned, though. I'm sure I won't hear a thing. I am so excited. Two whole nights to sleep in a real bed. I hope there are big fluffy pillows.

After using the bathroom, I walk in to see Jack lying across the bed, holding a belt in his hands. He's removed his shirt, shoes and socks, making him look like he's shooting a designer jean commercial. With a look that could melt my panties, he says, "Time to fulfill your fantasy."

"Really? We are in this room ninety seconds."

"I know. We wasted ninety seconds already."

He stands slowly, stalking towards me like he's about to have me for dinner. It's so sexy. "Baby, I need you naked."

"Then can I sleep?" He nods devilishly.

I raise my arms and respond, "Ok, go at it."

He shakes his head. "Nope. We are going to fulfill my fantasy today as well. And my fantasy is to watch you strip."

"Nuh uh...no way," I shake my head stubbornly.

Jack nods just as stubbornly. "Oh yes. I've been dreaming about it since the night you stripped after your farewell party. Even as drunk as you were, it was one of the sexiest things I've ever seen. I need a repeat." He sits on the end of the bed. "Come on, baby. Make my dreams come true," he pouts adorably.

I release a very heavy sigh as embarrassment takes over. "Jack, I'm not that brave without tequila."

"Come on, for me?"

"I hate you."

"I'll make it up to you."

"So you keep sayin'."

Kicking off my shoes first, I then slowly pull off my t-shirt, dropping it to the floor. Jack sits riveted, as if he's never seen my body before. I unbutton my jeans, sliding the zipper down with much ceremony. Actually, this is kind of fun. I'm turned on just from the look on his face. I would even entertain some stripper music right about now.

I turn my back and peel my jeans off of my legs, wiggling my ass in the process. I then step out of them and toss them onto Jack's lap. While looking over my shoulder, I unhook my bra allowing the straps to hang free. I hold the bra to my breasts and slowly turn to face him. Jack pins me with his smoldering gaze. The intensity in which he watches me causes every cell in my body to respond. He licks his lips and leans forward with his elbows on his knees. His reaction is completely spurring me on.

I pull the bra away one cup at a time and dangle it from my fingertips. As I drop it to the floor, I slowly slip my other hand inside my panties, leveling him with my stare.

Jack is on me instantly.

"You didn't let me fin..." He muffles my words with his lips. His kiss turns me inside out, leaving me breathless.

He lifts and centers me on the bed.

"Your turn. Raise your arms." Clasping my hands together, he loosely wraps the belt around my wrists, then around the headboard. "Ready, baby?"

When I nod, he pulls one of my scarves out of his pocket. "This will make it even better." Jack gently ties the scarf around my eyes. "Can you see anything?"

Shaking my head, he responds with a kiss on my lips.

He places a trail of kisses to my ear, down my neck and back up to my lips. He stops there for a few minutes, kissing me deeply. Being blindfolded heightens my senses. His lips feel softer against my own, his stubble burns against my face in a good way, and his scent is clean and masculine.

Pulling away, he moves lower and lower until I feel his breath on my left breast. He doesn't move, except for the puffs of air I feel against my hardened nipple. He runs his nose over it, and then his lips pull it forcibly into his mouth. Jack has sucked on my nipples plenty of times, but this time feels incredible.

I feel like I'm about to literally implode, the heat centered in my groin. "Jack, make love to me." He doesn't respond. Instead he starts the process on my right breast. By the time he moves further down, I'm panting uncontrollably.

He hooks two fingers into the side elastic of my panties and slowly drags them down my legs. He still hasn't uttered one word. It's doing unbelievable things to my arousal. Warm lips find me, while his fingers explore me. The combination brings me to an immediate orgasm. It takes hold and doesn't let go, rolling on and on.

As I'm trying to control my breathing, his lips are suddenly on mine, and his erection is pressing against my entrance. "I love you." He finally says, as he slowly slides into me. He releases my hands, but keeps the scarf securely tied around my head.

He snakes his hands behind my back, holding me tightly against his body. There isn't a sliver of space between us. Still being blindfolded, I can feel each of his hard muscles pressing against me. I can feel his fingers gripping my back, his abs against my belly, his breath on my neck, and his pants in my ear.

I reach orgasm first, and it's even more intense than the first one. Jack continues, quickening his pace until he shudders inside me.

"Holy fuck." He rasps out, as the shudders continue to move through him into me. I move my face to the left until my lips find his chin. I run them over his stubble before pulling his bottom lip in between my teeth. His groan rumbles right through me. I love that I can do this to him. I love he reacts that way towards me.

Jack pulls the scarf off, but doesn't pull out from inside of me. He looks so serious as he stares into my eyes,

"What's wrong?"

"Nothing. I've never felt this way before. It's overwhelming."

I know exactly what he means. "I know. Sometimes it scares me."

Jack gently pulls out, pulling me into his arms. "I can stay here forever."

"Me too." The lack of sleep from last night, and the two orgasms he just gifted me with take control of my body. Fighting desperately to stay awake, I lose the battle pathetically.

The last thing I hear is, "Sleep, baby."

I'm startled awake from a cursing Jack. "Damn it." Grabbing his jeans off the floor, he retrieves his phone. "Jen, you're on speaker. I'm with Leila."

"Great. I hope I'm not interrupting anything?"

"I wouldn't have answered the phone if you were."

"Ugh. I'm sorry I asked. Listen up. Dylan spoke to you about the security tapes?"

"Yeah." He stops for a second and continues. "I told him I still want security."

"Jack, there really isn't any reason for you to…"

"Jen. I want security."

"Whatever…I'm trying. So I'm flying in and I will be at the show tonight with Krista. We will also be joining you tomorrow at the radio station. I predict a lot of questions about you two. I want to be there to defuse them. Did I mention you have to be there at six-thirty and go live at seven?"

"Damn that's early. I'll need help to get Trey there."

"I'll get him there. See you tomorrow."

Jen hangs up and I immediately ask, "What happened on those tapes?"

"There was a guy hanging around the buses. From the description Dylan gave me, it couldn't have been Danny, too short. It was probably a roadie. But I still want security."

"I feel better about the tapes though, don't you?"

"Yeah."

♫ ♫ ♫

As I look around our pitiable crew, I'm grateful we are doing a radio interview this morning and not a TV interview. We are one sorry sight for sore eyes. Trey has on his shades, so there is no way of knowing how tired he looks. But the rest of us look downright pathetic, except for Jen and Krista. They both look as fresh as daisies.

After our show last night, Jen had arranged for a small after-party. She invited about a dozen of our fans, as well as the band, Patti, Mandy, Krista from the label, our roadies, our drivers,

Dylan, Will, our equipment manager, and some arbitrary chick that Trey picked up. This is the first time we've met Krista face to face, and I adore her. She is sweet and funny. I love that she has been assigned to Devil's Lair.

Jen had the brilliant idea of presenting backstage passes to random people in the audience. She really is a good agent. She had drinks and food set up for us and turned it into an intimate meet-and-greet. They took photos and autographs. Jen gifted them with Devil's Lair t-shirts and CD's.

It was really fun interacting with our fans so casually. They became real to us, to me. No longer the faceless people who did nothing but spew lies on the Internet. These fans were truly into Devil's Lair and loved everything we presented to them.

A few of the girls in the bunch flirted shamelessly with Jack and not being able to help himself, he flirted back. He would watch me give him the evil eye from across the room and wink. It was truly harmless and I was really just busting his chops, but it did leave me wondering which one of them he would have ended up with if we weren't together. That is one dangerous game to play in your mind, especially when a little tipsy.

Jack left the room for a few minutes. While he was gone, my cell phone buzzed with a new text. My sexpot of a boyfriend took a picture of his family jewels and sent it to me with the message - *you own this…find me.*

And find him I did.

We had a quickie in one of the empty dressing rooms.

Overall it was a really great night. The drinking until the wee hours when we had to be at the radio station by six-thirty in the morning was not so smart. So now we are all hurting. The upside is once the interview is over, we are free for the rest of the day and night. Even Jack conceded sleep is definitely in our plans today.

Shocker.

As we all sit and wait while yawning repetitively, Gregory, the station's morning producer, herds us into a large studio. I've never been to a radio station before. We are immediately fitted with headphones, given instructions on the *red light*, and a quick rundown of how the interview would flow.

Dean and Diane are chatting with Jen and Krista in the adjoining studio. I Googled the DJ's on WXLP, and I'm a bit star-struck. Diane and Dean are a team who have controlled the Chicago airways for years and are well respected in the Rock and Roll world. Dean looks like a well-aged rocker himself. He is extremely handsome and emanates a total *coolness*. Diane is a pretty woman with a trendy haircut and nerdy black-framed glasses. Except for the nose piercing, she looks more like a librarian.

They've interviewed everyone from up and coming artists like us, to The Stones and Springsteen. I now have six degrees of separation to Springsteen. The thought makes me downright giddy. A small giggle escapes, and Jack looks over amused.

"What's so funny?"

"I wonder if Springsteen's ass sat in this chair."

Smiling, he leans in. "His ass would be lucky to sit in your chair." Then he licks my neck.

I'll never get used to this man charming me. As I squirm my ass in the said chair, he smiles even wider and winks at me.

"Unbelievable."

He shrugs and says, "What?"

"This is fucking awesome," Hunter whispers loudly. "I am so excited, I could shit myself."

"Scott, switch seats with me," Trey mumbles.

The studio door opens and Dean, Diane, Jen and Krista enter. "Hi guys!" Diane boisterously says, like it's six-thirty at night and not in the morning.

Jack speaks first. "Hi. It's such an honor being here."

Dean comes up behind Diane. "We love interviewing new talent. We love to gloat once success is met and tell the world we were there in the beginning. We're not ashamed to say we also love to exploit your greenness."

We all laugh at his admission, while Diane says, "Shut it, Dean. You can't keep telling everyone how calculating we are."

Dean admits while shrugging, "Why the fuck not? Which reminds me…get all your fucks and shits and douche-bags out now. We only run on a ten second delay, but sometimes the guys on the dump button fall asleep."

Diane dramatically rolls her eyes. "You can see who the classier one is in this team?" She moves over to her side of the control desk. Once she's seated with earphones in position, she starts flipping some switches and my nerves start the stomach flutters and the leg jiggles to begin. Jack reaches under the counter and uses his hand to stop my jiggling knee.

Diane looks over and smiles warmly. "I'm sure you are all nervous, and there really is no reason to be. So what if hoards and hoards will be hearing you? Pretend it's just us. I know Shelly ran through the drill with you guys. We'll start off with a casual chat. Then we'll open the phone lines up to the fans. Finally, we'll end the segment with your live performance of *Committed*. Sound good?"

We all nod mechanically and Diane laughs. "Just like good little soldiers, right Dean?"

"Naïve, trusting good little soldiers." He smiles manically from his side of the control panel. I love these two.

Jen and Krista sit in the corner talking quietly. I feel a bit better they are here and they are on our side. Correction, I feel better Krista is here and on our side. In the few hours I got to know her, I already trust and like her a hell of a lot more than Jen.

After the DJ's talk to us for a few minutes trying to loosen us up, the Producer's voice comes over the speakers announcing sixty seconds to air. Jack takes my hand and squeezes it, running his thumb over mine. Looking over he smiles warmly and I return my own. This is a significant moment for all of us.

The timer on the wall counts down from five and then the red light glows from the *On Air* sign.

"Good morning Chicago. How are we today? I'm Dean Ratner here with Diane Jones, and you are privileged to be listening to the *Dean and Diane Morning Show*."

"*Diane and Dean Morning Show*."

"Whatever. Diane how was your dinner last night?"

"I'm lucky to be alive. I think he tried to kill me."

Laughing out loud, Dean then asks, "Finally? I mean, how?"

"Ha ha. He accidentally left the twine on the chicken and served me a piece that was wrapped in it. The Heimlich maneuver was required."

Dean laughs again and adds, "He meant well. You were the one who complained he never cooks for you."

"True. But I didn't want it to be my last meal. I still have a lot to live for. I could see the headlines. *CHICAGO DJ CHOKES ON CHICKEN TWINE*."

"That would be classic. The only thing to shut Diane Jones up is chicken twine."

"Hilarious, Dean. Besides, talking is my job."

"And thank God you have the gift of gab."

"Why don't you come over tonight and Luke will cook for you?"

"No, thanks. I like my life."

"What life?"

"Come to think of it, he did call me yesterday asking if I'd entertain changing the show to *Dean and Luke*."

"Great. I always knew my husband was jealous of my career. You all heard. If I turn up dead, Luke Jones for attempted murder and Dean Ratner as his accomplice."

"Whoa. I had nothing to do with the attempted murder this time."

This easy banter goes on between them for a few minutes as I silently sit wide-eyed, still awe-struck and nervous as hell.

Diane is the first to reveal our presence. "Listen up, Chicago. We have very special guests here with us today. Jack Lair, Hunter Amatto, Scott Malone, Trey Taylor and Leila Marino from Devil's Lair are in the studio. Welcome guys."

We all say a quick hello. Jack, as our nominated voice for most of this interview adds smoothly, "It's an absolute honor to be here." His sexy voice coming over my headphones is doing things to me. I've never seen him get nervous, not on stage, not now. Looking over at my calm boyfriend, I am in awe at how cool he is.

"You are quite a good looking bunch. Yum."

"Settle down, Diane."

"Just sayin'. So, what's new?" Diane asks in a singsong voice.

We all chuckle and Dean says, "Spill it, Diane. Just get it out, because we all know what you want to know."

"Ok, I'm not shy. Let's cut to the chase, then we can move on. Jack? Leila? What's the story?"

Jack laughs at her candor and looks over at me as my nerves go into overdrive. Jen watches like a hawk from the corner.

"What story?" Jack responds candidly.

"Funny. Did you take Dean's smart-ass pills today? What's going on with you two?"

"Diane, please leave the kids alone."

"Oh puhleezee. You were the one in the hall asking, 'So, how are you going to ask them? Huh? Huh?' You're such a gossip whore."

"I am not. I am asking for the listeners. You know, inquiring minds want to know and all that crap."

"Whatever, Dean. So, no one leaves here until you come clean. Spill it, you two."

Jack hesitates for a few seconds looking directly at me. "Um…well…Leila and I…um…yeah, it's true." He admits, smiling at me.

"If the viewers could see these two right now. Oh my God, so adorable."

"Calm down, Diane. How do you guys feel about these two?" Dean asks.

Hunter speaks first. "It's annoying."

Laughter fills the studio. "In what way?"

"I'll paint a picture. Cramped messy bus, two horny…wait, can I say horny?"

"Um, yes."

"Oh, good. Two horny rockers and a couple in love on a cramped bus. So much *fun*."

"We get the picture. Besides Jack, you boys aren't getting lucky? Wait, there are three of you."

Scott, Hunter both respond. "Trey is getting some." Trey shrugs.

"Lucky, Trey. What's his secret?"

"He's single. Our girlfriends haven't been able to join us until yesterday." Hunter admits.

"Ah, so now the horniness problem is solved?" Dean says.

"Yep, for now."

"Leila, how does it feel being the only woman on this bus?" Diane asks.

"Annoying."

Diane laughs and Dean asks, "And why is that? Don't tell me you are horny too? Jack, do we need to have a chat?"

"Really, Dean?" Diane chastises.

"What?"

"Ugh…anyway, why is it annoying?"

"No, Dean. I'm not annoyed for the same reasons as Hunter. I'm annoyed because they are all a bunch of slobs." My voice sounds a bit shaky through my headphones.

"I'm not." Jack admits.

"You are the worst of all of us. Don't lie." Scott says defensively.

"Well, I'm trying to change that." Looking over, he winks at me and Diane lets out a loud sigh.

Jack bestows Diane with his dimples and her eyes roll back in her head. "Oh my God! He has dimples. Jack, I'll leave Luke if things don't work out for you two."

"Diane…" Dean scolds.

"What…he's gorgeous. Sorry, Leila."

"I'm used to it."

Diane focuses on Trey in the corner. "Trey, how do you like traveling with this crew?"

"Annoying. No offense, Leila."

"No worries, Trey." I respond.

"So the gist of Devil's Lair tour is some of you are horny and most are annoying?" Dean asks.

"Pretty much." Hunter says arrogantly.

"Except, Leila…on both counts." Jack brags, smiling wide.

"Jack."

"Sorry, baby."

"Aw, that's so sweet." Diane says. "You two are just adorable together."

"Ugh…Hunter, I get your point now." Dean grumps.

Hunter shrugs. "Told you so."

The DJ's get down to the real interview. The guys all visibly relax as they speak about their true passion. Their knowledge and love of music comes through with every word they utter. Their eyes glazed and their faces serene as if they were discussing a really beautiful vacation spot they all shared. They reply easily to all the questions thrown their way. Laughing comfortably, responding honestly. It's a treat to watch, and it reminds me how lucky I am to have found this awesome bunch of men. Occasionally Dean or Diane will direct one question to me, as I try to answer with as much finesse as the guys. To my own ears though, I sound like a nervous wreck.

Things become a bit tense when the phone lines are opened. The fans shamelessly ask all sorts of questions, from the exact moment we fell in love, to when will we be getting married, to whether the guys prefer boxers or briefs.

Jack can't resist letting them know Hunter goes commando, Scott prefers boxers with cartoon characters on them, (as he snickers) and he prefers briefs. Trey is still a mystery. When another caller asks what I prefer, I place my hand over Jack's mouth just before he could embarrass me.

A few calls are cut short the minute the DJ's realize the callers do not have honorable intentions with their line of questioning. But all in all, it is a good interview. We end with a live rendition of *Committed* and considering the guys are working with borrowed instruments, we still sound really awesome.

During a commercial break, Dean stands and says, "We'll play *High Life* and *Nothing to Gain* when we return from commercial. Your agent also gave us a bunch of CD's to gift to the listeners."

"You guys were awesome. We'd love you to come back again." Diane moves around the counter to give us all hugs.

Dean nods behind her and says, "By then it may be The Dean and Luke show though."

"You're such an ass."

We say our good-byes before being ushered out of the studio. "Congrats guys! That was a great interview." Jen says, as we all congregate in the lobby. "You can all go and relax. I'd like to meet up for breakfast tomorrow before you take off. Let's meet in the hotel restaurant at check out. Band meeting, if you will."

"Are we in trouble?" Hunter asks, like he's a four year old.

"No…why would you think you are in trouble?" she smirks and leaves with Krista in tow. "Enjoy your day off people."

"We fully intend to!" Hunter yells back.

Jack pushes the elevator button. Minutes tick by and no elevators appear. One by one we all look at each other and all dart towards the stairwell, laughing uncontrollably the entire time. We all have one thing on our minds. Sleep.

Chapter 7 – Jack

Yesterday, after doing our radio show, I realized two things.

One...the evidence definitely proves our fame is exploding by the minute.

Two...I'm really happy.

Leila sleepily opens her eyes as I stroke her nipple with my fingertip. "Hey."

"Hey." I smile back, clearly showing her my euphoria.

"How can you be so happy in the morning?" She grumps adorably.

"Because the girl I love is naked in my bed."

I pull her closer, trying to transfer my want for her through a kiss. My cell phone buzzes and it effectively interrupts our moment.

"Damn it." I pull away to retrieve the stupid device. "What!?" She laughs as I aggressively answer the call.

"Dude, where the fuck are you? You're late." Hunter says through the phone.

"I was just about to make love to my girlfriend." I respond while she wraps her body around mine. I squeeze her tight, kissing the top of her head. She's finally comfortable with our relationship in front of the guys.

"Congrats, but you need to zip it in your pants, and get your girlfriend and your hard-on out here. You're lucky it's me calling you. Jennifer is about to barge into your room. There are some photographers outside, and Jen wants us to all leave together to maximize their efforts. Free publicity. So move your ass...now!" Hunter hangs up, and I look at the time on my phone. We're not that late.

"Damn he's bossy." Looking down at her, she looks totally freaked out. "What?"

"Photographers?"

"Yeah...so?"

"Jack, it's happening."

"The fact we are gaining fame? I know, it's awesome."

"Yeah, there's that and also all those people that heard our interview now know we are together and that we are having sex, thank you for that. The interview made it all so real, and it's one thing to post words, but it's another to say them out loud on a radio station that broadcasts to hundreds of thousands of people if not millions and millions, and it all just hit me and I really feel like I can throw up."

As she stops to take a much-needed breath, I tilt her chin up so she can stare into my eyes. "Baby?"

"Yeah?"

"Shut the fuck up." I bend to kiss her passionately with the intent to just distract her, but my lower half instantly gets the memo and comes to the meeting. Taking her hand, I place it over my pulsing dick. "Now look what you did."

"That's from one kiss? I'm good." She squeezes and smirks.

"Well, you have to do something about it."

"We can't…we're late."

"Your hand wrapped around it isn't helping."

She removes her hand. "Ok, problem solved."

Regretfully, I pull away with my massive hard-on in tow. "Jeez, you're such a buzz kill."

"Our agent is the buzz kill. Little Jack would hide if she came barging in here."

He considers my words. "First of all, not little. Second, it would take her at least four minutes to get up here."

"Jack."

"What?" She gives me a look. "Fine. You're right. We need to get downstairs. We'll boink as soon as we get on the bus."

"Boink? What are you eighty? Who says boink?"

"Come here, smartass." I attack her with groping, tickling and kissing. She giggles adorably, trying but failing to pry my arms and lips away from her body.

"Jack…stop." She gasps in between giggles. "Stop…we're late."

"Yeah, yeah...I know."

I reluctantly let her go and she finds her clothes before disappearing into the bathroom. I should follow her in, but remembering what we did in there last night, following a naked Leila into that bathroom right now would be asking for trouble. I'm at full mast and there's no time for a cold shower.

I throw on my rumpled clothes in record time. Once I'm fully dressed and adjust myself, I then knock on the door.

"Let me in."

"Are you going to be good?"

"Yes, I promise."

We move around each other like we've been together for years and not merely weeks. As we stand side by side, doing mundane things like shaving or brushing our teeth, I want nothing more than to do this for the rest of our lives. It's the normal, and the boring, that I most look forward to. I'm really not sure why. Maybe because I've never had someone to just *exist* with, to watch TV with, or make dinner with. I crave it now that I have her.

She watches me in the mirror. "I think I love you smooth as much as much as I love your stubble."

"Yeah? Which way do you prefer between your thighs?" She stares at me and then rolls her eyes. "For the record, I know I love you smooth."

"For the record, I used your razor last night." I gawk at her through the mirror as she smacks my ass and adds, "Hurry up."

Fuck, that's hot.

Leila goes to call the next elevator while I grab our bags. From down the hall, I can see her pacing and gnawing on her bottom lip.

"What?"

"I just remembered the photographers out there."

"Babe, they're just men who have cameras with very long lenses." We both enter an empty elevator when I rationalize, "They are overcompensating for their small dicks. Have some sympathy. It must be tough going through life with a tiny dick." I stroke her bottom lip with my thumb.

She looks up at me and takes a healthy bite.

"Ow. Seriously, what are you so nervous about?"

"Oh, I don't know, my face being plastered all over the Internet?"

"Just another thing you have to get used to. In a few years your gorgeous face is going to be on the cover of Rolling Stone. Mark my words."

"Your face will be right next to mine."

The elevator doors open just when I bend to kiss her. A family waits to get on as I attempt to lead her out into the lobby, but I stop when I feel resistance. "Are you ready?"

She nods, yet doesn't take a step. I stand at the open door with our arms outstretched between us. I smile apologetically as they patiently wait. Leila takes a few deep breaths. After a few moments, she finally follows me out of the elevator. She mumbles, "Sorry," as we pass them.

I can't believe how nervous she is.

The lobby is clear. Her eyes shift around the room on alert for photographers.

I decide to distract her. I bend and kiss her passionately in the middle of the hotel lobby. Her breath catches, she instinctively stiffens, but my lips moving over hers causes the undeniable spark to catch between us. I move my hands to her lower back and hold her up against me. She relaxes in my arms and completely submits.

When I break the kiss, she slowly opens her eyes and pants heavily against my lips. "Let's go, sweet lips."

She blinks repeatedly, while looking dazed and confused. Snapping back to reality, she takes a step backwards and pushes me away hissing, "You are so evil."

Raising my eyebrows at her, I smile and say, "What? You needed a distraction."

Ignoring the stares from the hotel patrons, the front desk clerk and the doorman, I grab her hand and drag her towards the restaurant to meet up with our band.

"Hey, gang." I focus on Jen and grin. She sits with crossed arms and a scowling face. Amanda and Patti look visibly uncomfortable and the guys are all smirking annoyingly.

"Relax, Jen. We're only a few minutes late." I say, as we both sit at the table.

"Twenty-six."

"Wait, back out and come back in. I want to get this on video." Hunter says, holding up his phone.

"Shut up, dickhead."

Hunter laughs out loud, continuing to point his phone at me. "Ooh, that was good. Insult me again, but put some meaning behind it this time."

Trying to hide my smile, I point at his phone. "If you don't knock it off, I'll shove it up your ass and you'll get plenty of meaning behind you."

"Grow up…both of you." Jen says impatiently.

"Yes, mommy." Hunter responds, and we all go into hysterics.

Jen continues to glare at us, waiting for us to act like adults.

"Ok, sorry. We'll behave." I placate our agent. "Can I order coffee before we have our band meeting?"

"Make it quick."

The guys have already received their food. Leila and I quickly order breakfast. Jen starts to speak, and I cut her off. "Please don't talk until I take a few sips of coffee. I can't promise I'll behave until I do."

Sighing she levels me with her gaze. "Sometimes I feel like I represent a bunch of preschoolers."

"Ouch." Trey responds.

Coffee, pancakes, eggs, bacon and a few more insults from our agent later, we are finally having an adult conversation.

"So, you all did a great job yesterday. I spoke to Gregory, he said the response the station has received from your interview was phenomenal."

Like the preschoolers we are, we all break into grins while fist-pumping each other.

"Don't get too cocky. Keep focused and do not let this go to your heads." She looks each and every one of us in the eyes. "I will not tolerate anyone screwing this up. Got it?"

"Loud and clear." Hunter responds for us, as the rest of us nod wordlessly.

"Good. There are a few photographers outside. We will all go out together. There are also a few fans. We'll sign autographs, we'll smile, and we'll take pictures, and you two…" She points to Leila and me, "…will ignore questions regarding your relationship. Smile and say nothing. Got it?"

Now it's our turn to nod wordlessly. "Good. Let's go."

As we shuffle out of the restaurant, Leila's nerves take control of her facial muscles. Her puckered forehead and her teeth gnawing on her bottom lip are complete giveaways.

"Smile, baby, or I'll distract you again." She plasters a big toothy grin on her face, making me laugh. "Perfect. But you have parsley in your teeth." She sucks in a breath, stopping her in her tracks. "I'm kidding."

"I hate you."

Winking, I respond, "No you don't."

The minute we hit the parking lot, the reality of our success hits me. Yesterday, when we boarded our buses, there wasn't a single soul in sight. Today, there are a handful of photographers all taking pictures while a couple dozen fans start screaming for our attention.

Not bad…

"Hey, you see the one in front with the two foot lens? He's probably packing three inches." She throws me a look and rolls her eyes.

We all do just as Jen asked, smiling, schmoozing and ignoring the relationship questions. As we move towards our bus, one of the photographers calls out, "How long have you been together?"

Trey deadpans, "Hunter and Scott would like their privacy during this stressful time." With that, he boards the bus, leaving the cameras flashing and Hunter and Scott open mouthed, red faced, and ready to kill him.

♫ ♫ ♫

"Hey, Liz. How are you?"

"Is this my famous brother who is too good to call his baby sister?"

"Ha…ha. I've been busy. Sorry."

"I'm teasing. I know fame is *very* time consuming."

"You're a riot today. So how are you?"

"I'm good. Busy. Where are you guys now?"

"We're in Des Moines. How are Mom and Dad?"

"They're great. They are so proud of you guys. Dad started a scrap book."

"You mean Mom."

"Nope. I mean Dad. He keeps it on the coffee table. It's so cute to watch him pull it out to add anything he can find to it. He has a page dedicated to each of you. Even Leila."

"He's finally gone off the deep end."

Lizzy giggles. "I agree. Hey, so they want to fly out to see your show in Miami. They'll combine it with a trip to see Grams and Pops. Don't tell them I told you. They'll kill me."

"I won't. Thanks for the warning. What about you? When are you coming out?"

"Well, funny you should ask, Evan and I are coming together."

"Great..." I mumble.

"What's wrong, big brother?"

"Evan, as Leila's best friend and brother, I'm excited to see. Evan, as the guy screwing my sister, not so much."

"How do you think Evan feels about you?"

"I hadn't thought of it."

"Exactly, because it's all about Jack."

"That's not true. I've changed. You'd be proud of me."

"Let me poll some of your band mates before I announce how proud."

"No confidence in me. So when are you coming?"

"Vegas. Are you ok with that?"

"Absolutely. We'll have a blast. We have three nights off. It'll be a big party."

"I know. I spoke to Jen to make sure there weren't any schedule changes. I know you added a show. We'll be coming for five days."

"I can't wait to tell Lei."

"No! Evan wants to surprise her. So keep your big mouth shut."

"Can I tell Hunt and Scott? They'll be pissed if they know we are planning a reunion and they didn't get to ask Mandy or Patti."

"Wow, look at you thinking of others. I am proud."

"Ok, smartass. I'm hanging up now."

Giggling, she adds, "Say hi to my future sister-in-law."

"It's all done?"

"Yes, Jack. All done. When?"

"I'm not sure yet. I'll keep you posted...and please keep it to yourself."

"Now I'm hanging up. You think I'm stupid?"

"No, just a dork. Love you Liz."

"Me too. Be good."

"Always."

As I hang up with Lizzy, I can hear Leila giggling uncontrollably. Curious, I walk out to the bus watching her with amusement. "What's so funny?"

"Nothing." Trey responds for her.

Sliding into the booth, I pull Leila towards me. "Tell me or I'll tickle you."

She looks over at Trey, shaking her head. I barely touch her when she falls into another fit of giggles and says, "Ok...ok, I'll tell you."

"Jeez, Leila. I hope I'm never with you while being tortured by the enemy." Trey says, pretending to be annoyed.

"He won't say anything. Promise me you won't tell Hunter or Scott."

Crossing my heart, I smile wide and say, "If you are fucking with Hunter and Scott, then I *absolutely* promise."

"Trey is going to tell Hunter and Scott the Internet is running rampant with rumors of their previous relationship."

"They won't believe you."

"A chick I banged dummied up a fake website page and sent it to me. I'll have it open on the laptop when they get back." Trey turns the laptop around to show Jack.

Looking at the page, it looks absolutely legit. "That's fucking awesome! They are going to shit themselves." The page shows pictures of Hunter and Scott. In one of them they are leaning in close to each other, and it looks like they just had an intimate moment. There is a write-up on their history and how they are tortured daily by their love for each other. "Priceless."

"Trey, I can't be here when you show them. I'll never be able to keep a straight face."

"Well, then you won't be here. You too, Lair. I need you to play along."

"Hell, I'm in. This is going to be too good to miss. Where are they anyway?"

"Getting food. They'll be back any minute."

Leila slides all the way around the booth and grabs her Kindle. "I'm out of here."

Trey and I patiently wait for the lovers to return. We can hear them before we see them, bickering as they normally do. "You're so full of shit, Hunter. Where do you come up with this stuff?"

"It's true. I read it somewhere." Hunter comes on the bus first, followed by Scott. Carrying two pizzas, he sets them down and grabs a slice immediately. He first looks at Trey and then at me. "What?"

"This isn't good man." Trey says.

"What did you do now, Jack?"

"Sorry dude, this time it's not me."

Scott takes his slice and sits across from me in the booth. "What happened?"

Trey shakes his head. "I guess the photographers in Chicago thought I was serious."

He turns the laptop, showing Hunter and Scott the webpage. Hunter throws his slice on the table. "Holy fuck."

Scott turns bright red, his mouth dropping open comically. He looks up as if lost. "Where did you find this?"

"I was checking out some of our blogs. It popped up on Google," Trey shrugs, "Jen's going to have to do some damage control."

Hunter pulls out his phone. I exchange glances with Trey, but he doesn't flinch.

"Jen. There is a website called Secret Rock Affairs that is claiming Scott and I were a couple." Hunter starts pacing the bus, back and forth. "No, I'm looking at it right now. Secret. Rock. Affairs. Google...Yes, Google...What do you mean you can't find it? It's the front page. There is...check Yahoo. Keep looking." Hunter waits while Jen searches. After a few long minutes he says, "What the fuck?" He glances over at me, while I'm pretending to analyze the slice I grabbed.

"I'll call you back."

He stops in front of Trey. "Give me the laptop, asshole."

Trey hands him the laptop. After a few clicks, Hunter realizes it's fake. "Fuck you."

Trey and I crack up. "Scott turned a new shade of red. That was fucking priceless."

"Just for that, you don't get pizza." Hunter takes the two pies and the slice out of my hand and leaves the bus. "Come on, Scott."

"Your boyfriend wants you, Scott." Trey says. Scott flings a pizza crust at Trey's head and follows Hunter off the bus.

"That was awesome! Best one yet."

Trey shrugs. "I know."

Chapter 8 - Leila

"Damn, Baby, it's freezing out here."

"We're in Denver, not Alaska. It's chilly at best." Dragging him down the street toward the Aquarium, I offer, "It's right down the block."

We have a few hours before rehearsals. We're staying in a hotel after the show tonight before we hit the road tomorrow for back-to-back shows in Salt Lake City, Boise, Spokane, and Seattle. Back-to-back shows mean nothing but arenas and the bus. I'm going stir-crazy just thinking about it and needed to get out. I convinced Jack to go to the Downtown Aquarium in Denver. It's only a three-block walk from the arena, and he's been complaining the entire time. "You live in New York, not the tropics. Suck it up."

"This feels colder."

Rolling my eyes, I pull him harder. "Once we are inside, I'll warm you up." Suddenly my boyfriend, who I've been dragging by his heels, picks up the pace.

We walk into the aquarium and he stops in his tracks. "Why are we here again?" he looks around apprehensively.

"I love aquariums."

"It reminds me of school, and I hated school."

"Come on, I'll buy you a stuffed shark."

The aquarium turns out to be a really fun day. Who knew there were so many dark corners to get lost in? The place was practically empty, so there weren't many young innocent grade-schoolers there to spy on us. We lost track of time, because Jack was mesmerized watching two penguins going at it and showed up over an hour late to rehearsals.

Out of breath, we both bolt onto the stage feeling like teenagers who missed their curfews. "Well, look who's here? Our lead singer, his girlfriend and his hard-on."

Jack looks at Hunter sheepishly. "Sorry, my phone died and we lost track of time."

"Uh huh…right."

I walk over to my keyboards with my head hung in embarrassment. "Miss Marino, I expect this behavior from him, but you?"

"I'm sorry, Mr. Amatto."

"Where were you? Marriot for a quickie?" Trey asks.

"No. We were at the aquarium."

"Hooo-kay, sure you were." Hunter says.

"I have a stuffed shark to prove it."

Hunter looks at me, "For real?"

Nodding, I say, "Scouts honor."

"Well, I stand corrected. If anything that I may have said gets back to the two of you, I plead the fifth."

"Ok, jackass, start drumming."

"We've already rehearsed. You missed it."

"Fine. Are there any issues you need to discuss? Sound problems? Lighting?"

"Nope. We each inserted a solo, though. Payback."

"You're serious?" Hunter nods. "Ok, I'm fine with that."

Will struts onto the stage. "You finally showed?"

"Jeez, my phone died and we lost track of time."

Will looks at Hunter. "Ok, I owe you twenty." Hunter concedes.

"You guys bet on us?" I glance from dickhead to dickhead.

Scott shrugs and admits, "I already paid Trey."

"Unbelievable."

♫ ♫ ♫

"Last night's show was awesome. I think we get better and better each night."

"We did sound great, and we didn't even rehearse," Jack responds, as he distractedly plays with my hair.

"Mmm. That feels good. Right here, you playing with my hair, on these kick ass pillows, is pure heaven."

We have a little more time before we need to check out. Personally, I wish we could stay here for days. "I slept so good last night. I'm trying to enjoy every minute we are in this bed, the next four days are going to be exhausting."

"We can handle it. If you want, I'll steal one of these pillows for you."

"You'd do that for me?"

"If I could take the whole bed, I would."

"We must be doing really well, our hotel rooms are getting nicer and nicer. This bed is heaven. I'm not sure I can leave it."

"Yeah, I may have had something to do with that. I complained and refused to stay in any more fleabag hotels. They said they would do their best to improve."

"Jack, they weren't fleabags."

"So I embellished. It got us a bigger hotel budget. Are you complaining?"

"Not at all."

"They can afford it."

"They must think you are becoming a demanding Diva."

He smacks my ass in response. "You know what I'm really looking forward to?"

"I can guess." I tease.

"Your mind is always in the gutter. I was going to say, I'm looking forward to living together…"

"We are living together," I interrupt.

"Not on a bus. In an apartment, in the city, doing normal things like watching TV or making dinner."

His comment surprises me. "Really?"

"Yeah. I've never had that. I loved those few nights we stayed at your place, when we first started seeing each other. I can't wait to do that again."

Turning towards him, I stroke his face. "God, I love you."

"Me too." He bends to give me a kiss.

"Wait, in the city? We aren't going to live in Hoboken?"

"Uh…no."

Feigning anger, I ask, "What's wrong with Hoboken?"

"It's not the city. I'll pick the location, you can pick the apartment."

"You're breaking up with Hunter?"

"Uh, yeah…" Kissing me chastely, he adds, "The minute we pull into New York, we are apartment hunting."

"My dad will not be happy if I move to New York or if I live with you in sin."

Jack pins me on my back with my wrists in his hands. "Well, then I'll have to make an honest woman of you before then." He kisses me deeply. "After I defile you."

"Defile away."

"Hmmm…what should I do to you today?" He skims his nose down mine, and then pulls my bottom lip in between his teeth. It's almost like his mouth is a jumper cable and I'm the battery. Instantly, I'm charged and ready to go. Rolling my hips against his in hopes he takes it fast this time, he looks into my eyes and shakes his head.

Nodding I respond with a "Yes."

"What has happened to you? Where did my shy girlfriend go?"

"I killed her. It was a very violent death, poor thing. She didn't have a chance."

"I would have sent flowers." He laces our fingers together, keeping our hands over my head.

I impatiently shift so he is right where I need him to be. Smiling he says, "Ok, your wish is my command." He bends to kiss me, deeply. It's my favorite slow, dry, deliberate kiss that I adore. My fingers grip his tightly, as he nearly gets me there with just his kiss.

I pull away and he looks down at me confused. "Did I ever tell you that I practically had an orgasm at your birthday party when you kissed me that night? It was just like it was now. Drives me crazy. So please, hurry."

"No, you never told me that." Looking into my eyes, without warning, he slips inside of me. "Fast enough?"

Nodding, I bite my lip from the fullness I feel, my muscles instantly contracting around him. "Yes. Now move, please."

"So bossy." He resumes his kissing, right where he left off. I bring my knees up in an attempt to get him deeper. The craving I have to consume him whole is unbearable. Jack pulls out almost completely, then slides back in torturously slow. His fingers are tightly gripping mine. He removes one of his hands, skimming it along the side of my body, resting it on the back of my thigh. He hitches my leg over his shoulder, simultaneously increasing his rhythm by moving in and out in the most delicious way. My free hand finds his hair, giving me something to latch on to as I shudder beneath him.

He drops his forehead to mine, staring into my eyes with such intensity that I know he's close. A few seconds later, he slows his pace, his moan and his eyes shutting, both indicators he is there.

Smiling at him, I'm in awe of this man. How did I get him? How does he feel the same about me?

As he opens his eyes, he smirks adorably. "Am I amusing you?"

"No. I can watch you have an orgasm all day. In fact, can I record it on my phone so I can watch it when we are apart?"

"If I can record you." He grins. "Let's make a sex tape."

"Sure. Tomorrow."

"Really?"

"No."

"Buzz kill." He pulls out, moving to lie on his side next to me. "I adore you, Leila Marino. I can't wait to make you my wife. I can't wait until we belong to each other completely."

"I can't wait for that too."

"Leila Lair."

My heart flips at the sound of that, but I tease, "It sounds like a porn star."

"Leila Lair does Jack." He purses his lips and says, "It kinda does."

"We'll be Mr. & Mrs. Marino."

"Uh, no."

"You wouldn't take my name?"

He shakes his head. "Nope."

"Old fashioned, are you?"

"Not at all. But you taking my name would make me extremely happy. The Lair's. Leila and Jack Lair. It works."

"Hmm. We'll see."

"On what?"

"How big the ring is."

Chapter 9 - Jack

"Why am I in trouble this time?" I ask over the phone, as Leila gets dressed a few feet away.

"Am I on speaker?" Jen asks.

"Yes."

"I needed to talk to you two." Jen doesn't beat around the bush. "*Rock MY World*'s website is reporting, *Jessa Perez is pregnant and scorned by Jack Lair, front-man for up-and-coming rock band Devil's Lair*."

My heart halts in my chest. "What?" I ask panicked.

Jen continues. "There is a whole write up, a picture of her, of you and Leila from our website. It's pretty bad. She is playing the role perfectly."

"Fuck...!"

We can't catch a fucking break. I am so angry I want to hit something.

Rock MY World is an entertainment show that caters to the rock and roll world. It can be watched on cable television, but their claim to fame is their website. They are known to stalk rock stars, getting all sorts of gossip and compromising photos of them at their most vulnerable.

"Jack, this is not good." For the first time since meeting Jen, I can hear the disappointment in her voice.

"Jen, Leila and I are the only ones who know about the baby. I don't know if it's mine. She could be lying."

"The article says it's yours." Leila and I stare at each other. She looks pale.

"Jack, you should have told me. This changes a lot. Krista and I are flying to the label. I'll call you when we get there. I don't know what she wants, but we need to spin this just the right way. We need to prepare a statement. I'm not going to lie, this can be a fucking disaster."

Leila gives me a knowing look as she sits heavily in a chair. She was so right.

"You need to mention there is a possibility it's not mine." I pathetically cling to that chance.

"I will. I'm not sure that will help. I suggest you tell the guys. You owe it to them to tell them yourself."

"I know, " I say, while scrubbing my hand over my face. Goddamn her.

"Then call Jessa. Try to figure out what angle she's going for. It will help us predict which route she is taking. I'll call you once I speak to Krista."

"Okay." Jen ends the call and I look over at Leila. Her hands are buried in her hair and she is staring into space.

"I'm sorry, baby."

She looks up sadly. "I've had plenty of warning, plenty of time to think about this, but it's still hard to hear."

"I'm sorry you have to deal with this. It's breaking my heart that you are involved in this mess." The hurt, mixing with the pure hatred I feel towards Jessa right now, is making for a dangerous situation. "I do need to tell them, now, before they see it."

"I dread this."

"I know. Let's get this over with."

A few torturously long silent minutes later, we board the bus. Hunter and Scott are arguing as Trey sits in the passenger seat looking like he wants to kill them.

Expelling a burst of air, Leila visibly relaxes once the bus door closes behind us.

Hunter looks up briefly. "Leila, you alright?"

She shakes her head and sits heavily at the table.

"What's wrong?" Scott asks.

"Um…I just got reamed out by Jen."

"Leila, we need you to keep his ass in line. He's acting like a lovesick idiot. He's not thinking with the right head right now."

"Hunt, back off."

"You were an hour late yesterday, and you…"

"I said back off."

"Why?" Hunter shows his annoyance.

I stall, trying to figure out how I can tell them. He loses his patience and asks again. "Jack, what the fuck is going on?"

Wordlessly, I open the laptop and load up *Rock MY World's* webpage. "I need you all to see something." Standing, I first pass the laptop to Trey. He'll be the easiest to deal with. Trey wordlessly reads the article, handing it back to me. I then give it to Scott.

Scott looks stunned. "Is this for real?"

"Afraid so."

He passes it to Hunter. After reading it, his expression turns furious. "You're fucking kidding me! Tell me this is a joke."

"It's not a joke."

Hunter stands, looking from me to Leila and back. "When did you find this out?"

"Opening night."

"Fuck, Jack! Didn't I tell you to stay away from her? Didn't I tell you to grow up and stop thinking with your dick?"

"I fucked up. I don't need you to remind me. It doesn't affect you."

"No? The fuck it doesn't. And what about Leila? Does it affect her?"

Stepping closer to where Leila is sitting, I respond quietly, "Leave her out of this."

"Jack, are you fucking crazy? This is not just about you and that manipulative tramp you knocked up. Do you think she is quietly going to go away? This will haunt you forever, thus haunting us too!"

I have nothing to say to Hunter. He is absolutely right. Sitting heavily, defeated and exhausted, I wait to accept whatever he is going to unleash on me.

"How do you know it's yours?"

"I don't. She was waiting for results of the paternity test. I guess she got them."

"She never even told you the results yet? She just told her story?"

Nodding, I look over at Leila. She stares back, but I can't tell what she's feeling. Hunter follows my gaze and sits next to Leila. "How are you with all of this?"

"I'm not happy about it. I've been consumed with fear wondering how this will affect our success. But I'll support Jack. We all need to support him." She gives him a pointed look.

"What does she want, Jack?" Scott asks.

"I don't know."

"I can tell you what she wants…either you or money. Let's hope it's the money." Hunter grumbles without apology. "Fuck, she finally got her hooks into you."

"She has nothing in me. This doesn't affect my future. I'm with Leila."

"The woman is dangerous. You know that. You know she is like a fungus that won't go away."

Reaching for Leila's hand, I mumble, "You really need to shut the fuck up, Hunt."

Watching Leila with concern, Hunter's facial expression softens for the first time. "I'm sorry. The last thing you need is me on your ass."

"I get it, I do. I'm sorry I let you all down. Most importantly, I'm sorry I let Leila down. But it is what it is. I can't change it or stop it. I'll have to deal with it."

We all sit quietly, lost in our own thoughts. Trey breaks the silence first. "Something's up." Every eye on the bus turns towards him. Even Steve is sneaking glances from the driver's seat. "Too much ceremony."

What?

"Keep the noise down." We all watch as Trey walks to the back of the bus and draws his privacy curtain.

"What the fuck is he talking about?" Hunter finally asks with a straight face. In spite of the situation, I can't help but laugh.

"I have no fucking clue." Sliding into the booth next to Leila, I take her hand and kiss her palm. "I love you." I whisper quietly.

"Me too."

"I have to make a phone call. I want to hear why she did this."

"Ok."

I place a soft kiss on her lips before walking to the bedroom without a word to anyone else. Jessa answers on the last ring.

"What the fuck did you do?"

"What are you talking about?"

"Knock it off!"

"Jack, I honestly don't know what you are talking about. If you called to give me crap, save it, I'm not in the mood."

"I don't give a crap if you're not in the mood. Are you trying to tell me you didn't tip off *Rock MY World* about your pregnancy?"

"What? Why would I do that?"

"Stop with the Goddamn games, Jessa."

"Jack, I am trying to convince you I love you. Why would I go and purposely piss you off?"

What the hell?

"So if not you, then who?"

"I don't know? I've told a few people. It could be anyone. Maybe it was Danny?"

"How does Danny know?"

"My brother maybe?"

"They still talk?"

"Yes."

"And it's true?"

"Yes."

"Why didn't you call to tell me?" The fury rises again.

"I haven't had a chance. I just found out."

"And yet it's plastered on the Internet already? Email me a copy of those results." I hang up on her, not wanting to spend one more second listening to her voice.

I immediately get a text. "I'll be in touch."

I throw my phone against the wall and numbly watch as it crumbles in pieces to the ground.

Chapter 10 - Leila

Sleep, wake up, rehearse, perform, sleep, wake up, rehearse, perform.

Every day...since Denver, through Salt Lake, through Boise and through Spokane.

Four days total. The four days I was dreading, because we wouldn't be getting a break, has turned into four days of torture. Four days, where the guys try to act as they normally do. Four days, where Jack and I haven't had sex. Four days, of me pretending life is fucking fantastic on this tiny cramped bus. Four days may not seem like a long time, but to someone like me who loves her boyfriend with all her heart and hates seeing him so miserable, to someone like me who is addicted to him and every part of him, it's a fucking eternity.

Since Jessa's news broke, it has covered us all like a wet blanket. Before, what I most worried about was how it would harm our success. Well ironically, that was all unnecessary.

The irony of our situation is almost comical. In four days, our popularity has only increased. Jessa's news really hasn't damaged our fame. Our fans are still loyal. Others are curious about the *bad boy rocker who got his ex pregnant before dumping her*. Our songs are being downloaded daily. Our album is steadily climbing the charts. Our top three songs are being played on radio stations. Even my haters are sympathetic to the fact my boyfriend knocked up his ex.

Four days of irony.

The label is ecstatic. They are milking the attention to a fault. We should be off the wall excited right now. I'm sure on the inside the guys are. They are respectfully containing their excitement, always cognizant of Jack and my secret hell.

We aren't fighting or bickering. In fact, Jack is still very attentive and affectionate. Our lovemaking has been replaced with holding, caressing, and lots of silence with a few sporadic words. At least the words are of love, of need and of support. I've tried to initiate intimacy. He said he needs time, so I don't push. His words are the only indication I get as to the torment he is feeling.

"You deserve better."

"I'm so sorry you have to go through this."

"Damn her."

"I need you."

"I love you."

"Don't give up on me."

His guilt controls everything in him, from his attitude towards our fame, to his once raging libido. It's like an ice cold shower on our relationship. All I can do is to be supportive. I love this man, and it's all I can do right now to help him.

Jessa has been quiet. She emailed Jack the test results the next day. I called the DNA lab she used in New York City and confirmed it was a legit place. Part of me hoped she would be deranged enough to falsify the tests. No such luck. So now that we know it is Jack's baby, I have replaced the *what if's* with the *what now's*.

Of the four days, I would say half the time I spent feeling our love is rock solid. I pictured us years from now, married with children. Then there is the other half I spent feeling vulnerable, exposed to Jessa and her conniving intentions. Not that I believe Jack would ever be with her over me, but what would she do to get me out of the picture?

The pregnancy is still an elusive thing to him right now. Once it becomes a tangible thing, a live baby, how will he feel? I fell in love with him because of his heart, his compassion, and his tenderness. The animosity he feels towards Jessa may all go to pot once his child is born. I would never keep Jack from his child. I'm banking that Jessa will use his child to her advantage.

I've avoided calls from home. I wasn't getting off that easy with Dad or Evan. Not surprisingly, their phone calls were pure hell. Dad is no longer on Team Jack. He hounded me to rethink this whole tour and come home. I told him he was being ridiculous. He didn't argue that point. I also said, he didn't raise me to be a quitter and most importantly, I love Jack. I'm going nowhere. I defended Jack and threw in how unfair it was to judge him on one mistake. By the end of the call, Dad wasn't threatening to come get me and said he would support me even though he wasn't happy about it.

He called Jack as well. Jack took it like a man, letting my dad get it all out, responding respectfully with "Yes, sir." "I understand." "Yes, sir." His last words to my dad were, "I love your daughter."

Evan was even worse. First he unleashed all his harsh words and criticisms towards Jack like a semi-automatic. He said Lizzy stopped him from flying out to beat the shit out of Jack. The rest of the conversation consisted of me repeating myself over and over that I loved him more than anything and begging Evan not to bad mouth Jack to my dad. I then texted a thank you to Lizzy.

All my other friends were flooding my phone with texts and voicemails of concern and support. The last time I spoke to Lori, she assured me the gossip was all pretty much contained to our website, our bloggers' websites, and a few entertainment websites. She said it hasn't hit the national news or anything…yet.

Knowing she set Google alerts for Devil's Lair, as well as our individual names, I'm depending on her to let me know if anything awful shows up. I've completely avoided the Internet. I can't be consumed by what I might see or read. So I'll let Krista, Jen, Dylan and Lori police it for me. Our performances these past four days have been somewhat robotic. The integrity of our show hasn't changed. We still give our fans their money's worth. The playful bantering and joking around is what's lacking.

We have a show tomorrow night in Spokane. It's only a four-hour drive from Spokane to Seattle, and since we are doing so well with sold out shows, the label had pity on us and gifted us with a night in a hotel. This works perfectly with my plan of having a heart to heart with Jack and trying to tear down his wall. I haven't pushed him, but it's time I do.

"Hey, babe. What are you doin'?" he asks, as he comes into the bedroom.

I've been spending a lot more time alone in the bedroom, reading my Kindle to escape our reality.

"Reading a trashy novel." I respond, watching him closely. He lies beside me on the bed, wraps his arms around my thighs and lays his head on my lap. My Jack would pounce on the fact I was reading a trashy novel.

I gently run my fingers through his hair. "You ok?"

"I am now." He says, holding me tighter. "Babe, I love you. Don't give up on me."

He's said this many times these past few days, but combined with his vise grip, he is now worrying me. "Hey…what's going on?"

"Nothing."

"Jack, tell me."

"I just spoke to my parents again. I know they love me, but I can't help but feel I've disappointed them so much. Between my career choice and now this. I feel like…" He squeezes me again, leaving his sentence hanging between us.

"What do you feel?"

"Like a complete fuck up."

"Jack. Jack, look at me."

He loosens his grip and moves up to sit next to me on the bed. "You aren't a fuck up. Baby, you are giving her control. You need to come back to me and to the guys."

"Lei, I don't want to be a father to her child. I don't want to be connected to her like that. My parents are giving me a good dose of guilt, and all I want to say to them is I don't care that it's mine."

He shifts back down, resting his head where it was previously. I don't know how to comfort him. Trying with my touch, I run my fingers through his hair again, bending to kiss his head, while fighting back my tears.

"Jack, that baby is part of you. You need to separate your feelings towards Jessa from your feelings towards your child. Otherwise, you will be consumed with guilt far worse than you have ever known."

He doesn't respond. He's done with words and moves back behind his shield of silence. I let him retreat, once again. It breaks my heart that he is so distraught. I know I'm part of the reason for his misery. I know he is so overcome with regret for that one stupid night, he doesn't know how to deal with the ripple effect it has on our relationship.

Through the window, I watch as the bus pulls into the hotel lot. A minute later, there's a soft knock on the door. "Come in."

Hunter slowly opens the door. "Hey. We're here. We're going to go grab dinner. Do you guys want to come?"

Jack shakes his head, otherwise not moving or responding. Hunter looks at me, almost begging for me to overrule him. "We'll pass. Thanks, Hunt."

Hunter doesn't leave, but instead comes into the room and closes the door behind him. "You need to snap out of it, man."

No response.

"Jack, dude, this is border line psychotic."

Still no response.

"Leila, talk to him."

I sigh loudly and nod, "I think we need some time alone. Is that ok?"

Hunter gets my message and stands to leave. "Ok. Call me if you change your minds." Once Hunter closes the door behind him, I resume running my fingers through Jack's hair.

"Babe."

"Hmmm?"

"Let's go in and get settled. We'll order dinner and maybe watch a bad movie?"

"Ok."

But yet he doesn't move or say anything else. It takes me an hour to get him off that bus and into our room. The moment I close the door behind me, Jack grabs the remote and lies on the bed. I can stall, but then it will be a long night. I rather get this over with.

I sit on the edge of the bed facing him and get right to the point. "Babe, can I say something?"

He looks at me expectantly. "Of course."

"Hunter is right. You really need to snap out of it. You can't keep shutting everyone out and suppressing your feelings."

He looks at me blankly. "I don't know what you want me to say."

"Say what you're feeling."

"Trapped. Cornered. Desperate. How's that for starters?" His tone is laced with annoyance.

"Good start."

He looks at me like I've lost my mind and resumes watching the TV. Pulling the remote out of his hand, I add, "How can I help you?"

"You can't. This is all on me." He meets my gaze, challenging me to disagree. His smoky eyes are glazed over, distant and cold. I know it's not towards me. It's the same look he gets whenever the subject comes up.

I caress his face and plead. "Please. Tell me."

"I don't want the baby. What kind of person does that make me?" He breaks eye contact, the muscles in his jaw clenching subtly.

"It's a normal reaction, Jack. That does not make you a bad person."

He gives me another incredulous look. "Leila, I…" Sighing, he stops his words again.

"What? Tell me."

Shaking his head, he focuses on the TV. This approach isn't working. I need to change tactics.

"Take a shower with me."

A tiny spark in his eyes gives me hope, but then his words kill it instantly. "Maybe later."

"No, now. Jackson Henry Lair, get your ass up so I can screw you in the shower!"

The corners of his mouth twitch slightly. Taking this as a good sign, I pull my shirt off over my head, engaging him in a stare down. Arching my eyebrow, I challenge him to ignore my advances.

He runs his fingertip across the lace edge of my bra, then retreats. I reach behind, and unclasp my bra, allowing it to fall off my shoulders. His eyes slowly take in my naked upper half. He uses the same fingertip to trace over my nipple.

I lean in until I am pressed up against him, and whisper seductively in his ear, "I miss you."

He wraps his arms around me. "I miss you, too."

"I'm right here."

I pull back to kiss his lips gently, then more forcibly, urging him to respond. After a few minutes, Jack gently pushes me away. These past four days, I've let him. I've let him stop us from getting physical and allowed him to instead hold me as a substitute. But today, I refuse to stop. So I keep trying. I keep kissing him, nibbling his ear, licking his neck, biting his bottom lip, subtly placing my hand on his erection. I'm pulling out every erotic trick I have up my sleeve.

Thank the Lord above he starts to respond. It's slowly at first, but then he goes from a taciturn-moody-ass to a raging-sex-God in seven seconds flat.

He takes me on the bed, against the wall, in the shower, in a chair, on the bed, and it's still only nine p.m.

Sitting in bed, eating room service burgers, he says, "Long four days."

"Long ninety-six hours."

He laughs out loud, with a face full of fries. "I love you so much."

"Promise me you won't deprive me like that ever again. I need my Jackson fix daily."

"Wow, I've turned you into quite the nymph."

"Complaining?"

"Fuck no, you're my nymph."

"Completely yours." Feeling confident his mood has changed for the better, I brace the subject again. "Are you ready to talk?"

Shaking his head, he says, "Nope." He watches me watch him from the corner of his eye. "Babe, I've admitted I have tremendous guilt because I don't want this baby, and I feel trapped. That sums it all up. There really is nothing left for me to say." He places his plate down on the end table and takes mine from my lap. Pulling me into his embrace, he strokes my hair. "I am sorry I allowed it to affect us though. I shut down. I acted just the way I keep asking you not to. I'm such a hypocrite."

"I understand. I just felt so helpless. I still do."

"Just don't give up on me and keep loving me. That's all you can do to help me."

♫ ♫ ♫

The next morning, Jack was in the shower when my phone rang with a number I didn't recognize. Ignoring it, a few seconds later I received a disturbing voicemail message.

"It's Jessa. I would like to talk to you. Please let me know when you have a few minutes to chat...alone."

My gut instinct was to tell Jack. He would tell me not to talk to her. However, I'm extremely curious as to what she wants and what she has to say. I convinced Jack to go down to the bus before me, to smooth things over with the guys and talk to them about his recent behavior. He argued at first, but then he thankfully agreed.

With shaking fingers, I texted the evil witch back.

Free to talk. It has to be now as we are pulling out soon.

Sitting on the edge of the bed quickly becomes unacceptable to my nerves. So instead, I start pacing the room, over and over like a caged animal.

A few minutes later my cell rings, cutting the silence viciously.

With my heart pounding in my chest, I answer the call. "Hello."

"Hello, Leila. How are you?"

"How did you get my number?"

"A mutual friend."

Liar. She is probably stalking me.

"What do you want Jessa?"

"I have some news."

Sighing, I'm already exhausted with this conversation. "What news?"

"I had my first sonogram. It's a boy."

Jack will have a son?

My stomach lurches from the reality of this situation. A small gasp escapes, but it's loud enough for her to hear it. "Are you ok?"

"Yes."

"I have a dilemma."

When I don't respond, she continues.

"I'm not sure if you know anything about me."

"I know enough."

She laughs condescendingly, as if I amuse her. "Well, what you may not know is I was raised by a single parent. My mom raised my brother and me all alone. Our dad took off and never looked back."

"I'm sorry for your loss."

"Thank you. I never really thought of having kids. Life is funny that way. You never know what it will throw at you. Having been raised by a single mother, I refuse to repeat the path she was forced to take, struggling, alone, practically penniless. It aged her. It changed her. I will not have that happen to me.

Remaining completely silent on my end of the call, she continues.

"I love Jack. I'm not stupid enough to think he loves me and will leave you to be with me. He's made that very, very clear. In fact, our last conversation left me troubled with his role towards our child. I listened as he adamantly stated he wanted no part of this. It was noble of him to offer financial support, though." She stops to let out a short, clipped laugh. "That would help, but it wouldn't be enough. Not knowing my own dad, I want our baby to know his and to have him in his life."

"Jessa, what are you trying to tell me?"

"The part I'm struggling with is I feel Jack would have eventually welcomed a son into his life with open arms, before you at least."

A chill runs down my spine as I realize what she is getting at. I feel sick to my stomach. This woman is beyond conniving, beyond manipulative. She is evil.

"Funny, just a few weeks ago I considered terminating this pregnancy. I felt no connection to it."

"If you were debating an abortion, you would have done it."

"My friends talked me out of it. Honestly, I'm glad they did. Now knowing that it's a boy, who is half me and half Jack, I now feel connected to it."

As this bitch rambles on, Jack tries calling my cell. I'm sure it won't be long before he comes looking for me.

"What does this have to do with me?" I whisper weakly into the phone.

"Leila, you seem like a smart girl. Jack isn't the kind of person to walk away from his own child. Beneath his cocky, God's gift to the world attitude, he does have a heart. I'm sure he is being torn in half right now, being ripped apart from the inside. If I know Jack, he's struggling with doing the right thing versus his commitment to you. Sometimes Jack needs a little shove in the right direction. He will adamantly claim this is the way he wants it. But over time, his guilt will kill him."

"Jack wouldn't just move on with his life, like you hope he does. He would hate and resent you even more than he does now. He feels trapped by you. That will never go away."

"Yes, it will. Jack marinates over things. He mulls things over. Time and Jack have a mutual understanding. If you had said after our break up that we would once again have sexual relations, I would have called you nuts. But we did. I think his guilt would change his decision. Fast-forward ten years. His son would be at the age where he'd be playing sports, growing up. Jack would absolutely regret not being a part of that. He just needs someone to help him realize that."

"That someone being me."

"That's correct."

"Jack is a stubborn man. I can't make him do something he refuses to."

"Oh, I think you can."

"You think I'll just break up with Jack because you want me to?"

"No. I want you to realize the different paths his life can take. Being with you, or knowing his child."

"And he can't have both?"

"Nope. Another thing you need to know about Jack. His vision is limited. As long as you are in his life, you are his life. If you weren't, he would focus on the next thing. He can't look past his own contentment."

"He isn't going to buy this. There is no way he'll allow me to walk away."

"Couples fight all the time. I'm sure you two do as well."

"Really we don't."

"How lucky of you. That's so sweet," she patronizes.

"I'm not walking away from Jack just because you threw around some empty threats."

"You love him, correct."

"Stupid question."

"You wouldn't want to harm him, correct?"

"I'm about to hang up, Jessa."

"Fame does have its disadvantages. It's called the Internet. It can be a major advantage, as well as a disadvantage."

"What are you saying now?"

"A really hot rock star can't keep his dick in his pants. While drunk and high, he literally pushes himself onto his ex-girlfriend, who has never gotten over him. The kicker is, after taking advantage of her, he abandons her in her time of need. This shit gets eaten up all the time. It could ruin him."

A chill runs through my veins. "That never happened."

"I was there and Jack was extremely drunk. He's a womanizer. He's not the monogamous type, and he most definitely is not the boyfriend type."

"You're a bitch."

"Just pulling out all my defenses."

"What do you want?"

"I want Jack."

"How could you do that to him?"

"I'm protecting my unborn child." She sighs into the phone. "You heard what I had to say. Make your decision, Leila, and soon. I'm not a patient person. Please don't be stupid enough to tell Jack. His temper is uncontrollable. I have connections and I'll know." With that she hangs up.

I've never wanted to kill someone before, until now.

She has no problem taking Jack down to get what she wants.

My anger boils towards her for ruining Jack's life and towards Jack for ruining everything for one meaningless night with that tramp. She has me completely cornered. It's like she did her research, focusing on Jack's guilt for not wanting the baby and my insecurities with being in the public eye.

Ignoring this would be all she needs to make a phone call to a sleazy tabloid. No one would question her when the evidence is her pregnant belly.

Realizing I've wasted a lot of time, I quickly text Jack as tears blur my vision.

hey...on my way. be there in a few minutes.

I then make a necessary phone call. There's only one person I can talk to, who can calm me down.

Chapter 11 - Jack

Knocking on her door, it takes a few seconds for her to answer. "Hey, babe. What's taking you so long? We gotta go or Jen will have my ass."

"Sorry. I got distracted."

"Without me?" I pull her into my embrace.

When she doesn't respond to my joke, I pull back slightly to look into her eyes. "Why were you crying?" Her silence has me worried. "Leila?"

"I need to talk to you."

Without a word, she pulls away to sit on the bed. As I close the door behind us, I move to sit next to her.

"What is it?" I gently take her hand in mine. "Lei?"

"Jessa called."

"What? I don't want you talking to her."

"Jack, she considered ending the pregnancy because of me." A quick flash of relief passes through me. Leila sits motionless.

"This doesn't surprise me."

"You could have lost your child because of me. Things would be different if we weren't together."

I immediately become suspicious with this conversation. "You're serious? She is totally pulling you into one of her little games."

"She knows you'll never be together. But she feels you'll never commit to them as long as you are with me."

"WHAT THE FUCK, LEILA?" Is she pulling this shit again?

"Jack..."

"Don't Jack me. What the FUCK?"

"Jack, this wasn't meant to be. I've changed my dreams to be with you. You're denying a child to be with me. We are forcing things to happen that clearly aren't supposed to."

Reaching for her she pulls away. "I can't."

"You can't what?"

"I can't be the reason you won't accept your child."

"Holy shit! I can't believe I'm hearing this. Ok, I'll be there for the kid. Is that what you want to hear?"

"Yes, but I don't fit into that scenario."

"Yes, you do!"

"I don't want to fit into it."

"You don't want me."

"I've lost track of what I really want."

"I can't believe you're saying this to me."

"I spoke to Evan. He reminded me how much I wanted to become a solo artist. He reminded me that I've abandoned all my dreams to be with you. I love you, but he's right. I know in ten years, I'll resent what I gave up and you'll resent what you gave up."

"What are you saying?"

"After the tour is over, I'll be leaving the band. I hope Malcolm will still represent me so I can follow my dream."

"You're leaving me?"

She stares at the floor, avoiding my eyes. "This has to end."

I viciously grab her upper arms, forcing her to look at me. Her eyes instantly well up with tears, spilling relentlessly as I continue to stare into them. "You said you wouldn't leave me."

"Let go of me." She whispers through her tears.

"NO!" As she looks away again, I grip her tighter.

"Jack, you're hurting me. Let go."

I release my grip, but only slightly. "Leila, please don't let her do this to us."

"She isn't doing anything. This is all me. This has been lying just under the surface. All Jessa did was help it to bubble up."

"You regret being with me?"

She doesn't respond and just sits numbly.

"You can flip a switch that easily? You can just turn us off?"

"No, I can't. This is tearing me up. But I made a promise to my dad before leaving. I promised to be true to myself. I haven't been. The more I convince myself things are just as they should be, the more life throws a fucking dart at our heads. Someone is trying to tell us something."

"Who are you? I don't even know who you are right now."

"I'm still me. This is me, before you. I was motivated, determined, focused."

This isn't my Leila. She isn't the same person. Something has seriously changed. She looks detached, distant, and cold even. She looks like a different person.

"You think I'm going to walk away? Fuck no…I'll call Evan, I'll call your dad, I'll call whomever I have to, to talk some Goddamn sense into you."

"It won't change how I feel. I need you to stay away from me. I can't be near you. I can't let you continue to control me."

"I've controlled you?"

"Yes. My heart, my head, my life. You completely took over and I need to take it back."

"I can't believe what I'm hearing."

She sits totally unfazed. She truly couldn't give a shit that she's cutting my heart out and feeding it to me for lunch.

"I need you. I can't be without you."

"You'll get over me, and I'll get over you…eventually."

"Baby, we love each other. Nothing else matters."

"Sometimes love isn't enough."

"Wow. You've basically decided our fate, and I clearly have no say in the matter."

"I've decided my fate. My fate happens to align perfectly with the fate you are meant to live. More of the universe trying to tell us something."

For the first time since being with Leila, I don't want to be near her. I feel the walls closing in, her demeanor a slap in my face, her posture a knife through my heart. I feel like I'm drowning in my own blood.

Seeing my silence as an opportunity to twist the knife, she adds, "I think it's best if one of us moves to the other bus."

"One of us? Like me?"

"Unless you'd like me to go."

"We need to be around each other. We need to perform together. We still have months left on this tour."

"We don't have to live together. You, yourself said to me you couldn't possibly live on the same bus with me and not be able to touch me or be with me. I agree."

"You really thought of everything. Amazing. I leave you alone for what, twenty minutes? And in that short amount of time you've rewritten our lives like it's a fucking fictional novel."

She doesn't respond. She doesn't move.

I continue to stare at her, willing her to come back to me. She finally meets my gaze, and there's nothing there. Her eyes are still moist, but otherwise absolutely nothing.

Kneeling before her I desperately try one more time. "Leila, you are my world. I don't care about anything else. I'll do anything you want. You can do anything you want. Please, just don't give up on us."

"I can't be who I want to be if I stay with you."

"Yes, you can. I won't stop you."

"Jack, I totally lose myself when I'm with you. Unintentionally, you would stop me."

"So this really has nothing to do with the baby."

"It's a combination of all that has gone wrong since we've started our relationship. The baby, her not wanting it, you not wanting it, me sitting in the sidelines as a culprit, my forgotten career. It's become too much drama. I can't take it anymore."

She turns away from me. Then says, "It's time I think of myself," putting the last nail into my coffin, she adds, "you need to let me live my life."

I've lost her. She's gone.

"I love you. I'll always love you, and I won't stand in your way."

I open the door and walk out of the hotel room feeling like the knife she used is still protruding from my chest.

♫ ♫ ♫

de·spair -di´spe(ə)r/

- noun – the complete loss of hope.

Synonyms: hopelessness, disheartenment, discouragement, desperation, distress, anguish, unhappiness.

-verb – to lose hope or be without hope.

Synonyms: lose hope, abandon hope, give up, lose faith, lose heart, be discouraged, be despondent, be demoralized, to resign one self.

You can go through life never really thinking about a word, its origin, its true dictionary meaning. I never gave the word despair a moment of thought. I never really had to. It's not a word that's presented itself in my life. I guess I can say I thought I felt despair during my college years, when my dreams of becoming a rock star were so far away, when I had absolutely no hope they would ever come true. But no, that wasn't despair. That wasn't the true word for word dictionary meaning of despair. That was more like the word immovable…stuck.

I did feel a touch of it the last time she pulled away from me, but even then, it pales in comparison to what I am feeling now.

This, what I'm feeling now, this is fucking despair. The despair I feel now is suffocating. It literally took hold of my chest in a crushing grip. It spills over everything like a toxic sludge that immobilizes me.

Our show last night in Spokane was the first show since she stabbed me in the heart. This morning, it was on every blog site that's been following us, spreading like a pool of blood from a stabbing…my stabbing.

I made a lot of mistakes last night. I wish I could have ditched the show, but Hunter threatened to beat the crap out of me. I was actually torn, deciding which fate was worse. Seeing her on stage, or getting pummeled by my best friend. So I fueled up with tequila and appeared on stage drunk for the first time in my singing career. It was a huge mistake, in hindsight. I spilled the beans to twenty-two hundred fans that she stabbed me in the heart. Every time she shared a mic with me, every time she looked into my eyes during a song, every time she walked towards me on stage, the knife she left wedged deep into my heart moved slightly. It moved just enough to once again cripple me with pain and for the hemorrhaging to resume.

The second our show was over, Leila stormed out of the arena and it took every fiber of my being not to chase her. I'm surprised with myself for giving up so quickly. I've threatened I would never let her go. But her eyes were void of all feeling, all the love I thought she felt for me. It was gone.

Remembering that void once again starts up the stabbing pain in my heart. I needed to extinguish the pain immediately. So I grabbed a bottle of booze and retreated to my bunk.

My new fucking home, with Dylan, Will, five roadies and our alternate drivers. This bus doesn't have a bedroom in the back. Nope, only bunks, wide open, no privacy, no door, with just a curtain to hide you from other humans. I've developed a newfound respect for my buddies, who have been living this way for the past five weeks.

The guys were stunned yesterday. They had no idea how to act or what to say to either of us. Hunter said she hid in the back bedroom, completely avoiding them. He said the only time she communicated was during the rehearsal, which I ditched.

Jen for the most part has left me alone. When she called me before tonight's show, she did throw out the predictable '*I told you so*' and the '*I knew this would happen*'. I told her to fuck off and she quickly apologized. I asked her to pass the news onto Malcolm that Leila was interested in a solo career. I meant it when I said I wouldn't stand in her way.

My sister, my mom, my dad, and Trini called, which I ignored. I feel bad I avoided Trini. Not only is she my ex-fuck buddy, but she's also been a good friend to me. But I really didn't want to talk to any of them. I did call Evan in a desperate attempt to get her back. I listened while he ranted, yet again. He said she is extremely upset and I need to respect her wishes. What a bunch of bullshit. He then said I was toxic for her, twisting the knife even further.

Whatever...

"Jack?" Hunter jerks open my curtain. "Really?" He says after eyeing my bottle.

"What do you want?"

He grabs the bottle out of my hand. I don't even attempt to fight him. I'll get more as soon as he leaves. "You're coming with us."

"Fuck off."

"Let's go."

"Leave me alone, Hunter. I'm tired. I'd rather drink alone."

"Jack, we have a night off and you are coming with us."

"No, I'm not."

"Yes, you are. I will fucking drag you out of here myself."

My response is to pull my curtain closed.

Hunter yanks me out of my bunk with two hands.

"Jesus Christ, Hunter. Leave me alone."

He pushes me out of the bus without resistance. I could easily pummel him through the ground right now. I just don't have the energy. As long as this class trip includes alcohol, I guess I'll be fine.

"Fuck." I groan as my legs almost fail me twice, causing me to stumble like a drunk. Oh wait…I am a drunk.

"Move. The guys are around front hailing a cab."

Catching a glimpse of the other bus sitting twenty yards away, my heart instantly pounds in my chest. Is she in there? Is she watching?

"Where is she?" I motion towards the bus.

Hunter stops to look at me. "She left in a cab right after the show."

"Alone? Fuck, Hunter, she shouldn't be going anywhere alone."

"Jack, she left with Dylan."

Another twist of the knife.

"Whatever. Where are we going? I look like crap."

"Who gives a fuck what you look like?"

♫ ♫ ♫

"Ugh, fuck me." I groan pathetically. I have a killer headache, like someone jabbed an ice pick right through my temple. A soft groan causes my eyes to fly open. "What the fuck are you doing here?"

"You invited me."

Oh no. No. No. No. NO!

Fuck NO!

"Oh God."

"Ready to try again? I'm extremely patient." She sidles up beside me, her hands running down my body. "Well yay, it looks like you're finally ready."

"Don't touch me."

"You didn't have a problem with me touching you last night, Jack. After you came in my mouth, you passed out. You owe me an orgasm."

"You need to leave…now!"

I can't even make myself look at her. I can't remember her name, how she got here, or what the fuck we did last night. Frantically pulling on my jeans and t-shirt, I grab my phone and head for the bathroom. "Be gone when I get out."

"You're a prick."

Locking the door I dial Hunter's phone. "What did I do?"

"What are you talking about?"

"Who is this chick and why is she in my room?"

"Oh, fuck. You were alone when we dropped you off. I shut the door behind you myself."

"I can't remember anything. It's like I blacked out. How the hell did she get here?"

"I haven't a clue."

"Hunter, I'm so fucked. I'll never get her back now." My anguish is clear in my words.

"I'll be right there."

Not even a minute later, there's a knock on my door.

Hunter walks in and says, "Hey, Jeannie. It's time to go."

"What the fuck is going on with him? He invites me all the way over here, lets me in, lets me suck him off, passes out, and now kicks me out. I do not deserve to be treated like this."

"Jeannie, he was really drunk. He had no clue what he was doing last night."

"He was in a coma last night. The only reason I stuck around was because I was hoping to have some fun this morning."

"I'm sorry. You really need to go."

"Fuck off!" She screams, then the hotel room door slams shut with such force, it rattles the bathroom door.

"Jack, open the door."

When Hunter sees me, he shakes his head. "Jesus."

I'm sweating profusely and shaking uncontrollably. I barely make the toilet before I become violently ill.

"Jack, did you take something last night?"

"I don't know. I can't remember anything after we left the bar."

"I cut you off last night. This isn't just from alcohol."

With that, I throw up again for the second time. Hunter grabs a towel, drenching it with cold water and throws it at me. Using it on my face, I feel another wave of nausea rake through me.

"Feel better?"

"No." Trying desperately to remember what happened last night, panic takes over. "Hunter, I feel like I lost an entire night of my life."

Hunter tries to help fill in the blanks. "We were at the bar. Three chicks were hanging around with us. Jeannie and you were getting it on and I told her to leave you alone. I said you just had a bad breakup. She responded that she was just the thing you needed. Trey uncharacteristically lost his cool. He threw a fit claiming he was the best of us, because he doesn't allow a chick to drag him through life by his balls. He then left with one of the other girls. We ordered another round, but I cut you off. You stumbled to the bathroom and came back claiming you were sleepy and needed to go back to the hotel. So Scott, you and me left. I put you in your room and you passed out on the bed."

"I don't remember leaving, calling her, or her showing up. It's a total blank."

"She claims nothing really happened. That she only blew you and..."

"Hunt, that's bad. Plus, I almost fucked her." I completely lose it, as I slink to the floor watching Hunter watch me lose my fucking mind.

He lets me. He sits and waits.

When there's nothing left, I lift my head to look at him. "Hunt, I can't do this. I can't. I can't go on tonight. We need to cancel the show."

"Jack, we can't cancel the show," he says, as he follows me out of the bathroom. "You need to snap out of it. She's gone, man. You need to let her go."

"No! I refuse to believe that."

I crawl into bed, suddenly feeling exhausted. A bone crushing tired that takes hold of my entire body. I've never been this mentally or physically drained. The last thing I hear is, "Jack…Jack…"

The first vision that appears in my head as I close my eyes is of Leila walking away.

Chapter 12 - Leila

"Lei...Lei, open up."

I open the door a crack. "What do you want, Hunter?"

"Let me in. I need to talk to you."

"Not now." I really can't deal with Hunter right now. I'm spread too thin, and I'm about to crack at any moment. But the look on his face is hard to ignore.

"I need to talk to you."

I open the door and he flies into my room.

"What's wrong?"

"Sit."

I sit stiffly in a chair in the opposite corner of the room and wait for him to explain.

"Leila, he's losing it. He's never acted this way, not even when he dropped out of school. He's totally sabotaging himself."

My emotions start to take control. My heart falters in my chest. I quickly rein it in, letting logic take over. "Hunter, he'll get over this. With time, he'll realize this is for the best."

"For who, Leila?"

I look away before responding. "For both of us."

"You're lying. Don't lie to me."

"I can't be the reason he never sees his son."

"Son?"

"She's having a boy."

"Who told you?"

"Hunter, I really don't want to get into this. I've made my decision."

"Leila, you need to tell me. I can't sit back and watch the two of you torture each other or allow him to destroy himself."

"It has to be this way."

"Says who?" My silence fuels his suspicion. "I think you are doing this for the wrong reasons. That bitch somehow got into your head and you are killing him with this."

"Hunter."

"She threatened you, didn't she? You broke his heart because she threatened you?"

"She didn't threaten me. She eluded that Jack is denying his child because of me."

"She threatened you…that fucking bitch. How could you allow her to do this to him?"

"Hunter, I had to. She needed to believe we were done. I needed it to be convincible. I needed her to drop her guard and trust me. It was necessary."

"Why?"

"It's complicated."

"I need to hear all of it."

Sighing, I shake my head. "No."

"Leila, I'm not leaving until you tell me what the fuck caused you to break his heart."

"I can't tell you."

"Jesus Christ, Leila. Do you know what happened last night? I think he took something. I cut him off and I still had to practically carry him back to his room. This morning he called me in a panic. A chick, who had been hanging out with us at the bar, somehow came to his room and he slept with her. He's a mess."

I gasp and immediately well up with tears. I did this. I caused this. I cover my face with my hands, nausea taking hold.

"Leila, he doesn't remember any of it. She claims he…"

Hunter stops abruptly and my heart stops beating. I look at him, waiting for him to continue. When he doesn't, I beg, "Hunter, please tell me what happened."

"She gave him a blow job."

"Oh my God."

"Lei, he passed out. They didn't have sex but it came really close. I've never seen him like this. I worry he's going to do something stupid. He doesn't want to perform tonight. He wants to cancel the show."

Dropping my head back into my hands, I whisper more to myself than to Hunter, "I needed to protect him."

♫ ♫ ♫

As I sit on the edge of his bed, my heart breaks to see him like this. He looks awful. He looks like he's been through hell, and I put him there.

Glancing around the room, an unused condom lays on the floor near the bed. The bile rises at the thought of another woman touching him and he touching her. Her lips were on him, her mouth wrapped around him. And yet, even knowing this, I can't feel any anger. My Jack wouldn't do that to me. This Jack is someone I don't know.

If this is the damage I caused after only one day, I can't continue with my plan to be apart for a week. I had given myself a week to try and figure out what she was truly up to. I haven't even scratched the surface. Hopefully, Jack's reaction was enough to appease her. If that bitch follows through with her threat and I broke his heart unnecessarily, I'll kill her.

Unable to resist the urge to touch him, I run my fingers through his hair. He stirs slightly, mumbling my name. Eventually, he opens his eyes. "Lei?"

"Ssh, baby I'm here."

"Am I dreaming?"

"No. I'm really here."

"Why?"

"I have a lot to tell you."

♫ ♫ ♫

"Ev." I can't bear to say his name without breaking down.

"Lei? What's wrong?"

"Jessa just called me. She's claiming Jack forced himself on her and will play the victim unless I leave him."

"You can't be serious."

"I need to end it with him."

"This will kill him."

"I need her to believe I actually did it, and the only way *is* to actually do it. This will give me time to figure out what she's up to."

"He will never let you walk away. Look how he acted last time."

"I know…so I plan on telling him the baby is only half of it. I'll say you reminded me how I *gave up my dreams for him and I feel that you are right."*

"Well that isn't a lie. I do feel that and I do believe that."

"Evan...not now. Please."

"So what is it you want from me?"

"He may call you. I need you to confirm that we spoke. Tell him you feel he's toxic for me and it's about time I listened. I'm calling Ace to get his help. I'll fill you in after I speak to him.

"He's going to hate me."

"He'll get over it. Please?"

"Fine. Lei, I hope you know what you are doing."

"I do. It's not going to be easy. But I need to do this. Don't tell anyone."

"Ok. Please be careful."

"I will...I promise."

♫ ♫ ♫

"Ace, its Leila."

"Hey, sweet girl. How are you?"

"I'm ok. Congrats on that baby boy of yours. I hear he looks a lot like you."

"Yeah, he's a total mini me. What's going on? Everything ok?"

"I need your help. I don't have much time to explain. I need you to investigate someone."

"I'm all yours. Shoot."

♫ ♫ ♫

"Hi Lei, it's Ace. My buddy Lee is on the case. He's a really good Private Investigator who also runs a very successful security company."

"Ace, I'll totally compensate you and Lee for all of this. I promise."

"Leila, I don't want your money. I want you safe. These two are trouble. We'll find out what they are up to."

"Evan is up to speed?"

"Yeah, sweetheart. He is totally filled in."

"Thank you. I'll call you in a day or so."

"Lei, one more thing. Evan and I think you need to tell someone. Is there anyone traveling with you, that you can trust?"

"Um, yeah, Dylan. He's our tour manager, but he's also a friend."

"Good. You need to fill him in, as soon as possible...ok?"

"Yes. I will. Thanks, Ace."

♫ ♫ ♫

"What do you want Jessa? Haven't you done enough?"

"Just touching base. You're a smart girl, Leila. I knew you'd see this logically. You did the right thing. I was impressed you did it so soon."

"Have you bothered him? Please leave him alone."

"I'm not an idiot. He needs to calm down a bit. Time...remember, it's Jack's best friend. He'll come around. He'll slowly warm to the idea he's going to have a son, and you should be proud you helped him make the right choice."

♫ ♫ ♫

"Lei, it's Ace. Lee saw her entering an apartment building on West Fourteenth Street. The address is listed as Danny Sorenson's. She's been there all day."

"Oh my God."

"Is it possible it's not Jack's baby? I know she had an official document, but maybe it's a fraud?"

"I thought of that. The lab is legit."

"I'll keep you posted."

"Thanks, Ace."

♫ ♫ ♫

"Hi, Dylan."

"Hey, Leila."

"I need to talk to you. Can you and I grab a cup of coffee after the show tonight?"

"Sure. Is everything ok?"

"I'll tell you tonight. Please don't tell anyone."

"Ok...I've got to be honest, I'm a little worried."

♫ ♫ ♫

"Hi Ev. I can't talk. I have to get to rehearsal."

"Real quick. Jack called me."

"He did?"

"Yeah. I told him just what you asked me to. I had to do some damage control with Lizzy also."

"Oh, Ev. I'm so sorry. Please fill her in. I don't want this harming your relationship."

"I was hoping you would say that. I kind of already did."

"I understand. I'm really sorry for dragging you into this."

"Lei, he's a mess. You know I'd do anything to help you. I just hope you know what you're doing. He truly sounds distraught. Lizzy thinks we should let her dad know what's going on. We may need some legal advice with this mess."

"Why?"

"Ace told me he saw Jessa coming out of Danny's apartment. Maybe it's not Jack's baby. There are online services you can order paternity tests from. If Jessa used an online service, she could have sent in someone else's DNA and claimed it was Jack's."

"I called the lab. It's a legit place."

"But no legit lab allows someone to walk in with a sperm sample to be tested. Jack would have to be present."

"Really?"

"Yep. Most likely it was done over the Internet. If so, she could have submitted anyone's sperm under Jack's name."

"But how would she have results from the New York Lab I called?"

"No clue. But something doesn't add up. Jack would have to request his own test to be performed through a court order, but a judge would need a reason to order another test. Since she proved Jack is the father, what would Jack's reason be?"

"I don't know."

"Mr. Lair may know a way around this."

"Hold on telling Mr. Lair. I need to make a phone call."

♫ ♫ ♫

"Can I please leave a message for Mr. Morrow? Can you have him call Leila Marino tomorrow on this number?"

♫ ♫ ♫

"That was my last conversation last night, right before the show."

"I'm going to kill her."

"No, Jack, listen to me. We need to handle this the right way."

"You know she's lying, right? I did not force myself on her."

"I know."

He holds my chin to stare into my eyes. "Leila, I would never do that."

"I know you wouldn't."

He sits up, encircling me with his arms. "What the fuck?"

"Baby, we need to continue with this. If she claims you forced yourself on her that could destroy you. Also, we aren't even close to figuring out what she and Danny are up to. We can't be together."

"No, I'm not going back to that hell. I can't."

"We have to. You need to go on just as she thinks you will. She thinks you'll self-destruct and go back to your old ways. You even need to act surprised when she tells you it's a boy."

He closes his eyes, leaning back against the headboard.

"Jack, how do you feel about that?"

"I don't know."

"Are you afraid to say you care?"

"I'm afraid to say I don't."

"You don't mean that."

"But I do."

"You are detached to this child right now. You may change your mind once he's born."

"If it's even mine."

"We still need to proceed as if it is, unless we get proof otherwise. You have to assume you are going to have a son."

"Leila, all I feel is it was a mistake that never should have happened." He stiffens and says. "I did something awful last night."

"I know." He looks down at me, his eyes moist with emotion. "Hunter told me. It's why I'm here."

"If I hadn't lost it and he hadn't told you, would you have come back to me?"

"Probably not...not yet." His pained face causes my heart to ache. "Jack, I haven't even scratched the surface on what I wanted to find out. It's only been a day."

"One day too long. Look how much damage I've done in one day."

"Baby...."

"Leila, I could have made another huge mistake last night."

Trying to lighten the mood, I point to the ground. "Well at least you were planning on using a condom." He follows to where I'm pointing, his face now twisted from remorse, my plan backfiring. "Hey." I say while stroking his cheek.

His eyes remain sad as he shakes his head. "Lei, I don't remember one damn detail, which is scary as hell."

Now it's time for me to shake my head. "I don't want to talk about it. Please promise me we won't talk about it...ever."

"I promise." He watches me closely. He suddenly grips me tightly against his body. "You promise me you'll never leave me again?"

"I do. I promise."

Leaning in, he kisses me deeply.

I reluctantly break the kiss. "Baby, I have to go."

"No."

"I can't be seen with you."

"No one will see you."

"Jack, we can't be sure. I suspect someone on the tour is feeding her information."

Jack looks directly into my eyes. "Why?"

"She said something that didn't sit well with me."

"What did she say?"

"She said I shouldn't consider telling you the truth, because she had connections on this tour and she would know."

"This makes sense now. I wondered how she got backstage opening night. I could kill her with my bare hands."

I move closer to kiss his cheek. "I really need to go."

"Not yet. Did you mean any of the things you said about me holding you back and controlling you?"

"No, I didn't. I don't feel that at all."

"Leila, I would never hold you back, you know that, right? Never."

"I know. I had to make you believe this just wasn't about Jessa. You wouldn't have let me go if you thought it was."

"You're right. I wouldn't. God, that day, you looked so cold...so distant. I did believe you."

"I'm sorry. It was necessary."

He strokes my cheek with his thumb, then runs it along my bottom lip. "It was necessary to actually break my heart? You didn't trust I could fake it?"

"No. I'm sorry."

"No confidence in me?"

"Baby, you're a rock star, not an actor."

"So the drinking, the performing while plastered, the telling an arena full of people that you dumped me..."

"Yeah, that one was tough." I interrupt.

"Sorry. All of that was perfect for the plan?'

"Yes."

"What about the part I called Malcolm to tell him you wanted to pursue a solo career?"

"He already called me."

"That cocksucker."

"Jack...I'm sorry I..."

"Don't apologize. I really don't want to hold you back...ever."

"I know. I won't talk to him if you don't want me…"

"No. I want you to. You need to hear him out." He studies my face as if seeing me for the first time. "You put me through hell."

"I'm sorry."

Staring down at his chest, he holds my chin, lifting my head up to gaze into my eyes. "I forgive you." He kisses me gently, moving his hand into my hair, holding my face to his.

When he breaks the kiss, I kiss him one more time on the corner of his mouth. "I love you. I need to go."

"No, five more minutes. I'll call Hunter and ask him to be the lookout."

"This is why I needed you to believe I left you. I lied. You do have complete control over me. I can't resist you." Caressing his face, I add, "Babe, you look awful." I run my fingertips over the dark circles under his eyes, over his stubble, over his dry cracked lips.

"I feel awful. I don't have a clue what I took last night."

"You need to rest and I need to go."

"No. I've missed you so much." He clings to me, refusing to rush through our reunion. He pulls me closer, crashing his lips to mine, as if he's pulling his oxygen from my body, frantic and desperate.

He leaves me gasping for air and wanting him desperately. "Ok. Five more minutes."

"I might need eight." He kisses my ear, my neck, my chin, my lips.

"Ugh…you need to shower. I can smell her on you."

He gives me a horrified look, before darting into the bathroom and into the shower. Calling from the bathroom, he shouts, "My eight minutes haven't started yet."

Smiling to myself, his comment tells me my Jack is back. A few minutes later, a wet and naked Jack stretches beside me.

"Better?"

"You could have dried yourself."

"Waste of time."

Leaning in, I sniff him, then again and again. Smiling he says, "What are you doing?"

"You smell so good." I smell him one more time for good measure. "But I still smell her perfume. It must be on the sheets."

Jack jumps up, pulls me off the bed and strips it completely bare. Throwing the entire pile of sheets, blankets and pillows in the bathroom, he then loudly shuts the door.

"Ok?"

Smiling wide, I nod. "Good." He pulls my tank top off, then my pajama bottoms, raising an eyebrow because I'm completely bare beneath. "I'm sorry, I was in a rush."

"No apologies needed." He positions me on the bare mattress, kissing my body inch by inch.

"Babe, you probably have a raging headache. We can do this later." He ignores my comment and continues his journey. My moans get louder and more frequent. It feels like an eternity before his lips are on my most sensitive part. He parts me with his fingers. He teases me with his lips. He focuses on bringing me dangerously closer with each calculated lick, stroke and lap of his tongue. It's not long after he began his exploit when my orgasm takes over.

"Oh God...Jack." I bury my hands in his hair and writhe as my body spasms with total pleasure.

Once I relax, Jack moves over my body, slowly burying himself inside of me. I can feel the friction between us, his muscular hips rubbing up against my own. It's accelerating my excitement. "Jack, please..."

"Baby, tell me what you want."

"Faster...go faster."

Smiling, he flips us so I'm now controlling the situation. Moving over him in the most perfect way, I bring my second orgasm to the surface and then tremble from its intensity. Jack stares at me with his smoky grey eyes, causing it to linger longer than normal. Not breaking our eye contact, I return his gaze until his own orgasm takes over his body. His fingers digging into my hips are the only indication he isn't done yet.

Once he releases his grip, he wraps his arms around my waist and pulls me down onto his chest. As I kiss his chest, he whispers, "Don't ever leave me again. I don't care what the reasons are. You talk to me."

"I promise. I was caught off guard. I'm sorry."

"She doesn't have a clue what she's dealing with." His expression becomes somber. "Thanks for having my back."

"Jack, it may not have been the best way to handle things, but I truly was doing it for you."

"I know. I still don't agree, but I understand. If you just talked to me, I could have helped you figure her out."

"The dumber she thinks we are, the better for us. Your reaction was exactly what she was waiting for. She pegged it." Kissing him, I add, "It's over now. Nothing can come between us anymore."

"Does this mean we are still engaged?"

"We're engaged?"

"You said yes…remember?"

"I remember. I'm teasing. Yes, I still want to marry you. I don't know why you would want to marry me though?"

"You have been a royal pain in the ass." Holding my face with both his hands, he kisses my lips softly. "But you are *my* royal pain in the ass. Baby, there isn't a thing you can do to make me not want to be with you. I adore you and I can't live without you."

"I can't live without you either."

The relief he must feel shows all over his face. He commences kissing me again as if wanting a round two.

Breaking away I pant, "Jack, I do have to go."

"You're still a buzz kill though…"

"Ha, ha…" Unfolding his arms from my body, I move off the bed to put on my only two articles of clothing. My cell vibrates with a call. Jack and I look at each other, before I answer.

"Hello?"

"Hello, Leila. It's Mr. Morrow."

"Mr. Morrow? Thank you so much for calling me back."

"You're welcome. I was concerned with your message. Is everything ok?"

"Unfortunately, my boyfriend is in a compromising situation with his ex-girlfriend. She's pregnant and is claiming the baby is his. There is reason for us to believe she is lying. Would my boyfriend be able to order his own paternity test?"

"If he suspects the test is fraudulent, yes, he is able to court order a paternity test."

"The problem is we don't want to tip her off that we think it's fraudulent, just yet."

"Well, unfortunately there isn't a reason for him to have his own test ordered then."

"I need to look into this some more. I may need your help with this. Is that ok?"

"Absolutely dear. Just let me know how you want to proceed."

"I will...thank you." As I hang up the call, Jack moves closer to wrap his arms around me. He clenches me tightly to his body.

"Hey...what's this?"

"You really do have my back."

"I do...I'd do anything for you. Even temporarily break your heart to help you." He looks down at me, not at all amused. "I hate leaving you right now."

"I know. I'll be good and let you go. But only because I need to go replace my phone so we can communicate, and so we can sext each other."

"What happened to your phone?"

"You don't want to know."

I kiss him one last time and on my way to the door he calls out, "Wait." He rummages through his bag and pulls out a postcard.

"What's this?"

"I didn't know if you had a chance to pick one up."

I'm stunned. I literally ripped his heart out, fed it to him, and he worried I wouldn't have a chance to pick up my stupid postcard?

"Jack."

I'm overwhelmed with emotion as I stare at the picture through watery eyes. He sees my struggle and pulls me into his arms.

"I know." He says into my hair and I cling to him.

♫ ♫ ♫

After leaving Jack, I checked out of the hotel and locked myself on the bus until rehearsals. First item on my agenda was to get Dylan up to speed regarding my reunion with Jack. He met me in my dressing room. The look on his face was one of complete shock as I detailed what Jack did last night.

"Is he ok?" Dylan asks after my rundown.

"He is now."

"How did he react to the whole Jessa thing?"

"He wants to kill her."

"I can't wrap my mind around her real motive. Yes, she says she wants Jack. But to go through such lengths to get him doesn't make sense."

"It must have to do with Danny. I think we need to take him more seriously."

He considers my words. "Maybe I'll embellish a bit with the label to get us a security guard. It will help us figure out who Jessa is communicating with."

"Embellish how?"

"I don't know. A specific threat."

"Dylan, I won't let you lie to the label."

"What if I filled them in on a condensed version of what's going on? It may be a good idea to have them backing us."

"I don't want all the pain I've caused Jack to be in vain. The more people who know about this, the more she can find out."

"I'll speak directly to Charles. He's level headed and discreet."

"Ok. If you think it will help, then go ahead."

"I think it will. This is a lot for you to carry. You need help figuring this out. If they are trying to extort Jack, he'll need the label's legal support."

"Thanks, Dylan. I really appreciate it. You've become such a great friend to me."

"I care about you, Leila. I'd do anything to help." His eyes look sad as he stares at me.

"Thank you." He nods quietly, an uncomfortable silence falls between us. "Um…I need to get out there. Let me know once you speak to Charles."

Leaving Dylan, I make my way to the stage. The guys are all in position, Jack waiting impatiently at the microphone. "How nice of you to join us."

Maybe I was wrong. Maybe he can act. Ignoring him, I walk to my position, aware of every pair of eyes on me.

Jack begins rehearsals by barking orders, criticizing mistakes, losing his patience. It's a very convincing performance on his part.

Looking out into the empty arena, I first notice Jen sitting a few rows back with Malcolm. I've just about had it with the bitches in Jack's life. This one is so anxious to get rid of me that she's blatantly pushing her boyfriend onto my tail.

The roadies are hanging around the stage, as they always do during our rehearsals. Will and Dylan are also here. The upside of Jack knowing is I can now concentrate on something other than his stress. I no longer have to worry about him. This gives me the opportunity to scrutinize our staff.

Watching from a distance, I study each roadie, looking for any obvious signs of disloyalty. Of the five, three of them are young, early twenties. It wouldn't be hard for one of them to be seduced by someone like Jessa.

Jack cuts rehearsal short and pounces off the stage towards our agent. A few minutes later, he storms out of the arena.

"Leila." Jen calls me from where she is standing off the stage.

Showing my impatience on my face, I walk towards her and Malcolm. "What?"

"Malcolm would like to talk to you. Do you have a few minutes?"

"Do I have a choice?"

"Of course you do."

Malcolm watches, with an amused expression on his face. "Come on, I won't bite."

Sighing, I motion for him to lead, the guys are all watching from the stage wide-eyed. I follow him towards the dressing rooms and walk through the door that he politely opens for me.

"I have a proposition."

"I'm listening."

"A song just came through my office. It's a winner. Top ten, no doubt. I'd like you to record it. Sort of an experiment."

"Experiment?"

"Yes. I know you would be huge. Let's throw something out there and see if anyone bites."

"Sure, why not."

He raises his eyebrows in surprise. "Well. I'm extremely pleased, Leila. You are finally taking my advice."

"I simply don't have the energy to continue fighting you. And since I'll be unemployed in a few months, timing seems right."

"Awesome. You guys are in LA in a few days. I happen to know you also have a day off. I'll arrange studio time for us." He bends to pull a few papers and a CD out of his bag. "Here are the lyrics and the music. It's a perfect fit for you and your voice. This is going to be gold."

"If you say so."

"Trust me. I believe things happen for a reason. This unfortunate chain of events will lead to something good. I just know it."

Jen barges in, without knocking or asking. "So, are we on board?"

"Yes, Jen, *we* are on board. You'll have me out of your hair sooner than later."

"Leila, I detect hostility from you. I've never given you any reason to believe I don't like you."

"Jen, let's not play games or sugar coat your true intentions. I have been a problem for you since the day I walked into my audition. Stay out of my way, and I'll stay out of yours."

Grabbing the papers off the table, I walk out leaving Jen with her sleazy boyfriend. Ugh, I feel like I need a shower. But this will help circumstances. What better way to show Jessa we truly are done than to pursue my solo career smack in the middle of our tour?

I have an hour before our show starts. Just as I'm about to jump into the shower, my cell rings. "Hey, baby. What did the snake want?" His voice is muffled and he sounds like he's under water.

"Where are you?"

"I'm in the bathroom."

"He wants me to record a song in LA. He's arranging studio time."

"Ok. That's good, right?" Jack clearly wants to follow my lead.

"I guess. Helps with our breakup rumors. Are you ok with it?"

"Of course. I told you, I'll support whatever you want to do."

"I know. Thank you." Clearing my throat, I add, "Hey, um…I kinda had words with Jen."

"Really? Why?"

"I just got sick of her attitude. I told her off. I'm sure she'll tell you since she thinks I'm the enemy right now."

"I'll act surprised. Then I'll tell her off too."

"Jack…"

"Kidding. I'll act indifferent. How's that?"

"Good. You're better at this than I thought."

"See, you have no faith in me. You could have spared…"

"Don't…say it."

"Ok. I won't."

"Jack, Ace is calling me. I have to go."

"I'll see you in a few. Love you."

"Love you, too."

"Ace?"

"Hey, Lei. She was back at Sorenson's place again today. Only for about an hour."

"Have you seen him? Can you get a picture so I know what he looks like?"

"You can Google him. He has a mug shot. He's been arrested twice."

"For what?"

Ace pauses for a few seconds. "Sexual assault and battery."

My silence prompts him to add, "Hey, don't get scared. We'll figure them out."

"Thanks, Ace."

Chapter 13 - Jack

"Oscar will be traveling on our bus. The two buses will now be caravanning for the rest of the tour. We leave together, we depart together. If anyone sees any suspicious activity, over-zealous fans, anything at all that looks shady, please report it to Oscar immediately. Oscar will be interviewing each of you, so he can get to know you, exchange cell numbers, pretty much routine stuff." Dylan runs through some more specifics of Oscar's job responsibilities. Most of Dylan's speech has been rehearsed.

Since our interview in Chicago, our fans have been getting more comfortable with approaching us in public or hanging around the buses after shows to get autographs and pictures. The staff thinks the reason security is being added is due to the fans becoming aggressive, especially towards me.

Leila explained it was Dylan's idea to bring Charles into the loop and tell him exactly what was happening. I couldn't agree more. I'm impressed he came through.

Finally having security, I will be able to concentrate on exposing Jessa's true motives. I can relax and not stress over Leila's safety. Oscar Holden is ex-army and works for *Orion Securities. I'm relieved he will be traveling with us for the rest of the tour. Dylan filled Oscar in on the entire Jessa/Danny situation. He knows his purpose is not only to serve as security, but also to find out who amongst our crew has been feeding information to Jessa.

Glancing over at Leila as she sits as far away from me as possible, my heart swells with the amount of love I have for this woman.

Once the dust cleared, I was able to digest why she did what she did. I fell in love with her even more, if possible. She does have my back. Our relationship is her priority. I'm her priority, and she's mine. We lock eyes for a split second, before she looks away. It's been two days since our reunion in Seattle. I'm literally aching for her.

"So that's about it. Roadies, are we all packed up?" The five roadies all nod simultaneously. "Ok, let's head out."

As everyone files out of the holding area, Leila is one of the first ones out the door. I can't wait to sext her.

"Jack, you have a minute?"

"Sure, Dylan." He moves to close the door.

"I wanted to let you know Oscar wants to travel to San Francisco on the other bus."

My hackles instantly rise. "Why?"

"Mainly for some privacy, so he can do some investigating online. But also to pick Leila's brain on her conversation with Jessa. He would also like to bring the guys up to speed. Unlike Leila, he feels the more eyes and ears aware of the situation, the better."

"Hunter knows some details of the situation, but Trey and Scott have no idea. I hated keeping this from them. I agree they should know."

Dylan nods. "Good. Also, I wanted to tell you since it's only a few hours from Portland to San Francisco and we are pulling in fairly early, if you want, you can sneak away with Leila before anyone is up and about. I plan on having a sit down with the roadies and Oscar mid-morning to keep any moles busy."

"Really? Dylan, that's awesome. Thanks, man."

"Sure. I feel bad for you guys. You ok?"

"Yeah, I'm hanging in. The sooner this is over the better."

"I agree. We'll figure it out."

I can see the draw Leila has towards him. I was jealous of his relationship with her in the beginning, but now I truly think he's just a good guy. I feel bad I called him a prick so many times behind his back.

On our way to the bus, my phone buzzes with a text from Leila.

love you

want you

i know. soon baby.

real soon. good news. i'll text you details.

k. xxx

It's times like now when I wish I could hire a hit on Jessa. Besides the obvious, which is missing my girl more than I can stand, living on the other bus is aggravating for so many damn reasons. I have no privacy. I can't call anyone without fear of someone hearing me. I feel so helpless, so unproductive.

Snatching up Will's laptop, I head to my bunk. I need to move things along, maybe bait Danny. I Googled his name and was not surprised to see he's been arrested twice. The first article I read makes me feel sick. Danny sexually assaulted a woman in a bar. Charges were filed against him. He served nine months in prison with a stiff fine. The second arrest is for battery against a woman. The second time there wasn't any jail time since the charges were dropped, victim un-named.

If Jessa did get mixed up with him, she should worry. Not that I care, it would serve her right. I take that back, no matter how evil and vindictive she is, even she doesn't deserve abuse from Danny.

I haven't spoken to her. It's beyond frustrating to be sitting around waiting for these two to reveal their intentions. I decide to change tactics. If someone is spying on me, I'll give him something to listen to.

Keeping my privacy curtain drawn shut, I dial Jessa's number. "Jessa, it's me. Um…so I um, wanted to talk to you. Call me back." Knowing her, she will call me back sooner than later. This is the first message I've left where I didn't call her a fucking whore.

As I'm expanding my search on Danny, my phone buzzes with a call from Jessa.

"Jessa." I say in a normal tone of voice, allowing anyone on the bus to hear me clearly.

"Hey, you called?"

"Yeah, thank you for calling me back."

"Of course, Jack. Is something wrong?"

My gut instinct is to say, "*Besides you trying to ruin my life, you fucking bitch?*" Taking a deep breath, I need to tread lightly and handle her just the right way. "Have you heard from Danny?"

"No, Jack…not a word. Why?"

"Did you know he was arrested twice?"

There is a slight pause on her end. Knowing her, she's quickly debating the different routes a yes or no answer would take.

"Yes, I did. He's a very dangerous person, Jack. That's why I wanted to warn you about him."

"Well, be careful. He clearly hates women." I don't want her to get suspicious, so I add, "I know she isn't my problem anymore, but can you warn me if you hear him say anything about Leila?"

"Of course, Jack. I haven't heard or seen him, but I'll tell Max to keep his ears open. Once I told Max that Danny leaked I was pregnant to the tabloids, he cut all ties with him as well."

"Max is a smart guy." This bitch lies through her teeth. "How are you feeling?"

"Better. It was a rough start, but I feel better now."

"Ok. I'll guess I'll talk to you later." I hang up before she can respond. At this moment, I just know she is smiling wickedly, assuming her expectations of my behavior were dead on.

No harm in helping her out a little.

Plan B is to text Danny. A simple text that will show vulnerability on my end, maybe even a touch of fear.

what do you want from me?

Now, to sit back and let Frick and Frack speculate.

♫ ♫ ♫

At five a.m. I sneak off the bus and into the waiting cab. Everyone is still sleeping, but I still need to be careful. I have another cab arriving in ten minutes to take Leila to the same destination that I am heading to. The Inn in San Francisco. It's a Victorian Bed and Breakfast that has a private sun deck, a hot tub and a five star rating. I needed to book two nights since check-in is at two and we are arriving at the crack of dawn, but it's worth every penny.

The owner was very gracious to meet me so early in the morning to check us in. Once she tiptoed away, she left me waiting anxiously for Leila in the formal living room. I cannot wait to get my hands on her.

Watching from the foyer, I can see her pull up, as she adorably looks out the cab window wide-eyed and open-mouthed. I open the front door for her. She walks up the path towards me while smiling and shaking her head.

"How did you arrange this in so little time?"

"I got lucky. As soon as Dylan told me about Oscar's meeting, I made the reservation."

She steps in, looking around still in awe. "Jack, it's so beautiful."

"I'm glad you like it. Let's get upstairs, we don't have much time."

"Don't we have like ten hours before rehearsal?"

"Like I said, not much time."

Leila gasps once I open the door. "Oh, Jack. This is incredible."

There is a huge bed, a lit fireplace, and the bathroom has a tub big enough for two.

I step closer to wrap my arms around her and nuzzle her neck. "They have a rooftop deck with a hot tub. And we can arrange breakfast here or on the balcony." She swings her head towards the balcony doors, her ponytail brushing my chin.

"This is perfect. Thank you." She leans back, pressing her body into mine. "I missed you so much."

"Leila, you have no idea how much I missed you." As I'm kissing her neck, goose bumps appear over her body. "Do you want to take a warm bath?"

"I'd love to."

Leading her into the bathroom, I start filling the tub as she pours some of the complimentary bubble bath under the stream of steaming water. We undress slowly, each watching the other quietly. Closing the distance, I kiss her like my life depends on it. I lift her and place her in the tub, following right behind. She settles against me, her back to my chest, my arms around her body, our legs entwined and her hands caressing my thighs.

"Remind me to thank Dylan again."

"Mmm…yep." She agrees.

I suck on her earlobe, before whispering, "I love you." My hands find her breasts beneath the warm water. She arches her back, pushing herself into my touch.

"I love you, too."

I kiss her neck and move one of my hands down her body while the other molds around her breast. My hard cock invades the space between us. Slowly, I caress her with my fingertips and drive her to the brink of an orgasm. The instant I pull my hand away, she groans with disappointment.

"Ssh, baby…turn around."

Gently I turn her and arrange her thighs on either side of mine. The warm water spills over the sides, prompting her to giggle adorably. She instantly stills when she sees the heated look in my eyes. I pull her face closer, connecting our lips. When I stroke my tongue against hers, she moans erotically. The inside of her mouth feels like warm, wet silk.

Slowly, she lowers herself over me. A small gasp escapes her lips as I fill her so perfectly. Her hands rest on my shoulders while she controls my pleasure with her movements. Her eyes close for the briefest time. When she opens them, the intensity of her stare is overwhelming to me. She reaches climax soundlessly, as she rests her forehead on mine. Her fingers gripping my shoulders, her pants, and her body clenching around me are the only clues that she is coming undone.

A guttural groan is my giveaway that I'm coming as I tremble inside of her. Leaning my head back against the tub, my eyes close from the force of my own release.

"Holy shit."

"Will it always be like this?" She asks through her pants.

"What? Mind-blowing?"

"Yes."

"Of course."

"Even when we're old and grey?"

"Especially when we are old and grey." I pull her towards me to kiss her deeply.

When we part, she smiles. "How did I get so lucky?"

I shake my head before responding. "I'm the lucky one. You've had to deal with a whole load of crap because of me."

"You're worth it." She settles against me, wrapping her arms around my body. "I can stay here all day."

"We can. We can do whatever you want."

"Can we order food?"

"Hungry?"

"Starving."

"Your wish is my command."

Later, while sitting on the patio having breakfast, I decide to let Leila know I had a brief conversation with Jessa.

"I had an idea. I called Jessa today while in my bunk. I thought if someone were listening, it would fuel her fire. I found out Danny was arrested twice, once for sexual assault and once for battery. He served a short jail time for the assault, but the battery charges were dropped. I pretended I was warning Jessa to be careful and she bought right into it."

"I know about Danny. Ace told me yesterday," she replies.

"We really need to take this seriously. He is one fucked up son-of-a-bitch."

Leila nods thoughtfully. "What do you think he really wants?"

I sigh from her question. I don't want to scare her, but she needs to know what he is capable of. "I texted him yesterday. I basically asked him that exact question."

"Did he respond?"

"Not yet. Knowing Danny, he's watching our success carefully. After we fired him, news spread through the bar scene. I know he hasn't hooked up with another band since then. He got involved with a scary crowd. Last I heard, before this mess, he was using and dealing. That's probably how he makes his money."

"Can't we use that to get him arrested or something?"

"He'd have to be caught in the act, or carrying. Does Ace know any cops who could trail him around the city?"

"Not sure. But I'll definitely tell him he is involved in that."

"It wouldn't hurt." I take her hand in mine, kissing it gently. "What do you want to do now?"

She raises her eyebrows and looks towards the bed. "You."

"I was hoping you would say that."

♫ ♫ ♫

It took a while, but it finally came. Just after our rehearsal in San Francisco, I received a response from Danny.

paranoid?

I forwarded the text to Oscar, and he advised not to respond. Coincidentally, Jessa called me an hour later. She was feeling me out, testing the waters. She called to tell me I was having a son. I remained silent on the phone. She asked if I was excited about that. I pretended to be stunned and confused, repeating over and over, "It's a boy?"

She comforted me. She said she hopes our son looks just like me and has my musical talent. Truthfully, that part stung. If it truly is my child, I haven't allowed myself to delve into the reality of having a son. I don't have a doubt in my mind that Leila would love him as if he were her own. A flash of her holding my son filled my thoughts. But I'm still wracked with thoughts of not wanting this child.

Jessa's last question had me reeling. "Jack, do you mind if I come out to Vegas to see you?"

"I really don't want to see you."

"I would like to talk to you about the future. Specifically, our child's future. I don't want to do it over the phone."

"Should you be flying?"

"Yes, I'm still allowed to fly."

"I don't think so."

"Jack, there are things we need to hash out. Soon I won't be able to fly. This is the least you can do for me."

I shook my head at her audacity. "Least I can do for you? Help me understand why I should do anything for you?"

"Jack, we can do this in a civilized manner, or not. I need to talk to you, face to face."

"Fine."

"I'll text you the details. How long will you be there?"

"I can meet you the morning of the Eleventh. That's your only option."

"Ok. Let me know where you'll be staying."

"Nope. I'll let you know where we can meet. Public place and only on my terms."

She paused for a second and then she said, "Whatever."

I hung up and emailed Oscar details of my conversation.

Oscar responded immediately:

I'll fill Ace in once we get to LA tomorrow. He did some research on Danny's financial situation. He's broke. Not a penny to his name. Your ex isn't much better. She is carrying a huge amount of debt. Stay tuned.

Oscar and Ace have been introduced via phone conference and are working as a team on investigating Jessa and Danny. Oscar's boss, Mike Casiano, at *Orion Securities, has been very accommodating in helping to figure out what Danny's deal is.

If Jessa is indeed broke, it's clear why she didn't argue or refuse my offer to financially support her and the baby. It's funny how she gave me guilt that the money wasn't what she wanted or wasn't enough, though.

But why would she care if Danny were broke? How does this help him?

Since we left San Francisco, I also emailed Evan. I sent him a long, heartfelt letter containing an apology and a request to please talk to Anthony. I asked him to fill Anthony in on the details of our situation. I asked Evan to let Anthony know I would be contacting him myself, as soon as I was able to get some privacy. I informed him of plans I've made for Vegas, which include he and Lizzy. I ended with a request to Evan that he please not tell Leila about the email, or the details in it.

Evan responded with a short, to the point email. He's not happy about the secrecy, but he would honor my request. He made it clear he's only doing it for Leila. I hate keeping things from her, but this time it's necessary.

We arrived in LA early this morning. After cleaning up and getting dressed, I make my way out to the bus. Oscar is missing, since he alternates between our bus and Leila's. Dylan, Will and the roadies are all hanging around having breakfast.

"You guys are so fucking loud." I say grumpily, as I make myself a cup of coffee. Sitting at the table, I stare into space for a few minutes. Facing Dylan, I say, "Arrange a rehearsal at one."

Dylan looks confused. "Why so early?"

Giving him a blank look, I respond, "Isn't she recording her song with Malcolm today? I want to rehearse without her."

"Jack, do you think that's a good idea?"

"Just do it, Dylan." Grabbing my coffee, I head towards the back of the bus. I have an errand to run, and I can't waste any time just sitting around. A few minutes later, I exit the bus. But not before saying, "I'm going to check out the women in LA."

Chapter 13 ½ - Jessa

"Get up. I'm going to miss my flight."

"Fuck off. What do you want from me?"

"Do you know what you need to do?"

"Yes. You've told me a hundred times."

"You can't be high while I'm gone. You can't screw this up, Danny. I mean it. Make sure you send the picture that's not blurry."

"Just leave already."

"One more thing, when he sees it, he's going to flip out. Do not respond. He'll panic when he sees you've been following Lizzy. He'll be putty in my hands. We may not be able to get to his precious girlfriend, but his sister is the next best thing."

"This better work. I'm fucking sick of all your little schemes. You convinced me to sit back and let you handle it. If I don't get what I need, I'll kill you and him."

"It'll work."

Chapter 14 - Leila

Malcolm arranged a cab to pick me up at the arena. While sitting in the back seat, I receive a call from Jack.

"Hi, babe…good luck."

"Thank you. I'm nervous about this."

"Don't be. You'll be great. I can't wait to hear the song. Don't forget to ask Malcolm for the mp3 downloaded onto your phone."

"I won't. I'll text you when I'm done. Where are you?"

"I have a quick errand to run."

"Alone?"

"I'll be fine."

"Jack, please be careful."

"I will."

I wish he were here with me. He'd be soothing my stress, calming my nerves, and most likely making out with me in the back of this cab. I barely see a thing as LA whizzes by. I have too much on my mind. I've always wanted to see LA, but now isn't the time to get hung up on being a tourist wannabe. Jack will just have to bring me back here one day.

I've listened to the music and memorized the lyrics Malcolm gave me. It is a good song. It's upbeat and fun, but it's also not too pop and more rock and roll. He's right. It's perfect for me.

As the cab pulls up to the recording studio, I quickly check myself in the mirror, nerves taking hold. I'm torn between doing this for the wrong reasons and wanting this song to succeed at the same time. Malcolm was right. I am also a firm believer in things happening for a reason, so who knows?

"Leila, you're right on time." Malcolm greets me at the front door of the studio. He shakes my hand, smiling warmly. When he isn't in predator mode, he really is a nice looking man. With his dark curly hair, tall muscular physique and vivid blue eyes, he is downright handsome.

"Ok, let's get this over with," I respond impatiently.

He chuckles at my attitude. "Once this hits top ten, you will feel differently. Trust me."

"Malcolm, that's the only reason I'm here."

"Come, let's get started." He takes my hand and leads me towards the back of the studio. "Can I get you anything before we begin?"

"No, I'm fine." I subtly remove my hand from his, just as we enter a small room. Small is actually a generous word. It's miniscule, barely big enough for the both of us. A large, black mesh disc attached to a single microphone sits in the center of the room. Facing the microphone is a plate glass window separating us from the control booth. Two men sit at the control panel, waiting for Malcolm's instructions.

"Gentlemen, this is Leila Marino. She will be recording the demo today." Both men wave and smile, as I wave back. "Are we ready?"

"So that's it. I just start singing?"

He places a set of large, bulky headphones over my ears. "You'll hear the music through these. Let's start at the beginning and see where it takes us. I'll be in the control booth with Pete and Glen. We'll let you know if we need you to stop for any reason."

Nodding, I position myself dead center, waiting for my instructions. A few seconds later, I hear Malcolm's voice in my ears. "Ok, Leila, on three. One, two, three…"

The music filters through my headphones. The song is called *Constant Torment* and has haunting lyrics set to an upbeat rock tempo. It's good, and it's perfect for me. I close my eyes and sing the lyrics in time to the music. I keep expecting Malcolm's voice to stop me at some point during the song. But he never does. Once done, he turns towards the guys and says something. The only sound I hear is my own breathing.

"Leila, that was just about perfect. Can we try it with you singing the chorus a touch lower?"

"Sure."

We run through the song two more times with different suggestions. After the third time, Malcolm joins me in the studio. "The guys said they've never had a recording session go as smoothly as this one did."

"I guess that's a compliment?"

"Absolutely. This song is practically ready for release. We're done here. I'll let you know once it's been mastered and edited.

"So what's next?"

"Once the label listens to it, we'll decide on a course of action. Most likely we'll sample it with some key radio stations coast to coast, a sort of exclusive demo. Make them feel they've stumbled on you. It will make them loyal."

It's clear why he is so successful. He's a rat, but he's good at what he does.

"Hey, can the guys download the mp3 onto my phone. I'd like to listen to it myself."

"Absolutely. We'll also give you a CD. Come."

Malcolm leads me into the control room. Fifteen minutes later, I'm in a cab with my download and my CD.

hey baby...i'm done. on my way back. i think it went well. sending you the link. love you. xx

He texts back immediately.

can't wait to hear it. love you 2. one more thing. come to the arena and follow my lead.

k. xxx

As the cab pulls up to the arena, I can hear their music from the parking lot. It's a bit unsettling to hear our songs and not be on the performing end. I'm curious why the band is rehearsing and can only guess it has to do with our façade.

Walking closer to the stage, Jack's eyes settle on me as he sings the lyrics to one of my favorite songs. He abruptly stops and it takes a few seconds for the guys to realize it and stop playing.

"Back so soon?"

"Why are you rehearsing?"

"Just getting some practice in without our back-up singer."

"Would you like me to skip our show tonight?"

He laughs bitterly. "I would love you to skip our show tonight, but it's not my choice."

Without a word, I turn and head for my dressing room. His angry act is really turning me on. On my way down the hall, one of the roadies follows. "Leila?"

I turn to see Kyle walking quickly towards me. "Hey, I just want to say I think it sucks what's happening with you and Jack."

"Thanks, Kyle. It hasn't been easy."

"Will you be finishing the tour?"

"I don't have a choice. I can't break my contract. I would love to pack my bags right now and get the hell out of here."

"That really sucks. You are so talented. So is the band. You guys are all a great fit together."

I turn away and nod quietly. "Yeah, thanks." As I start walking away from him, he says one last thing.

"Leila, don't worry. Everything will work out."

Turning back, I nod again and smile shyly. "Thanks, Kyle."

♫ ♫ ♫

"We just want to ask you a few questions."

"Am I in trouble?"

Oscar takes a seat across the table from Kyle. Jack, Hunter, Scott, Trey, Dylan, Will and I are all around the table. Oscar smiles at Kyle. "Why would you be in trouble?"

"This looks serious."

"Kyle, we are just trying to figure out how some specific details have ended up online. We will be asking the same questions to all the roadies. Has anyone contacted you recently regarding the tour?"

Kyle turns all shades of red. He looks from Oscar to Jack. "What do you mean?"

"You know, gossip magazines or reporters? We believe someone on this tour is releasing information."

"Um...I...no. No one has contacted me."

"Have you heard anything or seen anything strange with the other guys?"

"No."

"The Internet was buzzing today with details of Leila's recording session in LA. Except for us, no one knew Leila was recording a song. We can't understand how some of our fans got wind of it."

"Sorry, I really don't know."

"There was also a post that claimed Jack kicked Leila out of the band during rehearsals."

Kyle shrugs. "Don't know."

"Ok, thanks for your time. If someone contacts you who isn't affiliated with the band, please let us know as soon as possible."

"Will do. Anything else?"

"Nope. Thanks, Kyle." Kyle gives a nervous glance around and exits the room. Once the door is shut, Oscar says, "I'm not convinced he is our guy. But he does know something. He may be covering for someone else. We still need to talk to Brian and Rich. Will, can you grab one of them and bring them in?"

Will leaves the room to find one of the last two roadies to question. With Will gone, Jack turns to Oscar. "This is getting out of hand. They even knew what time she was at the studio. Oscar, I want you spending more time on the other bus."

Oscar nods. "I agree."

Will enters the room with Rich. Looking totally unfazed, he takes a seat and looks around. "What's going on?"

Oscar gives the same speech he gave Kyle. Rich responds with an arrogant, "So?"

"Have you been contacted by anyone recently regarding the tour?"

"Yeah. Some chick called me. She said she was from Rock MY World. Wanted to know how their breakup was affecting the tour."

"Why haven't you said anything?"

Rich shrugs, "Didn't know I needed to. You said to let you know about crazy fans, not the media."

"True. Did you talk to the reporter from Rock MY World?"

"Nope. I told her I didn't know anything." Rich leans back in his chair and folds his arms, watching Oscar with a look of total boredom.

"Do you have her number?"

He pulls out his phone, searching for a number. "Nope, I deleted it."

"Can you please let us know if she contacts you again?" Oscar asks, eyeing him suspiciously.

"Sure, no problem."

"Thanks. Anything else you'd like to let us know?"

Rich shakes his head slowly. "No."

"Ok. Please tell Brian we ran out of time and we'll touch base with him after the show."

Rich leaves the room, leaving the door open when he does. Oscar turns to the guys, "Do you mind if I chat with Jack and Leila for a few minutes?"

"No, the less we hear the better." Hunter says, as he leaves the room. Trey and Scott start to follow. Trey stops and says, "Rich is hiding something."

"How do you know?" Jack asks.

"He never looked at anyone but Oscar. Kyle's reaction was normal."

"Thanks, man."

Trey nods and walks out the door. Dylan stands to close the door.

"Well? That really got us nowhere." Dylan says, as he sits again.

"I disagree. They know we are suspicious. That will make them nervous. Screw ups occur when someone gets nervous."

"Now what?" Jack asks impatiently.

"You'll meet with Jessa in Vegas. I predict she'll go the pity route and try to negotiate financial support. Take it all in and tell her you'll get back to her once you speak to your attorney. Also, ask her if your name will be listed on the birth certificate as the father."

"Why would I ask that?"

"Because if it is, and she falsified the test, she can be charged with a felony."

Oscar watches our reaction and then continues. "Basically, if it's money she wants, she'd have to confirm you are the father. By doing that, she is digging her own grave if it's not true."

"She is one piece of work." Jack says. "What the hell is she trying to get out of me?"

"My guess is you and money. Ace and I feel it may be necessary for you to wear a wire, just in case she pulls out her cards." Oscar replies.

"I don't like this one bit." Leila says out loud.

"You need to trust us."

"I trust you completely. It's her I don't trust. What if Danny comes with her and tries to pull something?"

"I'll be there with Jack. Ace will warn us if Danny is joining her and we'll be prepared."

"Danny must have something on her, this has his name written all over it." Jack says, shaking his head. "Unbelievable...huh?"

"Jack, people will go to great lengths for money." Oscar admits.

"Thank you for filling us in."

"Mr. Morrow has been a huge help. Thank Leila for calling him once this started."

Jack looks over and winks at me. "She knows how thankful I am. Let's discuss the getting back together part. When?"

Oscar chuckles. "Not yet. There is nothing to prevent her from accusing you of sexual assault. If that were to get out, it really would be lethal to your reputation. Even if it's not true, there really isn't proof otherwise and people will always speculate."

"Fuck."

"You really need to be patient. Leila was absolutely right in planning this."

"Ok. Patience."

"One more thing. When you meet with Jessa, tell her you would like your own paternity test done. Do not tell her why. Stay calm and do not get excited or angry at her response."

"I may need to take a Valium to keep from strangling her to death."

"Be careful who you repeat that to." Oscar scolds.

♫ ♫ ♫

"Hi, Ace."

"Hey, sweetie. So, Jessa boarded a flight in LaGuardia alone and is on her way to Vegas. I haven't seen Danny in days. She has been to his place, but he hasn't surfaced or left his apartment. I already let Oscar know."

"Thanks for working so closely with him."

"No thanks needed. He's a great guy and I'm glad he's there protecting you."

"I'm glad you're in Jersey protecting me."

"Me too. Bye, sweetie."

A smiling Jack busts into my dressing room and closes the door quickly behind him.

"What are you doing?"

"I'm visiting my girlfriend." He comes to stand behind me, watching me through the vanity mirror. "Ooh, are you naked under here?" He asks as he uses his finger to open my robe a few inches.

"Yes, and we don't have time. We're due on stage in fifteen minutes."

"Baby, have I not proven I work well under pressure? Lately we've never had enough time."

"How are you here? What if someone saw you?"

"Will has the roadies scrambling with a 'missing amp' issue."

"Did you have something to do with this missing amp?"

"Me? Of course not. I may have bribed Trey, though."

Laughing at his admission, I say, "What is Trey's price? He seems un-bribable."

"You'd be surprised. He wants a solo tonight."

"Well, good for him. We are in his home state."

"Yep. He's shrewd." Jack pulls me into a standing position. "Enough talking."

He goes right to it, nibbling on my ear, then my neck.

"Mmm…did you lock the door?"

"Of course, woman." Jack slowly kisses my lips. It's the kind of kiss that drives me wild, and now that he knows that, he torments me with them every opportunity he gets.

"So listening to your single got me all horny."

"Did you like it?"

"Yeah, babe. It's really good. I love it. The lyrics went right to my groin."

"What?"

"They're hot. When you sing about being in a constant state of torment, it does things to me."

"That could become a problem since we're apart right now."

"Cold showers. They fucking suck ass." He kisses my neck, as I giggle at his admission. "When does it debut?"

"Malcolm said to give him a few days. He's going to send it to some key radio stations."

He unties my sash, moving his hand around my waist to the small of my back. Pulling me into him, I can feel each of his hard muscles…every one.

"Men from coast to coast will want you. But you are mine. Don't ever forget that."

"And you're mine."

"Completely." He lifts and sits me on the edge of the vanity, moving to stand between my spread legs. He then pulls my already erect nipple in between his lips and swirls his tongue around its peak. One hand slowly skims my body and comes to rest on the inside of my thigh and the other gently kneads my other breast.

"Lean back."

I do as he asks, resting my back against the mirror. He kisses me and then disappears between my legs. Taking an ankle in each hand, he hooks my legs over his shoulders and goes right to it. His warm lips immediately send sparks through my body, his wet tongue lights the match, but then a knock on the door douses the flames.

"Oh my God. Jack!" I whisper loudly, in a panic.

"Ssh…don't worry. Don't say anything."

Here we are, Jack on his knees with his face buried in between my thighs, and I'm spread as if getting a pap smear. After a few seconds, whoever knocked jiggles the doorknob, then moves on.

Jack starts laughing, his body shaking while his face is still buried in my…

"Jack!" I push him away. "Stop."

"I…Babe…" He can't even complete a full intelligible sentence from laughing so hard. He straightens and slumps over me, pinning me with his weight.

"I'm sorry, baby. That was so funny."

"It wasn't that funny. And now I'm horny as hell."

"We still have a few minutes."

"No!" I push him away and point a finger. "Stay away from me."

I pull my robe closed and cross my arms, waiting for him to calm down.

When he hunches over and continues laughing, I move into the bathroom to get dressed. He follows me in, still apologizing profusely.

"If it makes you feel better…" He takes my hand and places it over his rock hard bulge.

"Good. Serves you right."

"Can I hug you for luck?" Dimples appear, and my crotch reacts.

"Fine."

He moves over to wrap his arms around me. "I really am sorry. I'll make it up to you."

"Yes, you will, Mr. Lair. You know how I get before a show. You've wrecked my routine and frustrated me."

"I'm sorry."

An announcement with our five-minute warning comes over the PA system. "Out!"

"Ok. I'll see you on stage. Time to hate you." He kisses my cheek and sneaks out. That man is going to be the death of me.

It turns out my horniness helps with my pretense to hate Jack perfectly. Usually, when he makes snide comments about me to the audience, I remain quiet, pretending to stew. Today, I fight back. During our first duet, I decide not to share a mic with him and instead choose to roam the stage and openly flirt with Trey during his solo. Trey takes the opportunity to bust Jack and responds perfectly towards my advances.

Jack begins his verse staring out into the crowd. He slowly turns his head to finally look at us. The look is heated and says, *"You are so dead"*.

I respond with my own glare, challenging him to *"Bring it on"*.

Towards the end of the song, I move to the center mic and purposefully keep distance between us. He leans in until his lips touch mine. He seductively snakes his hand into my hair, holding my head in place while sneering the lyrics to me. To the audience, it looks like we can't stand each other.

The rest of the show goes much the same way, our tensions causing our performance to look enraged. It's the first show since I broke up with him that we've interacted at all. The audience loves it. After our encore, they begin chanting, "Leila and Jack", over and over.

"They sure want you two back together." Hunter says, as we exit the stage. As usual, Will and the roadies are all at the stairs, waiting to pack up our equipment.

Jack uses the opportunity and mumbles, "Not gonna happen." He then disappears into his dressing room. He always turns me on when he acts this way. Once I'm tucked away in my own room, he texts me.

coming in

no. too risky.

His response is to barge into the room.

"Jack, you are going to get caught."

"They are breaking down the stage. No chance." He stalks towards me like he's about to eat me for lunch. "Trying to make me jealous?"

"Did it work?"

He places my hand right where it was before our show started. "What do you think?"

"I'd say that is a yes. Have you been sporting this for the last two hours."

"Uh, yeah."

"I'll help you take care of it if you'd like."

"That's the plan." He removes my jeans and panties, lifts me and places me in the same spot I was in when we were so rudely interrupted. He then drops his jeans to his ankles.

I look down and smirk. "Commando?"

"Just saving time." He slips two fingers inside, while using his thumb to stroke me. "You're so ready." He removes his fingers and thrusts into me fast and hard.

"Ah, fuck." He says with his lips on my ear.

He buries his face in my neck, muffling his grunts and groans. The ache he left me with earlier has intensified unbearably. I take hold of his ass cheeks to urge him to go deeper and faster still. He complies and with every lunge, he gets me closer.

He slips his hand between us and a few strokes of his fingertips is all it takes.

Jack groans and repeats a throaty, "Ah, fuuuck." Once he stills, he pins me with his body weight, not moving a muscle.

"You ok?"

"Hmm. I'm good." He murmurs into my neck. "You?"

"Very good."

"Glad to hear it." He says, but still doesn't move.

"You have to go." When he remains slumped over me, I poke his chest. "Jack."

"Hmm?"

"You have to go."

"Such a buzz kill." He pulls out and looks down at my exposed crotch. He runs the pad of his thumb over me, causing my breath to hitch and my hips to buck.

"This sucks."

"What?"

"Leaving you here, especially like this."

I grab his shirt and pull him towards me. "I know." I kiss him deeply and he inches closer, until he is pressed against my entrance again, erect and ready to go. This was a bad idea. I've riled him up again.

I push him away and shake my head. "No. No. No. You really have to go."

Taking matters into my own hand, I hop off the vanity, pull up his jeans, carefully zip and button him up, and shove him towards the door.

On his way out, he turns and admits, "I forgive you."

"For what?"

"For the cold shower I have to go take."

Chapter 15 - Jack

I have so much swirling in my head that it's causing a constant dull pounding in between my ears.

Ace confirmed Jessa flew out of New York by herself. Unless Danny is arriving from a different location, she is coming alone. She is staying at some dump on the old strip. My guess is she can't afford anything better.

I can't wait to find out why she called this little meeting. Being in the same room with her is going to be challenging. I already feel the impulse to strangle her, and she isn't even here yet.

Leila is not happy about this, and I can't blame her. She worries Danny will appear to complicate things. Oscar assured her that he would be there, hiding in the background.

Besides all the Jessa charades, I've had to juggle the secret hotel I booked for Leila and me, the surprise of having our siblings coming, and coordinate the other "thing", all while doing our show and pretending to hate the love of my life.

When did my life become such a fucking soap opera?

I booked a suite at the *Bellagio* overlooking the fountains. Vegas is costing me a fortune, but I'd gladly pay ten times the price to be with her. As a ruse, Leila and I have our rooms booked in the same hotel that the band is staying in. We will check in and then sneak out to the *Bellagio*.

Will gave the roadies the night off, since our first show isn't until tomorrow. We all predict they will be like kids in a candy store and most likely disappear the entire time. Oscar will be following Leila and me, in case Jessa's mole isn't as excited about being in Vegas as we hope.

I feel bad for running them ragged because we are staying somewhere else, but there's a reason for this madness. The Marriott is just not special enough for what I have planned. Everyone who is aware of our predicament has been nothing but supportive, including my band.

I received a text from Lizzy announcing that she and Evan have arrived and the suite is perfect. She helped to organize everything I needed for my private dinner with Leila. They are taking in the sights and will meet up with us later tonight, in time for the intimate party I've planned with the rest of the band. I tried to get Patti and Mandi to join us, but they just weren't able to come so soon since their Chicago trip.

We should be pulling into Vegas in a few hours. It's super early, and I can't sleep once again. It works out to my advantage since it's the only time I can sit on the bus with complete privacy. The rest of the guys are all sleeping in their bunks, and it's just our driver, the laptop and me.

I decide to take a chance and text Leila.

are you up?

When she doesn't respond, I check out some of the gossip sights to see if anything new has festered overnight. I Google Leila's name and the usual posts come up. Her haters are still spewing nonsense, but no one is really paying attention to them. Seeing her gorgeous face on the screen fuels my hunger for her. I miss her so much. I miss having my arms wrapped around her each night like I used to. There are some new posts from fans that heard her song on the radio. Just thinking about it causes my cock to twitch. Her voice does things to me. The song Malcolm chose for her is perfection. It's just a matter of time when every station from coast to coast will be playing her hourly.

Next, I open our website and am shocked at the number of followers we now have. Just a few short weeks ago we had a few thousand followers. Our numbers are now in the tens of thousands. They adore us. They call themselves The DL Sinners. Their loyalty to us is amazing. They jump on all our updates, posts, and pictures that Jen adds to our blog. They pimp us out tirelessly. They attack all and any haters. They have our backs, and it's humbling to know all these strangers would defend us, support us, and share our story just because they love our music. It's all the awesome support we are getting from our fans that keeps me sane.

As I enter my own name in the search bar, a new blog site pops up as the first entry.

Ah, *fuck*. The name alone tells me this isn't good.

A chick I banged created a blog for all the other chicks I banged. There are hundreds of followers, all detailing their connection to me. Scrolling through their faces makes me sick to my stomach. I don't even remember the majority of them.

Great, *fucking great*. This is just what I need right now.

hey babe, whatcha doin'? Leila responds to my earlier text.

um. nothing.

are you jerking off?

no. i can't. my stupid bunk squeaks.

lmao. i'm sorry, i wish i could help.

you could always talk dirty to me. I reply in a desperate attempt.

it kinda doesn't work over text.

attach a pic. that'll work. ☺

that's all i need. a naked pic ending up in the wrong hands.

just my hand. singular. my other hand would be busy.

where would your other hand be busy? your bunk squeaks and you are surrounded by men.

Damn it. let's stop talking about this.

you started it.

ok, smartass.

why are you up so early?

Couldn't sleep.

So, watcha doin'? She repeats her question from earlier.

I stare at her text for a full minute.

jack.?

do I have to tell you?

Yes!

i'm on the internet.

watching porn?

Ha ha. i'm googling.

Ugh. I don't want to know…wait- yes I do.

When I don't respond, she adds,

hello?

First off, i read about your new song. it's starting to be played.

Yeah, Malcolm sent me a text telling me.

You sound so hot.

You're biased.

True. But you do.

So second?

Huh?

You said first off. What else are you doin'?

Nothin'

Liar.

I once again stare at the phone. Jeez, how do I tell her all my ex-fucks have banded together to brag about their experiences with me?

?? waiting...

i'm telling you because I promised not to keep things from you - lairlovers.com

oh my god!

A few minutes pass and no additional texts come through. Now it's my turn to prompt her.

lei?

really jack?

i'm sorry !

i love jack lair...i love jack lair...he loves me...he loves me...

what are you doing?

reminding myself.

i do. i love you more than anything in this world.

i know.

i'll make it up to you.

Yes you will!

I wish you were here now! I admit.

Me too.

My girlfriend is so fucking awesome.

♫ ♫ ♫

The roadies are all yapping like a bunch of women. I sit watching them make their plans, while scowling. They are starting at one end of the strip and bouncing from go-go bar to go-go bar, until they make it to the other end. Will is joining them. This is perfect. We will not have to worry about them for hours.

On their way out, I threaten, "No one better get arrested tonight."

The minute they leave the bus, I call Leila.

"Where am I meeting you? Can you give me a hint?"

"Nope. Oscar will handle getting you there. See you in a few."

I hang up before she has the chance to ask another question.

Hunt, Scott, Dylan and Trey are all hanging together. The roadies think I'm joining them. Instead, I take a cab straight to the *Bellagio*. As I stand in the suite, I am filled with anxiety...not in a bad way. More like a kid on Christmas morning.

I have a few minutes before Oscar will get here with Leila. The candles are lit. The rose petals are scattered. The table is set facing the floor to ceiling windows affording a dead center view of the fountains. I have nothing to do now but wait for her to arrive.

If I were a smoker, I'd want a cigarette right about now. After watching seventeen long minutes tick away on the digital clock that sits on the end table, I start pacing the room. At the twenty-six minute mark, there is a knock on the door.

I release a deep breath and walk over to open it.

Leila stands alone, smiling shyly. "Hey."

"Hey."

"The *Bellagio* huh? There is no way the label approved the *Bellagio*."

"No, this is all me."

"You look so handsome." She appraises my button down shirt and dark denim.

"Don't look so shocked. I can clean up sometimes." I step back to admire her. She makes shorts and a t-shirt look amazing. "You look good enough to eat."

"I feel under dressed compared to you." She moves right into my arms. "Seeing you in this shirt makes me want to slowly unbutton it."

"You're such a tease." I kiss the top of her head and move aside to let her in. She takes in the room, with her mouth gaping open.

"You did all this for me?" She looks over to see me nodding wordlessly. "Jack, this is beautiful."

I shrug and admit, "I have some romance in me."

"I can see that. I love it."

I take her hand and pull her towards the couch.

"I wanted to make this special. Being apart has been pure torture."

"It's been torture for me too." She settles against me, as we quietly enjoy just being together. This girl completely changed me. I love it.

"Do you want to dance?"

She looks up amused. "I'd love to dance, Mr. Lair." I walk over to the mp3 player and hit the play list I created especially for tonight. The sound of Elvis fills the room and I hold my hand out to her.

She takes my hand and fits herself against me. While staring into my eyes, I bend for a kiss. I wrap my arms around her, pulling her even closer. "Do you like the song choice?"

"I love it. You sang this to me in Cleveland. I love to hear you sing. You've thought of everything to make this the perfect evening. Thank you."

"I have a few more surprises for you."

She looks up at me wide-eyed. "What are they?"

"You'll see."

We sway to the music, wordlessly. There isn't a reason to talk. We both know what the other is thinking. We both know what the other is feeling. We are two halves of one heart. As we cling to each other, I catalog the feel of her in my arms. I want to commit to memory the way her body fits up perfectly against mine. The way her hair feels like silk against my cheek. The way her skin feels against my fingers as I grip her waist beneath her shirt. The way the gold flecks in her eyes glisten when she looks up at me through unshed tears.

Once the song ends, I wipe away the tears that finally escape. "Happy tears?"

"Extremely."

"Good. Are you ready for your next surprise?"

She smiles and nods quietly.

I take her hand and position her at the windows, facing the fountains. She takes it all in. My heart pounds frantically in my chest, as I stand behind and possessively wrap her in my arms. She runs her hands along my forearms and leans back against me.

A few minutes later, the lights that illuminate the front of the hotel dim.

"This is incredible. They time the fountains to the music." I say directly into her ear. Goose bumps appear along her arms. I'm not sure if it's from the fountains or from the touch of my lips.

"I've heard of this, and I've always wanted to see it."

The dancing waters rise majestically just as the music begins. A few seconds into the song, she bolts around to face me. "Uhh," she sucks in a breath and adds, "That's my song." I nod while smiling. "How did you do this?"

"The label helped." I turn her around so she can see the show. It's beautiful. The way the water dramatically sways in tune to my chords. I move to stand beside her so I can watch her reaction. She clasps my hand in both of hers, wide-eyed and tightens her fingers each time the pillars of water shoot high into the air. The song comes to an end, and the fountains quietly subside. As hoards and hoards of spectators lining the perimeter start to move away towards their intended destinations, our view of the street becomes unobstructed.

I swallow nervously, as she turns to face me. Her eyes are glistening with emotion.

"Leila, I love you so much that it's sometimes hard for me to breathe. You have changed my life. You have altered every cell in my body. You own me, completely. By simply staring into my eyes, you can bring me to my knees."

I gently lift her hand, placing a kiss on her ring finger. "I know things have been difficult. I will have to live with the pain I've caused you. I still don't understand why you are with me. But I want you to know I will do everything in my power to make you happy. I will laugh with you. I will cry with you. I will keep you safe. I will remind you how much I love you every day for the rest of our lives."

A single tear rolls down her cheek. I gently wipe it away before dropping down onto one knee. "Leila Marino, will you marry me?"

Her nod begins before my sentence is complete. Her smile illuminates her face.

"Yes."

I reach into my pocket and pull out the ring that I've chosen for her. According to Lizzy, it's simple, it's elegant and it's stunning. As I slip it on, her finger trembles adorably. Still holding her hand, I stand before her.

"I love you more than anything in this world. It no longer matters to me if we reach fame or not, because my career has taken a back seat to you." We gaze into each other's eyes, my heart racing from the reality of our connection.

"Jack, I also love you more than anything in this world. Everything I do, I do for you. Everything that happens from here on in, I'll be standing right beside you, good or bad." She moves towards me and circles me with her embrace. I bury one hand in her hair, the other I use to press her into me.

"Promise me something." She whispers into my chest.

"Anything."

"Promise me you will say those exact words to me the day I marry you. I never want to forget them." She looks up at me as her eyes once again fill with tears.

"Oh, baby. I promise." I lift her chin until our lips touch. The kiss becomes passionate and heated. She pulls away gasping for a breath.

"One of these times, I'm going to pass out from lack of oxygen." She teases, as the tears continue to escape. I gently wipe them away, while taking in her beauty. She simply takes my breath away.

"I'll revive you." Bending to give her a chaste kiss, I ask, "Do you like your ring?"

She smiles adorably. "Oh yeah, I have a ring." She pulls back to inspect it as her eyes bulge in the process. "Jack, it's absolutely gorgeous. When did you do this?"

"A few weeks ago." I saw the ring online and tracked it down at Tiffany's in New York City. I had Lizzy pick it up for me. I used her mom's wedding ring as a size indicator and hoped for the best. This was all before Leila broke up with me. Afterwards, Lizzy kept insisting she should return the ring, but I wouldn't have it. At the time, she thought I was losing my mind. I guess my heart just knew we weren't over yet. As it turns out, my heart was right. Liz had to travel across the country with it.

"There's more to the story, but I'll tell you later. I just want to make sure you like it. I can return it if…"

"Don't say another word." She interrupts. "I absolutely love it."

There's a knock at the door. "That's dinner." I pull away to let the bellhop wheel in a cart that is filled with enough food to serve four. He wordlessly sets up our plates and pours the champagne. After I offer a tip and close the door behind him, I watch Leila as she gently lifts random lids. She grins when she sees what's under the silver dome. "Grilled cheese and fries?"

"Our first meal together at Leo's. Don't forget the apple pie. I could have gotten lobster, but this means more to me."

She gently pulls her bottom lip between her teeth before she whispers. "Why are you so perfect?"

I shrug and respond, "Because of you."

During our meal, the fountains start up again giving us another front row view.

"This has got to be the most romantic proposal ever orchestrated."

Shrugging, I admit. "Maybe."

"You are a man of many talents."

"What are your favorites?"

"What, talents? I have too many to list." She grins at me and adds, "So, what's my other surprise?"

"You'll see."

She stands and moves around the table. I shift sideways to pull her onto my lap. I am literally aching for her.

"When do you want to get married?"

"I don't know. We are kind of busy for the next few months. Once we get home we can see what dates work."

"Can you promise me it will be sooner than later? I don't know what kind of wedding you want, but my only request is it be quick."

"I'd be happy with our closest friends and family. I don't want something big." As I nuzzle her neck, she asks, "I have a request."

"Anything you want."

"Can you make love to me?"

Pretending to debate this torturous invitation, I smirk, "Hmm. Can I?" Standing with her in my arms, I carry her into the bedroom and deposit her on the king size bed. "I just need to text someone real quick. Don't move."

She frowns adorably. "Hurry."

I close the door and text Lizzy as quickly as my thumbs can move.

Ok. u cqn comr bavk and dont mke noixe

HUH? English please.

Huffing, I try again.

Keep up please. Come back and don't make noise. Text hunt too.

Oh. Ok.

When I open the bedroom door, my gorgeous fiancé is patiently waiting and she isn't wearing a stitch of clothing.

"Holy shit."

"What took you so long?"

"I'm sorry." I remove my clothes as if they are on fire. Leila watches me with a heated gaze. I never once break eye contact with her. Once I'm as bare as she is, I move to lie next to her on the bed. "You had asked me for something?"

"Yes, make love to me."

My response is to attach my lips to hers. As I hold her head still, I suck on her top lip, then her bottom lip, then both together. My tongue follows the pattern, running along the top, then bottom, then inside to stroke along hers. In an attempt to push me along, she moves closer, eliminating the sliver of space that is between us. I don't want to rush this, but the effort it takes to move at such an unhurried pace is pure agony.

She moans and wraps her fingers in my hair and then slides her leg in between mine. I can feel her nipples teasing my chest as she presses her breasts against me. All of her reactions are normally triggers for me. Today, I summon every ounce of willpower I have to continue with just this one kiss.

After a few more minutes, she begs. "Jack, I need you, now." Her plea causes me to surrender. I slowly position myself over her and she tightens her grip in anticipation.

Words cannot begin to describe the connection I feel towards her. There isn't one single suitable word. The closest I can come up with is severe, consuming, crushing, and maybe fierce? But even combined, they are still lacking.

I stop moving my lips over hers, and she slowly opens her eyes staring straight into my soul. I'm completely exposed to her in a way I've never been in my entire life. She has the ability to end me, the power to destroy me. My beating heart sits in her hands. I've never been this vulnerable to anything or anyone, and all I can do is surrender.

"Saying I love you isn't enough. There's so much more I feel. I don't know how to tell you." She nods quietly in agreement. "Even showing you isn't enough. It's simply not enough."

"I know. Sometimes I have moments of panic, moments where I feel so connected to you that being apart for even minutes makes it hard to breathe."

I contemplate her words. I know exactly what she means. It's sick, actually. It's obsessive and fanatical, but it's absolutely true.

"No one would understand this. I don't think anyone I know could relate to this. The constant need to touch you, to see you, to need you. I need you. More than air, or food or water."

She holds my face and strokes my eyelids, my nose, and my lips with her thumbs.

"*I* understand."

She pulls me lower to join our lips once again. I need more now. I need all of her. I slide into her torturously slow. Her eyes widen ever so slightly as she inhales me in every way. She raises her knees to take me deeper…and still it's not enough.

We've never gone this slowly. At the moment, there's no need to rush. We have the rest of our lives together and there's no need to quicken this for any reason. It's pure perfection. There have been times, and there will be times, when frantic and hurried sex will be our only option and we will still appreciate it. Today, we are savoring every rub, every caress, every kiss, and every thrust deliberately.

We each bring the other closer with subtle movements or shifts. She moans in frustration when I hold back, because I start to feel the familiar tightening in the base of my spine. But I am now at the point where I need to let go and more importantly, I need her to let go.

"Baby, please come for me."

She is right there, right at the edge, and my words are the gentle shove she's been waiting for. Her arms and legs encircle me. Her fingernails mark the skin on my back. Her muscles constrict around me, prompting me to tremble inside of her.

The more I quiver, the more she tightens her grip. She's pulling every emotion, every sensation out of me, until there is nothing left.

"I love you." She says, staring into my eyes.

"I love you."

Once we both relax from our climaxes, I collapse from exhaustion. What I just experienced crushed me physically and mentally.

Murmurs and noises coming from outside our door wake me up from a sound sleep. Leila is sleeping beside me, while wrapped in my arms. I don't even remember us moving positions.

The voices I hear tell me it's time for her next surprise. I watch her sleep peacefully before waking her.

I kiss the top of her head, gently running my hands up and down her back. She stirs and slowly opens her eyes. "Hey, baby."

"Hey. You feel so warm."

"You too. I could stay here forever, but we need to get up for surprise number three."

She stretches in my arms, smiling shyly. "You are spoiling me."

"Not nearly enough." I kiss her cheek and add, "Come, the next surprise wouldn't appreciate us naked."

She looks up confused. Putting on my best poker face, I move around the room adding items of clothing as I go. She starts to dress as well, but her brow is still puckered in confusion. When we both freshen up and are presentable for company, I take her hand and lead her to the door. She can obviously hear the noises on the other side.

She narrows her eyes suspiciously. "Will this be embarrassing to me?"

"No...of course not. Ready?"

"Yep."

I open the door to Hunter, Trey, Scott, Dylan and Oscar standing around talking casually and hiding in the back are Evan and Lizzy. Her eyes move around the room. It's obvious when they land on Evan.

She looks to me excitedly, while squeezing my hand. "Oh my God! I love you."

She runs past everyone else and straight into Evan's arms.

"What are we, invisible?" Hunter pretends to be offended.

"I see you each and every day." Leila quips back. "What are you doing here?"

"Surprising you." Evan states the obvious.

"How long are you staying?"

"Four nights. We are coming to your show tomorrow night."

"Hey, Lizzy. How are you?"

Lizzy and Leila hug comfortably. "I'm great. Welcome to the family."

Evan remembers what occurred tonight and adds, "Oh, yeah. I guess congratulations are in order."

She pulls away to show Evan her ring. Lizzy looks at Leila fondly, before meeting my eye. She's been great during this whole thing. I drove her nuts, and once again I owe her big time.

Evan and I exchange a handshake and I hug my sister tightly. "Thanks for keeping this to yourselves."

Evan nods. "I'd do anything for her. Hey, I'm sorry I gave you such a hard time."

"Don't worry about it. I understand." I wrap my arm around Leila and smile. "Thanks for prepping Mr. Marino for me."

Leila looks up at me and asks, "With what?"

"I called him to ask permission to marry you. Evan had a long talk with him beforehand." We both look at Evan and I add, "I really appreciate it."

"No problem. He really does like you. He just worries about her."

"I love her more than anything." I admit, looking down at her. She smiles and hugs me tighter.

"We know." Evan admits.

During our slumber, the drinks and food I had arranged were delivered, and my band already took it upon themselves to dive right in.

"Babe, do you want some wine?"

"Yes, please."

I leave her with Evan to grab our drinks. One by one my band mates come to offer their congratulations.

Hunter hangs back and is the last to approach me. "I can't believe you're getting married man. This is huge."

"It is."

"Scared?"

"About marrying her? Not at all." I take a swig of my beer. "I'm terrified of something happening to her."

"Nothing is going to happen. None of us would allow it."

"Hunt, I suddenly have a lot at stake. It's scaring the fuck out of me."

"I get it. Things change, you know. What was once important isn't so much anymore. Without warning, your thoughts get hijacked and there isn't a fucking thing you can do about it."

His analogy is dead on. I turn towards my friend surprised by his admission. "Missing Mandi?"

"You have no idea. That girl wrecked me." This is the first time Hunter ever hinted what he truly felt about Amanda.

Slapping him on his back, I agree, "Yeah, buddy. It happens to the best of us." I motion over towards where Leila is standing. "She wrecked me too. I can't imagine life without her."

He follows my gaze. "I'm really happy for you, Jack."

"Thanks, Hunt."

"Come here, you bastard." He pulls me into a typical man hug. Over his shoulder I catch Trey's eye.

"Trey is watching us."

Hunter pulls away and levels Trey with his glare. "Don't even think about commenting, I'll have your nuts removed."

"Then I'd be just like the three of you." Trey tilts his beer and takes a healthy mouthful.

"One of these days you're going to be licking a girl's ass just like we do and loving it."

He shrugs and says, "Not before she licks mine first and my attached balls."

Leila shoots us all a look. "Guys, we have guests."

"Sorry." Hunter mumbles quietly, but then shoots back at Trey in a much louder voice, "I have fifty that says you will fall the hardest of us all."

Trey walks closer and extends his hand. "I'll take that bet."

"Count me in." Scott volunteers. "Make mine double."

"You want in?" Hunter asks me.

"Nope, that's a sucker's bet."

"You're the smart one. These two are jackasses." Trey touts, while shaking his head and walking away.

Hunt and I exchange a glance.

"He's going down."

"I'm not so sure." I admit. "You just made it even more interesting for him."

"I just made it my mission in life." Hunter responds arrogantly.

Chapter 16 - Leila

"So tell me everything that's been going on." I've monopolized Evan since the minute I saw him. This was an awesome surprise. I had no idea he was planning on coming out at any point during the tour. It feels like I haven't seen him in years and not just weeks.

He and Lizzy are so comfortable together. They sit close, his arm around her shoulders. Every so often, he kisses her head or she strokes his chest. He looks different. I can't put my finger on it. It's not just the happiness that's written all over his face, it's something else and it suits him.

He admitted how much trouble Jack went through to make sure his proposal to me was perfect. It only caused the overwhelming love I feel for him to swell even more so.

Jack comes over with my wine and sits beside me on the couch facing them. "Thanks, baby. Ev was just about to fill me in on the Hoboken dirt."

"I got here just in time."

"Where do you want me to start?"

"How is the band?"

"Good. Lori is truly a force to reckon with. She's been working our asses. We played Granite last weekend."

"You didn't tell me that. How was it?"

"Awesome. I love that place."

"Nina is working out well?"

"She's not you. But she's great. Her voice works well with Matt's. Our fans are slowly warming to her."

"I hope they weren't nasty."

"No, just indifferent. You had quite a following, you know that. They are very loyal to you."

"I'll come by after the tour to see them."

"So, I decided to tell the guys about us."

I halt my wine glass half way to my lips. "You did?"

"Yeah. They deserved to know. They took it well, after the shock wore off."

"You can't blame them." Lizzy offers. "It's quite a revelation. Especially to them, they are practically family to you guys."

Evan nods at Lizzy before adding, "Lori claims she knew all along."

"She's full of crap. I'm surprised she hasn't contacted me."

"I made her promise not to. She wasn't happy. She said our connection was a natural result of our circumstance."

"She doesn't know what she is talking about." I shake my head while smirking. "That girl is too much."

Evan laughs. "Joe is upset that you are with Jack. He said he would have loved to become my brother-in-law."

"Joe has a thing for Leila?" Jack asks with a raised eyebrow.

"No. He just teases me constantly."

"He loves to bust on her." Evan confirms. "He loves to make her blush."

"I still need to keep my eye on Joe." Jack grumbles before taking a sip of his beer.

I look up to stare at him for a few seconds.

"What?" He asks, completely clueless.

Turning my focus back to Evan, I ignore Jack and ask, "So has Dad been behaving?"

Evan sneaks a look at Lizzy. "Um…"

My heartbeat falters slightly. "What's wrong?"

Evan immediately shakes his head. "No. Nothing is wrong. Probably the opposite?"

"Oh, thank God. You scared me. Ok, so tell me."

Evan scratches his head and makes a face, clearly stalling for time. After a dramatic sigh, he informs me, "He's with someone."

My mouth drops to my chin. "You are *shitting* me."

"No. I wish. I, um, kinda walked in on them."

"Shut. Up" The image of my dad and a woman pops into my head. "Ewww, gross."

Evan rolls his eyes, "Yeah, tell me about it."

"Wait, you walked in on him at his house?"

He shakes his head while smirking.

"Do not tell me my dad was having sex in public."

"Don't be ridiculous, or I hope not at least. Ugh, I just got another visual."

"Do I know her?"

He nods, but says nothing else.

"You're killing me. Who?"

He can't seem to get the words out. It looks like he's physically not capable, as if they are lodged in his throat. After a subtle nudge from Lizzy, he mumbles, "My mom."

"OH MY GOD!" Jack chuckles at my reaction. "It's not funny," I scold through gritted teeth.

"Yes, it is. It's classic." Evan shoots him a look and he adds, "Um. You're right. Not funny."

Now it's Lizzy's turn to laugh. "I think it's awesome." She leans up and kisses Evan's cheek. "You need to lighten up and be happy for them. I told you that."

Evan and I exchange an exasperated look. "They don't get it. Their parents have always been doing it. Ours have no business having sex...again." He grinds his palms into his eye sockets. "Crap, I can still picture it."

Jack lets out a deep belly laugh, until I wedge my elbow against his ribs. He then turns it into a cough.

"How the hell did you walk in on them?"

"I had to borrow my mom's suitcase. I didn't think to tell her, I figured I could run in and run out. No such luck. They were in the fucking kitchen!"

"What did they do when they saw you?"

"They were so involved, they had no clue I was standing there. I covered my eyes and when I tried to get the fuck out of there, I knocked over a lamp."

"Oh my God. Ev." Now it's my turn to laugh, and Jack starts shaking beside me trying to contain his mirth.

"It's really not funny. Anyway, they were mortified. Apparently it's been going on for quite some time. They never asked me to keep it to myself. My guess is they knew I would tell you, sparing them the agony."

"How long, like years?"

"No, they said it started right after our newsflash broke about being related. I guess the relief they felt opened the door to much more. I hate to admit, but they do seem happy. My mom is doing well, so I'd like to think it's helping her recovery."

"I'm sorry you had to witness it, but I guess I am happy for them. I did want this for them years ago."

"Yeah, don't remind me."

"Will you change your name to Marino?"

His response is to throw his bottle cap at my head.

"Well, I think it's great. Good for them." Lizzy looks up at Evan and leans in for a kiss. He complies readily, and Jack looks away.

"Don't like seeing your sister smooching?" I ask.

"Um, not particularly." He waits a few seconds, and once they pull apart he says, "Baby, do you want Liz to take the ring home with her? She can put it in the bank until we get home."

"Hell no!"

He grins at my response. "You can't wear it."

"I know. This ring is not leaving my body. I'll pin it to my bra if I have to."

"Ok. Whatever you want." He bends to kiss me when Hunter rudely interrupts us.

"Hey, Lair. This party is lame."

"So leave."

"You don't mind?"

"Nope."

Suddenly my three band mates plus Dylan bolt for the door as if someone pulled the fire alarm. The door slams shut forcibly behind them.

"Damn. I guess we were boring them." Jack says irritably. "Oscar, do you want to leave too?"

"No, I'm staying, unless you want me to." He has set up shop in the corner with his laptop.

"And you two?" Jack addresses Lizzy and Evan. They exchange a look. "What? Go. Don't worry about us."

"I'm just really tired. It's three a.m. in New York. Can we meet you for breakfast tomorrow?" Lizzy asks shyly.

"Of course. I feel bad I took over your night." I apologize.

"Don't be. We couldn't wait to get here." She exchanges a hug with Jack before I walk them to the door.

"I'm so glad you came out, both of you. Thank you."

"I've been plotting to come for awhile. Of course, I needed to see my baby sis on her rocking tour."

"Well, I hope we don't disappoint you tomorrow night."

I hug them both goodbye. On my way back into the living room, the look on Jack's face stops me in my tracks. "What's wrong?"

He hands me his phone. On the screen is a picture of Lizzy standing at a red light in Manhattan. "What is this?"

"It must have come a while ago and I just didn't see it. It's from Danny."

Oscar takes the phone from my hand. "There's no message."

Jack looks up completely dazed. "I think it's loud and clear." He sits on the edge of the couch and rakes his hands through his hair. "Fuck."

I have no idea what to say to him. My heart is in my throat. This man is scary as hell. The picture is in focus. He had to have been standing a few feet away from her to get such a shot.

"Oscar, how the fuck do we handle this?"

"Text that to Ace and me. We know Lizzy's safe while she's here. By the time she gets back home, we can try to figure out our next move."

"Can we contact the police?"

"We can, but there's no crime committed."

Jack stands and starts pacing the room. "I don't care. At least they'll know about it."

"I have a feeling none of this is coincidence." He looks at me impassively. "You're meeting with her tomorrow. Lizzy is here in Vegas. Tonight you get a text from Danny? It's strange."

"Do I tell her? I don't want to scare her."

"Before she leaves, you need to tell her." Oscar responds.

"Goddamn it." Jack looks completely lost. I move closer to wrap my arms around him and he reciprocates.

"Jack, we'll figure this out. We have a huge support system."

"She's right, Jack." Oscar grabs his bag and adds, "You two are fine here. I'm going to go make some phone calls. I'll be back in the morning."

As he walks by us, Jack places a hand on his shoulder. "Oscar, I really appreciate your help."

"I know." He nods and leaves the room.

Jack pulls away from me to sit on the couch. All of three seconds later, he stands and announces, "I don't know what to do."

The problem is neither do I, nor do I know what to say to him. I go into the bedroom to retrieve the laptop. Maybe we can find something online, anything. When I come back, Jack is downing a shot of tequila.

He shrugs apologetically, looking all kinds of adorable. "I don't blame you, babe. Have another if it helps."

He takes my advice and takes another shot before joining me on the couch.

"What are you looking for?"

"I have no clue. I can't just sit here." I begin by Googling Danny's name. A crap load of information pops up. I randomly open pages scanning them. It's like literally trying to find a needle in a haystack. But I refuse to just sit here and think about Danny possibly hurting Lizzy. That leads me down a dark path.

I open up Danny's Twitter page, not sure I know what I'm looking for. He has thousands of posts. Some so stupid, it sounds like a five year old wrote them.

Jack looks over my shoulder while I scroll through his most recent ones. Interspersed are dozens of comments to a guy named Hagler that all look like random nonsense with a lot of abbreviations.

"That's probably his dealer."

"What do you think these are, meeting points?"

"Possibly."

"He would be dumb enough to put this on Twitter?"

"There's nothing there. Unless you knew what you were looking at, it's not incriminating. If anyone was looking at his Tweets, chances are they are on to him."

I reach for my cell and call Ace. I know it's late in New York, or early rather, but I need to tell him tonight. We don't have much time.

"Lei?" Ace answers, sounding concerned.

"I'm really sorry to bother you at this hour."

"I'm up."

"Have you spoken to Oscar yet?"

"Briefly. He explained what happened tonight."

"I'm here with Jack. I'm on Danny's Twitter page. There are a lot of weird posts that don't make sense at all."

"Like weird how?"

"Ok, this one says, - *A168 dam*. There are tons of them all to a guy named Hagler. Jack thinks this is his dealer."

"Could be. I'll look around and see if it makes any sense. I'll have Lee check it out as well."

"Thanks, Ace. We don't have much time. Lizzy is only here a few more days. Evan is here with her."

"I know, sweetie. We'll do our best."

When I end the call, Jack pulls me into his arms. "Thank you, baby."

"For what?"

"For always having my back."

"You would do the same for me."

"And then some." He bends to kiss me gently. "You're right. We have a ton of support."

"I'm glad you agree. You shouldn't doubt the wife." I tease as I stand before him.

"Yes, dear."

"It's late, let's try to get some sleep." I tug on his hands until he is standing. Without warning, he lifts me into his arms. "What are you doing?"

"Just practicing." He says, as he carries me into the bedroom. "I love you, Mrs. Lair." The intensity of his gaze melts my insides.

♫ ♫ ♫

Jack looks exhausted. He tossed around all night, until he finally got out of bed. He insisted that I stay and try to sleep, but it was useless. So I joined him on the couch as we watched *The Hangover* and *Ted*. It was nice to hear him laugh and forget things, even if for a few hours.

To make things easier, we asked Lizzy and Evan to join us in our room for breakfast. Jack and I both decided to tell them this morning. They need to know and prolonging it isn't going to help matters.

As our breakfast is being wheeled in, Lizzy and Evan follow right behind the bellhops.

"Good morning, guys. How was your night?"

"It was good," Jack responds quickly.

"Just good?" Evan turns towards me, "Already acting like an old married couple?"

"Shut it, Miller." He chuckles and throws a strawberry at me. "You're so annoying."

Evan's antics help lighten the mood. The four of us end up having a pleasurable time in spite of Danny's bullshit.

"So what's the agenda for today?"

"We have all day, until rehearsals at five."

"Rehearsals? Haven't you been playing long enough to know the words?"

Rolling my eyes, I stare at him for a few seconds.

"What?"

"It's more like sound checks."

"Oh."

"I wanted to take Leila sightseeing, but I'm not sure that's a good idea," Jack says quietly. We exchange a look that Evan notices.

"What's wrong?"

"Um…last night I received a text from Danny."

"What did it say?" Lizzy asks.

"It was a picture." Jack sighs heavily before continuing. He opens his phone and turns it towards his sister.

Her gasp is heartbreaking. "When was this taken?"

Evan takes the phone and looks at me. "What the hell is this?"

"He's making a point."

"He's following me?"

"Yeah, Liz."

"I'll fucking kill him," Evan barks.

"Ev, Ace and Oscar are on it. They will come up with a plan," I say to try and calm him down.

He turns towards Lizzy and demands, "You're staying with me."

"Evan, I can't stay with you. I need to be in New York."

"I'll hire a bodyguard."

She moves closer and cups his face. "You can't afford that."

"We'll figure something out. Ace is going to the police to see if there is anything they can do." Now it's Jack's turn to try and comfort them with his words. "I'm sorry I had to tell you, Liz. I really didn't want to, but you need to know."

She gives Jack a sympathetic smile. "You can't always protect me Jack. I'm not a little girl anymore. You were right to tell me."

"What is the deal with this asshole?" Evan asks Jack. "Really, what does he want?"

"He wants to ruin me, anyway he can." Jack looks at me and then at Liz. "He knows my weaknesses."

"Your weaknesses both happen to be two people I care about very much. This is no longer between you and him. He just involved me as well."

My cell buzzes loudly on the coffee table. Jack leans over to pick it up for me. "It's Ace."

"Hi, Ace."

"Lei, we think they are meeting points. I don't know what most of them mean, but a few are obvious. *A168 dam*, might mean Amsterdam and 168th. It's a location for crack deals."

"So now what?"

"I'll keep checking for a new post. Hopefully he'll tip us off to the next meet. If it turns out to be what we suspect, we can call in a tip and maybe nail him that way. This post was weeks ago, and no new ones since. I hope he isn't using an alternate form of communication. We'll keep digging."

"Ok. Thanks, Ace."

"Also, Lee is putting a guy on Lizzy when she gets back. At least until we figure something out."

"Ace, I want to compensate him. I've told you this before."

"He really wants to do this. He's a fan and he said we'll worry about it later."

"Ok. Tell Lee thank you."

"What did he say?" Evan asks the second I end the call.

"They believe the posts are places to score drugs. They'll keep looking into it. Lee will be putting a guy on Lizzy when she gets back to New York. He wants to help."

"This is not necessary. He has paying clients he needs to worry about." Lizzy says stubbornly.

"Liz. He wants to do this and we are going to let him. Jack, tell her." Evan pleads.

"He's right. I have no idea what Danny wants. Again, this could all be empty threats. Who knows if he's just trying to fuck with me? We simply can't take that chance."

Lizzy glances from Jack to Evan and then concedes, "Fine."

Evan and Lizzy stay a little while longer before heading out to do some shopping. Once they leave, Jack sags on the couch in defeat. "It's my fault you are on his radar and now my sister. What the fuck?"

"Jack, none of this is your fault. He's a lunatic. You couldn't have predicted this was going to happen."

He pulls me into his embrace, holding me tight.

"I don't want you going anywhere without me or Oscar."

His request is a bit unreasonable. I am with him constantly anyway and decide not to argue. "Ok."

"I'm sorry our engagement has been tainted by that fucker."

"You gave me the best engagement a girl could ever ask for. I love you for that."

He allows me to pull his lips to mine. His kiss is demure compared to his normal response.

I pull away and search his eyes. He looks so tired. "You are exhausted. Do you want to take a nap?"

"Yeah, I think I need one."

I pull him towards the bedroom. "How long do we have this room?"

"Four."

"Plenty of time." I give him a salacious grin over my shoulder and he quickens his pace. Distraction is my best line of defense.

♫ ♫ ♫

I finished up with my preshow ritual quicker than usual. My ring is safely pinned between my breasts. My makeup and hair are done. I'm dressed and ready. I quickly text Jack my usual message.

I love you so much.

My nerves are getting the best of me. All I can think about is Jack meeting with that bitch tomorrow. It's going to be the longest few hours of my life. Evan offered to keep me well entertained, but I know my brain. I wouldn't be able to put on a happy face and pretend, so I declined. I feel bad I'm not spending as much time as I could with him. But no one could have predicted the crap that's been slung at us. I know Evan understands completely.

Tonight's show is bittersweet for me. I am so thrilled he is here in the front row with Lizzy beside him. They'll meet us backstage afterwards. Jen has arranged for another meet-and-greet, after the show tonight. This time there will be about one hundred fans mulling around at an after party. The one that we had in Chicago only had a few dozen people in attendance. This is not going to be fun for me. I'm sure of the one hundred attending tonight, at least half will be women. Fifty women will all be vying for Mr. Lair's attention, while he needs to pretend we are not together.

Oh, *yay*.

I hope to attach myself to Evan and Lizzy as much as possible, without them declaring me a leech.

hey, my wife. I love you too.

you're turning me on

I'll be right there

No!

Buzz kill.

A quick rap on my door makes me think his text was serious. "I told you…Oh, hey Dylan." "Can I come in real quick?"

"Sure." As I turn to shut the door, Jack and the guys walk past. A raised eyebrow and a subtle tilt of the head are my clues he saw Dylan entering my room. Ignoring him, I shut the door.

"So, what's up?"

"I haven't had a chance to tell Jack yet, because he's been surrounded by the roadies. Jen knows though. We got something on Jessa."

"You're kidding."

"No, I'm serious. Krista contacted the New York lab. That document is a complete fake."

"I had called the lab to be sure it was real. It didn't occur to me to check if the test was."

"We all assumed it was legit."

"Wait, so it's not Jack's baby?"

"Well, we don't know that. It can still be his. But the fact she had the test done by sending the samples in the mail to an Internet company opens the possibility it could be anyone's baby."

It takes a few seconds for his words to register with me. He waits patiently while smiling. He's definitely not prepared when I throw myself into his arms.

"You have no idea how happy you've made me. This changes everything tomorrow."

"It sure does." Dylan releases me and quickly steps away to put some distance between us. It occurs to me right then that I must have really hurt him. "Go, have a good show. I've held you longer than I wanted to. They'll be frantic soon."

I move towards the door, but then turn to touch his arm. "Dylan, I really am so grateful for all you are doing for us."

"I know." He gives my hand a quick pat and leaves the room before me.

That bitch. She must think we are complete idiots. So she's trying to nail this pregnancy on Jack. If it truly was his baby, she could have easily proved it by going through the proper channels. Why the hell would she take this route?

"What the hell?" Jack stands in a threatening stance at the stage steps as I approach.

"Relax, I'm here."

"Barely."

Fuck, I love when he acts like an asshole. I've got it *real* bad.

I really wish I could give him a signal somehow. It's going to have to wait until the show is over. The house lights dim, and the guys run onto the stage. Jack has been the first one on lately, and the fans have picked up on that. Even in the dark, the screams are always deafening the minute his feet hit the top step.

"Hey, Vegas!" he croons into the microphone. The lights haven't even come on yet and the response is still thunderous.

"Wow. Thank you. We're so excited to be here." The crowd agrees and he laughs a low, sexy, *oh my* - kind of laugh that goes right to my special place. "Has anyone slept at The *Bellagio*?"

Once they respond, he adds, "Those beds sure are comfy, or maybe it was the company?"

He's such a ball-buster.

"Anyway, I love this town! I might move here. Guys, do you want to move to Vegas?"

Trey responds with an ear-piercing chord on his bass. "Would that be a yes?" After Trey repeats the riff, Jack chuckles and says, "Ok, let's get this party started. I'm a bit hung over. I'm going to sit the first one out and have Ms. Marino take the floor."

He motions at the center mic and takes a seat near Hunter.

"Hey, Vegas! How is everyone tonight?" Once their cheers lessen, I motion for the band to start a song I've been singing off and on for the past few weeks. Jack loves it and begged me to add it to our show. The stage lights dim, except for a spot on me. Trey starts off the intro to Pat Benatar's *Promises in the Dark*. The first few times I sang it, I was a nervous wreck. I am now so comfortable with the song and with singing it. It's a part of our show that I actually look forward to.

Once I'm done, Jack appears by my side. He coldly thanks me and gets right back into douchebag mode. He does his usual shtick of flirting, engaging the crowd, and ignoring me. The only acknowledgement comes when we both share the same microphone. He'll glance at me every so often, without ever touching me. Of course, Jack always turns me on. It really doesn't matter what he's doing. But watching him perform just riles me up. Rock star Jack is fucking hot as hell. Another painful symptom of our separation is having to go back to an empty bedroom after our shows, while being a horny mess.

Since our "breakup", he has taken to singing my song directly to one of the girls in the front row. The first time he did, it stung, even knowing it was all an act. The way those girls stare at him and send him obvious signals makes me want to scratch their eyes out. The entire time I need to repeat over and over, "He's mine. He's mine." Jealous Leila doesn't appear often, but when she does, it's pretty ugly.

I have a feeling my jealousy will be lingering well into the wee hours of the morning. Mulling around in a room full of Lair-lover-wannabes is the last thing I want to do right now. More charades and more pretending. I'm exhausted with all this nonsense. I want to be able to show Jack my affection whenever I want. I want to be able to sleep with his arms wrapped around me each night. Having him all to myself last night was bordering on cruel. It reminded me just how much I miss him. I'm so sick of this.

I've been consumed by these thoughts most of this show, and it's amazing I sang and played correctly. We only have a few minutes in the holding room before the masses arrive. The roadies are busy breaking down the stage, so the second we step into the room Jack is on me like a moth to a flame.

"Mmm, you're nice and sweaty." He says as he licks my neck.

"You're gross. I need to…" He takes the opportunity to shut me up by slanting his mouth over mine.

"Can you two knock it off?" Hunter says as he helps himself to his first beer. Jack's response is to push me into the bathroom, shut the door behind us and snack on my neck.

"Jack. Jack, I need you to listen. Dylan has some news about Jessa, so make sure you talk to him as soon as he gets here. I don't have time to tell you the details."

He stops long enough to say, "Yep", and roughly pulls me closer, trying to consume me whole. He grips my ass with both hands and moves my body so it perfectly aligns against his bulging crotch.

"Jack, you're driving me wild. Please, I can't get all worked up right now and neither can you." I tout in a threatening tone. "You're not allowed to walk around this party tonight with a hard-on."

"Such a buzz kill." He pulls away reluctantly. "But you're right." After a few cleansing breaths, he adjusts himself and adds, "Ok. I'm ok." He tucks a finger in between my breasts and strokes the ring that is nestled there. "I really wish you could have this on your finger where it belongs."

"Oh, so do I. Especially with the hungry bimbos that are going to be walking through the door any minute."

"You have nothing to worry about, you know that."

"Except for your shameless flirting?" He pouts until I kiss his lips. "I know I don't. I still don't like them all thinking they have a shot with you, especially since we are broken up."

"I could say the same about the dudes that are going to be here."

A loud rap at the door comes before Hunter barks, "Get the fuck out here!"

"Jeez, he's back to being grumpy Hunter."

"I can't blame him. He misses Amanda." I check my appearance and move towards the door. "Ready?"

"Yep, I love you."

I crack the door wide enough to see no one has arrived yet. Two steps out of the bathroom and Hunter scolds, "Knock it off. You're going to screw everything up if you aren't careful."

"Relax. No one's here yet." Jack says, as Hunter paces around the room. "What's wrong with you?"

"Nothing." He snips.

Jack and I exchange a glance. I walk over to take Hunter's hand and lead him towards a couch. "Something's wrong."

He nods, with a firm "Yes."

"Is it Mandi?"

"We had a huge fight. She won't answer her phone." He abruptly stands and starts pacing again.

"What about?"

"She had dinner with her ex."

"So?" Jack asks clueless.

"SO." He repeats with bulging eyes, like we are totally missing the obvious. "They ended things on good terms. She's there, I'm here, and I'm not happy about it. I told her so and I told her I didn't want her seeing him. Things pretty much went down the shitter from there." He starts pacing again. "What the fuck? If there's nothing going on, then she would have no problem doing as I asked, right?" he directs his question to me.

"Hunter, I'm sure nothing is going on. She's probably upset because she thinks you don't trust her." He stares at me as if I just said that last statement in a foreign language.

"That's not it."

"Did you tell her you do trust her?"

"No."

"Then she probably thinks you don't."

Trey walks over and sits across from us. He points to his crotch and brags, "My balls are still intact and attached."

"Fuck off, Trey."

"Just sayin'."

"Hunter, you need to apologize and tell her you trust her. You could be pushing her right back into his arms."

I've never seen Hunter look so lost, confused, and sad before. He must really care about Amanda. He also must have upset her, because she isn't the type to be spiteful.

With that, the door flings open with the first of our fans to arrive.

"You'll call her in the morning and work it out." I add quietly.

He nods solemnly. "Thanks, Lei."

No sooner do I turn from Hunter than I see a swarm of females around Jack. He looks over at me and smirks.

Fucking Awesome.

The first hour of a meet and greet is like a feeding frenzy. Evan and Lizzy left shortly after they arrived, wanting to avoid becoming road kill. Every person in the room wants to be sure they get their pictures, their autographs, their free stuff, before they can actually settle in and enjoy themselves. Once that's over, a different aura fills the room. As they feel more comfortable, they get downright ballsy.

I'm standing at the bar, waiting for my Diet Coke, and two guys come up beside me. "Hi, Leila."

They flank me on both sides and I turn my head from one to the other. "Hi. You guys having fun?"

"Yeah, this is awesome. You guys really rocked it tonight. I'm Drew, this is Jason."

"Nice to meet you, Drew and Jason." I take my drink and start to walk away.

"Wait, can we get a picture?"

"Sure."

Jason steps away, with his phone poised and ready. Drew stands close and wraps an arm around my shoulders. Jack is watching like a hawk from across the room. Once the picture is taken, Drew asks, "I have a bet with my buddies. Would you mind a kiss?"

"Um. No, I don't think so. Sorry."

"Oh come on. It would mean the world to me. I have a hundred bucks riding on this. They know I have a huge crush on you. Please? Just a peck on the cheek, how's that?"

"Um, Ok."

Drew stares into the camera and just as I move in to kiss his cheek, he turns and meets my lips with his.

"What the hell?" I shove him away, and he raises his hands apologetically.

"Sorry, it was a reflex. Honest."

In one swift motion, Jack has his hands wrapped in the guy's t-shirt and thrusts him up against the wall.

"Shit, man, it was just a little kiss."

"Get the fuck out." He sneers and then releases him.

Oscar and Dylan appear immediately. "What happened?"

"This asshole was just leaving."

Jack turns to Jason. "Give me the phone." Jason wordlessly hands his phone over to Jack. A few seconds later, Jack hands it back.

Drew suddenly grows some balls and antagonizes Jack. "She's not yours anymore, dude. Maybe she liked it."

Jack grabs Drew's shirt and pulls back with his fist.

"Jack, no." I latch onto his arm, as it's in mid-air. He looks down and composes himself.

He releases Drew and snarls, "Get out."

Oscar takes Drew's arm and leads him out of the room. On the way out, Jason looks mortified while Drew looks smug.

"Bye, Leila. I love you."

Jack faces Dylan. "Great, I'm sure that prick will be blabbing about this within the hour."

"Don't worry about it. You just gave him a fantastic story to tell his friends. It would have been a whole different story if you had punched him though."

"Yeah, I lost my head for a second." Jack runs his hand down his face in frustration. "When is this over? I want out."

"We'll wrap it up." Dylan pats Jack on the back. "Go have a drink."

He walks away, leaving me at the bar. The incident changed the mood of the crowd. They are all cognizant of his or her behavior, not wanting to be thrown out as well. Even so, some of the girls still had the audacity to try and solicit Jack. He wasn't his usual flirty self. He was downright nasty towards them.

Soon after, Dylan and Will rounded everyone up. "Thanks for coming tonight. The band really appreciates your support." They waste no time in ushering the crowd out of the room. Once every last person is gone, Dylan shuts the door leaving us alone.

Jack sits heavily, releasing a burst of breath. "Fuck. I could have easily beaten that motherfucker to a bloody pulp." He pinches the bridge of his nose, while squeezing his eyes shut.

I sit next to him and take his hand in mine. "None of us would have let you. Babe, I'm sorry."

"What for?"

"I let that asshole convince me to kiss his cheek for a picture."

He throws me a stern look and responds, "Yeah, um…don't do that again." He bends to kiss me gently and then adds, "Ever."

The guys join us on the couches just as Dylan comes back into the room, shutting and locking the door behind him.

"You ok?"

"Yep."

He pulls up a chair to complete our circle. "Did Leila have a chance to tell you what we found out?"

Jack remembers what I said earlier. "No, not yet."

I move closer and wrap my arms around him as he kisses my cheek. I turn towards Dylan. "Tell him. He needs some good news."

"The document Jessa sent you is fake."

Jack looks from me to Dylan. "What?"

"She didn't use the lab on the letterhead. She sent the samples out in the mail. She could have sent anyone's samples, claiming it was yours."

"So, it's not mine?"

"Well, it still could be. But this definitely opens the possibility that it's not."

"That bitch."

Someone knocks on the door and Dylan opens it to let Oscar in.

"You ok?" He repeats Dylan's words to Jack, as he walks towards us.

"I'm good."

"I know you're exhausted, but we should go over your meeting tomorrow."

"Yeah, ok." He responds lethargically. I can see how tired he is. All this bullshit has taken its toll on him. When I glance at the rest of our band, I can see it has taken its toll on them as well. It makes me wonder if all rock bands go through crap like this. Is there always some lowlife waiting in the wings, trying to take you down? Is that the price of fame? I want no part of it, if it is.

Oscar says to the rest of us, "You guys can head out to the hotel. Chuck is a security guard here at the arena. He'll be escorting you."

Hunter stands and stretches. "What a fucking night, huh?"

I turn to face Jack. "Do you want me to stay?"

"No, babe. You're exhausted. Go get some sleep."

I kiss him and stand reluctantly. I want to be part of this conversation, but I'd rather not know the specifics. "Good luck. Don't let her aggravate you. Don't give her any ammunition. Please."

He nods. "I'll be good. I promise."

"I love you."

"I love you, too."

I walk towards Hunter, and he wraps an arm around my shoulder. He looks back at Jack as we walk out the door and mocks, "I'm just hugging a friend. Don't hit me."

Jack shakes his head and flips him off.

"Are you ok?" I ask Hunter on our way to the waiting van.

"No. But I'll call her and apologize my ass off and then hopefully everything will be good again."

"Aren't relationships fun?" I tease.

"Why would anyone want to go through all this crap? It's so not worth it." Trey puts his two cents in.

"Shut up, Trey." Scott says, as we pile into the van. "You have no idea what you are talking about. It is worth it. To have someone by your side, having your back no matter what, who would do anything in the world for you…all fucking worth it."

"I'm telling you Trey. One of these days you are going to fall hard, and I can't wait to be there." Hunter adds.

"Yeah, ok. Keep waiting."

Hunter and I exchange a glance. "Mark my words." He whispers to me. I can't help but wonder if Trey already has fallen hard, and the rejection he received is what hardened his tattooed heart.

The van is quiet on the short ride to the hotel. Once we each escape to our rooms, I first feel how exhausted I truly am. I thought I would be up pacing all night, worried about Jack seeing Jessa tomorrow. But the minute my head hits the pillow, I'm out.

Chapter 17 - Jack

Watching her stroll across the café like she owns the place instantly ignites the rage I've been harboring inside. It's literally smoldering in my chest and slowly creeping to the back of my throat. She looks exactly the same...cold and bitchy. There's no warmth, no spark, no nothing. What the fuck did I ever see in her?

Her pregnant belly is clearly visible. She's smaller than I thought she would be. She's probably starving the kid to avoid gaining weight. When she reaches my table, she smiles cunningly. I can't wait to wipe the grin off her face.

"Hello, Jack."

"Jessa."

"You look well." She says, as she takes the seat across from me. Right behind her head I can see Oscar having his lunch while reading the paper. He glances up quickly to make eye contact.

"What do you want?"

"Charming as ever, I see."

"You're lucky I'm here. I don't have time for this or you."

"That's a shame. Because I have a lot to say."

"So say it."

"What are we going to do about our predicament?" She asks coyly.

"I don't know what you mean."

"I'm going to be incurring a lot of expenses. I can't do this alone. You said you would be there financially for the baby. After thinking it through, my pride needs to take a back seat to the welfare of my child."

I keep my best poker face on, even though my muscles are coiled as if watching my prey and I am waiting to attack. "What is it you're looking for?"

"I feel half now and half after the baby is born would be the best course to take."

"And what price tag did you put on your child?"

She widens her eyes as if insulted. "Our child. This has nothing to do with that. I cannot care for him without your help."

"You could, if you got a job."

"Are you retracting your offer?"

"Possibly."

She takes in a deep breath, as if she is trying to cage her anger. "I've always known you to be a coward. Running away from our relationship was one thing. I guess I shouldn't be surprised you are now running away from your responsibilities."

"I still don't believe it's mine. Until I have solid proof, I will not give you one red cent."

She leans back and crosses her arms. "You'll use any excuse you can. I've proved you are the father. You can try to deny it, but it is what it is."

"Or not." I pull a copy of the paternity results out from my back pocket and smooth it out on the table. "Let's talk about your proof." I level her with my glare. She is doing a fantastic job at keeping her cool, except for the tiny vein that visibly throbs at her temple.

"So, tell me how this went down." When she remains silent, I continue. "Ok, I'll recap and you tell me if I'm right. You walked into," I look down to read the name of the lab on the letterhead, "Stemcorp. Correct?"

She rolls her eyes annoyingly as if I'm wasting her time. "You carried my sperm in what, a *Tupperware* container?"

When she doesn't respond, I smile and persist with my scenario. "You walked up to the front desk and asked for a paternity test of the contents? And they complied readily?"

Now I fold my arms and sit back, waiting for her to speak. When she doesn't, I add, "I can sit here all day. For this, I don't mind wasting my time."

"What do you want from me?"

"The truth. I happen to know you cannot order a paternity test like a *Happy Meal*. So who's sperm did you send in the mail for your bargain basement results?"

She sits across from me, mimicking my position and not saying a word.

"Nothing? Suddenly you are speechless? I thought you had a lot to say?" I lean forward and boast, "I am so onto you. Is it my baby?"

"I don't know."

"Jessa, I want you to tell me the truth right now or I walk out that door. I will contact the police claiming you tried to extort money from me and you falsified this test."

She takes in a shaky breath and levels me with her stone cold gaze. "It's either yours or Danny's."

"Now we are getting somewhere. Why the hell did you get involved with that fucking lunatic?"

She pauses, probably debating in her head what she should say. I prod her willingly. "I'm warning you…speak or I'm gone."

"Max was having a bad time last year. Danny got him hooked on heroin. He owed Danny a lot of money. I paid some of his debt. I thought I could handle Danny and control him. As you know, he is not a bright person. I was buying time until I came up with a better plan."

I barely blink. I don't want to give her an excuse to stop her confession. "After some time, Danny was losing his patience and threatened Max and my mom's safety."

"Why didn't you go to the police?"

"He said being in jail would be worth the satisfaction he got from hurting us."

"Jesus."

"One night, he was high on crack, spewing all the things he wanted to do to you for kicking him out of Devil's Lair. I told him it was his own fault. He became a raving lunatic. He slapped me around. Not bad enough to send me to the hospital, but just enough to scare the crap out of me. As he was hitting me, he told me he'd do worse if he got his hands on you. The entire time all I could think of was you. I always felt you and I weren't done yet. I felt we belonged together. I loved you so much. I still do, even if it is unrequited."

"You love me so much, and yet you want to fuck with my life?"

"I'm helping you." She ignores my incredulous look and adds, "I derailed him. I convinced him the best way to get back at you was to ruin your life, not take it. The night we ran into each other wasn't an accident. I planned on sleeping with you and I did. I was also having sex with Danny as well. I figured one of you would get me pregnant."

"There's the Jessa I know."

She smirks at my comment. "I knew what I had to do."

"So the crap you told me about freezing my sperm?"

"Didn't happen. I wish I had thought of it sooner and not when it was too late. I really don't know if it's yours or Danny's. When I did become pregnant, I knew my plan would work. You'd help me financially. I would be tied to you for the rest of our lives. I could get Danny out of my life. Hell, maybe you would even fall back in love with me in the process. You did love me before."

"No, I did not."

"I feel otherwise."

I clench my jaw, feeling my control slipping away.

"When I came to tell you my happy news, I wasn't prepared to hear that you had fallen in love since the night we were together. Of all people, you?"

"Karma's a bitch, like you."

She goes on as if she didn't hear me. "Danny was livid. He didn't agree with my plan and wanted me to have an abortion. After he slapped me around some more, I convinced him this baby was his cash ticket. Based on your love confession, I had to revise. I could have easily panicked, but I had too much at stake."

"So he knows you are here trying to get money out of me?"

"It's the only thing that's been keeping him patient."

"This isn't good for you. I'm not paying you a penny until I know if this child is mine."

"I don't have a doubt he will hurt me. If I come back without money, he will lose it."

"Then hide out and get some help."

The ice around Jessa's heart slowly starts to melt as her eyes well up with tears. But then again, it could be an act. "He'll find me. You must care about me enough to not want this to happen."

"You can't be serious. I should call the police right now. You tried to ruin my life!" I glance around the café after realizing that I raised my voice. Oscar watches from his table.

"Jack, this could be your baby. You would knowingly be putting him and me at risk. I know you aren't that cold and heartless. Not to mention Lizzy's safety."

"You know about that?"

She looks away for a second before responding. "He told me. It's his insurance policy."

Fuck...she still has me by the balls, yet again. "When do you leave?" I ask with complete contempt.

"Tomorrow."

"I need to speak to my lawyer." She nods silently. "I have another question. Why did you coerce Leila into breaking up with me?"

"As long as she was in your life, I knew you wouldn't do the right thing. I needed you to be vulnerable."

"Who's your mole?"

"What?"

"I know you have someone feeding you information. Who is it?"

She looks down and fiddles with a ring on her finger. "Rich."

"Is that who tampered with the bus opening night?"

"Yes."

"Why?"

"I needed to delay you guys so I could get Rich on board. He was an afterthought when I found out you were with Leila."

"How do you know Rich?"

"I needed a way in opening night. I hung around the arena the day before and propositioned him."

I give her a look of pure disgust. "You're ruthless. Did Danny know about this?"

"No."

I wait for her to look up. When she does, I smile deviously. "For the record, we're done. It ends now. Your threats of telling the gossip sites that I forced myself on you aren't going to happen. I have never forced myself on you. Correct?"

She nods.

"Answer me." I prod.

"Yes."

"Good. Now here's the good news. This entire conversation has been watched and recorded." She looks around quickly, as her nostrils flare ever so slightly. "And guess what? Leila and I aren't apart, she is now my fiancé."

She pales and looks like I just sucker punched her.

"Surprised? We played you as much as you played us. My sister will have protection in New York. My fiancé and I have security with us on this trip. We are not sitting ducks to you and Danny any longer. I'm only playing your game for now, because I am not going to be held responsible for hurting that child. And you better hope it is mine or your future will not be a pleasant one. Clear?"

"Crystal."

"Good. I suggest you do your homework and cooperate with us. We know he's dealing. Anything you know, we now know too. Got it?"

"Yep."

"Once you have the baby, we will have a real paternity test taken. If it is mine, I will financially support just the baby...not you. If it's not mine, you better hope I don't press charges. I want you to contact me when you get back to New York. I'll let you know what your next move will be."

She sits quietly for a few moments, taking it all in. When she speaks, her voice is filled with emotion. "Where did it all go wrong for us Jack?"

"Honestly? For me it was the day I met you." I stand and walk away knowing I've left her completely stunned.

Chapter 18 - Leila

"Jack, I'm dying here."

"You're not going to believe all I have to tell you."

"Where are you?"

"I'm in the car waiting for Oscar. I'll be back in fifteen minutes. Can you call Dylan? We'll meet you in his room."

"Ok. Are you ok?"

"Yeah, baby. I am. I love you."

"Me too." He hangs up and I call Dylan as instructed. After explaining Jack's conversation, I quickly dress and make my way to his room.

I've been sitting on the edge of my bed for hours waiting to hear from him. This has been the worse form of torture. He still sounds on edge, but I can hear the change in his voice. Like a weight has been lifted.

Dylan opens the door after hearing my knock. "Hey, Leila. Oscar just called and said they are on their way up. I think he's going to tell us some good news."

"I hope so. I'm so done with this." I take the chair by the small table and start nervously tapping my foot.

A knock accelerates my heartbeat. I can't wait to touch him. I miss him so much. Dylan opens the door to Oscar and Jack.

Jack comes right over to me, pulls me into his arms, and buries his face in my neck. He kisses my neck and pulls back to look into my eyes.

"Hi."

"Hi."

"You did good, baby. Because of you, I was able to derail her fucking plans."

I smile at him before kissing his lips. "I want to hear all of it."

He sits in the club chair in the corner and pulls me onto his lap. Oscar and Dylan each sit at the table facing us.

"She wants money. She came here looking for a payout. She wanted half now, half when the baby is born. She never gave me an amount. Once I said I would provide support, only if it is indeed mine, the conversation took a whole other course. She insulted me. So I pulled out the test and enlightened her with what we knew. I then demanded the truth. She finally let it all out. She is involved with that fucker. Her brother got tangled in drugs and owes Danny a lot of money. Jessa paid part of his debt, but tried to manipulate her way out of the rest. Danny wasn't as dumb as she thought. He hits her. He threatened her family. I asked why she hasn't gone to the police. Danny said he actually wouldn't mind jail time in exchange for hurting them. She decided if she got pregnant she could be tied to me, and I could help pay Danny off. She arranged to meet me, have sex with me, and I'd increase her chances to have a baby. I was her back-up plan. She isn't positive the baby is mine, since she was sleeping with Danny as well."

Jack glances at me quickly as I try to absorb what he's telling us. He rubs my back soothingly and continues. "When she showed up opening night, she wasn't prepared for Leila to be in my life. It threw her. She had to revise and revisit what she initially wanted from me. She concocted a story and convinced Danny the baby was his cash ticket. This appeased him, for now. The problem is, if she doesn't return with some sort of compensation, he will hurt her. She was quick to remind me that it still can be my baby, and by not helping, I would be putting him in harm's way. She also mentioned his fixation on Lizzy."

Oscar interrupts. "Paying her would be a bad idea."

"I agree. How do we handle this?"

"We need to get him arrested…and soon." Oscar responds.

Jack looks apprehensive. "I still feel we should go to the police. Tell them everything."

"Ace did inform them of the events up until now. I'll pull together what little evidence I have, the text message from Danny, the falsified paternity test. I'll call Ace to discuss our course of action." He pauses briefly and adds, "I'll also put a call into my buddy, Colt at *Orion. Maybe he can start some more invasive background checks on this asshole."

Jack remembers another part of his conversation with Jessa. "I found out who she used to get her info. Fire Rich, immediately. I want him ruined. I want his chances of ever working with another band killed."

Oscar shakes his head. "That doesn't surprise me. Did she mention anyone else?"

"No, but I thought of that. She was quick to tell me it was Rich. I wouldn't doubt there is another."

"Now that she implicated him, I can work with that. I'll take care of it today."

I still don't trust her. I still worry she will try to hurt Jack. "What about her claims that you forced yourself on her?"

Jack gives me a half grin. "I got her to admit it, and then I told her that her threats are meaningless and our conversation was being recorded."

"So now what?" Dylan asks.

"So now, I take my fiancé, my sister and future brother–in-law out on the town. I need fun." He looks at me and adds, "I'll see if the guys want to come too."

"Jack, maybe that's not a good idea."

He shakes his head at my concern. "We'll be fine. I told her we are together and you are now my fiancé. She's in shock right now. I wouldn't doubt she is still sitting at the table staring into space."

Relief floods my veins.

No more charades?

No more game playing?

He can move back on the bus with me?

I grin at him like a fool.

"What?"

"You can come back to our bus." I whisper enthusiastically.

"Damn straight I can." His fingers curl around my waist and he winks seductively. "Oscar can you drive us to the *Bellagio*? I would like to hang there until our show."

"Sure, I just want to make some phone calls first."

He smiles at me. "That works with my plans. Call Evan and tell him we'll meet them in an hour." I feel optimistic for the first time in weeks. I lean in to kiss his lips when he pulls away and demands, "Oh, and put that ring on." He palms my face and resumes our kiss passionately. Someone clearing his throat brings me back to reality.

"Jack!" He chuckles at my embarrassment as I hastily climb off his lap. "I'm going to call Evan."

I walk into the bathroom leaving him with Oscar and Dylan. First thing I do is to unpin the ring and slip it on my finger where it belongs.

"Hey, Evan."

"What happened?"

"It's good. I promise. Where are you?"

"We are being lazy."

"Ugh." Evan laughs into the phone. "Do you want to hang out or continue being *lazy*?"

"No, we can hang out. Right, Liz?" I hear her say yes. "Where?"

"Meet us inside the main entrance of the *Bellagio* in an hour."

"Ok. See you then."

When I walk back out, Oscar is gone and Jack looks like he's having a serious conversation with Dylan. "Sorry. Do you want me to give you guys some privacy?"

Dylan shakes his heads. "No, all's good."

Jack stands and takes my hand. "Let's go."

"We don't have to meet Evan for an hour."

"Exactly." I glance at Dylan in time to see his frown.

Jack literally drags me down the hall to his room. The minute we are inside, he pushes me up against the wall and crushes his lips to mine. I can feel all his tension leave his body. His hands roam over mine, not knowing where to touch first. He walks us backwards towards the bed and falls while pulling me with him. The bed is so hard that when we land, we actually bounce apart from each other.

"Oh my God." I giggle from the hilarity of the situation.

"This place is a dump."

"A few days ago we would have thought this place were a palace. You have turned into such a diva. We can't always be in a *Bellagio*."

"Make no mistake, baby. I would fuck you if we were in the men's room at Penn Station right now."

"Ew."

"Just sayin'."

"One day engaged and the romance is already gone?"

"There are two sides to my coin. You've seen both. Mr. Raunchy and Mr. Romance live side by side."

I move closer and align myself with his body. "And I love them both."

"Good, because right now Mr. Raunchy is in the room. I need to fuck you." He announces as he starts to pull off my clothes. I immediately reciprocate, pulling off his t-shirt. When we get tangled, we separate just long enough to finish stripping.

He pushes me onto my back and without any preamble, dives between my legs. The rush of air I release and the buck of my hips spur him on. His mouth covers me completely while his tongue flicks dead center. He draws his lips in and sucks the spot he was just teasing.

I can already feel the buildup in my thighs and in the pit of my stomach. Hell, I actually feel it in my toes and the roots of my hair.

He slowly pushes his fingers into me and twists them from side to side. He nibbles on me like he's having me for lunch. I dig my fingers into his hair, manipulating his movements for my own pleasure. I unashamedly use him to my advantage. He complies willingly and I completely lose it. I come so hard that it causes me to tighten my thighs against his head in an attempt to control their trembling. I can feel him smile against me, and it only encourages the tremors that are taking over my whole body.

Once I calm myself down, I throw an arm over my eyes and declare, "Holy shit."

"I'm not done." He flips me over and slides right in. My fingers instantly pull at the cheap, scratchy bedspread that is beneath me.

"Fuck." He says to no one in particular. His fingers grip my hips so tightly that I'll probably bruise. Mr. Raunchy is giving me one hundred and ten percent of himself, literally. With each thrust, I can feel his happy trail tickle the base of my spine.

He moves one of his hands around my hip to stroke me in front. In response, I hold onto his forearm just in case he decides to remove it. He gets my message and rubs me straight into my second orgasm.

Less than a minute later, he grunts and stills while remaining buried deep inside of me. He slumps over my back, once he returns to earth.

"Just what I needed," he mumbles into my shoulder.

"Yeah, me too...twice." I collapse onto the bed and he falls with me.

He moves to my side and immediately closes his eyes. I take the opportunity to stare at him…at every inch of him. How did I get so lucky? I'm going to be this man's wife. This is completely insane. I've known him less than six months, but it feels so right. It feels as if every decision, every choice, and every plan I made has led me right to him.

I scoot closer and he wraps his arm around me, but never opens his eyes. "Babe, do you want me to cancel on Ev and Lizzy? You are exhausted. You didn't sleep much these past two days."

"Mmm. No. Just ask for another hour. That's all I need." The rise and fall of his chest tells me he fell back to sleep. I quietly grab my phone to call Evan.

"Hey."

"Ev, we're running late."

"Why are you whispering?"

"Jack is sleeping. We'll meet at three."

"Ironically Liz is sleeping too. I was just about to wake her. This works out better for us too."

He quietly chuckles into the phone.

"What?"

"It seems the Marinos wore out the Lairs." He announces.

"Evan, T.M.I."

♫ ♫ ♫

Once we met up with Liz and Evan, we grabbed something to eat and decided to hit the casino. As we stroll through, hand in hand, I feel life is just as it should be. No more hiding. The guys are joining us soon. Jack decided to cancel rehearsals and arranged a small party backstage for Evan and Lizzy after our show.

Jen is arriving today with Krista and Malcolm. Dylan volunteered to meet with Jen as soon as she arrives to fill her in. She has been kept in the dark and will not be happy about it. Dylan has been so awesome to us. He really doesn't need to be. It just proves what an honorable person he is. Oscar is handling the Rich situation. He has remained steadfast in his commitment to us. His loyalty is unwavering.

"I want to gamble," I announce. Dragging Jack by the hand, I lead us directly to the slots.

"Here? Slots are for wussies." Evan leans closer and lowers his voice. "Look around. Everyone in this section is above the age of seventy."

I snort at his comment. My watered down complimentary rum and Diet Coke comes right out of my nose.

"That is totally disgusting." Evan says, wearing his poker face.

"Stop making me laugh." I use my sleeve to wipe my nose. "Jackass."

Jack reaches into his pocket and pulls out a five-dollar bill. "Here, baby. This should hold you for at least five minutes."

I snatch the money and sit at the first empty slot machine I find.

"You're serious? You want to play slots?"

"Shut it and sit. It'll be fun."

Lizzy takes the seat to my left, leaving Jack and Evan standing and gawking at us. "This sucks." Evan grumbles.

"You don't have to stay. Get lost." I say over my shoulder, "I say our five dollars on the slots will win us more money than your twenty on the tables."

"You're on. And don't cheat."

I shoot him a look. "Says the guy who cheated at every board game we ever played."

"I did not."

Jack leans over and whispers in my ear, "You seriously want us to leave?"

"Yes. I want to chat with Liz." I turn towards him, kissing his lips.

"Stay put. Oscar is in the area."

"Yes, Dad."

Jack pinches my ass and challenges Evan. "Let's prove them wrong, Evan."

As soon as they walk away, I immediately turn towards Lizzy. "We're cheating." She laughs at my admission.

"You're on."

"I'm glad they're gone. I wanted to spend some time with you."

"Same here. We're going to be related soon. I've always wanted a sister."

Her words touch my heart. "Me too."

"He's absolutely nuts about you. I'm sure you know that."

"I do. I am about him as well."

"You've completely changed him. My parents are off the wall excited."

My thoughts go to my dad and his feelings toward Jack at the moment. I need to fix that and soon.

"I really can't wait to get home. This tour has been exhausting in so many ways. I just want to do normal things. Your parents invited me to their house and I can't wait to take them up on their offer."

She giggles at my admission. "You're living the life of a rock star and all you want is a burger on the grill?"

"Sick, right?"

"No, I understand. After this tour, your lives may never be as normal as you'd like though. You guys have been pretty busy, living in that bubble on wheels, but things are happening out there. *Committed* is constantly being played on the radio. It's strange, I still can't get used to it. I even heard your single a few times."

"I know. I have no idea what to expect when we get home. I think Jack and I both treasure those days, before we left on tour so much, that we will make it a priority somehow to hold onto the mundane." The ringing of Lizzy's machine halts our conversation.

"I won." She watches the numbers on the winning tally. "Hey, I won fourteen dollars."

We look at each other and crack up.

"No, you won thirty-four dollars." I offer and wink.

"Oh, right."

"So you and Evan have been seeing a lot of each other?"

"Yes." She bites on her bottom lip and looks at me before continuing.

"What's wrong?"

"Oh, nothing. Can I confide in you?"

"Of course."

"I think I love him."

My smile splits my face in two. "Really? I'm so happy for you Liz. Does he know?"

She shakes her head. "I haven't told him yet."

"What are you waiting for?"

She gives me the trademark Lair smile. "For him to say it first, of course."

"Ah. I understand. And he should." I look at her profile until she turns and add, "I think he will."

Her eyes widen before she asks, "How do you know?"

"I've never seen him like this. He's different, in a good way."

She turns back to her slot machine, trying to contain her smile. "So am I."

"He is a romantic at heart." Lizzy smiles like a Cheshire cat at my comment. "Can I tell you another secret?"

She turns towards me in complete earnest. "Oh, yes."

"Evan once stood outside a girl's house, when he was in eighth grade, and sang *This I Promise You,* towards her bedroom window."

"N Sync?" Lizzy asks.

I nod without turning towards her.

"That's so romantic."

"It was, until a dog chased him off the front lawn and down the block."

Lizzy starts laughing so hard, she nearly falls off her stool. Her reaction spurs on my own bout of hysterics.

"What's so funny?"

We both clamp up and turn to see Jack and Evan standing behind us.

"Nothing."

"Marino, you have that look on. What are you telling her?"

"Nothing."

Jack cages me in with both of his arms on the slot machine. "You'll tell me later?"

"Maybe."

"You are back way too soon. How did you guys do?" Lizzy asks innocently.

"We both lost our twenty within three minutes."

"Ah ha. I told you so. I don't even have to cheat. I still have four twenty-five and Liz won fourteen."

"Awesome. Now you can buy us each a drink." Jack pulls me off my stool and steers me towards the bar. "The guys are waiting for us."

I turn back to see Evan and Lizzy going at it in the middle of the slots section. "I'm sure they'll catch up."

We can hear the guys before we see them. Hunter is hooting about something and Scott is telling him to shut up.

"Hunter is in a better mood."

"I haven't even had a chance to ask him if he has spoken to Mandi yet."

As we approach, he shouts over to us, "Oh, good. You can settle this. Jack, do you remember the chick who snuck onto our MACE tour bus?"

He looks down at me before replying. "Yeah."

"What did she have tattooed on her ass?"

"Hunt, really?" He responds, looking at me.

"Please, she doesn't care. She wouldn't be here if she did. I've got fifty bucks riding on this. Scott doesn't believe me. Tell him."

"So much for keeping it to yourself."

"It was a over a year ago. Statute of limitations is up. Tell him."

Jack sits on a chair facing them and pulls me onto his lap. "I apologize for these idiots."

"Now I'm curious. Spill it."

"Mrs. J. H. Lair."

"AH! Fifty bucks asshole," Hunter demands from Scott.

"Wait, some bimbo is walking around as Mrs. Lair?"

"Ridiculous, right?"

"More like fucking annoying," I mumble.

He leans in and nibbles on my ear before declaring, "There will only be one Mrs. J.H. Lair, my wife."

I turn towards him and kiss his lips. "God, I love hearing you say that."

"I love saying it." He shifts subtly under me and whispers, "Can you tell?"

I stare into his eyes, my gaze then moving to his lips. I simply cannot get enough of this man. I've never really considered myself a sexual person, but Jack has single handedly turned me into a total sex fiend. He watches me as I continue to stare at his lips. He pokes his tongue out and slowly licks his bottom one.

I press my lips to his ear and whisper, "I have to go to the ladies room." He watches as I raise my eyebrows, sending him an obvious signal.

"I'll walk you." Thankfully he gets my message. "We'll be right back."

"You just got here." Hunter shows his annoyance. "You dog."

"Shut up." Jack retorts, before leading me straight to the back of the casino. On our way, we catch a glimpse of Oscar loitering a few feet away, and Evan and Lizzy standing in the center of the slots still making out. We are all going to get arrested today.

"Oscar, stay with Liz please. We'll be right back."

He nods, a knowing smile on his lips. A few months ago, I would be absolutely mortified right now. I've definitely changed.

"Where are we going?"

"Don't have a clue. But I'll know when I see it."

He wordlessly steers me around the perimeter of the casino until he sees a storage closet. Nonchalantly, he turns the knob and it miraculously opens.

"Mr. Raunchy is back." He pulls me inside and immediately locks the door. My heart is pounding from the adrenaline rush of being inside a storage closet in the middle of one of the most prestigious casinos in Vegas, as well as from the anticipation of what's about to happen.

"We don't have much time."

"I won't need much time." I admit. He smiles wide and immediately unzips my shorts and drags them and my panties down and off my legs in one swift motion.

Once he drops his own jeans, he props me up on a counter in the corner. His fingers find me and he smirks adorably. "You are so ready."

Nodding, I push into his hand and he pulls my bottom lip in between his teeth. He then thrusts himself into me without any ceremony, whatsoever. My reflexes kick in. I wrap my legs around him, pulling him deeper with each thrust. His hands are gripping the counter on either side of my ass and mine are gripping his arms. I can feel the strain of his muscles and it's sexy as hell. I bury my head in his neck and moan when my orgasm hits me full force.

His movements become jerky and faster. It doesn't take much longer for him to come inside of me. I take hold of his face, pulling him towards me to kiss his lips. My mouth on his muffles his grunts.

He smiles seductively, once he's done. "Damn, that was good."

My smirk tells him I agree. "The smell of cleaning products may now be another trigger for me."

"Me too. My list is getting longer and longer since I've met you."

We quickly put ourselves back together and return to our band mates. Lizzy and Evan have since joined them. "So, where did you go?" Hunter asks smugly.

"I needed to show Leila a...slot machine." He squeezes my hand as he says it. He takes the only remaining chair and pulls me onto his lap.

"Yeah, ok." Hunter shakes his head. "Jen just called. She wants to see us."

"She can, after the show. I'm not changing our plans."

"She said to tell you it's important."

"So is having fun."

"Jack, she's probably pissed about the Jessa stuff. Don't make it worse."

Jack looks at me and sighs. "Fine."

"Whipped much?" Trey touts, and Jack throws him a look.

"Shut up, Trey Taylor." I counter. He smiles wide and winks. I've gotten so much closer to Trey and I really like our relationship. It's fun, easy, and unexpected.

"Let's all do a shot first. I'll need it to deal with her." Jack says while motioning over a waitress. Her eyes fixate on him and as if on cue, they then give me the once over. It always goes the same way. I can practically read their thoughts each and every time.

He orders us all a shot, then another, and then a third. When we finally make our way out of the bar, I am pleasantly buzzed. Evan and Lizzy decide to watch the fountains and the rest of us hail cabs.

"Now I'm ready to meet with Jen." He says to me, as we climb into a cab.

"Me too." I giggle.

He smiles wide. "Should I worry you are getting really good at taking tequila shots?"

"I still hate them, but I like how they make me feel." I bring my lips to his ear. "They make me horny."

Jack leans back and closes his eyes. "Fuck."

"No cursing in my cab." He focuses on the irate cabbie and whispers, "I'll get even."

♬ ♬ ♬

"Can you please focus?" Jen asks for the tenth time.

She has been trying to get us to behave and it's been close to impossible. Dylan, Malcolm and Krista are in the holding room with us. Dylan filled Jen in on all the Jessa drama. He said she took it fairly well, but then again, she may implode at any moment from the reality of it all.

"Ok, I'm sorry. Guys knock it off. Jen tell us what you need to." Jack takes control and motions for Jen to speak.

"Things are going very well. *Committed* is in the top twenty on the charts and your album is in the top fifty. Our goal is to be top ten for both by the time we play in New York. Krista is doing a fantastic job with publicity. We are having a contest for a chance to win a night with Devil's Lair. We will provide transportation to and from New York for a fan and their guest. They will have front row seats at our final show and hotel stay for two nights. They are eligible to win through our website."

"Wow. That's fucking cool." Hunter says what we are all thinking.

"Yes, Hunter, it is. Let's talk about the Internet buzz. It has been mostly positive. There are those who hate Jack and what he did. But we think it only increased curiosity that much more. Especially while you guys were supposedly broken up. Leila's single is also climbing. Malcolm would like her to start singing it in the shows. I agree that it will create fantastic buzz for her and us. You will have the sheet music for it by tomorrow. I'd like to debut it as soon as possible. Malcolm wants Leila front & center, solo spotlight while singing it."

The way she says "her and us" doesn't sit well with me. It's an obvious slip that says Jen does not consider me part of the band. The sudden interest in my solo career hits a nerve as well. Jack takes notice of the frown I am sporting and raises his eyebrows. I'm sure if I share this with him, he'll tell me I'm being ridiculous. Instead, I throw him a smile, which he returns immediately.

I'm a little perturbed that Malcolm is my agent by default. I'm torn between the want of solo success and the disgust of being tied to him. He *is* a master in the music industry. If I stick with him, I don't doubt he would help me achieve my goals, but at what price?

"Let's discuss Miami. There is a huge rock music festival which we will be part of. It runs for a month and the turnout is impressive. I have booked us a spot on the weekend that usually has the biggest turnout. Unfortunately, this takes away your only night off. MACE is headlining. We are up right before them. Cliffhangers will be performing that day as well." She looks over at me smugly.

"What?" I ask in complete shock.

Jen nods. "Your friend Lori reminds me of me. She has secured a spot on the same day. They play early in the lineup and we play at night, but she managed to get it done."

Jack looks over smiling. "That's awesome. Lei, did you know?"

"I had no idea. Neither Evan or Lori mentioned it."

"It was only confirmed yesterday. He probably wasn't told yet." Jen admits.

She drones on as I sit reeling from her news. I glance over at Trey. His posture gives an obvious indication of what he is feeling, because suddenly he sits forward and intently starts to listen to Jen for the first time since she started yapping. I pull out my phone and quickly text my best friend.

Awesome job Lor!

"Ok, that's it for all of you. I'd like to have a chat with Jack, Leila and Dylan."

"Ooooh, you're in trouble." Hunter ball busts on his way out.

"Get out, Amatto." Jack responds. Once they have gone, we turn our focus to Jen. Malcolm remains comfortably seated in the corner, making no moves to leave.

"I'm trying real hard to understand why I've been kept in the dark for these past few weeks. Anyone care to enlighten me?"

"It was important. The less who knew, the better." Jack responds with an attitude.

Dylan adds, "Jen, I've explained. The only reason I knew was because Leila's friend Ace felt it was important for her safety. I pulled Charles in to get approval on security faster. The studio was taking too long to make that decision."

"This could have been a complete disaster. You all should have filled me in, if for no other reason than to fill me in. So things with this Jessa bitch are under control?"

"For now."

"I'm making a call to Louis. He needs to know. Is there anything at all you haven't told me?"

Jack and I look over at Dylan. We really don't know how much he filled Jen in on. He confirms our thoughts. "I told her everything."

Jen watches our exchange and shakes her head. "That's ok with you two?"

"I guess." Jack smirks.

"You should be kissing my ass, Lair."

"Jen, all kidding aside. We are sorry we didn't tell you and we do appreciate all you do. Honestly. Thank you."

Jen's eyes widen fractionally before she says, "It's getting late. I'll see you after the show."

Malcolm stands and speaks for the first time. "If you want me to leak some dirt on this Jessa person, just say the word."

"I don't want to go that route." Jack responds.

"Dumb move." He turns towards me and leers, "You're song is about to explode. Stick with me, kid. You'll be huge."

Jack stands, coming eye to eye with Malcolm. "Her talent will get her there, let's be clear about that."

Malcolm smirks and pats Jack's shoulder. "Of course."

The minute Mr. and Mrs. Agent leave the room, Jack turns towards me and asks, "What's wrong?"

"Nothing is wrong." My eyes fly over to Dylan.

"I'll leave you two alone." He quietly leaves the room.

The minute the door shuts, he asks, "Are you upset that Jen now knows about Jessa?"

"Of course not."

My relentless fiancé pulls me into his arms. "You made a face before. I'll stand here all night. What's wrong?"

"You can be exhausting." He shrugs at my response, but doesn't deny it. He then slowly moves his hands to my ribs, flexing them deviously.

"NO. Don't tickle me. Have you heard from Jessa yet?"

"Nice change of subject. No, not yet. I'll give a day before I make a phone call." He bends to kiss me. Just as I start to respond, he breaks the kiss.

"Are you punishing me because of the cab ride?"

"You do need to be punished. We have just enough time to move my things back to our bus. And if we move fast enough, we'll have time for me to torture you with my mouth. To be continued. Let's go." He picks me up and throws me over his shoulder.

"Jack, what are you doing?"

"I walk faster than you do." He then breaks into a sprint, while I giggle uncontrollably.

Chapter 19 - Jack

On our way to Oklahoma City, I feel things are just as they should be. It's only been four days since Vegas. Leila and I are back together in our tiny little bedroom. Every night I fall asleep with my arms wrapped around her. We share a dressing room at our shows. We show affection in public. I've resumed singing her song to her on stage…and I make love to her each and every day. Most importantly, she proudly displays her engagement ring on her finger.

The guys, Leila, and I are lounging comfortably on the bus. I even welcome the annoying bickering between Hunter and Scott as they act like ten years olds while playing video games.

Miami is quickly becoming our next big focus. We have several cities to visit before we get there, but it's going to be an awesome time…a huge party of sorts. Mandi and Patti are coming. My parents will also be there. Cliffhangers, Leila's dad and Evan's mom, Lori, and even Liz are all attending. I'm hoping we will have enough time to celebrate our engagement. I want to speak to Jen and possibly have her arrange a dinner while we are all in one place at the same time and surprise Leila.

"Trey, you need to shut it, you whore." Trey is having a lengthy discussion with Leila, trying to convince her on the merits of groupies.

He laughs at her while she ignores him. I watch amused as the two of them banter back and forth. Leila brings a side out of Trey that the rest of us rarely see. Then again, Leila brings the best out of most people. Trey has also been in a much better mood lately.

Since Jen shared the news regarding Cliffhangers meeting up with us in Miami, he's been a different person. Hunter said he has spoken to Lori. Actually, Hunter had to endure the torturous phone sex session between them, as he lay wide-awake in the middle of the night in the bunk beneath Trey.

My gorgeous fiancé is on her laptop reading up on all the posts she's been avoiding for the past few days. The fans are thrilled we are together. Some of the haters still hate me as well as my involvement with Jessa. The news broke that I've abandoned my "Baby Mama" and left her high and dry. Leila's haters jumped all over that news story and have been spewing toxic lies on their blog. I am proud of how my baby is handling it. She never ceases to amaze me. My respect for her is insurmountable. When I tell her so, she quickly becomes embarrassed by my adulations.

A few weeks ago she would have been devastated by their words. Now, she shrugs it off and ignores it for the most part, or she's acting like she is at least.

Every so often a smile plays on her face and then a quick frown. She wears her feelings so obviously that I always know exactly what she is thinking. When she looks up and catches me staring at her, she wrinkles her nose.

"What are you reading?"

"About what a huge whore Trey is." She quips without looking at me. But the pucker between her eyebrows tells me otherwise.

"Liar."

I scoot around the booth until I'm up against her side. On the screen is the home page to Lair's Lovers.

"Lei. Why are you on there?" I murmur in her ear.

"I was curious."

"What are you on?" Nosey Hunter asks without even looking up.

"Trey is a whore.com." I shoot Leila a pleading look. That's all I need is for Hunter to know about this fucking website. I'll never hear the end of it.

"So? I own it." Trey shrugs.

Hunter looks at me as if he's about to say something. Unlike Trey, I don't want to own it. Because every time it is brought up, in a kidding fashion or not, it will hurt Leila.

Miraculously, Leila's phone buzzes. "It's Ace. I'm going to take it in the back." She answers the call as she walks away. Ace calling reminds me I still haven't heard from Jessa. This is not good. I tried calling and texting, but she hasn't responded.

I decide to join Leila. As I approach the closed bedroom door, I can hear her clipped words.

"Where could he be?" She looks up as I enter. I can immediately tell something is wrong. "Ok. Lizzy is being protected?" After a short pause she says, "Ok. Thank you. Please keep me posted."

"What now?"

"Danny is gone."

"What do you mean he's gone?"

"Lee's guy hasn't seen him in days."

I sit heavily on the bed next to her. "I still haven't been able to get in touch with Jessa either."

I pull out my phone and dial Oscar. He answers the call by saying, "I know."

"Do the police know?"

"Lee is working on it."

"My sister?"

"He's watching her."

"Thank him for me. What about Jessa?"

"We don't know where she is either."

"Fuck."

"Don't panic."

"Can you tell Dylan to arrange extra security if possible at each arena we play in?"

"He's working on it."

"Thanks, Oscar."

"Do you think he'll hurt her?" Leila asks as soon as I hang up the call.

"I don't know." I skim through my contacts to find Max's number.

"Who are you calling?"

"Her brother."

The phone goes right to voicemail. "Max, it's Jack Lair. I need to talk to you. Please call me as soon as you get this message."

Leila sits on the edge of the bed, nervously fiddling with her engagement ring.

"Are you freaked out?"

"Of course I'm freaked out."

I really can't blame her. I pull her into my arms and kiss the top of her head. "I would never let anything happen to you."

"What about you?"

"I'll be fine."

She strokes my face before leaning in for a kiss. "I can't even think about something happening to you."

"I don't want you to worry about things like that. Besides, for all we know he's lying face down in a gutter strung out on crack."

"I might go to hell saying this, but I hope so."

"I rather talk about something else. Have you thought about our wedding?"

"I really want to do something simple. Closest friends and family, maybe on the beach?"

"I'd love that. When?"

"Well, how about early June? We could arrange to be on our honeymoon for both of our birthdays."

"That long?"

"If we want to do the beach, then we'd have to wait 'til then." She kisses my pursed lips chastely. "We'll be living together anyway."

"I want you as Leila Lair."

"Jack, I'm yours…with or without your name."

"I know…but still."

"Ok, well then we'll have to do it indoors."

"No, I like the beach idea. Fine, early June. It's the month you and I started working together, the month you were born, and now the month I get to make you mine."

"I am yours."

"Legally." I shift our bodies so she's beneath me on the bed. "One more question."

"Yes?"

"Can I own you now?"

"Hmmm…I don't know? Can you?"

I move my hand under her shirt and skim my thumb over the lace that's covering her nipple. It instantly hardens beneath my touch. "Still debating?"

"I need more convincing."

I skim the shell of her ear with the tip of my tongue, while stealthily moving my fingers inside her bra to pinch and roll her nipple. She shudders beneath me and says, "Ok…you convinced me."

Just as I start to lift her shirt up off her body, my cell buzzes in my pocket.

"Damn it."

"You need to get that. It could be Max."

Groaning as I dig my phone out, Max's name ominously displays on the screen.

"Max. Where's Jessa?"

"Danny beat the crap out of her."

I sit up abruptly. "Shit, when?" Leila sits up as well, looking concerned.

"A few days ago. She's in the hospital. He left her unconscious and took off."

"How is she?"

"They have her heavily sedated. She's been in and out. He cracked some ribs, her face is pretty bad, she has a concussion and..." Max stops abruptly.

"What?"

"She lost the baby."

"Fuck." Guilt instantly grips me, making me feel sick to my stomach. I desperately drag my hand over my face. "Where is she?"

"N.Y.U."

"Max, do you know why he did it?"

"Yes. She tried to protect me and this is what she gets for it." Obviously, Max has no idea that Jessa manipulated Danny or Leila or me in the process, and it's not my place to tell him. "There's a warrant out for his arrest."

"Do they have any leads as to where he is?"

"No. I gotta go."

"Wait...Max, can you...um." I don't have a clue what I want from him.

After a few seconds, he impatiently asks, "What, Jack?"

"Um...just tell her I called."

"Yeah, sure."

Leila watches me wide eyed. "What happened?"

"He beat her up...bad. He cracked some ribs, messed up her face and..."

"Jack, what?"

I woodenly gaze into her eyes. "Um...she lost the baby."

"Uhh." Leila gasps, and her eyes instantly well up with tears.

"What should I do? Should I call the hospital?"

"I'm not sure they would tell you anything." She's right. There's no way a phone call, claiming I'm the baby's father, would get me the results I'm looking for.

"Maybe you should speak to your dad?" She suggests.

"Ok."

"I'll give you some privacy."

"Can you call Ace and ask him to fill in Lee and Oscar? There is a warrant out and Lizzy needs to be protected even more now."

She nods and moves towards the door when I reach for her. "Baby…"

"Yeah?"

"I feel…I." I hang my head not knowing what to say out loud. She runs her hands into my hair, holding my head against her body. The internal battle between caring and not giving a fuck causes confusion beyond anything I've ever felt. I'm torn between saying what I really want to versus what I should.

"I know," she says giving me an out. I wrap my arms around her waist, holding her tightly. She soothes me with her touch, waiting for me to be ready to let go.

When I release my hold on her, she palms my cheek and asks, "You ok?"

"I don't know."

"Jack, this isn't your fault. You can't be held responsible for what Jessa or Danny did."

"It's hard not to."

"You didn't manipulate him and you didn't beat her."

"She warned me this would happen. I could have done something to protect her better."

She sits next to me on the bed and takes my hand. "She's made it difficult to show her any compassion. She tried to ruin you. You responded and reacted just as you should have." She takes my face between her hands and adds, "Hey, you didn't deserve any of this. You are a good person and she is not. I'm sorry this happened to her. Mostly, I'm sorry she lost her child. But I won't let you sit here and take blame."

She leans in to kiss me and whispers against my lips, "I love you."

"Me too."

She kisses me again and leaves me alone in the bedroom.

With shaking fingers I dial my dad's number.

"Hey, son. How are you?"

"Dad, something's happened."

"Are you ok? Leila?"

"It's not us. It's Jessa." I proceed to tell my dad all the details. From the manipulating Jessa did to Danny's threats to Lizzy being stalked to Danny putting Jessa into the hospital.

As I ramble, his silence on the other end is beyond frustrating. I have no idea what he is thinking or feeling. The disappointment he must feel is affecting me almost worse than the guilt.

"Dad, please say something."

"You should have told me all of this sooner."

"I couldn't have imagined the lengths she would have gone through. Plus I didn't want to worry you."

"You are involved. Your sister is involved. We should have known. You and your sister are my priority."

"I know. I'm sorry. This is such a mess. I feel so guilty that all this happened."

"Son, this isn't your fault."

Relief floods my insides. I needed to hear him say it as well. I need my dad to support me now more than he ever has.

"Dad, I still don't know if it was my baby."

"Do you want to know?"

"I don't know."

"Son, you've been rejecting the notion that this was your child all along. Your mother and I laid the guilt on you pretty heavy, and I am so sorry we did that. You've been through some heavy emotional situations. It's ok, to not want to know. It's ok, if your closure is dependent on not knowing."

"I feel lost. Knowing the baby was mine won't change the fact I never wanted that child. It will only add to the tremendous amount of guilt I've already been carrying."

"I understand."

"If I did want to know, how would I be able to get that information? I have no legal ties to her or the baby."

"We have enough evidence to court order a paternity test on the fetus. But I'd have to act on it immediately."

"I want to talk to Leila about it."

"Go ahead. Call me back with your decision."

"Dad, I'm sorry."

"I know, Son. It's over. Now, I want you to worry about yourself and your fiancé. We love you." When he hangs up, I'm still swimming in guilt. I'm not sure I will ever lose the feeling. At the moment, it's laying heavily on my chest. I'll need to find a way to work through this somehow.

I take a deep breath and walk out to join everyone up front. Leila and the guys are all sitting around wordlessly. My guess is she told them and they have no idea what to say.

When Leila sees me, she smiles warmly. I slide in beside her and take her hand.

"You ok?" Hunter is the first to ask.

I give him a non-committal shrug in response.

"Did you talk to your dad?"

"Yeah, he said we could court order a paternity test, but I don't know if I want to know."

"You want my opinion?" Hunter looks from Leila to me.

After we nod, he adds, "Nothing good can come from knowing it was your baby. If she were to find out and share the results then so be it, but to chase them when there isn't a reason to know? That news is only going to torment you, man."

There's one person I care about. I turn to Leila and ask, "What do you think I should do?"

She looks down, avoiding eye contact with me.

"Lei, I want to know your opinion. I need to know."

She closes her eyes before she responds quietly, "I don't want to know."

I immediately sigh with relief.

"I'm sorry, Jack. It might be really selfish of me, but I want to believe she never had a part of you. I need to believe that. It may be a false sense of security, or just game playing, but I'd rather not have a definitive answer."

A single tear escapes. The look on her face breaks my heart. I pull her into my arms as she sobs into my chest. "Jack, I'm sorry and if you need to know, I'll understand."

"Ssh, babe. Please don't cry. Please." The guys all quietly leave us alone. Her sobs increase as I hold her and rock her in my arms.

"Baby, look at me."

She lifts her head and searches my eyes. I gently wipe away her tears and bend to kiss her lips. "Leila, this is over. No more. I'm done. I'm done hurting you. You are more important to me than anything. I know I am a bastard for saying this, but I never wanted to know anyway."

"We're awful."

"No, we're not. We're honest."

She leans against me while I stroke her hair. Her admission is exactly what I needed. The guilt slowly dissipates from her words. I'm tired of the toxic cloud that Jessa purposely suspended over us. I'm tired of feeling like I'm the asshole for not wanting that baby and for not wanting her in my life. I'm tired of carrying enough fucking guilt to fill a Catholic church. For the first time in weeks, I feel at peace.

Chapter 20 - Leila

"What's new with you?"

Evan waits a few seconds before responding. "Nothing."

"Hmm. Absolutely nothing? Boring life you lead, Mr. Miller." I happen to know he finally said the L-word to Lizzy. She texted me with much enthusiasm…there were five exclamation points attached. "How are things with you and Liz?"

"Good."

"Evan!"

"What?"

"You're such a guy. Tell me."

"You're a pain in my ass. What are you fishing for?"

"You know and I want you to say it."

"I love her, ok? Is that what you want to hear?"

"Yes. Was that so hard?"

"Yes."

"You're so annoying. I'm so happy for my big brother."

"Thanks. She's so great. I love everything about her. I thank God I found her."

"She's lucky to have you too."

"I've been spending a lot of time at her place. It also helps me feel sane. I know Lee has detail on her, but still."

"I get it. So, when's the wedding?"

"Ha ha. Let's get through yours first."

"So what else is happening out there? I spoke to Dad. He seems happy."

"Yeah, Mom too. They have been very discreet. You would never know they were doing it."

"Ugh. Evan."

"It's true. Not even a hand being held or a peck on the cheek in public."

"Whatever works for them, as long as they're happy."

"I guess. Did you speak to Lori about Miami?"

"Briefly. She's excited."

He pauses for a few seconds before saying, "I am telling you this because I know you hate surprises."

"Oh, God. What?"

"Everyone is coming."

"I know. You guys and Lor."

"No...everyone. Dad, Mom, Alisa, Patti, Mandi, Liz, her parents...everyone. Do not tell anyone I told you."

"Whose idea was this?"

"Jack...and Lori. She wants a huge debut for Cliffhangers and has been relentless. She found out that Lizzy and the Lairs were coming. That was all she needed to make it a huge party."

"So let me get this straight, everyone is coming?"

"What is wrong with you?" Evan asks impatiently. "Yes! We are all flying in the day before your show, and we are staying until the festival is over."

"I heard you. I just can't believe you are all coming. How did she manage this?"

"We are talking about Lori."

"True. Speaking of, what's going on with her and Matt?"

"It's so ridiculous. Total role reversal. He is sniffing her ass like a lovesick bloodhound. We can't figure it out."

"How is she treating him?"

"Like an annoying teenager. He dedicated a song the other night, to the sexy redhead who stole his heart."

"Oh my God!"

"It was hilarious. Logan thinks Matt has been abducted by aliens."

I start giggling uncontrollably. Jack walks into the bedroom and smiles. "What's so funny?"

"I'm on with Ev. He's filling me in on Matt and Lori." He kisses me and lies next to me. "Ok, so what else has the jackass done?"

"He keeps trying to get her to agree to dinner. She said she was seeing someone and wasn't interested."

"She said that? Trey?"

"I was going to ask you that."

Jack proceeds to run his hand under my t-shirt, inching it up towards my breast. I swat him away and he gives me an irritated look. "I know that they've been talking on the phone."

"And then some." Jack mumbles. He tries again, this time placing his hand directly on my breast.

"She told Alisa, who told Logan, who told Matt that she's not interested in a relationship and having fun is all she cares about right now."

"Reverse psychology. I'm so on to her."

"You think she's acting like she isn't interested?"

"Hell yes!" Jack lifts my shirt and kisses the swell of my breast. "Ev, I have to go."

Jack smiles against my breast and takes my admission to Evan as his green light.

"Ok. I'll talk to you in a few."

I turn towards Jack while he is manhandling my breast. "Really? We have like five minutes before we pull into New Orleans. You can't wait until we check in?"

"It's tradition."

"Huh?"

"Haven't you noticed, since leaving Albuquerque, we've been 'doing it' as we pull in to each stop?"

"We have?"

"Yes. Amarillo, Oklahoma City, Dallas, Little Rock and Jackson. It's become a goal of mine."

"Is that why you woke me up in the middle of the night in Little Rock?"

"Yes. Impressive, right?"

"I am impressed. I had no idea it was a pattern."

"Yep. And now, we don't have much time." He attaches his lips to mine while removing my shorts. "I was going to prep you a bit, but we may have to get right to it." He moves his hand to stroke me and adds, "Doesn't seem to be a problem, though."

"Is it ever?"

He removes his jeans and briefs and aligns himself over me.

"Coincidentally, I'm ready too." He whispers against my lips while he pins me with his smoky eyes. "I love you, Mrs. Lair."

"I love you, Mr. Lair."

In true Jack fashion, he slides into me torturously slow, one perfect inch at a time. By the time he fills me completely, I am anxious to increase our rhythm. He bends to kiss my lips, while hitching my one leg higher to get in deeper.

I wrap my hands around his neck to give me something to hold on to. Once I've anchored myself, I increase the movement in my hips. "Faster." I plead, as he continues his measured, penetrating thrusts.

When I move my hands to his ass to encourage him, he smiles at me, the bastard.

"Jack."

His response is to move his hand behind my knee and push my leg even higher.

"Oh God. More, don't stop." I plead in a hoarse whisper.

He complies, driving into me over and over. He traces my panting lips with his tongue and effectively does me in. The tremors that start to radiate through my body are bordering on being painful. My fingers grip him as I lose myself to my orgasm. I can't remember if Jack came with me or after me. I was completely preoccupied. When I come to, Jack presses his forehead to mine.

"That was a fuck-tastic quickie." He glances out the window behind my head. "And we are just pulling in."

"Good job, cowboy."

"Thanks. You barely made any noise this time. You're getting better at muffling your coming sounds."

"Practice makes perfect."

"Well tonight you can scream all you want."

"I don't scream."

"You moan. Mmm, I love your moans."

"You are riling me up again. Get up." When I move around the tiny room to throw the normal necessities into my bag, I turn to see Jack watching, amused and Little Jack is waking up again. "Jack, are you going to lay there pant-less all day?"

"Would you mind if I did?"

"Normally no. But I'm five seconds from attacking you, then we'll never leave this bus and I really want to see some of New Orleans before rehearsals." I pout.

"Fine." He jumps out of bed and pulls on his clothes.

"You guys still want to hang before rehearsals?" Scott asks when we walk out of the back bedroom.

"Yeah, as long as Oscar is coming."

"He is. Dylan also. We are going to meet in the lobby in an hour."

"Sounds good."

We quietly caravan to the hotel, check in and make our way to our rooms. Once inside, Jack sits on the edge of the bed staring at the floor. "Babe."

"Yeah?"

"Should I try calling Jessa again?" He has that lost look he gets whenever Jessa or the baby comes up.

"Yes, you *should* call her again."

"I don't know why I can't just move on."

"You need closure." He nods silently. I stand before him and he wraps his arms around me. "I love you."

"I know."

Jack's tried calling her a few times since we got the news. She keeps refusing his calls and ignoring his messages, making him feel even worse than he already does.

"Do you want privacy?"

"No."

This is a ritual. He stalls, finally gets the nerve to call her hospital room, gets shot down, and sulks for the rest of the day. Just yesterday, I called her cell phone myself. I didn't tell Jack, he wouldn't want me getting involved with her or her conniving ways. I wasn't expecting to speak to her. I left her a message that Jack was also a victim in this situation and the least she could do was talk to him.

After staring at his phone for ten minutes, he finally makes the call.

"Max, it's Jack...yeah...ok." He looks up in surprise and says, "She's getting on."

He pushes speaker and holds the phone away from his ear. "Hi, Jack."

"What made you finally want to talk to me?"

"Jack, I'm hurt, I'm upset. This isn't about you. Not everything is about you."

Jack shakes his head and gives me a look. If I could reach through the phone, I'd slap her. "Jessa, I'm not going to fight with you. I wanted to know how you are feeling and if you need anything. I've left you messages, and I'm sure you got them. But I wanted you to hear it directly from me."

"How sweet."

"I didn't do this to you. Let's be clear, here."

She sighs heavily into the phone. "I'm sorry. You're right. I'm taking out my anger on you."

"Thank you. How are you feeling?"

"I'm in pain, but the heavy duty drugs help. I guess that's the upside of not being pregnant any longer."

"Jessa."

"What? Too soon for loss of pregnancy jokes?"

Jack remains silent. He looks at me and rolls his eyes. I take his hand quietly and give it a squeeze.

"Guess so."

"Jessa, I gotta go. I just called to see how you are."

"Wait…I was debating on telling you this. I guess it's the least I can do." She pauses for a few seconds, takes in an audible breath and admits, "It wasn't yours."

Her words stun me. I was not expecting her to ever tell him. I can't believe she just blurted that out, the one thing that's been tormenting us for days.

"You there?"

"Yeah." Jack takes a deep breath and releases it. He gapes at me in shock.

"I have legit proof, if you need it."

"Why did you tell me?"

"I want to move on. I hope you can forgive me. I hope this will…" She pauses and sighs before continuing. "I don't know what I hope it will do, but I'm sorry."

We continue to stare at each other. He pulls my hand up to gently kiss it.

"Jessa, I'm sorry he did this to you. But that's all I'll apologize for."

"Yeah, I get it. Just watch yourself, Jack." She hangs up the call, without a goodbye.

"Un-fucking-real. So now we know."

"I can't believe she told you…and apologized."

"Yeah, you'd think she would have milked this for all the sympathy she could get." He shakes his head over and over. "All that fucking guilt and worry for nothing. I'll never forgive her for this…ever."

"It's over. She can't hurt you any more or us. We survived her lies."

"We did. I think it made us stronger."

"It did."

"I know I should call my parents and let them know. This has been hard on them. I just need to digest this a bit. I feel like a weight has been lifted."

"I do too." I stand and hold my hand out for him. "Let's go have some fun. We deserve it. We're in freaking New Orleans. I want to take on the town with my husband-to-be."

He pulls me onto his lap. "I know I've told you this before, but I really appreciate all you did to try and protect me from her."

I link my hands behind his neck. "I know. I'd do it all over again, and then some."

"Except the breaking my heart part, right?"

I shrug and he frowns. "It was necessary. I'd even go as far as kicking her ass for you, if she hadn't been pregnant."

He raises his eyebrows and smiles wide.

"Why do you look so surprised? I could take her."

"I know you can." He slants his mouth over mine for a lingering kiss. "You are so adorable."

A loud pounding on our door causes me to jump. "Put it in your pants, Lair. It's time to party."

"Fucking, Hunter."

I get up to let Hunter in. He's standing in the hall with Scott and Trey. "Let's go. We only have a few hours."

He links his arm through mine and drags me towards the elevators. "Wait, I need my bag."

"No you don't. It's on Jack."

Our hotel is smack in the middle of the French Quarter in New Orleans. We can walk from it to the *House of Blues,* where we are playing tonight, or to about fifty bars as well. From the lobby, all you see are droves of tourists walking by, some openly holding alcoholic beverages. It's a huge party.

The *House of Blues*, although one of the most famous places we are playing in so far during our tour, is also one of the smallest. With barely nine hundred seats, it will feel intimate compared to the arenas we've been performing in. As we wait for Oscar and Dylan, I'm bouncing with anticipation. The weather is fantastic. Except for seeing Los Angeles from the backseat of a cab, and what little I got to see of Vegas, this will be the first real tourist destination I've ever been to.

"Do we have to wait for them?" Hunter asks impatiently.

"You don't. I'm not going anywhere without Oscar. Where you heading? We'll catch up." Jack offers.

"Fine, meet us at The Abbey."

The guys head out, leaving Jack and me to wait for our security.

"Jack, *The Abbey* is a block away. We could have gone with the guys."

"Baby, I don't want you going anywhere without Oscar."

"I'm with you constantly. Where am I going? Oh, the ladies room. Does he need to come with me there too?"

"I'm serious, smartass. If I'm not with you, Oscar is. End of discussion."

"I love when you get all controlling on me." I lean over to nibble on his ear.

"I know what you're doing."

"What?" I trace his ear with my tongue, then move lower to suck on his neck.

"Lei."

"Jack, the poor guy already has to stand guard outside my dressing room. You have him trailing us like a puppy dog. What more do you want, for him to sleep on our bedroom floor?"

He holds my chin and tilts my head to look into my eyes. "Leila, I'm not kidding."

"Ok. I hear you."

He kisses me and continues to stare into my eyes. "I love you."

Oscar and Dylan come over to where we are having our moment. "Hey, sorry we're late."

"Everything ok?"

"I was on the phone with Ace. Nothing new, no sight of him."

"I was just informing my fiancé she goes nowhere without me or you."

I roll my eyes, and Jack catches me. "Really?"

"Leila, he's right." Oscar sides with Jack. Well, of course he'll side with Jack.

Realizing it will get me nowhere to crack a joke, I concede instead. "Got it. Now can we go have a drink?" I stand and hold my hand out to him, which he ignores, and instead wraps an arm around me.

My argument was valid. Our walk to The Abbey took less than three minutes. We find the guys in the back corner. A tray of tequila shots sits, waiting for our arrival.

The waitress comes over, focusing on Jack.

"Baby, what do you want to drink?"

"I'll have wine." She levels me with her glare, measuring me up. She is one hot piece of ass, and the old Jack would definitely be paying attention. My Jack barely looks at her.

She takes our orders and throws Jack a dazzling smile before heading off to get our drinks.

"What took you so long?"

"We were waiting for Oscar and Dylan." Jack looks at me briefly and quickly adds, "So, um…I spoke to Jessa."

They all wait patiently as Jack takes a few seconds to continue. "She told me it wasn't mine."

"Holy shit." Hunter speaks first.

"Jack, you must be relieved."

Jack nods at Scott and says, "You can't imagine." He squeezes my hand and adds, "It's over. I don't want to hear about it any more."

"Well, I've been staring at these entirely too long. Shot time." Hunter is quick to comply.

"I'll pass." I shake my head, as Hunter passes out the shots.

"Lei, this one is your shot. It's ginger ale." Trey holds up the tiny glass.

"Not funny."

He shrugs and smiles. "She asked me to do it."

"Leave my wife alone." Jack says, just as the waitress reappears with our drinks.

"You two are married? I don't see a ring on your finger." She asks, looking directly at Jack.

"Soon to be." He responds without looking up.

She leans over and says into his ear loud enough for us to hear, "That's a shame." Then hands out our drinks and saunters off towards the bar.

"Is she for real?"

Jack drags his chair closer. "Ignore her."

"She's hot as hell and hitting on you."

"Is she? I hadn't noticed."

"Hoo-kay," Hunter challenges. "We know you love Leila, but you are trying to say you didn't notice that hot piece of ass?"

Jack stares into my eyes and touts, "Nope."

"I believe you. But if she comes near you again, I'm going to get violent."

"Now that's hot," Hunter says, while smiling. "Two hot chicks in a fight? Wet dream material." Jack and I stare at him. "What?"

"You guys are too much." Oscar shakes his head before drinking his seltzer. "Don't you have a girlfriend?"

"Yes, and I love her. But just because I can't touch doesn't mean I can't look. I'm being honest."

"Hunt, how many chicks did you average a year since I moved in with you?"

"What's your point?"

"Been there, done that."

"So?"

"It doesn't interest me anymore."

"Are you saying I love Mandi any less because I look?"

"No. I'm just saying I no longer have the desire to."

"Oh, throw up. I'm not in love or attached or pussy whipped. I'm going to tap that." Trey gets up and stalks to the "hot piece of ass".

"He is such a whore." I say out loud. Besides what little I know of him from Lori, it occurs to me I really don't know much about him. "How old is Trey?"

"He's thirty-one." Jack responds. "Why?"

"I was just curious."

"Spill it." Jack eyes me suspiciously.

"Do you think he'll ever settle down and have a family some day?"

"No."

"Yes."

Jack and Hunter respond simultaneously.

"I don't know. I have to agree with Hunter. I think domesticated Trey is in there and just needs a nudge." I lean over to give him a quick kiss. "You've changed."

"For the better." We proceed to ignore all things around us and have one of our moments in the midst of this crowded, noisy bar.

Oscar notices and says, "You two make sure you keep this fire going. That's what kills a marriage…trust me. My wife and I didn't work hard enough at it. With me being gone in the beginning, we lost our connection. Even when I got home, we didn't work hard enough. I was detached, having been through hell and back while serving, and she didn't understand what I was going through. Whatever little passion we had, smoldered and died. After being together for almost ten years, we had nothing left."

I first notice sadness in Oscar's eyes. "Oscar, do you have kids?"

"No. We tried. Maybe things would have been different if we had been successful. But then again, my career choice would have probably done us in anyway. When I got home, I had gotten a boring desk job in an attempt to settle down and work at having a normal married life. I was miserable. After we split, I called my army buddy, Colt, and begged him to get me a job with *Orion. He spoke to his boss Mike, and they hired me. I was meant to do this. If I had discovered this line of work earlier, she would have left me much sooner."

"I am never letting you go." Jack says directly to me.

I smile warmly at him. He truly has changed. He's so open with his love for me. He's so romantic and sweet. Having heard many of the stories of how Jack used to behave, stranger things have happened than Trey finding love and settling down. I'm witnessing it every day that I'm with Jack Lair.

"You two are truly nauseating." Hunter says, before tipping back another shot.

"And you are such a hypocrite. When I was miserable, you and Mandi were God-awful to be around."

"Oh yeah. I forgot," Hunter smirks. "Still, if I can't be happy, no one should be allowed to be happy."

"Jackass." Jack says, before leaning over to smack the back of his head.

"You guys are very entertaining, I'll give you that much," Oscar admits. "You are the first rock band I've worked for. It's been a blast."

"You don't get tired of living on a bus with a bunch of men?" Scott asks incredulously. "I don't think I could do that if I weren't also doing what I love to do."

"I am doing what I love to do. I love my line of work. I love helping people." Oscar shrugs. "Dylan is in the same position. Do you mind living on a bus with a bunch of men?"

"Yes and no. I also love what I do, but it can be torture as well. This is my third tour. I can't see myself doing this for much longer."

"What would make you leave?" Scott asks.

"A family. If I had a wife and kids, I'd be in corporate behind a desk." Dylan glances up at me briefly before looking down into his beer.

An uncomfortable silence falls over us until Jack turns towards me and asks, "Are you ready to see some of New Orleans?"

I nod at his question.

"You guys gonna continue drinking the day away?" He asks, looking directly at Hunter. In response, Hunter picks up yet another shot and downs it.

"Oscar, do you mind leaving?"

"Of course not. It's my job." Oscar is always extremely professional with us.

"You two better not be shitfaced for our show tonight." Jack says to his band mates before standing and pulling me up as well.

"Can't promise that."

Jack shakes his head and leads us out onto the street that is crowded with tourists. The daylight hits me, causing me to squint. "I feel like we've been in a cave for hours."

"Me too. I needed air."

Jack, Oscar and I walk down the narrow streets of the French Quarter. I feel strange having Oscar trailing us like a chaperone. I hold my tongue anyways. We stroll into shops and Jack buys me a few little trinkets as souvenirs. I buy my postcard marking this stop on the tour. When we get to the Mississippi, he hands his phone to Oscar. "Can you take a picture?"

"What's gotten into you?"

"We need to build memories to tell the grandkids some day."

Oscar takes a shot of us with the river behind us.

"Great pic, you two. You are going to make gorgeous babies."

Oscar's words thrill me. Having children with Jack is a prodigious event I cannot wait to occur in our future...now more than ever.

Jack nuzzles my neck and whispers what I am thinking. "I can't wait for you to have my babies." His words send shivers down my spine and instantly turn me on. He may as well have asked me to fuck him right here on the side of the Mississippi.

"I'm done sightseeing."

He smiles at me and responds, "Well, yay."

It's about twelve minutes later when Jack and I stumble through our hotel room door, clamoring to try and remove our clothes while still attached at the lips.

He kicks the door shut with his foot before pulling away breathlessly. "God, I need to be inside you so bad."

"Stop talking." I rasp before pulling him back to me. The burn he started at the river has become an unbearable throbbing in between my legs. I yank off my clothes, and then assist in helping him remove his. Once we are completely bare, I push him to sit on the edge of the bed and straddle his hips.

I lower myself onto his shaft and he curses under his breath. I feel the same way. The fullness takes over my senses, the pressure instantly relieved. My insides are ablaze with pure ecstasy. I tangle my fingers in his hair and cover his mouth with mine. His moans rumble through me, further igniting my fire.

I take complete control over the situation, unashamedly using him to pleasure myself. I move over him repeatedly until a painful tightening begins low in my belly. It spreads to my core, controlling me completely. His breathless pants in my mouth indicate how close he is getting. I take his entire length and bury my face in his neck, fingers still tangled in his hair and surrender to my climax. It seems to go on forever and drains me completely.

Jack mumbles something against my neck and tenses beneath me as he digs his fingertips into my back, holding me flush against him. Once he slackens his grip, I remove myself from him and crawl onto the bed.

"I feel so used." He says, smacking my ass playfully.

"Sorry, baby. I need to take a quick nap." I murmur, my eyes closing heavily.

He aligns his warm body behind mine, pulling me close to him. His arousal is still obvious on my backside. I wiggle closer and he grumbles, "Knock it off or I'm fucking you again. Sleepy or not."

My giggle prompts him to slide his hand around my body towards my breast. He runs a fingertip around my nipple, and it responds under his touch. He tugs my earlobe between his lips and whispers, "Still sleepy?"

"Hmm, yes."

"Buzz kill."

"Just give me a few minutes." I mumble and bury my head in the pillow.

He traces a finger down my back over my ass and repeats the pattern on the other side. His touch causes me to break out in chills. Still struggling with an internal battle within me, between sleeping and attacking.

I turn to face him, still conflicted when he lifts himself and pulls the comforter over my body. The warmth and coziness I'm engulfed with, as well as his gentle caresses, take hold of my subconscious and I drift to sleep.

Chapter 21 - Jack

I can stare at her for hours. It still amazes me that she has managed to completely alter me as person. She has profoundly changed my life. How can that happen? I was never one to believe in soul mates. I was too ignorant to know that when you found the person you fall in love with, you lose all control. I was stupid to think that I could avoid it, that I would always call the shots.

I meant what I said to Hunter at the night of our engagement. The thought of ever losing her brings with it a panic that permeates every fiber of my being. My love for her is irrefutable, undeniable. It's a fear I've never known before, an anxiety that cripples me. I memorize the lines of her face, her swollen lips. Her beauty takes my breath away.

I gently run the pad of my thumb across her bottom lip and she stirs slightly before opening her eyes. "Hey."

"Hey."

"How long have I been out?"

"About an hour."

"I need to shower."

"Me too. I've been waiting for you." I wiggle my eyebrows comically.

She giggles and stretches lazily. The comforter falls away, exposing her from the waist up.

"Baby, you are so beautiful." I bend to take her nipple in between my lips. She buries her fingers in my hair, holding me to her breast. "We don't have much time." I say, before taking her other nipple next. My actions are belying my words, until I reluctantly pull away.

"Let's shower." I lift her and carry her into the bathroom.

"Multitasking again?"

"It's what I do." Seconds later, we are under a warm stream of water, lathering, groping and stroking each other wild. I wrap myself around her, pressing her against me from head to toe. My cock protruding between us is the only space I am allowing. I hold her head in my hand, tilting it up to search her eyes with mine. "I love you so much."

"I love you too."

I cover her mouth with my own, devouring her lips. She opens and gives me access, which I readily take. My tongue probes and mingles with hers. While kissing her passionately, I lift her and gently slide into her warm channel. She accepts every inch of me.

Her iron grip on me further escalates my salacious intentions. Her moans drive me wild as I pump faster and harder. She doesn't have to use words to tell me she is close. I can feel it. I can feel her taking hold and not letting go. She cries out as I hit her sweet spot over and over. My primal grunts echo off the tile walls of the shower.

"Fuuuuck." I croak as I empty into her with every spastic thrust I make.

"Holy hell." She whispers into my neck. "You truly are going to be the death of me."

"I can say the same to you, Mrs. Lair."

"We are out of control."

"So?" She unlatches her ankles and straightens her legs. Still keeping a tight grip on her, I slowly and regretfully pull out. "I can stay in you all day." I admit my thoughts.

"That would be interesting." She smiles and wipes the drops of water out of my eyes. "We're pruning."

I look down at myself and smirk. "Speak for yourself."

I watch as she follows my gaze and purses her lips trying to contain her laughter, but she fails miserably. I shrug and hand her a towel, helping her step out of the shower.

"You'd think Little Jack didn't just get some."

"You really need to come up with a better name, baby."

Her eyes on me have me growing stiff once again. She shakes her head, "Does he have a mind of his own?"

I laugh at her comment. "Unfortunately."

She smacks my chest. "Stop. We have to get ready."

While we scramble to get ready for rehearsals, she suddenly stops and says, "How about J.J.?"

"What?"

"Jack Junior."

"That would knock out calling our son J.J."

She shoots me a look.

"Fine. J.J. Happy now?"

"Yes."

"Good, now hurry up and put some clothes on, or J.J. is going to get restless."

♫ ♫ ♫

Leila and I walk through the lobby of the *House of Blues*, and she keeps looking around, taking everything in. "I can't believe we are in the *House of Blues*." she says for the eighth time.

She looks up at me and frowns. "Aren't you impressed at all?"

"Sure."

"But we are in the *House of Blues*." I can't help but laugh at the look on her face. "Let's get you a *House of Blues* postcard."

By the time we get to the stage for rehearsals, the guys are congregated on stage animatedly having a vociferous conversation.

"What's going on?"

"We're top ten!" Hunter yells at us.

"No shit?"

"No, man. Jen just called Dylan. We're fucking top ten!"

Leila and I exchange wide smiles. "This is surreal."

"I know."

Dylan appears with a bottle of champagne. "Congratulations, you two." He pats my back and gives Leila a quick hug.

"Which song?"

"*Committed* and *High Life*." Scott beams. "Two…two fucking top tens!"

Dylan pours out a round and raises his own cup to make a toast. "You guys should be really proud of yourselves. The studio couldn't be happier with your success. I spoke to Louis this morning. He would like to extend his congratulations. He also would like to tell you all there will be a celebration planned for us in Miami."

"Woo hoo!" Hunter yells.

Dylan grins at Hunter's enthusiasm. "You can invite anyone you like. Transportation costs will be on the studio. One more bit of good news."

We all wait expectantly at what Dylan is about to share. "You guys will have some special guests here tonight. Jessie, Liam, and Cruz from *Bayou Stix are attending."

"Are you insane?"

"Nope…Jen called to tell me. They are on a tour break while Jude is on his honeymoon and heard you guys were playing tonight. They will be coming backstage after the show to meet you all."

"HOLY SHIT!" Hunter roars and starts twerking to non-existent music as Leila falls into a fit of giggles.

"Jack, man…*Bayou Stix! Do you remember all the nights we sat listening to their CDs on our roof?"

"Yeah, Hunt. This is pretty amazing." It's true. It is amazing. It's sometimes hard to wrap my brain around all that is happening to us. These guys deserve this…we all do. Their excitement is palpable, and it's infectious. I watch my best buddies celebrating this awesome news and my fiancé being passed around among them, forcing her to join in their antics.

I also witness Dylan turn towards Leila while smiling warmly. There is sadness in his eyes as he watches Leila dancing with Hunter animatedly. Dylan looks away and locks eyes with mine. He turns and leaves us to our celebration.

What I just witnessed disturbs me. Our tour manager still has feelings for my fiancé. I trust Leila implicitly, but it upsets me knowing he still wants her.

As the group resumes their loud, boisterous celebration, Leila pulls away from Hunter and comes towards me still laughing.

"He's crazy." She frowns and asks, "You ok?"

"Yeah, I'm fine."

"I can't wait to talk to my dad about Miami."

"Hey, I sort of have a confession to make."

She looks up worried. "What's wrong?"

"I was going to surprise you. I already invited our parents and siblings to Miami."

She bites her bottom lip before responding, "Um. I know."

"What?"

"Evan told me." She looks up wide-eyed. "Sorry, baby."

"I wanted to surprise you."

"It's the thought that counts."

"Damn, Evan."

She drags me closer to the festivities. "Come on. We need to celebrate."

After a few toasts and a short unproductive rehearsal, Leila and I retreat to our dressing room to get ready for the show.

I am no longer allowed to solicit sex before our shows. Apparently, her routine takes longer than mine, and I was cutting into her prep time. I don't see what the big deal is. She's gorgeous and doesn't need all that fussing. When I said as much, she impatiently explained that having sex minutes before performing was messing with her frame of mind. She uses the time before our shows to relax and mentally prepare herself. I was upsetting that balance.

Whatever.

So now I sit in a corner, like a punished toddler, watching as she goes through her preshow routine. It's been hard as fuck. Knowing she is sitting there, practically naked, messes with my own frame of mind. By the time we hit the stage, I want to bend her over Hunter's drum set and fuck her senseless. It does add an element to our show, having me walking around horny as fuck. I'll give her that much.

"Hey, babe?" I call over to her while she is applying her makeup.

She looks up with her doe eyes and my cock twitches in my jeans.

"Fuck. Don't look at me like that."

"Like what?"

"Like you have no clue how much you are torturing me right now."

She smiles devilishly. "Ok, I won't look at you at all." She looks down at her cluttered vanity smirking. "What?"

"What?"

"Jack, you just were about to ask me something."

"Oh, yeah. Um, do you think Dylan still has feelings for you?"

She snaps her eyes to mine in the mirror. "What? Why would you ask me that?"

"Just the way he looks at you."

"He doesn't look at me a certain way."

"Yeah, he really does. I was curious if he's ever mentioned your relationship after we left New York."

She levels me with her gaze and shakes her head. "He's been nothing but professional with me. Jack, he also really cares about both of us…not just me. He is a friend and nothing more."

I walk towards her and place my hands on her shoulders. "Babe, I'm not bringing this up because I suspect something is going on between you. I just was curious if he's ever discussed his feelings with you."

"No. But if he were to, I would reiterate what I said in New York."

"I know."

The announcer gives us our ten-minute warning over the PA system. This is always her cue to get dressed. She kisses me chastely before she heads for the bathroom. Leaving me swimming with thoughts of what would have happened, if she and Dylan had started a relationship instead of us. When she emerges, I'm neck deep in a visual of Leila holding a baby with sandy brown hair and big blue eyes.

"What are you thinking about?"

"Nothing."

She wraps her arms around my waist, skimming them up my back soothingly. She looks incredible in her tight jeans and fitted top. Her topaz eyes search mine for an indication to my thoughts. Her lips beg to be kissed.

"You're lying. You have this scowl on your face like you just tasted something awful."

"Just the opposite, babe. The scowl is from the lack of tasting something sweet and delicious."

"Liar."

I slant my mouth over hers in a searing kiss. "Mmm, delicious. Not quite what I really wanted a taste of, but it will suffice for now."

Our five-minute warning is announced. She shakes her head subtly and says, "Saved by the bell."

"I can accomplish a lot in five minutes." I wiggle my eyebrows as she puckers her brow.

"No way."

"Buzz kill. Come, let's go tear up the *House of Blues*."

Chapter 22 - Leila

"Is this like a bachelorette party?"

"No. It's just me and the girls hitting a club and having a girls night out." I walk over to him sitting in a chair in the corner. Our hotel room is gorgeous. The studio went all out for us here in Miami. Jack is dressed in dark denim and a grey cotton t-shirt that always drives me wild. The color is an exact match to his eyes.

He opens his arms, giving me access to his lap. "Don't you trust me?"

"Of course I trust you. It's every cocksucker walking around with a major hard-on that usually frequent dance clubs in Miami that I don't trust."

"You've never been to Miami."

He shoots me a look, causing me to laugh.

"Sorry. Babe, we will be fine. No one will come near me with Juan trailing us. Please don't worry."

Juan is a huge hunk of a man. Oscar requested an addition guard from *Orion to escort us tonight. He convinced the studio he couldn't be in two places at the same time. Because of his sheer size, Oscar explained Juan would be better to escort the ladies tonight and Jack reluctantly agreed. But he is most definitely not happy about it.

Jack claims the man has the hots for me. How he can assess that after a ninety second introduction is absolutely ridiculous. I didn't want to further upset him. So instead, I slowly unzipped his jeans and lowered to my knees as he kept ranting about the way Juan's eyes focused on my body instead of my face. Once I wrapped my lips around his cock, he stopped talking.

Unfortunately, the effect of my blowjob has definitely worn off, because he's restarted his rant.

"Jack, I want you to go out with the guys and have fun tonight. Besides, you won't have time to worry about me. You are going to have your hands full warding off the ladies."

"Ha ha."

I cup his face, turning his head until he stares back at me. "I love you. You need a night out and so do I. Please promise me you'll enjoy yourself and not worry about me."

His eyes soften and he skims my bottom lip with his thumb. "Ok…I promise."

He kisses me like he's trying to sear an imprint of his lips on mine. His tongue probes and strokes, he buries one hand in my hair while the other travels up my side to cup my breast. His demanding erection beneath my ass announces its arrival.

The effect of his kiss immobilizes me for a few seconds until oxygen slowly creeps into my major organs.

"I'll see you later." He whispers against my lips.

"You don't play fair."

"There will be more waiting for you when you get home." He gives me one more quick kiss and pats my ass. "Ok, I got to go. Be good and have fun. I love you."

I stand to allow him to leave. When he reaches the door, he turns and says, "I'll be texting you sporadically. Please respond in a timely manner so I don't lose my mind with worry."

"I will. Go."

"Hey, Jackson." Lori croons as Jack walks through the door. She has taken to calling him Jackson to bust his chops.

He responds with, "Behave yourself tonight. If she ends up in jail, I'll hold you responsible."

"Well, that's not fair." Lori pouts.

Jack shakes his head and squeezes past the five females taking up most of the hallway. They all enter and start yapping instantly. Lori, Alisa, Patti, Mandi and Lizzy are dressed to the nines and look stunning.

I am so excited to have everyone here with us. My old band melds perfectly with my new band. When the shuttle deposited the lot of them earlier today, we caused such a commotion in the lobby that the concierge politely escorted us to an empty ballroom to contain the noise level. The only ones missing are Dad, Barb, the Lairs, Nina and her boyfriend…they are all arriving tomorrow.

It was Lori's idea to have a girl's night and in a reversal of roles, the guys all bitched and moaned about it. Lori accused them of growing ovaries and told them to shut it.

I personally am thrilled with the plans. They work perfectly with my surprise for Jack.

"Ok, let's blow this joint." Lori announces as she inspects her face in the mirror.

"We need to make one quick pit stop."

"Where?"

"The tattoo parlor."

They all look at me like I just grew a dick. "I want to surprise Jack. Please?"

"I want one, too," Alisa announces.

Lori shrugs and says, "Ok, I'm game. Tattoos first, then dancing."

We parade through the lobby to the portico where our limo is waiting. Juan stands at its side, waiting patiently.

"Who the fuck is that?" Lori asks as we walk towards the Latin god who is our protector for the night.

"That's Juan. Jack is not a fan."

"I am." She sidles up to him and says, "Hi, Juan."

"Evening," he responds, returning her smile.

He nods at each of us as we pile in. A group of men entering the hotel start whistling.

"You girls need dates?"

Lori leans out of the limo door and offers, "Sure. Meet us at the *Clevelander*."

She shuts the door and smiles wickedly.

"Lori. Really?"

"What? We aren't going to the *Clevelander*. We are going to *Mynt*," she smirks.

We take full advantage of the mini bar in the limo. By the time we arrive at the tattoo parlor, we are giddy with excitement. All six of us are getting tattoos. The girls scan the books anxiously looking for the perfect image. I know exactly what I want, so I'm the first one up.

There are three tattoo artists in the shop, two male and one female. Based on the location of my tattoo, I decide on Tamara to ink my body. I want to avoid a fight with Jack. Having another man's hands on my body will be hard enough for him to get over. Having another man's hands well below my bikini line would give him an aneurysm.

"So where do you want it."

I'm unable to stop the immediate flush of my cheeks. I point to my chosen location.

Tamara smirks and says, "Great spot."

As she preps me on the table, I nervously ask, "How bad will this hurt?"

"It's not terrible," she shrugs, "but this is a very sensitive part of your body."

"He better appreciate this."

"He? Hmm…too bad," she mumbles. "What are you going with for Mr. Lucky?"

I tell her my tattoo choice and she shakes her head. "I hope this works out for you two."

Maybe I should keep the fact Tamara likes women from Jack as well. She is covered in tattoos. She smiles as I shamelessly inspect her exposed skin. It doesn't stop me from looking. Some are hard to decipher. A jumble of color and swirls take up a huge patch of her arm. It must have taken years to get all those tattoos.

"Ready?" She asks, catching my attention.

I pull in a breath and close my eyes. "Yep, let's do this."

♫ ♫ ♫

Almost two hours later, we arrive at *Mynt* and the place is jammed. The techno music's pounding vibrations can be felt on the pavement outside the club.

"I have us on the VIP list," Lori announces.

"Of course you do."

"Don't doubt the powers of Lori Banzini."

As we move through the club, I'm not oblivious to the many pairs of eyes that follow our path from both males and females alike. I'm not sure if it's us, or the god who is protecting us tonight that solicits the stares. Lori squeezes us past writhing bodies on the dance floor to a corner table marked as "Reserved".

"How?" I ask in awe.

"Just enjoy it."

Lizzy leans over and says, "She's impressive."

"Ok, what are we drinking?" Patti asks.

"Tequila shots first." Lori looks directly at me when responding. She points a finger and adds, "Don't give me a hard time."

I roll my eyes and concede, "Fine."

As we wait for our drinks, I pull out my cell phone. "There is no service in here." I mumble.

"And?"

I look up to see Lori glaring at me. "We have Juan and he can spend a few hours away from you. Shut it."

I give her a dirty look before stashing my phone back in my purse. "Jeez," I grumble like a child who just got scolded by her mother.

Three tequila shots and a round of cosmos later, we work our bodies out on the dance floor. I haven't been dancing in ages. It feels so freeing and liberating to let loose. I don't know anyone here, thus helping with my normal inhibitions when attempting to move my body in a somewhat seductive manner. I've been told I am a good dancer, but I never quite believed it. I've always held back, sure that I looked like a fool. Tonight I dance the way I always desire to, letting the music control my movements.

Males who attempt to make contact with their physicality quickly encircle us. Lori is the only one who responds. She hones in on the best looking one in the bunch and aligns her body with his as if they have known each other for years.

"She's such a tramp," Alisa says through her smile.

"A loveable one, though," I shout above the music.

After a dozen or so songs, thirst, my throbbing feet and a hot flash hamper my desire to continue dancing.

"I need a drink." I half mime, half shout to the girls. Lizzy, Mandi and Patti nod in agreement, following me over to our booth. We order another round of drinks, my body sinking into the soft leather sofa already exhausted from the non-stop dancing. A few minutes later, Lori and Alisa join us.

"Five minute break to refuel," Lori says to no one in particular.

"Lor, this isn't a dance competition. It's ok if we skip a few." My toes agree with my declaration. They have been sending silent protests to my brain for the past hour.

"We haven't been out together in forever. Our asses will be out on that dance floor in five minutes."

It's never worth the argument when it comes to Lori and her demands. Alisa and I exchange exasperated looks and quickly finish our drinks afraid to be yelled at.

Lizzy and Mandi decide to stay behind when Lori drags Alisa and me back to the center of the floor.

"Glad you came back," her dance partner shouts. He immediately picks up exactly where he left off.

I dance with Alisa out of default. A few men try to make a move on us, but quickly move on when ignored.

I close my eyes and allow the music to control me. The alcohol has dulled my senses. The music isn't as punishing, my feet are now numb, and my movements are more exaggerated. I'm in a Jack induced daze. I imagine Jack and how he looks after we make love. How his eyes darken, right before he comes inside of me. The image sends pulses over my sensitive skin as if his hands were actually skimming over me. The alcohol in my system plays mind tricks on me, until a seductive breath in my ear jolts me out of my reverie.

Spinning around, I come face to face with Jack.

He gives me a sexy smile. "Hi."

"What are you doing here?"

"I needed to see you."

"You couldn't have come at a better time."

He pulls me into his hard body, his arousal evident against my belly. "Why is that? Is my girl horny?"

The way I focus on his lips is my dead giveaway. He pokes his tongue out and runs it slowly over his bottom lip. A smile lifts one corner of his mouth.

"Oh, God."

He starts to move us to the music. I wrap my fingers in his hair to pull his head lower. He stops right before our lips touch.

"Jack, don't tease me."

"I'm not, baby. I'm trying to figure out where I can fuck you in this place."

He crashes his lips to mine. I completely open my mouth, giving him full access, not caring one iota if anyone is watching. Plenty of other bodies have been entangled in seductive kisses all night. I could give a crap if we are now supplying the entertainment.

A tap on my shoulder and then another and a third irritates me. I shrug the invader away, never breaking our kiss.

"Why is he here?" Lori shouts in my ear.

I swat her away and Jack smiles against my open mouth. I've had my tongue practically shoved down his throat for the past few seconds. It's now his turn to visit my mouth.

"Your dad is going to see this on You Tube tomorrow."

I pull away wide-eyed and level my gaze with Lori.

"Go. Away."

"Just sayin'," she nods towards a small crowd of people all pointing their phones at us.

Jack clenches his jaw in frustration. "Come," he drags me by the hand off the dance floor and towards our table.

A few scantily clad girls brazenly follow us. "Are you Jack Lair?"

"No," he responds, not turning to look at them.

"Yes you are…and she's Leila."

The louder this chick gets, the more gather around our table.

"Get out of the way," Lori nudges her way towards our corner. A leggy blonde elbows Lori as she nears and Lori barks, "Bring it. I'm from fucking Jersey."

The girl startles and backs up, looking at Lori as if she escaped a mental institution.

"Let's blow this joint," Lori shouts as Juan stands guard in front of our tiny table. I feel like a circus animal. Girls are blatantly taking our picture, calling out to Jack so he would turn in time to get his gorgeous face in the shot. He pulls out his phone and calls Oscar.

"Hey, we have a situation in here…Ok, text me when you pull up." He hangs up and says, "Oscar said the limo had to circle around the block. He's on his way back."

Lori decides Juan needs her help and stands in front of our table, shoulder to shoulder with him.

"What is she doing?" Alisa asks me while looking at Lori's back.

I shake my head not bothering with a response. My head is now pounding as if someone hit me over the head. And then there is the unfortunate condition of my libido, which has shriveled as if a bucket of ice water was thrown in my crotch.

Jack possessively has me on his lap on the tiny couch, his arms wrapped around my waist in a death grip. "Jeez, this is ridiculous."

Lizzy looks at her brother incredulously. "I've told you…while you all have been living in your metal bubble, things are happening out there for you. You guys are wanted men."

He shakes his head as if in denial.

"Where are the rest of the guys?" I ask directly into his ear.

He responds into mine, "I left them at the bar. I told them I was coming to get you guys."

Jack's phone buzzes and he announces to our group that our limo is out front.

An intimidating bouncer makes his way to our corner. "Ok, move it people," he barks. Making his way through, he gently pushes female bodies aside and shoves the male ones.

"I'm with them," Juan announces when they come toe to toe. The bouncer looks past Juan at Jack and me. Recognition changes his scowl to a smile. "Devil's Lair?"

Jack nods hesitantly. "Our limo just pulled up. Can you get us out of here?"

"Sure, come with me." He and Juan create a people plow, pushing and moving bodies as we move towards the entrance.

The presence of Juan and the bouncer prompt people to move back to their own partying, making it much easier to get to the door. Once outside, we quickly scatter towards the limo and close the door to all the curious eyes watching our departure.

Jack lets out a sigh of relief. "Fuck, that was crazy."

"Thanks for ruining our fun, Lair." Lori quips with an attitude.

"Sorry. I just wanted to see my girl." He kisses the top of my head as I watch Lori scowl at him.

"I was having a great time 'til you showed up."

"I came to get you girls. The guys are all waiting for us in a private room at a sports bar. They miss you all."

Lori's features change to a smirk. "Ok, you're forgiven."

I wonder if it's the thought of Trey or Matt that put that smirk on her face.

When we make eye contact, she winks.

The drive is short, and we are at our destination a few minutes later.

Juan and Oscar escort us into the bar and back towards a closed door. The noise filters out of the sliver of space between the bottom of the door and the floor. They are almost as loud as the crowd in the sports bar behind us.

"Well, it's about time," Hunter yells from across the room. He and Mandi meet half way in a sweet embrace. Patti and Scott connect. Lizzy and Evan connect. Alisa and Logan connect. Lori looks at Matt and walks over to Trey.

Oh, fuck.

The look on Matt's face is priceless. Joe is also not paired off, since his girlfriend couldn't make it. He puts his arm around Matt and says, "I don't put out on the first date."

"Get off me, jackass." Matt pushes him away, grabs his beer and leaves the room.

"He ok?" Jack asks me.

"No, I don't think so."

The room has TVs mounted on two of the walls. Both are muted, one is on a female volleyball game in Malibu and the other is on a surfing competition in Hawaii. The music from the bar is being piped in. It's classic rock and hard not to sing along to. The guys are running a tab, and the flowing drinks are making us all loose and relaxed. It's not long after when my buzz returns and my horniness resurfaces.

Jack and I are dancing to *Light My Fire*, by the Doors. His voice is a smooth perfect match to Morrison's. Once the chorus starts, some of the others start singing along. Jack's hands are on my ass, pushing me into his body as we seductively sway to the long musical interlude in the middle of the song. He bends and pulls my bottom lip in between his own.

"I love you."

"Me too."

We dance through every song that is played...*Witchy Woman, Rhiannon, The Night Owl.* Some of our friends are dancing around us, some are loudly singing along with the music, and some are just drinking while listening.

Jack sings each song to me. His voice is doing things to my insides. As we sway to Journey's *Faithfully*, I can't take it any longer.

"You're driving me wild."

"What? My kisses, my hard-on?"

"Well, yes, but mostly your voice."

He swallows and his eyes become hooded with lust. "I can't wait to get you to our room," he says while watching my lips. We start making out like teenagers. After several long minutes, I suck in a much-needed breath.

"Ok, I'm ready." I admit.

Jack announces we are leaving. The rest of our friends enthusiastically agree that it is time to head back to the hotel. Obviously they have also worked themselves up while we weren't paying attention.

The short drive back is quiet. We split up into two limos. Ours include Evan and Lizzy, Logan and Alisa, Scott and Patti, Hunter and Mandi. I wish I were a fly on the wall of the other limo, though. Matt never returned. Lori and Trey are sharing the ride with Joe, Will, Juan, and Dylan. Poor guys.

We grumble quick goodnights and all head to our rooms. It's late. Tomorrow is a big day. The studio is hosting a luncheon for us with our friends and families. Then we have our normal concert scheduled. The following day is the music festival. Then we all separate and continue on with the tail end of our tour.

But at the moment, sleep is the last thing on my mind.

"Alone at last." Jack says, wrapping his arms around my waist, pulling me into his body. He nuzzles my neck, his lips sucking on the sensitive spot below my ear.

"Mmm. Let me freshen up. I have a surprise for you."

He turns me around to face him. "I hope you didn't pay a ton for it. It's going to be on the floor in a few minutes."

"I can't take this one off." I walk away, leaving him confused.

After quickly freshening up, I open the door to find Jack completely naked on the bed.

"Oh, yum." I admit as I lean against the door jam.

"Oh, Christ." He quips back. I am wearing a black lace bra and matching panties.

I unhook my bra and remove it, throwing it on the floor. "That was in the way." He caresses me with his gaze. When his eyes come back to mine, I move forward and lie next to him on the bed.

He pulls a nipple between his lips, swirling his tongue around its stiff peak.

"Is this my surprise? I think I've seen these before."

"No."

He moves lower, kissing along the way. He skims the lacy edge of my panties with his tongue from end to end.

"Is this my surprise?"

"No."

He hooks two fingers under the narrow side straps, easing them off my body in super slow motion. His eyes are glued to mine as he removes them, until he shifts his gaze to my sex.

"What's this?" he asks, touching the narrow white gauze bandage covering his surprise.

"Open it and see."

He peals off the bandage and gasps. Below my panty line dangerously close to my pussy, is my new tattoo, *The ONLY Mrs. J.H. Lair*, in a delicate script ending with a tiny red heart.

"Holy fuck."

"You like?"

"I fucking love it." He blinks repeatedly, touching the skin above and below, but not the tattoo.

"Did it hurt?"

"A little. This is why I insisted we separate tonight. The girls all got one too."

"Who did this?"

"I knew you were going to ask me that. A really hot guy covered in tats."

He levels me with his gaze. "Lei."

"I'm joking."

"That's not funny."

"A girl named Tamara. I totally planned ahead. However, she is a lesbian."

"Her loss."

The tat is about two inches above my clit. No one will ever see it, except Jack…and my gynecologist.

"So, do you like it?"

He spreads me wide, planting a whisper of a kiss on the mark that forever brands me to him.

"I love it. Thank you."

With his eyes still pinned to mine, he lowers his mouth over me. All the sexual frustrations I've pent up all night bubble up to the surface. Jack uses his tongue masterfully to bring me an instant orgasm. He doesn't pull away, instead repeating the process…twice more.

When he stretches beside me, he kisses me deeply. I can taste myself on his lips. "Straddle me, baby. I don't want to rub up against your tat."

"Aw, you're so sweet."

"In a few minutes, I won't be."

He impales me, no pomp, no circumstance. The fullness I feel takes hold of my already sensitive nerve endings. I clench and he groans.

"Can I move? Jack, I need to move."

His eyes are closed and his mouth is gaping open. He nods and says in a voice filled with lust, "Go, baby."

I take control, stabilizing my shaky body by holding onto his shoulders. He grips my hips, rocking his hips up when I move down. He flexes his fingers, emitting a groan with each thrust. I can feel him move his hand. I can feel his fingertip skim over my swollen bud ever so lightly. That's all it takes. I'm done. Completely unhinged. Totally falling.

When my internal muscles grip him, he mutters, "Fuck."

He uses both hands to keep me lowered over him as he viciously spasms inside of me. The benefit of climaxing first is I get to watch this gorgeous man lose his shit while he comes apart at the seams.

The first thing he sees when he opens his eyes is my love encompassed smile.

"Hi."

"Hi."

Not wanting to break our connection just yet, I lower my upper body over his. I can feel his pounding heart against my breast. He buries his hands into my hair, holding my head in place when he kisses me.

"Thank you."

"For rocking your world?" I tease.

"For loving me."

Chapter 23 - Jack

"Baby, are you almost ready?"

"Two minutes." She calls out from the bathroom.

"We're gonna be late."

"That's totally your fault."

She's right. I couldn't keep my hands off of her today. Granted, I always have a problem keeping my hands off of her, but what she did for me last night was such a turn on. I can't get the image of my name on her body out of my fucking mind. Especially because of the location of where her tattoo is.

The bathroom door opens and I'm stunned into silence.

She frowns adorably and asks, "You don't like it?"

"We're not going."

"What? Why?"

"I need to have you again."

She smiles wide and walks towards me. "You like?"

"I love. Leila, you look beautiful." She always looks beautiful, but she just took my breath away. She is wearing an incredible dress that skims her curves in a pale pink color. Her hair is loose and wavy. Her lips are begging to be kissed. "Fuck." I mutter as I adjust myself inside my jeans.

She runs her hands up my chest towards the collar of my shirt. "I also love. You look so handsome in a button down."

I pull her into my arms and skim my hands up her back into her hair. When I tilt her head back, her lips point towards me and I simply can't resist. I pull her bottom lip between my teeth, groaning in the process.

She kisses me deeply and pulls away. "We really need to go."

"You're right. I know Jen went through a lot of trouble for us."

"I'm really amazed she organized such an elaborate engagement party."

"Yeah, so am I actually." She spared no expense. We are heading to one of the trendiest clubs in South Beach. The label has rented the space out for our friends and family. They even went so far as flying them all down at their expense. Besides our engagement, it's also a party to celebrate the tour's success. We've sold out in every venue, and the fans are begging for more dates to be added. Our two singles are still top ten on the charts. Leila's single is now, as well. My song to her is top twenty. We have just about a month left to the tour. I can't believe how fast it went. It feels like we just left New York a few days ago. On the other hand, so much has happened, I feel like it's been years since we've been home.

"Ok, I'm ready."

"You really look beautiful, Lei."

"Thanks, baby."

I bend to gently kiss her lips. I can't let it get any further than that, or I really will not let her out of this room. She looks too gorgeous to keep her here locked up for myself. She doesn't say much on our way down to the lobby and while in the cab. Juan sits stiffly in the front seat, Oscar is with Lizzy and Evan.

"You ok? You're so quiet."

"I'm just really happy." She says while gazing into my eyes. Hers are moist with emotion. I squeeze her hand in mine. "I can't believe what has happened in my life these past four months. It's crazy how things have changed for me."

"For the better, I hope."

"Jack, I would never have imagined finding my dream job and man all at the same time. Yes, definitely for the better."

"Me too. I thank God every day for you." I finger her engagement ring before bringing it up to plant a kiss on it.

When our cab pulls up, Juan opens Leila's door and holds his hand out to help her out. The way his eyes skim her body doesn't go unnoticed by me.

Prick.

I follow her out and possessively hold her to my side. Once inside, our friends and family rip us apart from each other. Leila is pulled into her father's arms while my parents take hold of me.

"Son, you look well. How are you?"

"Good, Dad…real good."

My mom wipes the lipstick off my cheek. "I can't wait to get you two home. You look too thin."

"Mom, I'm fine."

My eyes follow the path of my fiancé's. My mom notices and smiles warmly. "I am so happy you have found her. She's a delight, Jack."

"She is." My mom returns my wide smile and pulls me in for yet another hug.

"Have you discussed the wedding?"

"We think June. Small and intimate."

"Oh, that sounds perfect. Dad and I want to help with all expenses. We have spoken to Anthony and he declined. We understand. But anything else that you guys need is on us. Ok?"

"Thanks, guys."

Leila comes over with a beer for me and wraps her arm around my waist. "Hi Mr. and Mrs. Lair."

"Leila, darling. Please call us Peter and Renata, or Mom and Dad."

She smiles shyly. "Ok. I'll try."

"We were just telling Jackson, we would like to help you out in any way. I know it's hard to plan a wedding while on the road. Please use Lizzy and I for anything you need."

"I will definitely take you up on that, since I have no clue how to plan a wedding. Thank you." She looks up at me and asks, "Can I introduce you to someone?"

"Sure, baby."

She pulls me towards her dad and a pleasant looking woman beside him. She looks familiar. "Barb, this is Jack."

"Jack." She wraps her arms around me in a crushing hug. "I am so happy to meet you."

"Same here. I've heard such great things about you." Anthony tilts his drink towards his lips, keeping his eyes on mine.

"Mr. Marino. It's great to see you."

He doesn't respond. A few long torturous seconds later, he impulsively throws an arm around me bringing me in for a hug.

Leila smiles at us as he pats my back affectionately.

"Can I have a few minutes with you?"

I swallow and nod. The look on my face prompts Leila to say, "Dad, be nice."

"I will. I just want to chat with my son-in-law."

From the corner of my eye, I watch Leila introduce my parents to Barb. In the meantime, Anthony leads me to a quiet corner in the back of the club.

He motions for me to sit across from him.

"Ok…here's the deal. I love that girl more than anything in this world. I will not apologize for my behavior. Put yourself in my shoes. My only child is traveling the country on a bus full of rock stars and one of them got another woman pregnant."

The way he depicts our story causes me to cringe. He nods at my reaction. "Yeah. Sounds as bad as it is."

"Mr. Marino, I…"

He holds up a hand and says, "Let me finish. I also put myself in your shoes. I'm sorry for what you went through. I never considered how the situation was affecting you, and I apologize. I'm sorry for how things ended. In spite of the circumstances, a life is a life. You were assumed guilty and I apologize. No one should ever have to go through the nonsense that woman put you through."

"Thank you."

He nods. "I now get it. I now know how much you love my daughter. I now know how she has altered you and your world. I now trust that you will take good care of her."

His words shock me. I was prepared for a full-blown lecture. He watches me closely, waiting for my response.

All the words I want to say are clogged in my throat. It means so much to me that he accepts me. I think mostly because it will make Leila so happy.

"Sir, I also love her more than anything in this world. She's my life."

He measures me up before nodding, "I know."

He offers his hand across the table. I earnestly accept and make peace with my father-in-law.

"Ok. Let's go before she thinks I'm burying your body out back." A nervous laugh escapes, and he shakes his head, "Just kidding."

As we rejoin our friends and families, I feel a weight has been lifted. I was dreading the chat I knew was inevitable. Having had it, I now feel much more relaxed. Anthony Marino is a good man. Leila has an incredible heart. She may look like her mom, but she is who she is because of her dad.

The rest of our luncheon is filled with laughter, reminiscing, and celebration.

Jen makes a speech on our behalf. She informs our guests of the success we've achieved so far and the future plans of the band and goes as far as congratulating us on our engagement.

I watch my girl among her closest friends. She is completely relaxed, comfortable, laughing. Every so often our eyes meet and she gives me her incredible smile.

I saunter over and casually drape an arm around her shoulders.

"Hey, baby. Having fun?"

"Yes. Evan was just telling me about a bar they played in a few weeks ago."

Lori jabs, "Stop complaining, Miller. Blah, blah, blah. Exposure is exposure."

"You could have warned us, is all I'm saying."

"And miss the looks on your faces? That was the best part."

I watch them argue back and forth, clueless as to what their issue is.

"What are you talking about?"

"Lori booked us at a gay, biker bar. We had no clue, until we took the stage."

Leila giggles uncontrollably and Lori bites her lip to contain her mirth. "Priceless."

The look on Evan's face is beyond funny. Leila buries her face in my chest to cover her laughing, and I lose control. Lizzy covers her mouth with her hand to contain her giggles from escaping. Evan realizes he lost the battle and shrugs.

"Whatever. It was worth seeing Matt getting manhandled, literally."

We all fall into hysterics. Our response draws a crowd, and before long, half our party is now hearing details of the night that Cliffhangers played at "The Man Cave".

"The name alone should have been a clue," Leila reveals.

Evan shoots her an irritated look. "What? A man cave is a cool place that men hang out."

"Ugh." Joe covers his eyes and responds, "Can we puhleeze change the subject?"

"Hey, everyone," Jen's voice interrupts our private party. Based on the time, I'm sure she's about to remind us to all get back to work…ever the agent.

Once all heads turn towards her, she continues. "I just wanted to thank you all for coming. I have tickets and passes for each of you for our last show in New York. I have one more announcement to make. We are all aware of the semi-monthly publication, *Rolling Stone Magazine*. I'm happy to announce, Devil's Lair will be interviewed for the first May issue."

We all gape at each other in shock. Hunter, Trey and Scott come closer to where Leila and I are standing frozen in disbelief.

Applause erupts, and still Hunter, Trey, Scott, Leila and myself stand with our mouths hanging open, immobilized by Jen's statement.

Jen laughs and adds, "I can see my band is in shock. Jack, did you want to say anything?"

"Um...How about holy shit!"

Laughter fills the room as the rest of us slowly come out of our stupefied states.

I shake my head as if to clear the haze. "Wow. First I want to thank you all for coming down and supporting us. It means so much to the guys, Leila and me. We kind of forget the outside world while traveling the country, and you all keep us grounded and humble...so thank you. I also want to thank my band. These guys are tireless in their trade. They eat, breathe, and sleep Devil's Lair. I couldn't be surrounded by a better group of humans."

I look down at Leila by my side. "I also want to thank my fiancé. She has been a rock to me. She has had my back. She has shown me nothing but support, love, and understanding. I adore this woman and I can't wait to make her my wife."

Applause erupts as she looks up at me. Her eyes are misty with emotion. I smile at her and kiss her chastely. "I love you."

"Me too." She smiles and squeezes me tighter.

"Ok, enjoy the show tonight, as well as the festival tomorrow." Jen dismisses us before coming to stand with Leila and me.

"Congrats, you guys," she smiles warmly.

"Jen, how long have you known?" Hunter asks what we are all thinking.

"A few days."

"Thank you," I bend closer to kiss her cheek.

"You're welcome. I'll see you after the show."

"Yes, boss," I kid, as she walks away.

"I can't believe this," Scott says. "I feel like we should be dancing on the tables, but I'm still in shock."

"Fucking Rolling Stone!" Trey confirms. Lori comes over and snakes her arm around his waist. "Fucking Rolling Stone, Lor."

"I know. I'm so happy for you guys. Don't forget to mention your up and coming rock band friends named Cliffhangers." She points a finger at each of us.

"Always working it," Leila says, while shaking her head.

"You know it, Marino."

"I do. I knew you would be perfect for them."

The rest of our families and friends approach us with their congratulations, kisses and praise. As our guests leave one by one, we are left to contemplate how much our lives are really about to change. We *have* been living in a bubble.

We still have a whole lot more partying and fun coming these next two days, but this party was the perfect start to mark our celebration. I appreciate what Jen and the studio has done for us, as well as our friends and family for supporting us. I appreciate our success, my guys, and our talent. Most importantly, I appreciate this woman who is at my side, riding the wave with me.

Chapter 24 - Leila

"Hey Miami, how are you?" Jack yells into the microphone. He throws them his dazzling smile. His back is towards me, but I always know when he graces the audience with his dimples, simply by watching the girls in the front of the stage. I can practically see the smoke billowing out of their ears.

"We don't have much time together. So let's have fun, ok? What do you want to hear?"

A mass of unintelligible gibberish assaults us.

"Trey, did you get that? Start us off."

Trey starts plucking on his bass the intro to *You Broke Me*.

Jack saunters back and forth on the stage. During this song, I remain at the keyboards while singing back-up. He makes his way towards me, leaning over and hitting random keys as he sings in my ear. As he walks away, he pinches my ass.

Our twenty-minute set goes by way too fast. Trey and Scott change positions. Jack and I sing our duets lips to lips. Jack lets the guys fool around with their solos and skips around our set list. Jack even asks the crowd if they saw the Cliffhangers earlier in the day and informs them they are good friends of ours.

As we take our final bow, I am throbbing with excitement. This was one of the best shows we ever played. The response we received was awesome. I had so much fun. This festival has a different vibe from our other shows. It is much more relaxed and laid back and fun to be part of.

We need to rush off the stage, as there is only a fifteen-minute break between bands. MACE is up next and they are the last band to play tonight. I am looking forward to being a regular fan, while hanging out with all our friends and my gorgeous fiancé.

As we congregate side stage, Jen hands us each an all-access pass so we are able to get backstage after the show.

"I want dead center for MACE, hurry people." Hunter barks, as he sprints towards his destination.

"Hunter, we have passes, we will be dead center." Scott speaks to him like he is a child.

"There are like twenty of us. Only one person can be dead center."

Trey, Jack and I watch as Hunter and Scott run towards the VIP section in front of the stage.

"I want to grab a beer. Babe, do you want something?"

"I'll take a Diet Coke."

"Trey, come with me." Jack searches the crowd pointing out Oscar standing at the entrance of the VIP section. "I'll be right back. Go find Oscar."

"Yes, Daddy."

He smacks my ass in response to my comment.

As I make my way towards the crowd, I can see the tops of Hunter and Scott's heads. Oscar is chatting with the security guard in our section. A flash of my badge gets me past most of the fans towards the front edge of the stage.

"Where's your other half?" Hunter asks as I approach.

"He went to grab a beer."

"I hope he grabs us one."

"He took Trey with him." I glance around, trying to see over the many heads surrounding us. "The others aren't here yet?"

"I just texted Mandi, they went to grab drinks. They are on their way back."

"I was going to wait for them, but I really have to pee."

"Wait for Oscar."

"He's over at the entrance. I'll be right back."

When I get to the passageway leading to the bathrooms, Oscar is no longer anywhere to be found. I quickly scan the crowd, not seeing him.

"Fuck." I mumble, frantically searching for him. I can't bear to wait any longer and hurry towards the Ladies Room so I can get back before MACE takes the stage. As I turn the corner, the line is twenty deep. There is no way I'm waiting and quickly move towards the back parking lot where our bus is parked, deciding Tom or Steve should be able to let me in.

"Don't scream, just walk." A sharp point in my side and a vicious bark in my ear cause my blood to run cold. He slipped his hand under my shirt, concealing the knife he is holding. To any bystander, we would look like a boyfriend who is embracing his girlfriend. His arm is possessively wrapped around me, his fingers digging into the flesh of my waist. It's too dark to see any other details, such as the look of terror on my face. My mind instantly goes to Jack and how angry he is going to be with me.

"Who are you?"

He doesn't respond. He just steers me towards the front parking lot near the festival entrance. As my heart pounds frantically in my chest, I force myself to focus. Distraction. I know that distraction is key in situations like this.

"Are you Danny?" He drags me faster, practically lifting me off the ground. "Did you come to hurt me?"

"And then some." His admission and his voice in my ear make me sick to my stomach.

"Why?"

"Shut the fuck up." He digs his knife into my side a fraction deeper to emphasize his request.

Anger now mixes with terror. But a wrong move on my part would be all he needs to finish what he so desperately wants to.

"Danny, this isn't going to get you what you want. You're talented. You can use that."

He pushes me towards the parking lot. Panic takes hold of my brain function. If I allow him to get me into a car, I'm done. There are several security guards near the ticket booth chatting. I contemplate screaming, but he could so easily plunge his knife deep into my side before they were able to reach me.

Otherwise, there isn't a person around as the festival is still in full swing. I can hear the music begin. I can visualize our group congregated in front of the stage. It'll be a matter of seconds before Jack realizes I'm not back. It's not helping with my concentration. Even seconds may be too long of an amount of time. By the time Jack reaches me, I could be long gone. The image of Jack's face isn't helping with the level of my panic either.

He pauses, looking around frantically. "Fucking, prick. Where is he?" He rushes away from the entrance, cursing under his breath. I stumble once as he drags me along, the tip of his knife now causing a painful pinching in my side. After my second stumble he barks, "Move!"

"These shoes are too high. I need to take them off."

He stops for a second, keeping his knife wedged against my flesh and his arm tightly around me. "Do it."

I flip off each shoe, now standing shorter and barefoot. He immediately starts a quick pace. I have no idea how fast he is and what he would do to me if he caught me. But I can clearly picture what he will do to me if he were to get me alone.

My right arm is pinned to my side under his arm. My left is between his body and mine. I desperately try to come up with a plan when I faintly hear my name. Danny must not have heard it, as he continues on his course, forcibly dragging me along. We are getting further and further away from the entrance and I need to make my move, now.

A black, beat up van pulls up at the end of the aisle a few car lengths away, just as my name is called again, but only louder this time. Danny stops and turns. I ram my elbow into his groin with all my strength. He doubles over and I run as fast as I can towards the voice.

"Jack!" I scream back. He responds with my name. I can hear Danny behind me, tears now blurring my vision.

I can tell he's gaining distance, but I can't get my legs to move any faster. Jack is running towards me with a few people behind him. Danny grabs my hair and yanks me towards him. The excruciating pain shooting through me stuns me. He pulls me into his body, slicing into my side. At first I feel nothing except for wetness, then I feel a painful stinging.

"LEILA!" Jack screams louder as Danny drags me in the opposite direction. My thoughts are no longer on Danny's intentions towards me. I am now consumed with terror, because Jack is quickly approaching. I shake my head in hopes he'll stop…as I'm doing it, I can hear sirens in the distance. I have no idea if they are heading this way. My sobs control my body. I am completely helpless.

Just as we approach the van, the side door swings open. Danny throws himself into the back, taking me with him. My head hits the hard metal floor with such force my teeth rattle. The last thing I see is Jack running towards us. I can't make out his frantic words before I pass out.

Chapter 25 - Jack

"LEILAAAAA!" My heart is racing as I watch him lift her and throw her into a van. "NO! LEILA!"

The van pulls away just as I reach it. Oscar and the guys followed me out. I have no idea where they are, as I continue chasing the van as it speeds away.

"Jack!" Oscar's voice calls out to me. But I refuse to stop. I can't stop. He has my life in that van.

The sirens are getting louder, giving me a sliver of hope. A security truck sails by me as it chases the van, and still I continue to run. My mind is a flurry of visions…bad horrific visions of what he is doing to the love of my life.

In the distance, the van picks up speed and exits the parking lot onto the main highway. The helpless feeling that takes over is crushing, causing my legs to give out as I fall to the hard ground.

The pain I feel in my chest is indescribable. The voices calling me are just noise. Time literally suspends…it just stops. Nothing. Nothingness surrounds me and the only thing I can see behind my closed eyes is her face.

The sound of shrieking tires, crunching metal and blaring sirens jolt my still heart. A black car pulls up beside me. When I turn my head, Oscar is leaning out an open window shouting something. Is this what shock feels like? I'm so disconnected from my body, I feel like I'm hovering above, watching what is transpiring below.

Oscar stands before me, "Jack, get in the car!" He yanks me up and drags me to the open door. "Get in!"

The breath I've been holding finally breaks through. Gasping for air, I watch as Oscar drives us towards the chaotic noises that are playing on a constant fucking loop.

The scene is worse than what I envisioned. A black van smashed into the side of a police car, people moving around as if in slow motion. A few bodies are scattered around the wreckage, Danny among them. For a split second, I debate heading towards him.

Until I see her.

"LEILA!" I fly out of the car as it's still moving. When I reach her, she is laying lifeless, bleeding from a wound in her side and one on the top of her head.

A human approaches as I pull her across my lap and into my arms.

"The paramedics are on their way. Her pulse is strong, but she's unconscious."

I look up towards the voice, gripping her to my chest.

"Sir, please don't jostle her. We are unsure of her injuries."

I blankly stare at the person before me. He's a cop. His uniform tells me that much. I continue to hold her tightly, refusing to let go.

In my head, I start pleading.

Baby...please, wake up. Please. Babe, I'm here. I'm not leaving. I'm never leaving. I need you, please. Please, baby. Please. I love you. Leila, please.

She feels so small, so cold.

Another human approaches.

"Sir, we need to check her vitals. Please let us do our jobs."

The noise level increases. Sirens, voices, beeping. I refuse to look around. I refuse to pull my eyes from her face. I trace her closed eyelids, her nose, her bottom lip with my thumb.

Wake up, baby. Wake up.

"Sir."

I look up at the male and female hovering over me. They gingerly remove Leila from my grasp and lay her flat on the ground. The ground is hard and unforgiving. I remove my shirt and place it under her head. As they probe and touch and poke, I hold her hand in both of mine, repeating my mantra.

Wake up, baby. Wake up.

Another human wheels a gurney over and lowers it to the ground. She's lifted and placed on top before they raise her and wheel her towards an ambulance. I think it's an ambulance. It could be an ice cream truck for all I know. Still gripping her hand, I walk along with them as we approach.

"Sir, are you her husband?"

I nod.

"Ok."

I settle in beside her as someone slams the doors shut and the vehicle shoots forward.

"She has sustained a head injury, and she'll need stitches on her side. It's a superficial wound, more of a slice than a stab. She's very lucky. Her blood pressure is low. When we get to the hospital, the main priority will be her head wound. They will rush her to trauma to be sure there isn't swelling on her brain."

I wish I had someone here with me, as I didn't hear a thing this man just said. I lower my forehead to her shoulder and start silently praying.

God...I need you. I'm sorry I've been absent. But I need you. Please, please let her be ok. I need her to be ok.

Minutes later, or possibly hours, the vehicle stops and the humans start frantically moving. She's ripped away from my grasp and I frenziedly chase after, trying to touch her again. I might be her lifeline, and I need to make contact. Just as I grab her limp hand, we approach two doors and stop.

"Sir, you can't follow. We will find you once we assess her situation."

I stand rigidly, still clutching her limp hand in mine.

"Sir." The female pries my fingers off of her, and they move through the doors leaving me on the other side.

I watch through the small, square window as they disappear into another room.

Terror takes over from being this far away from her. She needs me or I need her...whatever. I just know I need to be touching her.

"Sir, can I have your name please?"

I turn towards the voice, staring blankly. "Your name?"

"Jack Lair."

"And the victims name?"

"Leila Lair. I mean Leila Marino."

"Is she your wife?"

"Fiancé."

"She's in good hands. Can you follow me please?"

I numbly follow the woman towards a counter, or desk, whatever. "Mr. Lair, would you mind putting this on?"

She holds something white out to me. I take it from her not knowing what she wants me to do with it. "You've lost your shirt, can you put this on?"

I glance down and first notice I am naked from the waist up. The other females behind her are all staring at me shamelessly. It annoys me. It angers me. I want to scream at them. Instead, I wordlessly slip the thing in my hand over my head.

"Ok, I'm going to ask you to take a seat. The doctor will be out to update you shortly."

I continue to stare at her and she points behind me. I slowly turn to see several rows of chairs and robotically move towards them. I sit in the corner, put my head in my hands and resume my praying.

A flurry of activity snaps me back to the disgusting, ugly, cold waiting room.

"Jack, how is she?"

Faces…some standing before me, some on the sides, some still walking into the ugly room. I shrug.

Someone takes my hand and sits besides me.

"Son, she'll be fine." Mom.

"Jack, do you want something. Do you want me to get you water or a drink?" Dad.

"She's strong. She is stubborn as hell. She'll be ok." Lori.

"Just leave him be. Stop hovering and give him space." Hunter.

"Maybe we should all wait outside. He looks like he's about to freak out." Scott.

"I'm not going anywhere." Evan.

"Ok, let's all leave her immediate family alone and give them some privacy. Anthony, we'll be in the lobby." Barb.

A rush of bodies leave the small room and I turn my head to see five chairs occupied. My parents, Anthony, Evan and Lizzy all sit quietly, staring into space.

Should I be saying something to them? I don't know what to say. I resume my praying and ignore the other five humans in the room.

Every so often, my mother rubs my back. Otherwise, I would have no idea that other people were here in this ugly room with me. It's quiet. No noise. I imagine Leila lying on a table, scared, and alone, and in pain. I pull my hand out of my mom's and storm out of the room.

"WHAT'S HAPPENING?" I bark at the woman who gave me the thing I put on my body.

"Sir, someone will be out to see you as soon as possible."

"STOP CALLING ME SIR!"

She gasps at my outburst and gawks at me like I'm a wild animal. A set of arms encircles me and a male voice says, "Son, come."

He leads me back to the ugly room and towards the chair I was previously occupying.

I pull away and shake my head. A vision of Leila haunts me. She needs me. I need to be there. I can't. I...

"I need to..."

I pace the room, over and over, back and forth.

Two men in uniforms enter the room.

"Mr. Lair?" I turn towards the person calling my name. He and the other man step closer. "Can we ask you a few questions?"

My dad stands and approaches the cops. I guess they are cops.

"What do you need, Officers?"

I continue my pacing. If they need me, they can stop me. My dad speaks to them in low, hushed tones, occasionally glancing over at me. They both nod and leave the room.

My dad comes over and rubs my back. "I gave them all the details I knew. I directed them to speak to Oscar."

Good thinking, Dad. But I don't say it. I nod and resume pacing. I'm sure I'm driving them crazy. I really don't give a fuck. That is until my pacing starts to irritate me. Then I slump to the ground, staring at the ugly puke colored rug. The helplessness is back. The tears blur my vision, making it impossible to see anything before me. I rub my eyes until they burn from the friction.

"Mr. Marino?"

I snap my head up to see a male in putrid grey clothes. I am instantly in the man's personal space. There's blood smeared on his shirt.

Leila's blood.

Bile rises quickly in my throat. I feel like someone plugged my nose and mouth and I'm suffocating.

"I'm Leila's father. This is her fiancé."

The man nods at us. "She has suffered an extradural hematoma on her left frontal lobe. The contusion is small, and surgery wasn't needed. We were able to drain the hematoma through aspiration. We cut a small hole to remove the clot with suction. There is no pressure to her brain, nor any damage that we can see. We have her on Mannitol to prevent further brain swelling or seizures. She also has a concussion from a surface swelling on the back of her head. She received a few dozen stitches to her side from a knife wound. She's extremely lucky. The wound just missed her large intestine. She will need to be monitored closely for the next several hours due to her brain injuries."

"She's alive?"

"Yes, she is alive and stable."

Relief floods my body like floodwaters over a seawall. The force is so volatile, it causes my knees to buckle beneath me.

"Is she awake? Can we see her?" Anthony asks.

"She is still sedated, but yes, you both can see her."

I turn towards my parents. "I need to go."

Evan steps towards me. "Go."

Anthony and I follow the doctor through the doors towards Leila. "Thank you," I mumble to no one in particular. God, I guess or whoever listened to my pleas.

Anthony places his hand on my shoulder and squeezes affectionately.

I pull in a jagged breath as we walk towards her door. Anthony walks into her room before me.

The bed looks massive. Seeing her lying there attached to tubes and wires scares me to death. In spite of all that, she looks peaceful. She looks like she's sleeping. A large bandage covers her head above her temple. I move to her left and Anthony moves to her right. My brain function slowly returns. Consciously, I know I should give Anthony some privacy. This is his daughter...his only daughter. But I can't leave her. I can't offer to leave or apologize for being here.

"She's good. She's good." Anthony says, as if he needs the words to ensure that she is.

We each pull a chair up towards her bed and settle in. It's obvious that neither of us is leaving anytime soon.

I rest my head on her arm, while holding her hand and resume my praying.

Chapter 26 - Leila

I'm struggling to wake up. I'm struggling to stay asleep. Stuck in between, not sure which I want more. Warm lips kiss my hand, helping me decide what I want more.

Jack.

I want Jack. I continue to struggle, willing my eyes to open, willing my mouth to speak. The best I can accomplish is a subtle shift of my aching head.

"Baby." He squeezes my hand. He saw it. He saw me move. My head is killing me. My whole body hurts. My side stings uncomfortably. The touch of his hand dominates over all the pain.

Slowly, I regain control of my body. I can flex my foot. I can lick my lips. I can return his squeeze. The last to cooperate are my eyes and my voice. I need to see his gorgeous face. I need to say - I love you.

"Lei, we're here. Your dad and I are here. Come on baby, wake up."

I take a deep breath, wincing from the pain, and slowly open my eyes. He looks directly into them.

"Baby."

I'm unable to keep them open and they flutter shut. Frustratingly, I try to force them open again and continue to squeeze his hand to communicate that I'm trying. I'm desperately trying to come back to him.

"Leila, come on baby girl. Wake up." My dad's voice sounds hoarse, raw. I'm causing them so much pain.

I blink a few times and focus on first Jack and then Dad. Dad looks older. I move my eyes back to Jack. He looks so tired.

"Hey, baby." He coaxes, gently caressing my hand that is sandwiched between both of his. My dad moves to a button on the wall and pushes it.

"Thirsty."

Jack flies up and grabs the pitcher to pour me water. "Here, baby." He puts the straw to my lips, wiping my chin when a few drops escape.

My dad holds my face in between his hands, placing a lingering kiss on my forehead.

He pulls away, his eyes moist with emotion. "You scared me, kiddo."

"Sorry." I rasp, barely audible to my own ears.

He chuckles and shakes his head. "I'll go fill everyone in. I'm sure Evan wore a hole in the floor by now." He kisses my cheek and leaves Jack and me alone.

"What happened?"

"What do you remember?"

The whole experience comes rushing to my memory. "My last memory is of you running towards me."

Jack frowns, as if he is in pain. He pulls his chair closer so we are merely inches apart. "The van took off. I couldn't get to you. I tried desperately, and I just couldn't." He swallows before continuing. "Baby, the scariest thing I've ever witnessed was watching that van pull out of the parking lot."

He lowers his head and rests his forehead on my arm. "That was nothing compared to the horrific sound of the van crashing into something."

I search my memory, unable to picture what he's describing.

"I don't remember any of that."

"They think you hit your head when he threw you in the van. You were unconscious when they pulled you out."

"Where's Danny?"

"I don't know." He tightens his jaw, failing to hide the rage that I can see so clearly in his eyes.

I squeeze his hand encouragingly. "Jack, it's over. I'm here and we need to move on."

He levels me with his gaze. "Leila, the only thing that stopped me from killing him was you. I had to tend to you."

A nurse stalks into the room. "So how are we feeling?" She asks me in a calming voice, as she flips switches and turns knobs on a computer next to my bed. She looks so sweet and it calms me. She is short and portly with grey hair and rosy cheeks.

"My head hurts."

"I know, dear." She pulls a wire off the side table that is attached to an I.V. "You push this when the pain becomes too much to handle." She places the thing in my hand, patting it before resuming her inspection of the monitors.

"What time is it?"

"It's six a.m." Jack responds.

"Six?" I just lost seven hours of my life. "Where is everyone?"

"They are in the lobby."

"I've ruined their night."

"Lei." He chastises. "Please."

I want nothing more than to continue to stare at him. But I'm so tired and my eyes betray me by closing heavily.

"Sorry. I'm so tired."

"Ssh. Sleep, baby." He says quietly. Now that I have his permission, I slowly slip into a deep sleep.

♫ ♫ ♫

Dr. Williams stands at the foot of my bed reviewing my charts. Jack is in his usual spot, in a chair pulled up to the side of my bed. He has refused to leave. I've been in this room for three days and I am ready to leave. I've had a parade of family and friends coming through the day after the accident. I was so out of it, I barely remember any of the conversations.

We've had to cancel our shows in Jacksonville and Atlanta. I have horrible guilt over it. The guys and Jack have all taken turns telling me off. Regardless, I can't help how I feel.

"So, Miss Marino. Your vitals are good. How do you feel?" He glances up from the clipboard and smiles.

"I'm ready to get out of here."

"Sounds like a plan."

"Are you sure she is ok?" Jack asks in his usual threatening stance, arms folded, eyebrows puckered with concern.

"Yes, Mr. Lair. She is absolutely fine. She will need to have those stitches checked in a few days, but otherwise she's good to go." Jack continues to frown as if not believing him.

"Miss Marino, I am discharging you."

"Thank you."

"Isn't it too soon?" Jack questions.

"Stop."

"What? I want to make sure they are not pushing you out because they need a bed."

"No, Mr. Lair. She's ready to be discharged…but, I'd like you to remain on bed rest for a week or so."

"I can't."

"The fuck you can't."

"Jack."

"Sorry. But there is no way you aren't following doctor's orders."

"He's right. Take the time to mend. You can resume all normal activity in a week."

"Thank you, Dr. Williams." My fiancé patronizes. Once he leaves my room, I roll my eyes.

"Don't give me that look."

"Jack, I'm fine."

"I. Don't. Give. A. Crap." He leans closer, enunciating each syllable.

Angry, unshaven, sitting in a hospital room for three days – Jack looks fucking hot.

"I know I am better. Do you want to know how I know?"

"How?"

"Because I want to jump you right now."

His cheek twitches as he tries to contain his smile.

"If I wasn't all yucky from being in this room for three days, I would pull your hot ass into that sterile bathroom and devour you while on my knees."

"Fuck."

"Yeah. So stop. I'm fine."

"Ok…you're better, but you are still going to be on bed rest," he quips.

"So what's the plan?"

"No sex for a week."

I gape at him while blinking.

He widens his eyes in exasperation. "What?"

"I meant with the band. But why?"

"Doctor's orders."

"He never said no sex. Go. Go out there…go and ask him!"

Jack smiles at my panic. "Fine, I'll clarify. But if he says no sex, no sex."

I huff out a frustrated breath. "This sucks ass." I mumble to myself.

"What's that?"

"Nothing. What about the band?"

"I'm calling Jen. She'll have to cancel Nashville, Charlotte and Richmond. We'll fly home tomorrow. Rest up, and pick up the tour in D.C."

"Goddammit."

"Stop."

"Jack, we were doing so well. This isn't going to go over well with our fans."

"What is your point?"

"We can continue with the shows. I'll rest on the bus and perform at night. Please, go ask Dr. Williams."

"We will make up the dates next tour. Stop being so difficult."

"Please?"

He growls and leaves the room in search of Dr. Williams. There is no way I'm going to have this band cancel a total of five major cities.

Jack comes back with Dr. Williams in tow. "Ok, ask him."

"You have questions?"

"Um. Yes. I was, um…" I bite my lip as I feel my cheeks flush with embarrassment.

"She wants to know if we can have sex?"

Dr. Williams laughs at Jack's question. "This is a good question. Yes, you can have sex. Just be careful with her side wound."

I smirk at Jack and he blatantly ignores me.

"Anything else?"

"Yes. If I promise to do nothing else, can I please perform at our shows?"

"When's your next performance?"

"We are supposed to play in Nashville day after tomorrow and Charlotte the next day."

"I'll tell you what, you cancel Nashville, then you can resume in Charlotte, but no other activity. Please schedule a follow-up appointment in a few weeks."

"I will. Thank you, Dr. Williams."

"Sure, dear. Anything else?"

Jack and I exchange glances. "No, I think those are the two most important things."

"Ok. Good luck to you."

The minute he leaves my room Jack barks, "I am furious with you right now."

"Why? You get to get lucky because of my insistence."

"I'm talking about the tour."

"Jack, I sit at a keyboard and I walk ten steps to you and then I sit at a keyboard. I can handle that."

I hold my hand out and he surprisingly takes it.

"Don't be mad." When I pull him closer, he sits on the edge of my bed. "Kiss me." He bends and plants a chaste kiss on my lips, and then another.

"Am I forgiven?"

"Do bears shit in the woods?"

"Thank you. Now get me out of here."

♫ ♫ ♫

"Oh my fucking GOD!" I exclaim, but yet again. He laughs at my enthusiasm and brings my hand up to give it another kiss.

"Jack, he walked right here. He stood right here. I sat right out there, and there, and there." I point out to the various empty seats at the far corners of the concert hall.

"I know, baby. You keep telling me."

"I'm not a Springsteen fan, but I have to admit this is pretty fucking exciting," Hunter says from his drum set behind us.

I make another round on the stage, committing to memory what he has seen the many times he's played here. I cannot believe we are at the Asbury Park Convention Center. Last stop on our tour before New York City. We pulled in late last night. We're home. We are back in New Jersey, and we are finally home.

Since the "incident" in Miami, Jack has been extremely protective...to the point of lunacy. Danny is in jail awaiting trial, bail denied. The charges wracked up against him will hopefully have him there for the rest of his life. I am not looking forward to his trial. I don't want to see him ever again, nor do I want Jack anywhere near him. But our presence is necessary and we will have to testify. I'll worry about it when I need to.

Jessa also decided to press charges against Danny. Besides assault, kidnapping and attempted murder, he is facing aggravated murder charges on Jessa's unborn baby, possession of heroin with the intent to distribute, and grand theft auto. The van used to try and kidnap me was stolen earlier that day. Jack has not pressed charges against Jessa. I agreed with his decision. She has suffered enough. Dragging her through the courts is not something I want to take on. She is grateful that we are moving on. She has decided to as well and will move to Los Angeles to pursue her modeling career.

Good riddance.

Jack still feels Danny can try and hurt us from the confines of his jail cell. It's unnerving to have to go through life with such fear. I cannot allow myself to be in that constant, unproductive state of vulnerability. We've had a few arguments over it. Jack feels Danny has not accomplished his goal, and we need to be cognizant of that.

The upside of Jack's paranoia is he hasn't left my side since the "incident".

The downside of Jack's paranoia is he hasn't left my side since the "incident".

I confessed I didn't want us getting sick of each other. We each have to have our separate lives, interests and ventures. Another argument later, and he slowly backed off...slowly.

To placate him, I suggested we go to my apartment tonight and hibernate in Hoboken until we are due in New York City for our last two shows in a few days. We will have a mini vacation of sorts, take-out, pay-per-view, and sex on every flat surface, all the things we desperately craved while on tour.

We haven't had time to go home yet. As a favor, Lori and Alisa are heading over to my place to stock the fridge and romanticize for our secret rendezvous.

"Maybe he'll be here tonight," Scott says nonchalantly.

"What? What do you know? Tell me? Is he coming?"

"Holy shit, Leila. I was just speculating."

"Do not speculate!"

Hunter blatantly laughs at him and Scott mumbles under his breath. I feel bad I yelled at him, but Springsteen attending our show is no joking matter.

"Babe, I tried to get Jen to arrange it. He's in Europe."

"Ok. That's good. I would be a nervous wreck if he was here tonight."

He measures my facial expression and quirks one side of his mouth in disbelief.

"Honestly. Thank you for trying."

"Are you ready to rehearse?" Jack asks tentatively.

I nod distractedly, my mind now wondering if he would have come if he were in the States.

Chapter 27 - Jack

The fantasy I had months ago, the one with the big ass stretch Hummer and screaming fans chasing us down the street? Yeah, it's a reality now. Well, we don't have screaming fans chasing us yet, but we are recognized daily now.

Our tour ended last week in New York City, five months after we embarked in September. The media coverage we received was insane. Being endorsed by several rock bands such as, *Bayou Stix and MACE, as well as one of the top music critics in the industry catapulted us to the number one spot on the charts. Our album is selling so well, the label feels we may achieve Gold status within the year. My song to Leila is in the top ten. Leila's single is as well. We've made it. We're there. The fans are aggressive, interrupting us constantly for a photo-op or an autograph. It's a strange, scary feeling knowing someone is always watching you. I sometimes feel like we are living in a fishbowl. But I wouldn't trade any of it. The best part is having Leila right by my side.

In the few days since coming back to our normal lives, it has been anything but normal. Leila and I have been bouncing between my place and hers due to commitments Jen arranged with reporters. I still feel homeless and out of sorts.

I will be an official Hoboken resident as of tomorrow. I'm not exactly thrilled with the situation. Leila knows all about my Jersey induced affliction. She just rolls her eyes and reminds me it's temporary. Truth is, I'm not as upset as I am letting on. I really am just trying to conjure up some sympathy from her. The more guilt she feels from dragging me across the Hudson, the more sex I get. I get a hard-on just thinking of living with her, in a real home, with many rooms at our disposal. I could care less what state we live in. Besides, it's only a few months until we get married, and she already knows the day we return from our honeymoon, we will be apartment hunting in the city.

I will miss living with Hunter. It was a blast. I owe him so much. He was there for me many years ago when I was lost, confused, and scared as all fuck with my career decision. The label of best friend isn't adequate. He is a brother to me.

Hunter and the love of his life, Mandi, will soon be roommates as well. She plans to move in within the next few days. Scott is planning to propose to Patti soon. She isn't aware of it yet. I told Leila the day it happens will undoubtedly spawn a five-foot-four blonde bridezilla.

Trey and Lori are officially through. They both maintain it was mutual. She has succumbed to Matt's endless pursuit. They are officially a couple. I unfortunately know more details than I need to. Lori held nothing back a few nights ago while visiting. That girl has no shame. Hearing her play-by-play was both unnecessary and enlightening. I actually tried a few of her descriptive moves on Leila later that night.

We have all grown in so many ways. Mainly in our careers, now that success has found us. Granted, we worked our asses off for it. We have also all significantly matured in the relationship department. Even Trey has morphed into a different person. Not one with marriage on his doorstep, but he's softer, more approachable, more sensitive. Hell must have frozen over.

My priorities have most definitely shifted. My future ambitions are now altered to include domestication, something that was not on my radar less than a year ago. No one could have predicted the path my life has taken, myself included. While sitting in said Hummer, I glance from face to face, watching my band mates all animatedly reminiscing the highlights of our tour. Besides us, Dylan, Will, Oscar, Mandi, Patti and Krista are here. Krista and Dylan have been having a quiet conversation in the corner as they flirt shamelessly. When they migrated towards each other, my eyes collided with Leila's in shock. Watching them from the opposite corner of the Hummer, I'm secretly hoping something comes of this. Besides their looks mimicking a Barbie and Ken doll, their personalities and careers are perfect for each other. Not that I ever worry anything would come from Dylan still harboring feelings towards Leila, but still.

"Hey, baby. Are you ok?" Leila asks while nestled against my side.

It's hard to verbalize what I'm feeling. How do I convey in one word the feeling of complete and utter contentment and happiness like I've never felt before, excitement for our future, terror of something ever happening to her, anticipation of the children we will have some day, and gratefulness for my absolutely fucking perfect life?

"I am more than ok, baby. I'm…complete."

She runs a fingertip over my bottom lip. "I love you." She lifts her face until our lips touch. Our kiss progresses, each trying to consume the other, each trying to infuse our irrefutable desires into the other.

This woman rocks me to my core.

"You two gonna screw in the Hummer?" Hunter asks annoyingly. "I call dibs second." Mandi elbows him as she blushes.

"What? Why should they have all the fun?"

"You're such as jackass," I announce.

We are just pulling up to Granite. The label is throwing us an End-of-Tour bash. Our friends and families will be here tonight, as well as some select reporters that Jen personally invited. The normal line of club hoppers wraps around the building. Their noise level increases when we pull up. They have no idea who's inside, but the presence of a Hummer elicits their curiosity.

"You guys ready to party?" Hunter asks as he literally bounces in his seat like a five year old.

"I can't wait to have Jell-O shots." Leila announces.

I raise an eyebrow and ask, "Jell-O shots, huh?"

"Yep, many. I love them." She leans in and whispers directly into my ear, "Plus, they make me really horny."

"Tease."

When Oscar opens our door, Hunter is the first one out.

One loud female on the line screams his name, drawing attention to the occupants of the Hummer. He raises his arms, soaking up every ounce of attention. As we each exit, the screams recommence.

"Do you think they truly know who we are?" Leila asks, gripping my waist tightly.

"Some. Some are just copying the motions." She becomes understandably uneasy in public lately. I can't blame her. It's hard to get used to. My instinct is to turn around to see who they are actually screaming for, not quite believing it's for us.

Once inside the door, Leila visibly relaxes at my side. I've missed Granite. This place was our go-to place for fun. It's also the place I first realized I was falling in love with Leila. My cock twitches thinking of our heated kiss on the overhang. I'll have to re-enact that tonight.

"You look so fucking hot." I rasp in her ear as we walk into the bar. Her legs, her fucking beautiful legs go on forever. "Don't bend over, this skirt is way too short. I don't want anyone looking at what's mine."

She quirks one side of her mouth up and rolls her eyes. "Killjoy."

"Hey, smartass."

On the elevator ride up to the roof, I position her directly in front of me. I slowly skim my hand up the back of her thigh feeling nothing but smooth skin.

I press my lips to her ear and whisper, "Commando?"

"Thong."

"Fuck."

Her response is to push back against me, moving her hips slowly from side to side, spurring an instant erection.

"Fuck." I mutter again, taking hold of the hem of her dress and pulling it down in an attempt to cover her more.

She giggles at my frustration, beating me at my own game.

I don't have time to retaliate. The doors open to applause and cheers. I experience a brief moment of déjà vu from the night of my birthday party.

Charles from the label greets us at the door. "Congratulations on all your success. Louis sends his regrets, but wants you all as guests on his yacht this summer."

"We are there." Hunter speaks for all of us.

Jen opens the night by making her usual speech. Charles follows with a speech of his own. A video montage is played, some photos from our performance, some candid silly shots from life on the buses and backstage. Krista tells our guests of future appearances, cover stories on schedule, and an honorable mention of our upcoming feature article in *Rolling Stone* this coming May. Once the pleasantries and plugs are out of the way, our party truly begins.

Our parents are here, as well as Cliffhangers and their significant others. Leila and I are working the room, side by side when Trini comes over.

"I have missed you!" She exclaims, throwing her arms around me. I've missed her too, as a friend. So much has changed since the last time I saw her. I tactfully remove her arms from around my neck, and she thankfully understands my discomfort.

"Sorry, Jack."

"No worries." I smile shyly. She returns my smile. I've been in some compromising positions with this little pixie and there is a strange dynamic between us now.

"Um...Trin, you remember Leila?"

"Hey, Leila. Congratulations on your success and your engagement." She graces Leila with the same hug she just gave me. "You take good care of him, he's a catch."

Leila laughs and accepts Trini's embrace.

"Thank you, Trini. I intend to." She looks up at me amused.

Trey walks over to join us. "Hey, Trin."

"Hey, handsome. How are you?"

"Good. Real good. You off tonight?"

"Yes, can you imagine?" Trini is not sporting the signature Granite uniform of tight black shorts and matching vest.

"I requested the night off. I wanted to party with you guys, celebrate your success properly."

Trey nods with a small smirk on his lips and commands, "Walk me to the bar."

A slow, sexy smile spreads across Trini's face. "I thought you'd never ask." She quips and takes his hand, dragging him across the room.

"Huh." I mutter out loud.

"Are you jealous?" Leila teases.

"No. I'm stunned. Didn't know they had a thing for each other."

"Trey probably kept it to himself out of respect for you." She watches them from across the room. "They are a pretty good match."

I follow her gaze and stare at Trey and Trini standing close, flirting openly. "They kind of are. Who knew?"

Lori saunters over and nods towards Trey. "Who's she?"

"An ex-fuck of Jack's." Leila blurts out.

"How many Jell-O shots have you had?" I scowl.

She giggles adorably. "A few." I continue to frown when she adds, "Why are you mad? You are most definitely going to get lucky tonight."

Before I can respond, Lori impatiently says, "Yeah, yeah...Jack is going to get lucky. Woo hoo. So, why is Trey flirting with Jack's ex-fuck?" Lori folds her arms over her ample chest and glares at me.

"Hey. You are in a relationship now. Knock it off." Leila shoots back, in my defense.

"I miss him." Lori remembers her current dating situation. "Fuck. You're right, but that man is good in bed."

"Thanks, babe," Matt says, as he moves behind Lori and wraps his arms around her.

Lori's eyes bulge a bit when she realizes Matt heard her last comment. She shoots me an evil eye look when she sees that I'm trying to contain my laugh.

"I can't get used to you two together." Leila mutters before downing another shot. I raise my brow in question and she sees my annoyance. "Oh, please. I am so over him." She smacks Matt on the arm forcibly.

"Yeah, feeling's mutual." Matt responds.

Lori turns in his arms planting a kiss on his lips. "I'm it for you. I'm your forever after. Even if we break up, I'll wreck you for anyone else."

Matt swallows audibly and simply nods in response.

"Aw, that's hot Lor." Leila slurs. She comes closer, wrapping her arms around my waist. As she nibbles on my neck, I first notice how buzzed she really is. "You want to get some air?"

"Are we gonna make out?"

"Possibly."

"Then, yes please." She turns to Lori and Matt and brags, "I'm gonna get some too."

"Good for you, Lei Lei." Lori smiles at her tipsy friend.

I take Leila by the hand, leading her towards our special place. Visions of my surprise party fill my head. She was so drunk that night and so sexy. I become aroused from the memory of her surrendering to my advances on this very balcony.

"God, that night I wanted you so bad." She admits, reading my thoughts.

"Me too. You have no idea how much." I turn her body to mimic the position we were in that fateful night of my birthday party. She tilts her head, staring straight into my eyes, into my soul. She literally turns me inside out. I'm completely exposed from just one look.

"You are so beautiful." I voice my thoughts. I trace the shape of her lips with the pad of my thumb. Her lips part just as her eyes darken with desire. A flush appears on her cheeks, and her chest is rising with each breath she takes. She grips my shirt between her fingers, pulling me even closer. Our bodies pressed against each other are like two perfect puzzle pieces. Our lips are just an inch apart.

"Jack, kiss me." She pants breathily.

I lower my head, closing the distance. I swear I felt a tingle from the connection. So strong is my draw to her. So powerful, that after all the kisses we've shared, and all the caresses I've bestowed, and all the times I've sunk deep into her proclaiming my love, it still always feels like the first time.

I duplicate the kiss she claims she loves. The one she said she uses as a bench mark for all kisses. She duplicates her response by sliding a leg in between mine, lacing her fingers in my hair, and opening her mouth to allow me access. It's perfection. This woman is perfection, and she's mine.

♫ ♫ ♫

Since we got home from our tour a week ago, life hasn't stopped to take a breather for one minute. Leila and I have bounced back and forth between her place and mine, still living out of a suitcase. The good news is today I official move into her apartment in Hoboken. Seems fitting that it's also Valentine's Day, and our first one together. Initially I wanted to take her away for a few days, just the two of us. But I hate inflicting more travel and suitcase living on her. So after much thought, I decided the best way to celebrate this day would be to give her a romantic night at home…our home.

Last night was our end-of-tour bash at Granite. We had a really nice time, in spite of all the publicity and marketing crap Jen inundated the night with. I get it was necessary, and she constantly needs to work us. This is how it is now, and we all may as well get used to it. We aren't complaining by any means.

Cliffhangers and MACE played an impromptu short set for our guests. The night was the perfect ending to our tour and the perfect segue to our futures. My band got rip roaring drunk. Hunter needed to be carried out, but not before a very public twerking display. The highlight of his night was seeing Trey and Trini hitting it off. You would think the man had invested his life savings in waiting for the day that Trey finally finds love, and not just a measly hundred bucks. I have to give Trey tons of credit though. He laughed and ignored Hunter's antics, not letting it spoil his getting acquainted with Trin.

The whole Trey and Trini thing blew me away. I have no ill feelings towards them hitting it off and getting together. Trini and I were nothing more than friends with benefits. However, I sat and wondered all those times I was hooking up with her, what was Trey thinking in his head.

My gorgeous Leila was also very tipsy. She just loves those Jell-O shots. Our rendezvous on the back patio brought us as close to public sex as we've ever gotten. We almost needed a firehouse to break us apart. I had to fight the overwhelming desire to drag her into the restroom to take her. Instead, I suffered through an unbearable hard-on for the rest of the night, appeased only by thoughts of getting her naked and fucking her senseless. The irony was, once I got her back to my apartment, she passed out fully clothed on my bed.

Her hangover could have hampered our morning romp and our packing and moving day, but it did no such thing. After screwing for a solid hour, she jumped up and started the day. She plastered a smile on her face, excited as all hell to get me to Hoboken. Hunter and Amanda helped pack my stuff. Scott and Trey offered to help as well, but since all my belongings were able to fit into a half dozen boxes, and they both wanted nightly solo's on our next two tours, I told them to take a hike.

We caravanned to Leila's place, her little Honda and Hunter's piece of shit on wheels loaded up with my stuff. We had me settled and unpacked in a few hours time. Hunter and Amanda stayed for a bit, relaxing with us as we reminisced on the tour highlights, filling Amanda in on Trey's antics. They left a little while ago, having Valentine's plans they needed to get ready for.

Having my own scheme that I hatched up in my head, I had Lori insist Leila come to her place to approve her outfit choice for her date with Matt tonight. Leila, being difficult, asked her to text pictures of the choices to her, exasperated with her demands. Lori, being Lori, ranted and yelled on her end of the line loud enough for me to hear the gist. I listened quietly to their conversation. When Leila hung up, she huffed with little explanation and flew out the door. I owe Lori, big time. I'm guessing I have about an hour to get things ready.

Leila thinks we are relaxing quietly...and we are. But I also have a few surprises for her that I know she will love. Mr. Romance is here tonight, and I don't want to disappoint her. I watch from the window as she walks to her car, gets in and drives off.

Like a man possessed, I bolt out of the apartment, needing to pick up some last minute things. As I zip line across four Hoboken blocks, I load up with flowers, a card, champagne, chocolates, and a box of cannoli. Lori's text of warning is my only line of defense that she is on her way back. The text comes just as I'm lighting the candles.

I'm no cook, so take-out will have to do. It should be arriving shortly after Leila does. I've dressed up for her, wearing my blue button-down that she loves so much. I have my playlist ready and waiting on the mp3 player. When I hear the key in the door, I hit play.

Her smile spreads slow and sexy on her gorgeous face. "What's all this?" She scans the apartment, the candles flickering giving off all the light needed in the room. The music is playing softly in the background. The table is set for two, displaying her flowers, waiting for our meal to arrive.

"Happy first Valentine's Day, baby."

She drops her bag and melts into my arms. "Jack, this is so sweet. It's just perfect."

"You're not disappointed that we didn't go away somewhere?"

"No…this is where I want to be."

"Good…me too." I kiss the top of her head gently and ask, "Did you help Lori choose a dress?"

"How did you know that's what she…" she narrows her eyes suspiciously at me and asks, "wait, you did that?"

My response is to shrug.

"God, I wanted to kill her. Seven…seven dresses she made me sit through and three sets of lingerie."

"I'm sorry, baby. I had things to do."

She relaxes in my arms, and smiles warmly. "I forgive you."

When I skim her lips with my thumbs, they part automatically just as her head tilts up towards mine. Her response to me is immediate, my response to her as well. It's an automatic, involuntary reflex.

When I bend to connect our lips, the current runs right to my cock. I will never tire from the feel of her lips against mine. I've kissed this woman thousands and thousands of times. I can't explain how the touch of her lips can still send jolts through me as if it's the first time all over again.

Still standing in the same locked embrace, the kiss quickly builds as we grip each other with clenched fingers in an attempt to eliminate the space between us. The door buzzer loudly interrupts.

She pulls away first, panting audibly. "Holy hell."

"I know. It's insane what you do to me."

The door buzzes again. "Who can that be?"

"Our dinner?" I shrug apologetically. "Sorry, babe, I didn't want to ruin our night by forcing you to eat my horrible attempt at preparing a meal."

She kisses me again before I go to retrieve our Valentine's takeout.

When I get back inside, she's waiting for me on the couch, holding a large box. "What's that?"

"Your present."

"Baby, you've already given me my present. The day you accepted my proposal."

She smiles shyly and shakes her head. "You're so damn perfect. Here, open it."

The box is practically as big as she is. As I tear the paper and lift the lid, I'm stunned to see a brand new high-polished *Fende*r acoustic guitar. "Babe."

"Do you like it?"

I run my hand over the shiny wood, it's dark and striking and gorgeous. "I love it."

"Look at the back."

When I flip it over, etched into the back of the body is a quote from her song.

"There isn't a doubt, my love runs too deep.

With my blood in my veins, it controls my heartbeat." ♥ *LML*

A small lump lodges in my throat at the amount of thought that she put into this gift. I skim my fingertips over the words.

"Thank you," I say, as my emotions swirl in my head, forcing any coherent thoughts to fail to rise to the surface. She takes my face in her hands, tilting my head down so we are eye level.

"You're welcome," she whispers, understanding what I'm struggling with.

"This is the best gift I've ever gotten, besides you."

Her response is to kiss me gently. "I love you, Jack Lair."

"Me too. So much." I pull her into my arms, holding her tightly. My body pathetically responds to her being in my arms. "Come, let's eat so I can show you how much I love you."

We eat our meal with light conversation. She tells stories of when her and the guys started Cliffhangers. I tell her of similar tales with my own crew.

"I'm really glad they all get along so well."

"Me too. I look forward to how our futures will progress. You're friends are on their way. They are very talented."

She smiles proudly. "They are. I'm really happy for them. I feel sometimes I abandoned them."

"You didn't babe."

She shrugs. "Yeah, I sort of did. But I know they don't feel that way."

"Are you ready for your present?"

She nods enthusiastically. I head to our room to grab her gift. When I hand it to her, she looks up wide-eyed like a kid on Christmas.

She unwraps her box to find several more wrapped inside. The first is a sexy lace teddy that gave me a hard-on just imagining her in it. I'll have to share that store visit that I took with Hunter and Scott with her later. I felt like I was shopping with two ten year olds.

"Is this for me or for you?"

"Me, of course."

She nods knowingly and touts, "I thought so."

Her next gift is a framed picture of us at the Mississippi. "I love this."

"Me too. It's my favorite picture."

"It reminds me of what followed."

The memory of our lovemaking once we got back to the hotel floods my mind at her admission. "Yeah, me too. Hurry, open the rest." I request impatiently, wanting to get her on our bed to re-enact that memory.

There are a few more wrapped trinkets in the box. A CD of our playlist, a gift certificate to a fancy spa in the city, a few sex toys…those are for me also.

The last present is an envelope. She looks up curiously while gently opening it. Inside is a confirmation of the two-week honeymoon I booked for us on a private villa in Antiqua.

"Two weeks?" she asks earnestly.

"Two weeks."

She throws herself in my arms. "Jack this is the best present ever. Can we go now, can we leave today?"

I chuckle at her request. "I wish we could, but we have a little thing called a wedding to hang around for."

"Oh, yeah," she concedes and smiles warmly. "Thank you babe, I love it. I can't wait to go on our honeymoon."

I take the paperwork out of her hands before lifting her and carrying her into our room. "Time for the best present."

"Do you want me to model my teddy?"

"Yes, please."

"Are we using the toys?"

"Definitely later."

As she leaves me to change into the scraps of black lace I gave her, I light candles in her room and patiently wait for her.

The sight of her in the doorway simply takes my breath away. "Oh, fuck."

"Good choice, Mr. Lair," she croons as she comes closer. "Do you want to remove it for me?"

I meet her halfway, before nodding wordlessly.

My eyes rake over her, taking in every inch of her beauty. I skim the outline of her breasts with my fingertips, causing her eyes to close and her chest to heave from my touch. I run my hands over her shoulders, and down her arms. Turning her, I gasp at the sight of the black lace skimming her curves, barely covering her ass.

Gently, I lower the thin straps until they hang loose. "Sweet Jesus, this looks incredible on you." I wrap her in my arms, pulling her back and shamelessly pushing into her ass to show her how much her body affects me. Dragging my lips from her shoulder up to her ear, she tilts her head to give me better access. The goose bumps that appear over her arms tell me how my lips are affecting her. When I turn her around to face me, her eyes are hooded with desire. While pinning her with my gaze, I slowly peel the lace off of her until it pools at her feet.

Taking her hand, I help her step out of it and lead her to our bed. I worship her, every part of her, from her head to her toes. At times, she grips the comforter under her fingers. At times she grips my head as it's in between her thighs. At times, she grips my thighs as she devours me. When I sink into her, she grips my face, staring straight through to my soul.

She clenches around me, prompting me to join her. Her orgasm is silent but profound. Her response makes my own climax earth shattering.

She smiles when I return to earth. "I love you."

I nod silently, causing her smile to widen. She knows what she does to me. She knows how much she completely wrecks me…and I know I'll love this woman more and more each day, for the rest of our lives.

Epilogue ~ Leila
June 7, 2014

I'm not even nervous. Normally, I would be freaking out knowing one hundred people were about to watch me walk down a sandy beach. But nerves are not what I'm feeling at the moment. Pure exaltation, joy, happiness and bliss are what I'm consumed with. I am about to become Mrs. Jackson Henry Lair.

As I stare out the window of my bridal suite, over the beach that is prepped for our wedding ceremony, I close my eyes and imagine Jack as clear as day.

I can envision him standing under the floral trellis, in his simple black tuxedo, smiling wide, dimples showing. My heart flips in my chest at the visual. I can only imagine what it will do when I truly lay my eyes on him in less than a half hour.

The girls all left to let me dress in solitude. Actually, I asked them for that favor. I needed to remember every minute as I prepared myself for my future husband. I knew that wouldn't be possible with the commotion of five giddy girls fussing over me.

I examine myself in the mirror. My dress is a simple sleeveless scoop neck that is fitted to my waist and billows down to the floor in a full skirt. There is beading at the waistline. I have a fingertip veil with a pearl encrusted comb tucked into my hair, which is swept up into a classic bun. I also have on the three presents Jack gave me…my heart necklace, my new bracelet and my engagement ring. I glance down at my engagement ring as it sits on my hand and once again thank God for letting us get to this day. So many things could have gone wrong. So many times, we could have lost each other. I will not take one day with Jack for granted…not one.

"Baby," Jack says, as he gently knocks on the door.

"Jack, you can't be here."

"I just needed to hear your voice. Did you get my present?"

"Yes, Lizzy gave it to me. Jack, I love it." I glance down at the beautiful bracelet that sits on my wrist.

"I can't wait to see you." His voice sounds desperate through the door.

"I can't wait to see you, too. I'm sure you look totally hot in that tuxedo."

"What are you doing out here. Get lost, Lair." Lori's scolding tells me Jack just got busted.

"Calm down, Lori. I can't see her. Baby?" he asks through the wood panel door that separates us.

"Yeah."

"I love you. I'll see you at the alter."

"I love you, too…and I can't wait."

"Blah, blah, blah…now get lost." I hear shuffling in the hall before the door opens.

"You two can't be trusted."

"We're allowed to talk."

"I don't doubt that if I hadn't shown up, one of you would have caved and opened this door." She firsts catches a glimpse of me and her eyes soften. "Oh, Lei. You look so beautiful."

"Thanks," I reply shyly, "you do, too."

She truly does. My maid of honor looks stunning in the blush colored simple cocktail dress that we all chose together. Her hair is loose and wavy. She's a complete knockout.

Lori pulls me into her arms.

"I'm so happy for you, Leila."

"Thank you, Lori."

"He truly adores you. I hope to have that some day."

"You will. Matt really cares about you. I've never seen him like this."

"Part of me still feels he's going to break my heart. If I gave up that hot rocker, and he fucks me over, I'll kill him."

I laugh out loud at the scowl on her face. "You didn't love Trey. You love Matt."

"I know, Goddammit."

"You can't help who you love."

"Don't I know it."

"Lei, can I come in?" My dad's voice outside the door interrupts our moment.

"Yeah, Dad." The door opens and he slowly walks in. His eyes immediately well up with tears.

"Oh, my baby girl. You look so beautiful." He moves towards me as Lori turns to leave.

"I'll go round up the girls." Lori says and closes the door behind her.

My dad wraps his arms around me. "I wish your mom were here right now."

"Dad, don't make me cry." I fan myself to attempt to stop my tears.

"Ok, ok…sorry. I came to bring you something." He reaches into his pocket and pulls out a small box.

"What's this?"

"Mom was saving this for your wedding day."

The warning I gave my dad about making me cry flies right out the window. My eyes well up and the big, fat tears begin to flow relentlessly. My dad wipes them away as I wordlessly hold the tiny box in my hands.

"Go on, open it."

I gently open the box to reveal a beautiful pair of classic pearl earrings. "Your something old. Her mom gave them to her and she wore them the day we got married."

"Oh, Dad." I cling to him as I silently cry. The absence of my mom is an unbearable ache on what is the happiest day of my life. I know she would have loved Jack, and he would have loved her. I mourn for her as if it just happened. I mourn that she is not here with me on this day. I mourn that she will not see my children grow up. I start to tremble in my dad's arms from my sobs.

"Hey, enough. She is here and she is with you. Maybe not in body, but in spirit."

I turn towards the full-length mirror to check my appearance. Silently, I thank Lori for buying the industrial waterproof mascara that cost a small fortune.

At that moment, Lori walks in with Patti, Lizzy, Alisa, and Mandi.

"Lei, my God!" Alisa throws her tiny frame at me and wraps me in a tremendous hug. "I'm no longer mad at you for beating me to the alter." Alisa has been holding a small grudge. Her smile tells me she is now over it.

"Thanks, Lis. Your day is going to be amazing."

"I know," she shrugs and hugs me again.

Lori catches one glimpse of my face and frowns, "Anthony? What did you do to her?"

"Sorry," my dad mumbles, as Lori comes over and starts dabbing at my face.

"Can you put these on for me?" I ask Lori. She takes the pearl earrings from my trembling hand and fastens them to my ears.

"Your mom's?"

I nod wordlessly.

"Ok, sit. I need to fix this." She pushes me towards a chair and repairs my makeup. The rest of my bridal party all surround us. Their compliments and chatter causes the noise level to rise with each squeal.

My dad looks completely out of his element. He sits on the couch, watching the five animated girls as if they've escaped from a mental institution. I am not a girly girl, never was. My childhood was filled with baseball and rock and roll. He has no clue how to react towards this.

Lori finishes up with my face and stands back to admire her work. "Perfect. Do not cry again or I'll hurt you."

"You don't want me to cry on my wedding day?"

"No. Please don't be difficult, it's not an outrageous request."

I shake my head as I gawk at her.

"What?" she asks snippily. "Ok, inventory. Something old?"

"My earrings."

"Something new?"

"My bracelet."

"Something borrowed?"

"And blue. Alisa lent me her blue garter."

"Good."

The door opens and Mrs. Lair pokes her head in. "Can I come in?"

"Of course." I motion for her to join us.

"Oh, Leila. You look stunning."

"Thank you. I love your gown." She is wearing a classic Grecian gown in midnight blue.

"It's not every day my first born and only son gets married." She is a complete knockout. From the corner of my eye, I can witness my dad's eyes bulge a bit.

I turn towards my mother-in-law and ask, "Have you seen him?"

"Yes, dear. He is busting at the seams. I've never seen him this happy."

Her words accelerate my already pounding heart. "I was sent to see if you are ready."

I look at my dad and ask, "Dad, are you ready to do this?"

He nods slowly as he gnaws on his bottom lip. "I'm ready." The look on his face crushes me. I need to look away to stop myself from completely bawling.

Lori points her finger into my face and commands, "Stop."

"Whew…" I take in several deep breaths, desperately trying to corral my anxiety. After a few long seconds, I voice, "Ok, I'm ready. Let's go."

"I'll go tell them we are about to start." Mrs. Lair leaves the room and five female bodies sheathed in blush colored silk all frantically move around grabbing bouquets, fluffing out my veil, slipping my feet into my shoes, and getting in last dabs at my watering eyes.

Lori, the self-appointed ringleader announces, "Ok, people…show time."

The girls line up before us as we file out of the bridal suite into the hall. We chose a beautiful Victorian bed and breakfast on the Jersey shore, because it reminded us of the place we stayed at in San Francisco. It sits on the beach and has a quaint patio where we will be holding our reception. It's simple and understated, just like Jack and me.

As we get closer to the French doors that lead out onto the beach, I subconsciously shake my legs in anticipation.

"You ok, sweetheart?"

I choose to nod instead of speak for fear I'll get yelled at by Lori. The lump in my throat would clue her into my threatening tears.

The change in music tells our guests that the ceremony is about to begin. They all look towards the back of the big Victorian house, waiting for us to approach. First one out is Alisa, followed by Mandi, Patti, Lizzy, and finally Lori. The minute Lori walks away from us, I get my first glimpse of Jack.

Our eyes lock and I lose all the air in my lungs. As I try to pull more air in, my chest constricts painfully. I don't see the faces watching us walk down the aisle or the ocean behind him. The only thing I can see is my future husband looking more beautiful than I even could have imagined. The closer I get, the less I see. I'm in a vortex with everyone, everything spinning around me and at the opening is Jack.

"Who gives this woman for marriage?"

"I do." My dad places my hand in Jack's and kisses my cheek.

My feet carry me up the step to stand before the minister.

Lori takes my bouquet out of my hands.

Our eyes remain locked on each other. His smile is now gone, in it's place a heated, intense stare. His hands grip mine as we face each other.

"Hey."

"Hey."

"You look incredible."

"So do you."

The minister begins the ceremony as Jack and I keep our eyes locked in a trance.

It could have been a minute later or many when the minister says, "Jackson, please recite your vows to Leila."

Jack rubs his thumbs over my knuckles as he still clasps my hands in his.

"Leila, I love you so much that it's sometimes hard for me to breathe. You have changed my life. You have altered every cell in my body. You completely own me. By simply staring into my eyes, you can bring me to my knees. I want you to know, I will do everything in my power to make you happy. I will laugh with you. I will cry with you. I will keep you safe. I will remind you how much I love you every day for the rest of our lives."

He repeated the words he said to me the night of our engagement. Yet still, I feel like I've heard them for the first time. My emotions overwhelm me as I stand before him on our wedding day.

"Leila, please recite your vows to Jackson."

"Jack, I love you more than anything in this entire world. In times of sickness or in health, in success or failure, in plenty or want, I will be standing beside you. I will be your partner, your wife, your lover and your best friend. I promise to always cherish you, respect you, and support you. I give you myself, my heart and my love for all of eternity."

His eyes glaze over with unshed tears and a small smile plays on his lips. I return his smile, not able to stop my tears from falling. He reaches over and wipes them away, keeping his hands on my cheeks. I can feel my heart pounding frantically as it swells in my chest.

"If any man can show any just cause why Jackson and Leila may not lawfully be joined together, let him speak now, or else hereafter forever hold his peace." Jack's eyes move to my lips and then back up to my eyes, igniting me from the inside.

"May we please have the rings?"

Lori hands me Jack's ring as Hunter hands Jack mine.

"Leila, please place the ring on Jackson's finger and repeat after me. I, Leila, give you this ring as an eternal symbol of my commitment and love."

I repeat his words quietly, staring into Jack's stormy grey eyes. As I slip his ring on, he entwines our fingers tightly.

"Jackson, please place the ring on Leila's finger and repeat after me. I, Jackson Henry, give you this ring as an eternal symbol of my commitment and love."

Jack repeats the minister's words and slides my ring onto my finger. He pulls me closer and whispers, "I love you."

"I love you."

"By the powers vested in me by the state of New Jersey, I now pronounce you husband and wife. You many now kiss the bride."

Jack instantly wraps his arms around my waist, eliminating the space between us. My hands find his hair. Our lips collide and we forget our guests, our wedding party, and the minister. His lips move over mine in a heated dance, and I willingly respond, enthusiastically respond, to the point of indecency.

The minister clearing his throat and random chuckling filtering through the air is what brings me back to earth. Remembering where we are, I am the first to pull away. Our guests applaud while we remain locked in each other's arms, nose to nose. As I gaze into my husband's eyes, I know this man will completely own me every day for the rest of my life. I wonder how I will be able to spend any time away from him. I've become so spoiled, being with him as much as I have been. It's almost unhealthy.

"You are going to kill me." I murmur against his lips.

"No way. I need at least seventy five more years."

"Let's go, party time. Save it for later." Hunter interrupts rudely.

We pull away long enough for me to take my bouquet from Lori. Jack then tucks my arm in his and leads us down the aisle, beaming like he just won the lottery. My dad steps out as we near his row.

"I love you...both of you."

"Love you too, Dad."

He grips me tightly as Jack watches on. As he looks over my shoulder, he smirks, "Go, we're holding up your impatient best man."

No sooner do we step onto the patio than Hunter, Trey and Scott surround Jack with shots. "First one you have to do with us." Jack and I are still arm in arm when they all tip back their tequila shots effortlessly.

Lori hooks her arm into mine. "Our turn." She pulls me out of Jack's hold, dragging me away to the opposite side of the patio.

"Where are you going, wife?"

"She'll be back." Lori says over her shoulder.

"Don't get her too plastered, please. I need her coherent later."

"Like that would stop you." I say as we walk away.

"Let's go, Lei Lei. No ginger ale for you tonight."

She ushers me to join the girls at the bar for our own round of celebration. "First Lei, then Lis, who's the next to find their bliss?"

"What?"

"Just go with it." She says, as she drinks her shot.

"Ooh, yum. What is this?"

"Yay, I found a shot you like. Lemon shooters."

"Yes, I'll have another."

Strong arms wrap around my waist from behind. "I need you, my wife." He whispers into my ear.

"Jeez, she just got here. One more." Lori hands me another as I tip it back.

Jack turns and kisses me. "Yum, what is that?"

"Lemon shooters, aren't they good?"

He kisses me again, this time driving his tongue into my mouth. "Delicious. Come, our parents want to talk to us."

Jack drags me over to where his parents and my dad are standing.

"Welcome to the family." Peter Lair pulls me into his arms. He passes me off to his wife next.

"Ok, so what did you guys want to tell us?" Jack asks, as they stand smiling at us like they have a mad secret.

Renata hands us a key. "Our wedding gift."

Jack and I exchange a glance. "What is this?"

"It's to your new apartment." She shrugs while smiling. "We wanted to give you your honeymoon, but Jack beat us to it."

I search my dad's eyes for any signs that this could be a joke.

"No way."

He smiles warmly. "It true. It's perfect for you guys. It's near the studio. It's nice and roomy. It'll make a great home, until you wake up and decide you need to leave the city because it's no place to raise a family and should really be back in Jersey where you belong."

"Dad...really?"

"What?"

"Guys, this is unbelievable. Thank you. I was worried we would be stuck in Hoboken forever."

"Hey."

"Sorry, babe."

"It comes with a condition," Renata says, while smiling.

"Two conditions," my dad threatens.

"I'm afraid to ask."

"One, you need to visit us on the Island and Anthony in Jersey frequently."

"And two?" Jack responds suspiciously.

"We want grandkids...soon."

"So, this is more a bribe than a gift?"

None of the three have the decency to deny it.

"Good Evening, Ladies and Gentlemen. How are we tonight?" The D.J. interrupts our moment. "Can we get the bride and groom on the dance floor for their first dance?"

"The D.J. just saved your asses," Jack smirks.

I quickly hug our parents, kissing them and thanking them again. Jack follows suit and leads me to the dance floor.

As everyone applauds, the opening to my song begins to play. Jack pulls me close as his voice resonates around us clear as a bell. He sings the lyrics into my ear, making me love him more with every line.

"It just took one kiss, to claim me as yours.
I see no one else, you've closed all my doors."

The D.J. announces for the rest of our bridal party to join in on the first dance. Seeing our band dressed in tuxes is so endearing. They all look so handsome. I scan the patio, taking in all the smiling faces as they watch us. Soon after, all are invited to join us in our dance. Dad dances with Barb, with his hand possessively holding her back. She whispers close to his lips. Our friends are all dancing intimately with their partners, lost in each other's eyes. Even Trey and Trini are having a moment while dancing to our first song. I was both pleased and surprised when he announced they were coming together. Hunter and Scott are secretly plotting how long before they would be getting their bets paid off.

Dylan is here with Krista. They just started dating. Of course Jen is here with Malcolm. She is now engaged. Her ring as big as her attitude. Although she has softened considerably towards me, I still don't care for her.

Today doesn't only signify the joining of Jack and Leila…it signifies the joining of Devil's Lair and Cliffhangers forever. Our two worlds have meshed perfectly. I picture us all involved with each other's lives, more weddings to come, and many children to be born.

"I can't believe we are married," he says, staring into my eyes.

"You mean you didn't foresee this when I literally stumbled into the studio?"

He chuckles at the memory. "No. I saw a gorgeous girl who literally gave me a hard-on when I heard her sing."

"Shut up."

"It's true. Can I confess something?"

"Oh, yes, please."

"After I met you, I kept envisioning you when I was with other women."

"Ugh. Jack, really?"

"What, it's a compliment."

"I'm supposed to see the flattery in hearing my husband pictured my face when screwing dozens of random women?"

"Hey, hold on. It was three women. I told you, as soon as I got to know you and once I tasted your lips, I went on a dry spell."

"For some reason, I find that endearing."

"You should. You totally fucked with my head."

"Are you sorry?"

"Lei, I thank God every day for finding you. I love you so much."

I lean up to kiss his lips.

He groans against my mouth. "Is this over yet?"

"Ten minutes into our reception and you are ready to ditch?"

"Yes, baby. I'm ready to celebrate you becoming Mrs. Lair." He kisses me deeply, not caring who's watching us.

"Can you feel me?" He presses himself into me and I nod wide eyed. "I'm literally aching for you. Your plan of not having sex for a week was one of the hardest things I've had to endure. Sleeping next to you each night and not being able to fuck you was torture. So yes, I want this to end. I can't wait to peel this dress off of you. I can't wait to touch and lick every inch of your body. I can't wait to drag my tongue over your tattoo. I can't wait to sink into you. I can't wait to make slow, passionate love to my wife. I can't wait to wake with you in my arms as my wife for the first time. I can't wait to make love to you again, before taking you on our honeymoon. I can't wait to get you to our private beach, swim naked in the warm waters, kiss every part of your body while you lay on a chaise lounge in the sun, and make love to you over and over and over again."

I gape at him, unable to process any words. The only thing I can muster is, "Grrr."

He smiles wide. "What?"

During the rest of our reception, while dancing with my dad, celebrating with our friends, mingling with our guests, taking our portraits, while tossing my bouquet, feeding him cake…all I can think about are Jack's plans for me. The vision of Jack's lips on my body is what keeps popping into my head. I thought I was hot shit cutting him off, hoping to make our wedding night special. He just effectively put me in my place, the bastard.

By the time he carries me through the door of our honeymoon night suite, I'm horny as all hell.

The room is prepped with candles, flowers, and a roaring fire.

I turn towards my husband to see him watching my every move. "I know you want to peel this off of me, but I need to freshen up."

He nods, continuing to watch me hungrily. "Hurry."

I move closer to kiss him. "I will."

Lori was with me when I chose the pink scraps of silk I'm wearing under my wedding dress. I gingerly remove my dress and headpiece while keeping on the lingerie, silk stocking thigh highs and my wedding pumps. I brush out my hair, brush my teeth and check my face.

Not being able to stand another minute away from him, I quietly open the door.

Jack is lounging on the bed, wearing black silk boxers...and he looks edible.

He widens his eyes, scrolling from my head down to my toes. "Holy shit."

"You like?"

"I love. Turn around."

He meets me half way and slowly wraps his hands around me, pressing his silk covered arousal into my backside. "Part of me doesn't want to take this off."

"That would make things difficult."

"You're right." He slowly slips the thin straps down over my shoulders, letting them hang limply. He kisses my neck and pulls my earlobe in between his lips.

I lean against him, mainly to feel more of him, but also so he can help support my weight. The simple kisses he is placing on my neck are making me weak in the knees.

I slowly turn and wrap my fingers into his hair. "You are driving me insane."

"By merely standing here, I can say the same for you." He runs his nose along my jawline and places a kiss in the hollow of my neck, my exposed shoulder, and the swell of my breast.

He skims his hands up my back and starts to slowly untie each of the satin ribbons that hold it all together.

A few seconds later, I'm standing before him in a tiny G-string, stockings and heels.

"You are the most beautiful thing I've ever seen in my entire life." His voice is husky and raw. His eyes devour me.

He lifts my left hand, placing a kiss over my wedding rings. "You've made me the happiest man on earth today. I can't wait to spend the rest of our lives together."

I lift his hand as well. "The sight of this ring on your finger does things to my insides. It's sexy as hell knowing you are my husband."

Jack lifts me and carries me to the bed. He places me dead center and lies beside me. I pull him towards me to kiss him passionately, running my tongue inside his mouth while taking hold and stroking his erection. Uncharacteristically, he pulls away before I do, panting heavily.

I move down his body, tasting every inch of him. I completely become unhinged from the act of pleasuring my husband. His hands gripping the duvet as my hands remove his boxers and my lips move over his entire length, causes my own insides to pulse and constrict. I bring him to the brink and slowly release him, moving back towards his lips. I end, where I began, swirling my tongue in an erotic dance with his.

He looks into my eyes and declares, "Tease."

Jack takes his revenge out on me. He proceeds to do everything he promised on the dance floor. His hands caress and explore. His lips cover every inch of my body. He tastes me as if for the first time. He pulls away, leaving me a heaving mess. While giving me a sexy smile, he wraps his strong arms around me and slowly joins us as one. He makes love to me, giving me pure ecstasy. I am overwhelmed by the sensations he is causing within me. I am overwhelmed with the amount of love I feel for this beautiful man.

As he stares into my eyes, he connects us in every way a man and woman can possibly be connected. As he kisses my lips over and over, he declares his love. As we consummate our marriage by doing something we've done hundreds of times before, this time feels different.

This time, I can see our lives spread out before us.

This time, I can see our home and our kids.

This time, I am Mrs. Jackson Henry Lair.

~ The End ~

The story of Jack, Leila and all their friends continue in the conclusion of
The Back-up Series, Encore ~ coming summer of 2014.

Follow A.M. Madden

Please support all Indie-authors and leave a review at point of purchase. Indie-authors depend on reviews and book recommendations to help potential readers decide to take the time and read their story. This Indie-author would greatly appreciate it.

Xo

A.M. Madden

You can contact A.M. Madden at:

www.ammadden.com

https://www.facebook.com/pages/AM-Madden-Author/584346794950765

https://twitter.com/ammadden1

https://www.goodreads.com/author/show/7203641.A_M_Madden

The Back-up Series Playlist ~

Reason I Am is an original song created for The Back-up Series. Lyrics - A.M. Madden, music - Mike Martone, vocals - Tyler Cohen, guitar - Randy Newberry, and recording engineer - Dennis Arcano. The song Reason I Am will soon be available for download on Reverbnation and iTunes. Follow status on www.ammadden.com for exact release date information.

The songs listed below are both personal favorites and inspirational tracks that I played on a constant loop while writing The Back-up Series. I'm sure it's not a revelation to hear that I adore music, especially classic and modern rock. I did write a book about a rock band, after all. These songs helped set my tone, helped create my moods, helped inspire me. Every Avenue has a special place in my heart. If Devil's Lair were real, this is what they would sound like. I never tire of hearing them, which I feel makes the mark of a true masterpiece. Follow A.m. Madden on Spotify.com to find The Back-up Series playlist.

Dream On ~ Aerosmith
Promises in the Dark ~ Pat Benatar
Tie Me Down ~ Every Avenue
Only Place I Call Home ~ Every Avenue
I Can't Not Love You ~ Every Avenue
Come Undone ~ My Darkest Days
Shadow of the Day ~ Linkin Park
A Story To Tell Your Friends ~ Every Avenue
The Reason ~ Hooberstank
New Divide ~ Linkin Park
Touch Me ~ The Doors
Rhiannon ~ Fleetwood Mac
Tell Me I'm a Wreck ~ Every Avenue
Brown Eyed Girl ~ Van Morrison
Jersey Girl ~ Bruce Springsteen
Layla ~ Eric Clapton
Fall Apart ~ Every Avenue
Mindset ~ Every Avenue
Faithfully ~ Journey
The Night Owls ~ Little River Band
Can't Help Falling in Love ~ Elvis

Bayou Stix: Arena Tour 2014 Press Release

Bayou Stix is steadily topping the charts. Their onstage presence, chemistry with fans, and God given talent have made this rock band, based out of Baton Rouge, Louisiana, a household name.

Jude Delecroix, Lead Singer, Jessie Adams- Lead Guitarist, Liam Christianson- Rhythm Guitarist, Dade Rodriguez- Bass Guitarist, and Cruz Ellings- Drummer are selling albums, traveling the country, front-runners on Billboard, and have big plans for the future.

A brand new endeavor will be put into play in 2014 as Bayou Stix breaks into arena tours.

Stay tuned for dates and details. This is one Tour you won't want to miss.

***Bayou Stix is a sexy, adult romance written by Skye Turner.

Acknowledgements

It's a miracle my family hasn't murdered me. It was hard on them the first time around when I set out and started writing Back-up. The difference was I really wasn't taking it very seriously. It was something I wanted to do, but I had no expectations whatsoever. I'd write at night, after dinner, after homework, after the dishes were done. Writing Back-up really didn't cause any disruption to my family…sort of.

Front & Center caused complete and total neglect. I now had expectations. I now had a vision, a goal, a dream. Throw in social media and all it's demands. Throw in the obsession to finish a novel and publish it sooner rather than later to appease my readers. Throw in a husband and two teenage boys who barely saw their wife and mother. Throw in an author with tremendous guilt…you get an accurate glimpse of what my life was like these past few months.

That being said, I would do it all over again in a heartbeat. I want to thank my best friend, my husband. You have been nothing but supportive throughout this entire process. You encourage me. You make me laugh. You watch me cry (while rolling your eyes). You are the best. I love you J.D.

My boys. My loud, passionate, raging-with-hormones, teenage boys. You guys have been super supportive with my project. Thanks for understanding. Thanks for accepting. Thanks for being the best things that have happened to me. Love you guys so much.

I want to thank my immediate family. My mother was my first reviewer. My sister, the best damn agent anyone can ask for. My brother, sister-in-laws, brother-in-laws, you all routed me on tirelessly. I love you and thank you for your support.

Mike Martone…we've never met, but I adore you regardless. You were able to take my song lyrics for Reason I Am, add the perfect melody and turn it into a beautiful ballad. With the help of Tyler Cohen, Randy Newberry, and Dennis Arcano, I am now the owner of a beautiful love song. Thank you, from the bottom of my romantic heart.

My friends. The Get-together Club, Camille, Renee, Michael, Jane, Diana, Rebecca, and Rhetta. You all know who you are. Instead of rolling your eyes and sighing when you found out this loon wrote a book, you raved about loving it, you hugged me for my efforts, you supported me to a fault. Thank you. I love you all.

I have met the best people in this industry, and most of them are Bloggers. An indie-author is as good as her exposure. Bloggers are the key to helping an indie-author get their works noticed, read, reviewed, and talked about. They do this for no other reason than for the love of reading. They use their own resources, spend hours of their own personal time, to promote us to the many potential readers that may one-click based on their recommendation. I appreciate each and every one I've met during this process. I adore you guys.

To my Facebook friends and confidants, Trisha H., Kathy C., Karrie M., Yamara M., Kathleen Y., Jessica B., Christine D., Kimberly T., Miranda, Geri, Tiffany Marie, Melissa, Alexis B., Ashley M, Rachel H., Desiree G., Jodi M., Stephanie M., Stephanie F., Darcy, Karen, Marjorie, Megan, Marina, Savannah, Kellie K., Joanne S, Janett G, and Jamie C., thank you so much for your help, your advice, your support, your pimps, your teasers, and your unconditional love of Jack & Leila.

To Pedro Soltz, my handsome muse for Jack Lair. You allowed me to use your gorgeous face on my teasers, you allowed my fans to connect to Jack personally, and you have no idea how much I appreciate that. Thank you so much for trusting me. To Kim M., our Pedro connection brought us together, our newfound friendship was a bonus.

To Trish H. ~ girl, I am so glad I found you. Your positive attitude, your loyalty, and your ability to figure out a way to make it happen, are all so appreciated. I love you.

To my Beta Readers ~ thank you...thank you...thank you!!! I couldn't have found a better team to work with.

To my nephews, J & A for helping this old lady to learn the ins and outs of social media.

To my Street Team. Your tireless pimping has put me on the radar of many potential readers. I found great friends among you and I adore my "Mad Chicks" to death. Thank you so for all the kick-ass, sexy as fuck teasers, and thank you so much for always having my back.

To my personal IT guy, Mr. Magic ~ Go Yankees...kidding. Thank you so much for all your help. You've helped this technically challenged, clueless author with everything from Facebook issues, (they do hate me), to website issues, to super-loops, (whatever that is.)

To my cover artist, Sarah, @ Sprinkles on Top Studios, thank you for really awesome covers, and a kick-ass logo. To Alicia, @ AVC Proofreading, you've been a Godsend and have become a friend. I'm so glad I found you. To Andrew K, for my band logo, I love you cuz.

To my cheerleaders ~ Linda, Lina, Josephine, Antoinette, Barb, Laura, Elise, Maryanne, Kim, Jeanette, Tammy, Rose, Rita, Joyce, Jessica, your help on Facebook has been tremendous. Sharing, Voting, Pimping…no matter what the circumstance calls for, you are there. Thank you.

To my author pals and life-long Sinner-sisters ~ Christine Davison, Ann Vaughn, L.L. Collins, J.M.Witt, Ren Alexander, Tricia Daniels, A.D. Justice, & Skye Turner~ I adore each and every one of you. I love our late night bantering, I love our camaraderie, and I love that we support each other tirelessly. We have a mutual understanding, and I hope some day we can have a Sinners girl weekend getaway. I need to hug each of your gorgeous asses. Thank you for becoming such great friends.

To all the fellow authors I've met during this process, you all rock. Thank you for answering my questions, no matter how stupid they were. To Ann Vaughn for lending me Mike Casiano and Colt Harris at Orion Securities©. Ann Vaughn is the author of Long Way Home, Finding Home and A Home for Christmas. You can find Ann's ebooks at Amazon.com.

To Skye Turner for lending me Bayou Stix©. Skye is the author of Alluring Turmoil, Alluring Seduction, and her new Novella, Alluring Ties. You can find Skye's ebooks at Amazon.com, paperbacks are available at skyeturnerauthor.storenvy.com

Ann and Skye, I am so excited your characters have met Devil's Lair and look forward to their budding friendships.

To Cassy Callahan Witthar – winner of my "Quote" contest for Front & Center. Her quote was added to Chapter 5 in a very steamy scene between Jack and Leila. "Hang on…it's going to be a bumpy ride."

Finally, to my readers. You guys have been unbelievable. Your emails, messages, and reviews have carried me and lifted me and reminded me that my goal as a writer is for someone to pick up my books, and hopefully find an escape for a few days. Hopefully, they'll fall in love with my characters, and their journey. Hopefully, they'll walk away wanting more, and counting the days until the next book comes out. You have made me feel I achieved my goal and more.

Thank you.

Interested in becoming a Mad Chick? Contact me at am.madden@aol.com. I'd love to have you.

Made in the USA
Lexington, KY
02 October 2014